GRAVES

KATELYN TAYLOR

Published by Katelyn Taylor
Cover by Booklovedesigns
Edited by My Brother's Editor
Proofreading by Lyndsey Goss
Formatting by Midnight Designs
Graves is a work of fiction.
Names, characters, incidents, and places are used fictitiously. Any resemblance to real people or events is coincidental.

DEDICATION

This is for the babes who enjoy an unhinged MMC who is completely obsessed with the FMC who has a twin brother who is also head over heels for her. Why should you choose between this one and that one when we know that you can have both? This one is for you, ya little slooter.

TRIGGER WARNING

LAST CHANCE TO RUN

This is it. Your last chance to run. Please tell me you've read and considered the triggers. Please know that you are about to enter a story that is dark, twisted and at times completely fucked up. We don't yuck anyone's yum, especially when it is this delicious, but there is nothing wrong with this book not being for you!

Alright, that was it, your last warning. Sit down, grab any *ahem* tools you may need to enjoy this read, and prepare yourself for the Graves brothers.

PLAYLIST

Solitude by Billie Holiday

You Put a Spell on Me by Austin Giorgio

Angel by Toby Mai

Fly Me To The Moon by Frank Sinatra

Collide (Feat. Tyga) by Justine Skye, Tyga

Gangsta by Kehlani

Easy to Love by Bryce Savage

Formaldehyde Footsteps by BertieBanz

Going to Hell by Bryce Savage

Be Your Love by Bishop Briggs

Gasoline by Halsey

RUNRUNRUN by Dutch Melrose

Breathe by Kansh

Toxic by 2WEI

save me from the monsters in my head by Welshly Arms

lovely (with Khalid) by Billie Eilish, Khalid

Evil Beauty by FATE

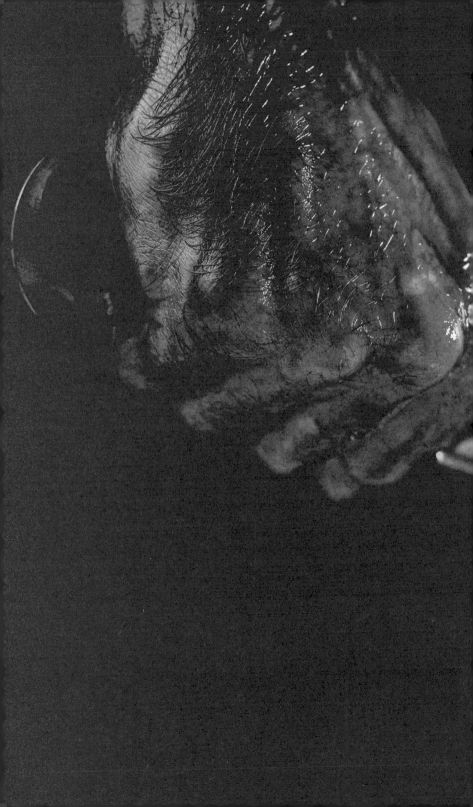

PROLOGUE

ZAYDEN

Both of my feet hit the concrete as I drop from the second-story balcony. The overweight security guard is surprisingly fast, given his size. This was supposed to be a quick job, in and out. That's what Dominic said. We didn't account for the fact that the target was going to hire private security over the last forty-eight hours. I'll beat the shit out of him for it later.

"Stop!" the man rages as he lands on the ground of the concrete alley and tears after me.

He's pissed, obviously. It's probably his first day, and I just killed his boss. Whoopsies.

With my mask in place, it's not like he knows who I am or even my skin color. My brother and I have been at this for what feels like our whole lives. Dominic does it for the power it brings us, but I do it for the fun. The thrill that courses through your veins when you hold someone's pulse in your hands, teetering on that edge between sparing them and snapping their neck in two. Of course, I can't say I've ever felt inclined toward the former.

It's intoxicating and erotic, and it's never enough.

Fuck, I'm still hard from taking out tonight's target. Once I take care of this security guy, I'm gonna need to find the nearest warm hole and sink into it.

My steps pound against the ground as the alley finally opens up and reveals the street. Before I can devise where to lure my prey, though, a sharp sting rips through my back. I stop dead in my tracks before whipping around.

There, I find the profusely sweating security guard only one hundred feet from me, his hand shaking as he holds a Glock .45 with a silencer on the end. I take even, measured steps toward him until he shoots me again, this time in the ribs.

My body jerks, but that is the only impact I allow him to see. I let my mind go to the darkest recess I can reach, allowing the inky black memories to wrap me up like a warm cocoon, numbing the pain and allowing me to push forward.

The man's eyes widen as he shoots me for the third time, this one in the thigh. My body is already too cold, too numb to register the pain. The only thing I feel is the cool metal of my knife against my fingertips as I reach into my pocket and pull it out.

My prey's body begins to shake, a look of horror as he watches me walk toward him with ease. He turns to run, but I'm too close to him, and he's out of time. I wrap my uninjured arm around his head, gripping him with my gloves as I turn his neck up to expose the carotid.

He squeals like a spring pig as I plunge my blade into his throbbing pulse, but the squeals quickly turn into a harmonic gargle as I slide the knife across the front of his neck like butter. There is only a small piece of skin and his spine to keep his head attached to his body before I drop the bleeding sack of shit to the ground.

I look down at my blood-soaked hand and knife before I begin rubbing my fingers together, momentarily mesmerized by the warmth soaking into my gloves. It soon turns cold, though, and I've lost interest as I turn on my heel and walk toward the street.

Pulling out my phone, I shoot off a quick message to our cleanup crew that there is another body to take care of. Dominic says that if we don't clean up our own messes, we are able to operate even smoother without the risk of ever being tied back to anything. Really, I think he was just tired of cleaning up after my playtime. Our cleanup crew understands the risk. Should they ever get placed for a job, they will take whatever charges they give them and do it with a smile on their face and their lips sewn shut. They know that turning on the Graves brothers would be a fate worse than death. I'd make sure of it personally.

The next step I take twinges, and no matter how much I block out the pain, it comes back in a crashing wave. Looking down at my leg, I curse. Motherfucker nicked my femoral.

As if acknowledging the wound was all the permission my body needed to feel the pain, my head begins to spin. The next thing I feel is the cold, hard cement beneath me. I assess my surroundings, but I'm still a good fifty feet away from the street and a quarter mile from the car.

I feel a warmth begin to seep all around me as I look down to see blood soak through my black shirt and pants. Shit, can't say I've been this fucked up in a while.

My hand shakes as I attempt to shoot off a text to Dom, my blood-soaked fingers slipping and flailing across the keyboard. I hit send, or at least I try to before my vision spots.

Doing my best to banish the spots away, I peel my eyes open when they catch on to a figure. I couldn't have bled out that quick, and there is no way in fuck I'm getting into heaven. But right before my eyes, I swear to fuck it's an angel.

Her hair is so light it's practically white, flowing at her sides in an ethereal way I've never seen before. She has a large pair of headphones covering her ears as she walks naively down the road, not even slightly aware of all the danger that surrounds her in this city. The danger that is bleeding out just feet from her.

She's perfect, better than perfect. Her creamy skin shines in the moonlight, and I fucking hate that I'm too far away to see what color the angel's eyes are. Her long legs take each step with purpose, and soon she's fading from my view.

GRAVES

My sight begins to dim as darkness begins to cloud over me. If I don't make it out of this, at least I got a glimpse of an angel before I burn in hell. If I do, then that angel is *mine*.

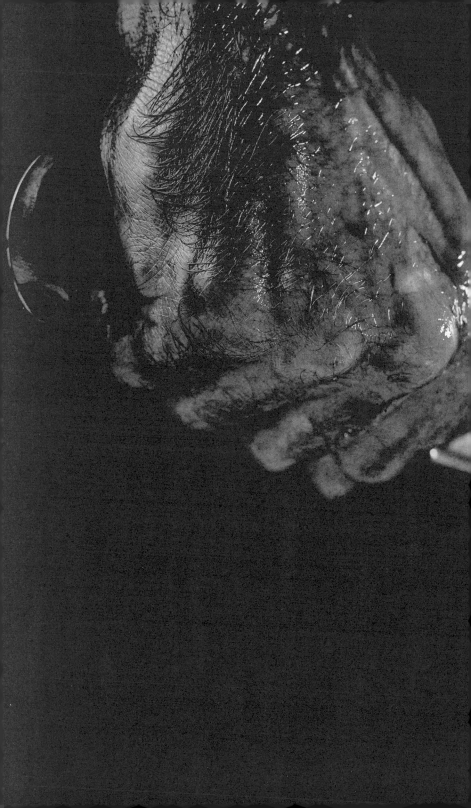

CHAPTER ONE

ZAYDEN

THREE MONTHS LATER

My fingers tangle through her silky strands as her body slowly rises and falls. My angel is such a heavy sleeper, which is a dangerous thing. What if there was a fire, carbon monoxide poisoning, or an intruder? I wrap my arms around her tighter, plastering my body against hers as I press my lips to the crown of her head.

She doesn't need to worry about any of that ever again, not when I'm here.

Three months ago, I almost died. The closest I ever got, for sure. Dominic got my half-jumbled text, and he found me out cold in the middle of the street. He said he tossed me into the car and drove me to our doc, where he worked on me off and on for about a week. I don't remember any of that week. The only thing I did remember was her.

At the first chance I got, I snuck out from my brother's watchful eye, and I tracked my angel down. It didn't take me long. She works at a bar just down the block from that alley, and I followed her back to her apartment, which was another mile down the road.

It took virtually no effort to break into the bar and find the schedule in the back. I memorized it and have been sure to make myself available during all her shifts. She's so oblivious, it's infuriating. Every day she walks to and from the bar with those fucking headphones on, her head up in the clouds, not looking around at the countless predators ready to sink their teeth into such perfection like her.

It's been three months, and she hasn't met my eye a single time. Not on the way to her work or from. Not when she goes out to lunch with her one and only friend Gabrielle Aranda, and not even when she finishes washing her face before crawling into bed.

I've been tempted on more occasions than I can count to show myself to her, allow her to rest easy now that I'm here. I want her to know that I'll never let anything tarnish her, but I think I like it better this way for now. This way, she can't fight me, can't attempt to stop me. I'm free to come and go as much as I please without any protests falling from her ruby-red lips.

18

Lips I've savored over and over again when she's at the deepest part of her REM cycle. The way she doesn't kiss me back, the way I have to work harder for it only makes me want her more.

Sometimes it seems that I'm too late, though. That the darkness of the world has already marred my precious angel. The whimpers she makes some nights, the scrunching of her nose, and the trembling in her body tell a story deeper than words ever could. It's a pain only I could ever understand, and the first night I saw it, I knew we were going to be bound to each other for all of eternity. Even if I had to drag her to hell with me.

I allow my fingers to dance over her bare shoulder, skimming over her intricately done tattooed sleeve on her right arm. It's beautiful, just like her.

My phone, resting on her dresser, flashes to life. Only one person has my number, and he knows not to call me when I'm away unless it's urgent. So begrudgingly, I release my angel and slip out of bed, grabbing my phone before stepping out into the hall where I can still keep my eyes on her.

"What?" I answer tersely.

"Where are you?" Dominic asks.

"Out."

"Obviously, why the fuck is your locator off?"

"What do you want, Dominic?"

He huffs in irritation before speaking.

"We have a problem. They are going to take in the manager at the shop in a few hours. He called them about an anonymous tip he wanted to make."

I fucking knew it.

From the moment Dominic hired him to run the business, I didn't trust him. I could practically see the words "little bitch" tattooed across his forehead.

I'm seething mad. Not because I need to go take care of this pathetic excuse of a man before he costs us everything, but because this means I can't stay until the sun comes up with my angel. That's enough to send me into a blind fucking rage.

Turning to her balcony door, I slip outside before locking it behind me. Normally I would kiss her goodbye, but I'm in no mood. I don't want her to think I'm upset with her. So I'll make it up to her tomorrow night and instead focus my rage on the person who deserves it most.

———————

THE SLAM OF A CAR DOOR HAS ME TURNING MY HEAD. A man in a matching skeleton mask walks up to me, clapping his gloved hand on my shoulder.

"You disabled the street cameras and their surveillance system?" I ask.

He nods his head, his eye roll practically visible through the mask.

"Of course. We have one hundred and eighty seconds before the police are notified, two hundred and forty before they get here."

I step into the unlocked house easily, walking down the hallway and to the right before opening the second door. As soon as Dominic hired this guy, I memorized his place just in case a situation like this came up. I also learned that he has a congenital heart defect, so this will be a lot cleaner than I typically prefer, but given the time crunch we are on, it'll have to do.

Dominic steps in front of me, always needing to be the one running the show as he grabs Arnold's face, slapping him awake with the other hand.

"What the hell! What the—oh f-fuck," he shouts before stuttering to a stop.

Dominic turns his head to the side slightly, his face obstructed by the mask, but based on the chill that runs through Arnold, I'd say it was intimidating enough.

"W-who are you? What do you want?"

"I think you know exactly who we are." I grin behind my mask.

His eyes flash to me, fear and confirmation practically drowning out his normally murky brown color.

"I-I don't understand. W-what have I done to you guys? Did someone put a hit on me?"

"Yes," Dominic says. "The Graves brothers."

Understanding passes across his face as he tries to run. Dominic overpowers him immediately and slams him back against the bed.

"P-please. It wasn't personal. I needed the money. A cop came by a few months ago, said if I could ever pass over useful information that I'd be taken care of. I have a sick mom, I was desperate!"

What the fuck?

Dominic and I share a look. That's not fucking good. Why the hell are cops snooping around our front? We are nothing but an upstanding business to the naked eye. It's been a useful mechanic shop to launder our money through over the years and we've never so much as sneezed out of line there. So what the hell is going on?

"What was the cop's name?" Dominic asks.

"Sanderson. U-uh...James. Jimmy, I think. Yeah, Jimmy Sanderson."

I nod at that, tucking away that name for later.

"Thank you. That's very helpful," Dominic says.

Arnold exhales in relief, and I can't hold in my laughter at the fucking idiot. I step up beside my brother, forcing him to release the sad sack of shit on the bed, my gloved hand gripping his neck tightly as I pull out the syringe from my pocket, biting off the cap before spitting it into Dominic's waiting hand.

Arnold begins to thrash under my hold, but it's almost too easy to keep the man down. I sink the needle right into his heart, his eyes going wide as I allow my smirk to bleed through in my voice.

"Night, night."

I push the extremely high levels of potassium in, forcing it directly into his heart and causing his entire body to tighten almost immediately. A little bit of potassium for the average person is no big deal. A good amount of potassium for the average person can be deadly. A lot of potassium directly injected into the heart of someone with a pre-existing heart condition is immediately lethal and just the kind of clean kill we need today.

It will present as a heart attack, and by the time they beat down the door, declare him dead, and get a tox screen, the potassium will be out of his system.

Dominic hands me the syringe cap back, and I place it on the needle before sliding it back into my pocket as we make our way out of the house. My brother glances at his watch as we get to his car.

"With seventeen seconds to spare before the police are notified of the outage."

"Yippee, what do I win?"

"Your freedom," he says dryly as he slips into the driver's seat while I sit in the passenger's seat. We are gone in seconds, and once we are a few blocks down the road, Dominic does something on his phone, assumingly turning the street cameras back on. I wish I had power at the touch of my fingertips like that.

He weaves in and out of the streets of Seattle with ease as he takes a left toward my warehouse in town. I could have gotten an apartment or a house if I wanted, but this place has a loft upstairs, a place for me to park my car inside, and a hidden room where I have all my toys.

Dominic parks the car outside the door, keeping the car locked as he takes off his mask. Looking at a carbon copy of yourself should be strange, that is if I hadn't lived with it for the last thirty-one years. We have the same black hair, the same six foot five build, the same sharp chin, and the same dimples when we smile. The only difference is that I have blue eyes, while Dominic has brown.

In identical twins, the odds of having different eye colors are 0.1 percent. Probably the same chance that that set of twins would grow up to be full-fledged mercenaries. Or the same chance that we would turn out semi-normal given our background. Though I think my proclivity for bloodlust and his for overpowering control shot those chances in the face.

"Where were you?" Dominic asks.

I don't pretend to act stupid because he's too smart for that, but I'll also never tell him about my angel. She's too precious for my brother to lay eyes on. She's too precious for me to have laid eyes on her, but it's too late for that.

He clearly understands I won't be giving him any information, which only confuses him more. His brows furrow as he turns his head to the side.

"What is going on with you? Ever since that night in the alley, you've been...off."

"Worry about who this cop is and why he is looking into a business *you* guaranteed would be the perfect front, brother."

His eyes narrow on me.

"It is perfect. There is no way he was telling the truth. Cops don't just show up to places and try to bribe the manager to give them intel. For all a cop would know, he would be the owner of the place. He was lying."

I nod. "Well, I trust you to handle it then."

"Always do," he mutters.

I roll my eyes at his dramatics before unlocking the car door and throwing it open.

GRAVES

"Text me when we have a job."

He nods and takes off before I've made it inside. I unlock the door and deactivate the security system before grabbing my bike. I walked from here to my angel's work today, and I could take my car back over there, but I haven't ridden the bike in a while, and our window is closing on riding weather in Seattle.

Tossing my leg over the two-hundred-and-fifteen horse-powered beast, I race across town toward her apartment. I still have a few more hours before her alarm clock goes off, and I'm gonna savor every fucking second.

CHAPTER TWO

BLAKE

There is so much blood, a deep crimson like an inky stain that won't fade. My hands scrub together under the water, but it's no use. They're stuck like that. Forever.

When my eyes open, that same creeping feeling sinks in. It's hard to describe, things just feel...off. They have for months now. I'm beginning to think this apartment is haunted or something.

My eyes bounce around the room, coming up empty as I look for anything even slightly out of place that could be the cause of this strange sensation. I never feel it at night before bed, only when I wake up in the morning.

Running my hands through my light-blonde hair, I let out a soft exhale before tossing the covers away from me and walking like a zombie to the bathroom. I begin washing my face for the day when my eyes in the mirror catch my attention. They seem to catch everyone's attention, and almost never for the good of it.

I heard it all growing up. Freak, monster. I was even called devil spawn by some old bag who clutched her pearls when she got a good look at me. People are fucking great.

I know it's uncommon, but heterochromia is not so rare that people don't know about it. My left eye is brown, and my right eye is blue. That's the small genetic condition that made my already dumpster-fire childhood just a little bit worse.

Genetic. Sure would love to thank Mom for passing it along. Kinda hard to get in touch with the land of the dead, though. I grew up hearing how it was a miracle I survived. That at first glance, I seemed halfway dead. I've felt all the way dead for years now, though.

I do my best to mask it. Nothing sends people running faster than someone with obvious mental health struggles. At least that's what I've learned. And don't get me wrong, I'm twenty-eight now. I'm not exactly looking for the perfect family to adopt me, but I wouldn't be opposed to a small group of close friends that would care if I was kidnapped in the middle of the night.

I do have Gabby, though. We met when we were seven back

in Chicago at the foster home we were both placed at. Gabby was only there for barely eight weeks before she was adopted by a nice family and moved out to Seattle. I wasn't as lucky.

About six months ago, I dumped my asshole boyfriend, but since the house was in his name, I had nowhere to go, and Chicago really had nothing but bad memories. So, Gabby and her rich husband moved me out here. I refused for weeks before she literally showed up, knocked on my car window, and forced me onto the plane with her.

I know that I should have my shit together more than I do at twenty-eight, and trust me, I'm trying. It just seems like no matter how hard I try, the universe says, "hold my beer" and kicks me back down. But this time is going to be different, it has to be.

Gabby and Christian tried to get me to stay with them when I came here, but that's where I drew the line. Gabby always thinks she knows best, and while I appreciate it, they just had baby Alison last month. There was no way I was going to intrude on the little growing family.

I did, however, accept the job Gabby hooked me up with at a bar called Hooked & Sinker. Not really sure if the owner was playing with the whole nautical vibes Seattle has going for it or if he's talking about hooking the local drunks and sinking them to their lowest lows. Either way, that seems to be what happens around here.

Our clientele wasn't the most pleasant at first, but now that I've been here a bit, everyone seems to have in some way accepted me, and it oddly feels...comfortable. I don't know. It's just a rundown bar, but the owner, Mark, is always throwing extra shifts on me, and if I'm a few minutes late, he doesn't give me more than a stern look before getting back to what he was doing. I'm not gonna work here forever, but for now, I'll sock away the money until I can get the ground under my feet.

Despite the exorbitant housing prices in Seattle, I was able to get this cute little one-bedroom apartment. It's very minimalist, and I didn't have much to add to it, but it's mine. In my name, paid with my money. It feels good, like a step in the right direction for once.

I wish I didn't have to get up so early after closing last night, but Mark fired two of our day shift bartenders that he caught stealing, and I really would love to buy a new car, so I'll take the money.

After I finish my morning routine, I throw on a clean black T-shirt and a pair of jeans before grabbing my purse and heading out the door. I was lucky enough to snag an apartment that actually has parking while still being relatively close to downtown, but because there is literally no parking lot at the bar, I walk.

Pulling out my headphones from my purse, I slip them on before opening up my playlist. Billie Holiday comes on, crooning softly in my ear as I make my way down the street. I'm not sure why I've always liked older music. I think it has to do with the family I was briefly placed with when I was six, the Harrisons. They were a nice older couple in their sixties who never had kids of their own. Mrs. Harrison would sing Billie Holiday and Frank Sinatra until her voice was hoarse, and Mr. Harrison would smile lovingly as he watched her the whole time.

Unfortunately, when I was eight, they got into a car accident on their way to pick me up from school, and both died immediately. Then I bounced around a bit before I landed at my last house.

Somehow, throughout all the bad times, a song from those days with the Harrisons seems to make everything a little brighter, a little softer, and I try to lean into it with everything I have.

When I get to the bar, I step in through the back, waving hello to Mark, who is pulling down chairs from on top of the tables, as I throw my purse and headphones into the office.

"Thanks for coming in, Blake," Mark says as he finishes the last table.

I nod as I move to the register to clock in.

"No worries. I appreciate the extra shifts."

"Well, you can have them all since you're about the only person I trust in this place," he says gruffly.

I raise an eyebrow at him as I shake my head.

"What poor life decisions did you make to land you in a position like this? Me, your only trusted ally? Yikes."

A throaty laugh escapes him as he scrubs at his silver beard.

"Tell me about it."

I grin at him before I start the opening process. The nice thing about closing last night and then working the next morning is that I know the closer did all the closing tasks, and I'm ready to start my shift. Only fourteen hours to go.

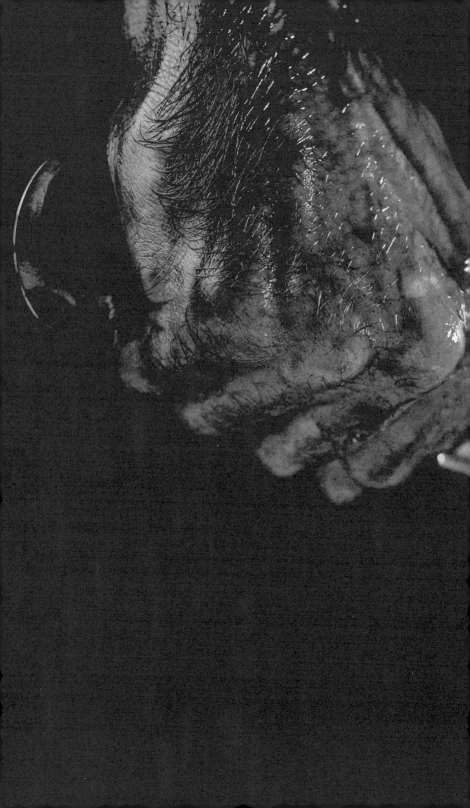

CHAPTER THREE

ZAYDEN

Something was off. I knew it before I even got to her block. I couldn't feel her near me anymore. The heavy sensation I feel in my chest when she's not close was in full force. Like an elephant sitting on my chest, not allowing me to fully catch my breath until I at least see her. Though it doesn't fully go away until I press my skin to hers.

When I got to her apartment to walk her to work like the gentleman I am, I saw her car there, which is normal. The piece of shit Nova is on its last leg, and there is no parking at her work, so it makes sense why she leaves it. I'll need to buy her a new car soon, though, something nice. I think she would like something red.

From there, I climbed up the fire escape to her balcony and let myself into her apartment. The bathroom was in disarray, just how she always leaves it when she sleeps in a little too much. She wasn't supposed to meet with Gabrielle today. The last time they texted was two days ago about getting together on Saturday. I only have her text messages wired to come directly to me, but maybe I need to set up another tap so I can get her phone calls too. Dominic is more of the tech wizard in that aspect, and asking him for help with something as important as this is too risky. I'll figure it out.

With the most likely places of her whereabouts crossed off the list, I went straight to Hooked & Sinker. I flipped up my hood, acted like I was texting, and walked past the dive bar. The window gave me only half a second view of my angel behind the bar, but it was enough to allow oxygen to fill my lungs for the first time since I left her this morning.

Nodding to myself, I move across the street, taking up residence at my spot in the alley across from the bar. It gives me just enough visualization to watch through the window without being noticed. She's not ready to meet officially just yet. I need more time with her first.

My phone suddenly begins buzzing in my hand, and I can't help but groan before answering it.

"What could you possibly need now?"

"Where are you? We were having a discussion. You went to

the bathroom, and now you're gone."

I shake my head as I pull out a cigarette, putting it between my lips before pulling out a lighter.

"Oh, did I forget to say goodbye?"

"Knock off the attitude, Zayden. What are you up to? Have you been prospecting without me? Do you know how dangerous that is? You don't think, you just kill. You have to be smarter than that, or you're gonna get us both locked up."

I roll my eyes at that as I take a large inhale of my cigarette.

"I'm not prospecting a job."

The phone goes quiet for a few seconds before he speaks again. "What *are* you up to then?"

I stay silent as I watch my angel smile at a man in his late forties. She hands him a beer, and he gives her a wink in return. My jaw clenches so tight that my molars begin to crack under the pressure. I feel the familiar rage begin to tingle every nerve ending in my body. These men shouldn't even be looking at my angel, let alone winking at her. I memorize everything I can about him, so it'll be all the easier to hunt him down later and pluck his eyes straight from his fucking head.

"Zayden?" Dominic asks.

"Watching over an angel," I snap before ending the call and turning my phone off.

She needs to get the fuck out of that place. I won't allow it anymore. She can finish her shift tonight, but after this, she is fucking done.

I'M FLICKING THE BLADE OF MY FAVORITE KNIFE OPEN and closed when the back door of the bar opens and my angel steps out, headphones on as usual, as she makes her way to her apartment. I pull out my phone, tapping into hers with ease before the familiar sound of Frank Sinatra rings through my ears. I love watching the way her hips sway to the beat, like the old music physically moves her.

I'm a good hundred feet away from her on the other side of the street, but she wouldn't notice if I was right on her as she practically dances her way home. The way her body moves so freely has my cock hardening to a pipe. I'm always hard when she's around, and the way her lips feel against the head of my cock is like touching fucking heaven.

I can't lay in bed beside her and not get turned on. I usually just rub it out as I rest my head against her neck, but a darker side got the better of me the other night. I rubbed myself against her lips for just a moment. I hoped she'd wake up. I hoped she'd taste me and see how perfect we are together, how destined we are. Unfortunately, she didn't. Doesn't mean I didn't come into my hand in front of her face so hard I blacked out.

For a moment, I'm so lost in the memory of her, her scent, her skin, that I don't see where he comes from. There is a man walking behind her, a sinister smile on his face and dirty clothes on his body. The look he has as his eyes rake over her sends white-hot anger searing through me. He's too close to her, and I'm too far away.

Darting through a few parked cars, I sprint to the other side of the road. My feet are quick but light, barely making a single sound. It's an art to be mastered when you are as large as I am, but it's one I've perfected.

He's practically twenty feet from her, and my heart is pounding with fury as I close the final steps between us and slip my arm around his neck. My hand covers his mouth to muffle his screams, though I know my angel plays her music entirely too loud to hear regardless.

Taking my knife from my pocket, I flick it open before plunging it into his side, right into the kidney. Even through my hand, his scream is piercing. He reaches for the knife, gripping the handle, but I smack his hand away as I pull my knife from his fingers and push him to the ground. I jump on top of him and begin letting out my wrath on this worthless waste of life. He was going to touch her, hurt her. He'll never even get the chance to set eyes on her again.

I grip the sides of his face, digging my thumbs into his eye sockets until I hear a loud pop in each, and his screams fill up the night air. My eyes flick forward to see my angel crossing the street, completely unaware of the scene behind her as she makes her way to the front of her apartment building. Good. I wouldn't want her to set those unique beauties on someone as unsightly as this man.

"Freeze! Hands where I can see them!" a voice shouts from over my shoulder.

Are you fucking kidding me?

I have two choices at this moment. I could grab my knife, turn, and have it lodged in the cop's jugular in less than two seconds, but based on the sound of the passenger door opening,

I'd say he has a partner with him who will no doubt get a few bullets into me before I can get to them, and honestly, I still walk with a slight limp since the last time I was shot.

My second choice is to play victim until Dominic can get a crooked enough judge to get me out of no doubt an attempted murder charge. I don't like that one at all, but it seems to be the only one that gets me back to my angel the fastest, so I'll make it work.

I quickly slide into character, leaping away from the scum as I scramble across the ground and hold my hands up shakily.

"P-please, help," I stutter. "H-he attacked me. Tried to stab me with his k-knife."

The cop holding me at gunpoint pauses for a moment, his eyebrows dipping as his mind tries to catch up with the curveball I just threw him.

"Looked like you were the threat, not him," he says, still holding that gun on me as he looks at the other guy.

I look to his partner to see a hardened judgment in his eye as he too holds out his gun. My mind starts racing with a plan to get out of here when another cruiser pulls up and two more cops get out. Fuck. Looks like my angel will have to sleep on her own tonight.

When they slap the cool metal handcuffs onto me, my eyes flick up to the second window to the left on the third story. The light flicks on in the same moment, and a small sense of ease settles that she's safe, at least for tonight.

I'll see you soon, angel.

CHAPTER FOUR

DOMINIC

I roll up the cuffs of my black shirt to my elbows as I sit in the metal chair and wait on the other side of the plexiglass window for my idiot twin. What the fuck was he thinking?

He didn't tell me much.

Last night, I got a phone call from him saying that he got arrested at the corner of Thompson and 47th at 1:15 a.m. I knew what he was saying without saying it. So I pulled up the street cams and wiped the footage of his attack, made it look like a technical glitch, and erased my footprints in case they dove deeper into the issue.

The question is, what the hell was he doing?

For the last few months, there has been something off about him. Don't get me wrong, there was always something off about my brother. We lived the same life but dealt with the events of that life in two totally different ways. I internalize and only allow out what is absolutely necessary, where Zayden feels everything. He feels so deeply and so wildly that he jumps over the line of crazy and lives in full-on psycho town. It's a miracle he hasn't gone all Jack the Ripper on the world these days. I think our line of work keeps the demons inside him at least semi-satiated, so I make sure the work is steady and the plans are iron-tight.

Which is why I still can't, for the life of me, figure out why a highly skilled killing machine could make such a reckless and careless attack on some random drug addict that came out of nowhere. The video didn't make sense to me the first time I watched it, but it only took one rewind for everything to become much clearer.

It was her. Something about that girl set him off. The man was obviously about to harm her in some way, and I watched my brother intervene, no, annihilate the guy before the girl even had a chance to look over her shoulder.

I've seen my brother's control slip. His irrational actions take over from time to time, but never like this. Never to the point where he got arrested. Because of what we do, it's important we maintain perfect records, that way we are never suspects. Well, pair that bullshit lie about a cop being onto us, a cop who doesn't even exist, might I add, with my brother's idiocy, and I've had enough of this shitty week.

The door in the back buzzes before it opens, allowing several guards to escort inmates to various phones. The last inmate is the tallest, with inky black hair to match my own, two arms filled with tattoos differentiating us, and an entirely too-casual demeanor for being where he is at this moment. Zayden towers over his guard by at least a half-foot, and the guard looks far more intimidated by Zayden than he should.

If only he knew how scared he really should be.

Zayden plops down into the chair across from me, picking up the phone while I do the same. I raise an unimpressed eyebrow at him, which only causes him to roll his eyes and lean back into his chair.

"What?"

"What?" I parrot. "How about, what were you possibly thinking?"

"He attacked me. It was self-defense." He shrugs.

I let out a humorless laugh as I shake my head.

"Yeah, self-defense would have ended before you gouged the man's eyes out and stabbed him in the kidney."

"He pulled a knife on me, what was I supposed to do?" Zayden asks, his face serious, but a flicker of mirth only I seem to be able to detect in his ice-blue eyes.

Seriously, does he really expect anyone to believe that he was the victim in this scuffle? I guess it's the only angle he has to work at the moment, and he's milking it for all it's worth.

"So, when do I get out?" Zayden asks.

"You don't."

The mirth in his eyes evaporates instantly as a flicker of the cold-blooded killer he is comes to light.

"What?"

"You've been denied bail. The official report is that you appear to be too mentally unstable to be trusted. You're a flight risk. So, no bail until your hearing."

"Who said I was unstable?" he practically snarls. "It was that little bitch detective, right?"

"Easy," I say in a way that seems to snag his attention.

His eyes are filled with fury, but he understands what I'm saying. Not here, not like this.

"I've contacted the best defense attorney in the state, and he's agreed to represent you. He's working on getting you a hearing in three months."

"Three MONTHS?" he shouts before closing his eyes and shaking his head.

"I can't be in here for three months. I need to get out, now," he says, a dangerous look filling his eyes that has my head cocking.

"What's going on in there? Everything okay?"

He shakes his head. "It's not about in here, it's out there. I need to..." He pauses for a moment, sinking his teeth into his lower lip.

"I can't be in here for that long. I..." He trails off again before clenching his jaw tight. "If I'm going to be in here for that long, I need you to do something for me."

I nod as I let him continue.

He glances over his shoulder at the security guard, who is obviously eavesdropping but pretending not to be.

"There is something I need you to watch over for me at Hooked & Sinker. You'll know it when you see it."

"Time's up!" one of the guards shouts to the room.

Inmates begin lining up as their loved ones say goodbye and walk away until it's just Zayden and me on the phone.

"Promise me," Zayden demands, a strange note of desperation in his tone that has me nodding my head.

He exhales, but it doesn't look like it's in relief, per se. His eyes flick up at me once more as I go to stand, still gripping the phone.

"Take care of my angel, brother, or I'll end you."

With that, he walks away and lines up, giving me a lethal look on his way out the door. My interest is officially piqued. We've never kept each other in the dark about anything before, ever. Whatever or whoever this "angel" is has somehow been able to turn Zayden into their own personal guard dog, and based on the way he was following her before she was attacked, I'd bet my life she doesn't have a clue.

CHAPTER FIVE

BLAKE

"What can I get ya?" I ask the scruffy-looking man who reeks of malt liquor as he teeters on the barstool.

"Whisker, er. Whiskeyer. Whatever," he slurs.

I raise an unimpressed eyebrow as I shake my head.

"Not gonna happen, buddy. Stumble outside to the corner, grab a Seattle Dog from the cart, and when you sober up, you can have a drink."

He grumbles in irritation, but does as I say, bouncing around like a pinball between the tables before he's out the door. I honestly don't see the appeal to the things. A hot dog smothered in cream cheese and grilled onions? I'll pass, but people seem to love them. One night, I actually saw a woman full-on fight a group of men over the last one. Nothing like downtown Seattle at three in the morning.

"You tell him, honey." Bonnie, one of our regulars, cackles before she takes a healthy sip of her boxed wine merlot.

I laugh with her as I suddenly notice a large man sitting in the booth tucked away in the furthest corner. I didn't see him come in. I honestly don't know how I could have missed him. The guy is massive. I'm five foot eight, but it still looks like I would come up to under his shoulder if I stood side by side with him.

His eyes lift from the phone in his hand, clashing with mine instantly. A feeling rips through me from my head to my toes. There is something in those eyes, so deep and heavy. The way he watches me is like nothing I've ever experienced. He watches me like he's been waiting for me his whole life.

Mkay, Blake. That is the last time you fall asleep to some Hallmark bullshit on TV.

Shaking the ridiculous thoughts out of my head, I make my way around the bar top, moving to the corner where the man sits before I stop a foot or so short.

"Hey, sorry. I didn't see you come in. What are you drinking?"

The deep browns of his eyes flick between my own for a moment. I expect him to make a face or look away, but instead he continues to stare. It gets to the point where I think he's a mute before he finally answers.

"Scotch, neat."

"Gotta favorite brand?" I ask.

"Whatever you think," he says, still not taking his eyes off my own.

"That's a dangerous game. You don't ever trust a woman to pick out your liquor," Marty, another regular, shouts from the table beside him.

"Shut the hell up," I scoff with an eye roll before turning back to face the man in front of me.

His mouth twitches just slightly, like he wants to smile but won't let himself before he nods.

"I'll take my chances."

Something about the low timbre of his voice sends a shiver up my spine. I nod softly as I turn on my heel, my normal confidence dimming softly as I feel his eyes track my every move. Slipping behind the bar, I grab some Blue Label and pour it into a fresh glass before carrying it over to him.

I set it down in front of him before giving him a quick smile. "Let me know if I can get anything else for you."

He nods as he lifts the glass to his lips, taking a small sip before humming his approval. He doesn't verbally say anything, but that hum has vastly inappropriate images flickering through my head.

I do my best to get back to work, but for the rest of the night, every time I steal a glance in his direction, he's already watching me. It's both unnerving and exhilarating. The customers begin to wean out as closing time approaches fast, with every single person leaving except for him. His drink is untouched apart from the single sip he took, and something like disappointment dips inside me at that. It's not like I made the scotch, so I don't know why the hell I'm disappointed.

"Did you not like it?" I ask.

His eyes move down to the full glass before lifting it up and tossing it back in one go. He swallows easily before looking back at me.

"I did."

I nod at that. Not sure if he did that to spare my feelings or not, but either way, does it matter?

"Good. We are closing soon. Anything I can get you?"

"Wasn't last call half an hour ago?" he asks.

"Well, yeah. I just...you're still here."

He raises an eyebrow. "Is that a problem?"

"I mean, kinda. I need to close, and to do that, I need no customers here. Plus, the way you're just staring at me, waiting for everyone else to leave, it's giving off serial killer vibes."

An amused huff escapes him at that.

"My apologies. I didn't mean to put you on edge. I just wanted to make sure you had a safe way to get home."

"And the creepiness continues," I say, only half teasing.

He shrugs his shoulders but doesn't say anything in his defense, which again is creepy. Hot or not, I know how this works. I saw the Ted Bundy movie.

"I'm good. You can go."

He pauses for a moment like he is about to say something, before he nods his head and stands. His height keeps going and going until, I swear, it looks like his head is about to hit the ceiling.

Okay, not really, but he is extremely tall, his shoulders are wide, and his hands alone are nearly the size of my face. Something twists inside me, a warning, a memory, a fear. Whatever it is, when he takes a step closer to me, I take a step back, visibly shaking as I bump into a table and send the thing toppling over.

Logically, I can tell he doesn't want to hurt me, but tell that to my racing heart.

He frowns at that as he bends down and rights the table, not immediately getting up as he speaks to me while crouched.

"Have a good night."

With that, he slowly stands, turning away from me before he can fully tower over me as he steps out the door. I let out a shaky breath when he's gone and lock the door behind him. I press my back against the heavy wooden door as I try to control my breathing. Jesus. I haven't gotten triggered like that in a long time. I don't know if it was his size or demeanor, or maybe something in my intuition, warning me that he was bad news.

I don't think it was the latter, though, because there is an equally loud voice in my head telling me there is something different about him. Not necessarily good, but not entirely bad either.

CHAPTER SIX

BLAKE

For the last three days, he has come into the bar. Every day he sits down in the same booth, orders the same drink, and proceeds not to drink it until it's closing time. We haven't spoken outside of basic pleasantries since that day, and honestly, I'm not sure why I'm not more bothered by his silence. I should be creeped out, right? The way he watches me and studies me. The way he is very clearly following my work schedule. I should be alarmed. This is the part where I call the cops and file a restraining order, right?

Instead, though, when he's here, I feel...safe, I guess. As safe as one could be when they are practically alone, in a large city, working in a dive bar until the early hours of the morning. I'm filling up a couple of college guys' shot glasses when he steps inside. I give him a head nod in greeting, and he does the same.

I pour his drink without hesitation and drop it off at his table.

"Thank you," he says simply.

I nod my head in response as I turn and go about the rest of my shift. The night goes pretty easy, and I'm thankful because last night I had to clean someone's puke off the bathroom floor. Ten out of ten, don't recommend.

"Hey, sugar tits! Another round!" one of the rowdy college boys shouts through the bar. His dumb friends all laugh, like it was the funniest thing the pack of hyenas had ever heard, as I begin filling up their next round.

Gritting my teeth together, I slip past the center tables and come up to the guys. I set the class clown's glass harder than the others as I lean down until I'm eye-to-eye with him.

"You pull any shit like that again, and you're all out of here. Got that?"

His friends all nod, but he just rolls his eyes lazily.

"Ah shit, calm down, baby. I'm just messing around. Besides, what do you expect when a pretty little thing like you comes to work at a place like this?" he says as his hand reaches behind me, slapping my ass so hard the sting is instant.

Outrage and disgust fill me as I get ready to throttle his ass. Unfortunately, I'm too slow. A black blur comes out of nowhere, tackling the frat boy to the ground. I recognize my silent customer instantly.

His fists drive into the guy's face in perfect synchronicity, throwing in an elbow to the nose for good measure before his hands are wrapped around his throat, squeezing so hard his knuckles are turning white.

Several of the guy's buddies are yanking on him, trying to pull him off their quickly dying friend, but they all fail. My eyes begin flicking around the room nervously, not sure what to do to stop him before he literally kills the kid.

Crouching down so I'm in front of him, I shake his shoulders, trying to get him to let go or at least look away from him, anything.

"Let him go. Stop! Please," I say, all of which seem to fall on deaf ears. The silent giant doesn't relent. It's like he's not even here right now, like he can't see anything except for the guy in front of him.

I hesitate for a moment before gently reaching my hand out to his face. It's the equivalent of trying to pet a rabid wolf, but as soon as my fingertips touch his skin, something snaps. His head whips up so fast it actually startles me, sending my stomach plummeting to the floor as his deep brown eyes collide with mine. They are so dark, they're practically black right now, and for a moment, a chill runs up my spine at the look in them. So vacant, so hollow. It's like nothing I've ever seen before.

"Please," I say again softly.

He blinks hard once before that empty look slowly recedes, allowing that rich brown color to return as he eases off the limp guy beneath him and goes to stand. The guy's friends all rush around him, shaking him until he groggily wakes up.

The man doesn't pay any attention to them, though. Instead, he gives me his hand as I stand up with him. When I go to pull my hand away, his grip tightens for a moment, his thumb running against the back of my knuckles as he looks down at me.

"Are you okay?"

I can't help but let out a humorless laugh.

"Me?"

He nods seriously. "He touched you."

Something about the simplicity of his words, the possessiveness, the protection. It gives me far more comfort and not enough fear. I should be running fast and wide from someone who is obviously so out of control. He's dangerous, clearly, and he's fixated on me for some reason. I should already be entering witness protection at this point. Instead, something in me is savoring the feeling of his large hand tenderly holding my own, the clean scent of his cologne swirling around the space between us, as the face that could rival a god stares down at me with concern.

"I'm fine, but you should probably get out of here. They look like the kind to call the cops," I say as I nod down to the guys who are half-tending to their friend and half-watching him like he's a crazed madman.

"I suppose you're right. Look after yourself," he says before dropping a hundred-dollar bill onto the table and releasing my hand at the last possible second as he makes a swift exit out of the bar.

"Hey! Wait! Where is he going? The cops are on their way!" one of the guys shouts out with the phone up to his ear.

"Why?" Marty asks from the bar top as he takes a sip of his beer. "Your friend had too much to drink, slipped, and busted his face to shit."

"What?" another one of the guy's snaps. "That's not what happened! He was attacked."

"Not what I saw," another customer chimes in. "He sexually assaulted Blake here, and then when he tried to follow after her, he slipped and got all fucked up."

A collective nod passes through the bar, apart from the group of guys. The reality of the situation around them begins to sink in as they panic. They should have gone downtown for their night out if they wanted justice and all that jazz. We don't even have a working camera inside the bar. The people around here are kind of like Luxembourg, they govern themselves.

THE COPS SHOWED UP A FEW MINUTES LATER AND TOOK reports from the guys as well as a few of the customers and then me.

"Let's cut the shit, lady," the cop says to me. "There is no way he slipped and fell. He has bruising around his throat that are clearly fingerprints. Now, who did it, and where did they go?"

"I don't know what to tell you, officer. I've given you the

full story," I draw out lazily.

Even if I wanted to help them find him, I wouldn't, because this cop is a grade A asshole. He's talked down to me ever since he's gotten here and has either called me girl or lady. Neither name I will be responding to, so instead I just stand here and stare at him.

The cop curses, flipping his notebook shut before grabbing his partner and storming out of the bar. The "victim" and his friends left a while ago when their buddy was toted off in an ambulance. Once all the excitement was over, all of our customers left, until it was just me and the police. Now that they are gone, I can finally get to closing.

It doesn't take long to get everything put away and shut down for the night. I'm sure I'll be getting a phone call from Mark first thing in the morning when he hears about all of this. I'll give him the same story I gave the cops just for cohesiveness, though knowing Mark, he'd probably want to high-five the guy for laying the little shit out.

As soon as I'm done for the night, I lock the back door, pull out my headphones, and begin to slip them on when I see a hooded figure leaning up against the wall. My stomach tightens in anticipation before I fully make out who it is. Letting out a soft, relaxed breath, I tuck my headphones back into my purse as I step up to him.

"What are you doing here?" I ask him.

Those brown eyes swing down to me as he straightens up to his full height. God, giant isn't much of an exaggeration. I never thought I'd feel so dwarfed by anyone. Instinctually, I take a half-step back just for good measure, and based on the way his eyes track me, he doesn't miss it. Goddammit, I hate how weak I can be sometimes.

"I wanted to make sure you were okay. Did the cops give you any trouble? They seemed to stick around for a while."

I shake my head. "They were just assholes. I didn't tell them anything, none of us did."

"Wouldn't matter if you did," he says.

He's got a point. Aside from the fact that he likes scotch and is available most nights, I know nothing about this guy. Not where he lives or his job. I don't even know his name.

"Can I give you a ride home?" he asks.

I think about it for all of two seconds before I shake my head. "No need. I live just up the road."

He doesn't say anything for a moment before he nods.

"Would you mind if I walked you? It will give me peace of mind that the guy or his friends aren't going to jump you for tonight."

"Are you going to start stalking me if you find out where I live?" I laugh teasingly.

He doesn't laugh, though. Instead, he just shakes his head seriously, causing me to swallow down my laughter as I look him over. Am I stupid for talking to this virtual stranger in a dark alley? Yes. Am I even dumber for contemplating allowing him to walk me home and discover where I live? Absolutely. So, tell me why, when I look into his eyes, all rational logic flies out the window and I nod my head yes as I begin my walk home like normal, sans headphones.

I hear his steps behind me at a close yet respectful distance. Neither of us say anything until we get just outside my building, and I can't take the silence any longer.

"Why did you do it?" I ask as I turn to face him.

He pauses his movements as he tilts his head slightly.

"Do what?"

"Attack that guy, beat his ass, whatever you want to call it."

One of his eyebrows lifts in what looks like curiosity.

"He touched you. You think I was going to allow that?"

"Well, why wouldn't you? We don't know each other. You don't owe me anything."

He doesn't say anything for a few moments, like he's choosing his words wisely.

"We don't know each other," he agrees. "What I did probably came across as aggressive and out of line, and perhaps it was." He pauses again, taking a half-step closer to me, lifting his bear paw of a hand up to my face before brushing a piece of hair away from my eye. "I do know that you're special, and you deserve to be protected."

"I can take care of myself," I say as his fingers tangle in my hair.

"I know, I've seen you hold your own just fine. It doesn't mean you should have to."

Something in his words stirs a feeling inside of me. One that I haven't felt in literally decades. It shakes at the countless locks and doors I have guarding that part of me. The part I vowed to never show again. Now, I'm not dumb enough to allow my guard to drop just like that for a perfect stranger just because he feels protective of me, but I can't deny that his tone, his words, and the sincerity on his face are rattling the chains a bit.

Not knowing what to say, I swallow roughly at that before glancing from his lips to his eyes. The air between us is practically buzzing, my chest fluttering in anticipation of having this dark knight's lips on mine. I flick my eyes up to see him watching me with a complicated expression. He doesn't make a move, but he doesn't pull away either, so I muster up all the courage I could possibly have and go for it.

Lifting up onto my tiptoes, I bring my hands up to his face, resting them on his cheeks as I drag him to me. He comes easily, but when our lips meet, he doesn't kiss me back. A buzzing feeling practically rips through me from just a single brush of his lips to my own. It starts from my mouth and runs all the way down to my toes before settling between my thighs.

I've never felt such an exhilarating feeling in my life, and he's not even kissing me back. At that thought, I go to pull away as the buzzing fades and embarrassment at literally throwing myself at this stranger takes up full residence inside me. I don't get far though before his hand on my face wraps behind my neck and his other arm winds around my lower back, forcing my body flush against his as he deepens the kiss.

His lips smash against mine before his teeth sink into my bottom lip. I let out a soft moan as the pain quickly ebbs into pleasure. His tongue wraps around mine, like he's trying to relish the taste of me. His hands grip me to the point of near pain, like he needs me to stay exactly where I am, right in his arms, or we will both snap in two. It's all enough to fry my senses completely.

When he pulls away, his chest is heaving as he rests his forehead against my own. His eyes are clenched tight, and I furrow my brows as I run my hand through his dark locks. At that, his eyes fly open, completely focused on me before he whispers roughly, "I have to go."

Disappointment fills me, but I nod softly. He takes me by surprise as he leans in for one more chaste kiss against my lips, as if he were savoring me one more time, before he leaves.

"I don't even know your name," I breathe out with half a chuckle.

He gives me the start of a smile, but his eyes are anything but happy as he looks down at me. "You don't need to."

He straightens up and takes a step away.

"Please," I say simply, not knowing why I need the tangibility of a name at this moment but asking all the same.

He rolls his lips together as he watches me carefully.

"Dominic."

I can't help but smile at that. "Dom."

Something flickers across his face at that as he gives a short nod.

"Goodnight, Blake."

CHAPTER SEVEN

DOMINIC

I broke a promise to my brother. Something that I've never done in my life. I promised him that I'd look after her, but I can't. Since that night almost a month ago in front of her apartment, I knew I had to keep my distance.

I still watch over her from a safe distance, but not for as long as Zayden would insist upon, I'm sure. I make sure she gets to the bar safely and home safely, all the while she's none the wiser.

I can't be near her. She's too consuming, too intoxicating.

From the moment I laid eyes on Blake Carlson, I understood why Zayden was so obsessed, why he was so hell-bent on keeping her for himself. She's practically magnetic, the soft rasp of her voice, the supple curves of her body, and those intriguing eyes, all wrapped up in a package that would bring the most disciplined man to his knees.

After the first night, I looked into her, and though there wasn't much that came up, what I did find was less than pleasing. No doubt Zayden has done deeper research than I have, and I can only imagine what went through his mind when he saw those photos.

I did my best to keep my distance, to observe but not engage. And then that went to hell real fast when that piece of shit smacked her ass. I had someone look into him, and apparently he has neurological deficits from how long his brain was deprived of oxygen. The police are looking for what his friends described as a big, scary dude with tattoos. I almost laughed at his friend's incompetence, but it was nice to know there wouldn't be any heat coming down on me for my rash action. Zayden seems to be bringing enough heat for the both of us.

His lawyer called me and said that he got the hearing moved up to today. He also told me that Zayden has been in three fights since he's been incarcerated. Which, of course, is not surprising, but it sure as hell is unhelpful to his plea of being the victim.

The smooth-talking lawyer I hired was able to get me a ten-minute conference with him before he had to go to court. He said that I need to talk some sense into him. Obviously, he doesn't realize my twin doesn't have the capability for anything of the sort.

When the door buzzes open in the cold jail conference room, my stomach dips in anticipation. I haven't seen Zayden since the first time I came here. Mainly because I haven't wanted to see him since I kissed his sole obsession. He's observant, too observant. What I did was despicable, no matter how much he doesn't deserve her and how delusional he clearly is if he thinks he could ever really be with her. Either way, it doesn't matter. He saw her first, he claimed her first, and I broke my brother's trust.

Swallowing over the guilt I have building inside me, I school my face as Zayden comes strolling into the room with a nice, clean blue suit on. He sits down at the table as the guard stands in the corner.

Zayden's eyes are on me instantly, narrowing in accusation. "You haven't come to visit."

I give him a bored look as I tilt my head.

"Sorry, I've been running a business, several actually, just trying to keep things going since my partner got himself locked up."

Zayden doesn't drop his accusing look, though, his eyes tracking me like a hawk.

"Did you expect me to come every day so we could chitchat? Have some brotherly bonding?" I scoff dryly.

"You were supposed to be giving me updates on her," he says as his jaw clenches.

"You didn't specify that," I say as I glance at my watch.

"Fuck you!" he snarls as the guard takes a warning step toward him. Zayden blows out a calming breath before looking back at me. "You knew I would want updates. Why haven't you come?"

Choosing to sidestep his question, I redirect the conversation.

"I hear you've been causing trouble in there."

"Only a little." He smirks in a sinister way that would make any normal person's skin crawl.

"Yeah, well, your little bit of trouble is going to cause you big problems when it comes to sentencing, you fucking idiot."

He rolls his eyes at me and shakes his head.

"The lawyer and I have it all planned out. They were all self-defense. You know how jail can be. They tried to take advantage of me," he says as his entire demeanor shifts and he allows his voice to shake and his eyes to fill with terror.

My god, he's a fucking psychopath.

"Hope your acting classes have paid off because you're gonna have to sell it hard."

He waves me off, dropping the scared act as he adjusts his seating.

"Now, back to my angel. How is she?"

I nod. "Fine. I assume you know the routine by now. To and from the bar, an occasional lunch with her friend. Fairly mundane life."

"Any problems?" Zayden asks.

"Actually, yes," I say, causing Zayden's eyes to snap up to me.

"There was an incident at the bar. A guy was harassing her, and then he slapped her ass."

I hear one of Zayden's molars actually crack as his jaw clenches to the point of steel. His chest is heaving as he stays silent, no doubt trying to control his rage.

"And?" he practically growls.

"And he was discharged from the ICU two weeks ago with long-lasting neurological deficits."

The fire in his eyes dims a bit, returning to a calm smolder.

"Excellent news, brother."

I dip my head in thanks as I pull my wallet out, removing the Polaroid photo I took for him. When I set it on the table, he grabs it instantly, lifting it up in his shackled hands as he stares at it reverently.

"My angel," he whispers underneath his breath.

I don't know why he calls her that, she isn't his anything, but if you tried to tell Zayden that, I'm sure he'd rather cut out your tongue than accept the truth.

His eyes trace over the image for several more seconds before he tucks it into his pocket and nods his head, closing his eyes tightly. When he opens them up again, a clarity I haven't seen in years fills them. For a moment, if you didn't know better, you'd almost think Zayden was normal. He's calm, composed, and not a ticking time bomb eager to go off at the slightest inconvenience, just for a taste of blood.

"Let's go. Sooner I can get out, sooner I can be in bed with her," he says as he stands.

I frown at that.

"You've been in her bed? Zayden," I say with a curl of my lip.

"We're soulmates," he says simply, like that is the most basic piece of knowledge there is in this life.

Instead of arguing with him, I shake my head and turn to walk out of the room as the guard escorts him through his door. The courthouse is just next door, so I make quick work of exiting the jail and stepping into court.

Once I'm through security, I find Zayden's lawyer pacing the hall. As soon as he sees me, he hurries over.

"Tell me you calmed him down. I tried to talk with him the other day, and he fucking lost it on me."

I nod. "He's calm."

"Good." He nods. "If he plays his cards right, we *just* might be able to get him out of this with house arrest and probation."

"And if not?" I question.

He gives me a sharp shake of his head that has me cursing under my breath.

Fucking hell, Zayden.

———

THE JUDGE RATTLED THROUGH THE CASE INFORMATION way too fast. Judge Martinez barely looked at Zayden as he put on the performance of a lifetime. Honestly, I almost believed him, and I know him better than anyone in the world. For some reason, it doesn't seem to affect the judge in the slightest.

"Zayden Graves, rise for sentencing."

Zayden stands, that same innocent look splashed across his face as he stares up at the judge hopefully.

"For the charges of first-degree assault with a deadly weapon, I find you guilty and sentence you to five years in the Washington State Penitentiary, with the possibility of parole after three years."

With that, the gavel is banged and gone is my calm and collected brother. A roar rips through him as he attempts to jump over the table. I'm not sure what his goal was once he got over, but several prison guards rush him immediately, slamming him to the ground before wrapping him up in even more restraints as they haul him out of the room.

His screams are heard even after the door is shut, and his lawyer shakes his head as he packs up his briefcase.

"Sorry, Mr. Graves. Looks like the judge had his mind made up before we even showed."

I look at him but don't respond as I stare at the judge. Judge Allen Martinez. I'll come up with his home address later and make sure to check on him. I heard there was going to be a terrible gas leak.

CHAPTER EIGHT

BLAKE

It's been over a month since I last saw Dominic. He gave me an earth-shattering, heart-palpitating kiss and then said he had to go. I didn't know that he meant forever. I can't deny that I was more than a little disappointed when he stopped coming around. But that's just the way it is, I guess. People come and go, right?

I pop my car trunk as I fill it with the groceries I've just bought. Today is my first day off in a while, so I'm just going to go home, stock the cabinets, and then waste the rest of the day watching trash TV. It's gonna be glorious.

When I slide into my seat, I put the key in the ignition and turn, only for nothing to happen. What the fuck? I try it again, but still nothing. No lights pop up on my dash, but those things only work half the time anyway. Letting out an irritated exhale, I pop the hood and throw my door open.

As I lift my hood, I quickly realize I have no fucking clue what I'm looking at. I see some wires and I try to wiggle them. I don't know, maybe it'll do something.

"Need some help?" a familiar voice asks from behind me.

I startle for a moment before I look up to see Dominic staring down at me. He's wearing a black button-down shirt tucked into black dress pants. I don't know what he does for work, but he's always dressed nicely. Never suit-and-tie style, but just clean and put together. Oh, and hot as fuck.

"Hey. What are you doing here?" I ask.

He holds up a single bag of groceries, effectively making me sound like an idiot.

I don't know, Blake, what is he doing at a grocery store?

"Car won't start?" he asks.

I shrug. "Guess not."

"Can I try?" he asks.

"Be my guest." I nod as he attempts to sit in the driver's seat. I say attempt because he's so tall and my car is so small that his head literally has to bend just to fit inside it.

He goes to turn the key, but nothing happens yet again.

"It's probably your battery," he says as he steps out of my clown car. "I have a shop in town that can get you set up with a new one and do a once-over on your car if you want."

"Thanks, but I don't think I can afford all that right now. I hardly use the thing anyway."

"I insist. I know the owner, money is not gonna be a problem."

I hesitate for a moment before I relent. Fuck it, if he wants to help me get my car fixed, who am I to say no?

He nods before I can even respond, apparently reading my face or something, as he pulls out his phone and shoots off a text.

"A tow truck will come pick it up within the hour. I can take you to the shop now, or maybe we can get you lunch?"

I tilt my head at that. "Just me?"

"I could eat too, I suppose," he says with a slight twitch to his lips.

I shake my head as I toss my hands at my sides.

"I'm sorry. I know you're trying to be nice, but what the fuck?"

"Excuse me?" he asks.

"You're confusing. One minute, you're showing up at my work every day, watching me like a hawk. Then you beat someone half to death just for touching me. Then you kissed me like the earth around us was shattering, and then you ghost me. I mean, the ghosting thing is whatever, but now here you are showing up like a savior, ready to whisk me away to lunch? So, yeah, I repeat, what the fuck?"

He opens his mouth like he's going to speak before he closes it and shakes his head.

"I'm sorry that I've upset you. It wasn't my intention."

"I'm not upset," I practically snap, clearly contradicting my words. "I'm just confused."

Dominic nods but doesn't say anything in his defense. I'm ready to just say *fuck it* and walk home when he speaks.

"That night, it took me by surprise. I haven't felt so... connected to someone in a long time, ever maybe."

I cross my arms over my chest as I look up at him.

"Is that a bad thing?"

"Yes," he says flatly.

My eyebrows knit together at that before I nod.

"C'mon, let me take you to lunch. It's the least I can do."

"What about my groceries? They're going to spoil if I leave them all day," I say.

He glances toward my car before pulling out his phone, his fingers flying across the screen as he speaks.

"I'll have him put them into the shop fridge when they get your car back there."

I frown at that. "You have that much pull?"

He shrugs his shoulders but doesn't respond. I tilt my head to the side, assessing as I speak again.

"Why now? Is it okay to be around me because you don't feel connected anymore, or...?" I hedge.

"I've recently decided a little bad isn't always bad for you."

"Has anyone ever told you that you're super fucking cryptic?"

A surprised laugh bubbles out of his chest. It's deep and throaty and it's the most joyous sound I've ever heard come out of someone. Or maybe it just sounds that way because I've never heard anything like it come out of him. I can't help but smile that I made him do that.

"Okay, where are you taking me?"

———

DOMINIC ENDED UP TAKING US TO A REALLY GOOD THAI restaurant on the other side of town. They had the best shrimp chips I've ever had, and I may or may not have shoved the rest of them in my purse, wrapped in a napkin, obviously.

We talked about where both of us grew up, me in Chicago and him in Seattle. He's an only child, just like me, and unfortunately, just like me, his parents died when he was young. Now he owns a few businesses around the city that he mostly oversees, which I'm pretty sure is code for *I'm so rich I don't have to work, I have people work for me.*

When we get to the mechanic shop, I see three open bays, all with cars on the lifts. One of them is my piece of shit with two guys underneath it and parts scattered everywhere.

"Uh, what are they doing?" I ask as Dominic puts his Lexus into park.

He glances over to where I'm looking.

"A once-over, remember?"

"Giving something a once-over is checking it out with your eyes. Not ripping the thing apart."

Dominic reaches over, wrapping his hand around my thigh as he looks at me.

"Take a breath. I told you I'm gonna take care of it. Trust me."

Blowing out a heavy breath, I nod. I'm not sure how I feel about the way he can calm me down so easily and the way he makes me feel so seen with the simplest gestures. Or the way he seems to know exactly where my insecurities are and shines light on them like they deserve it.

He squeezes my thigh once more, sending a rush of that same buzzing feeling through me before he opens the car door and strides around to get my own. I thank him as I step out, and he rests his hand on my lower back as he guides me into the auto repair shop.

As soon as we step in the door, the receptionist practically bounces to her feet, a wide smile on her face as she stares at Dominic.

"Mr. Graves, I didn't know you were coming in today."

"Carl is looking at a car for me. Call me when it's ready," he says as he continues ushering me up the stairs to the right.

"Of course! Let me know if there is anything else I can do for you," she says with her hidden innuendo plastered across her plastic face. She doesn't miss the opportunity to send me a withering glare, though, before she goes back to her computer.

"Where are we going?" I ask as we continue up the stairs. The waiting room was clearly next to the receptionist.

"My office."

"Your office?" I say over my shoulder. "So when you said you knew the owner, you meant you really know him? Share all your meals with him, grew up with him and all that."

He gives me a crooked smirk as he nods. When we get to the top of the stairs, he reaches around me to input a code into the keypad on the door. As soon as it opens, an airy room is in front of us. It has a few windows, one looking over the shop and another looking out over the parking lot. A simple desk and chair along with a few cabinets, are really all that fill up the room. It doesn't give much insight as to the person who occupies it, but then again, I think that's just who Dominic is. Quiet, reserved, mysterious, and all.

"What?" he asks.

I turn to see that he's watching me from the corner of the room.

"Huh?"

"You have a look on your face," he says. "What are you thinking?"

"Oh, nothing."

He walks away from the corner, shutting the door behind him as he closes the distance between us.

"Tell me."

"I was just thinking how the room doesn't give much away. You're as much a mystery now as you were the night I met you."

He hums under his breath as he slowly reaches out a hand, running it through my hair. My eyes fall closed on instinct as he continues weaving his hand through the strands.

"I'm not so sure I'm the mystery between the two of us."

I opened my eyes at that, to find him staring at me hungrily. Anticipation thrums in my veins as his grip on me tightens just slightly, pulling me in closer, as his other hand goes to my hip.

"What do you wanna know?" I tease with a soft smile.

He doesn't smile back, though, as his eyes practically drill me into place.

"Everything," he murmurs.

My heart beats out of rhythm at that, and the next thing I know, my lips are on his. I don't know who initiated it, but all I know is I never want it to end. Our tongues are battling for dominance, our hands everywhere and anywhere. Just like before, the kiss is rushed, frantic, and ravenous. It feels as though he's attempting to consume my very soul with this one kiss, and God willing, I'd let him.

I feel the palm of his hand glide over my back before resting on my ass. His other hand takes up the same position before I'm suddenly being lifted into the air. My legs wrap around his torso as he carries me several feet before releasing one of his hands. I hear the sound of things clattering to the ground as he swipes his desk clean before laying me down on top of it.

My back isn't even flat on the desk before he's at my leggings, bunching up the material in between my thighs before yanking hard. A rip sounds out through the room that has me gasping in surprise.

"Did you just rip my pants?"

He nods as he pushes my panties to the side, pulling his cock out in the next second before lining up to me.

"Condom!" I shout.

He pauses, quickly rifling through a drawer in his desk before he pulls out the foil wrapper. I don't even want to know why he has them at the ready in his office. If I think about it too hard, then I come to the very obvious conclusion that I'm not even close to the first woman he's fucked against this desk, and right now I want to pretend that I am.

As soon as the condom is rolled on, he's inside me. His thrusts waste absolutely no time, stretching me as he buries himself inside me.

I let out a squeal as he bottoms out before pulling out and doing it again.

"T-too tight," I pant.

"You can take it," he says as his hand slips through the hole in my pants, his thumb finding my clit almost immediately before rubbing quick circles in rhythm with his thrusts.

A rush of pleasure begins to run through me at his touch. He's so aggressive, so primal. There is no tender lovemaking or whispered promises. This is a good old-fashioned fucking, and I can honestly say it's been far too long since I've had one.

One of Dom's hands snake up my body, dancing across my skin before wrapping around my throat. My pulse thunders in surprise as his eyes come to meet mine. With his aggressive movements and practically mute conversation, I'd expect to find them blank, hollow, and animalistic. Instead, they are soft, light, and looking at me like I hung the moon.

"You feel better than I imagined," he says as I lift my hips slightly, causing his eyes to roll into the back of his head for a moment.

"You've imagined this?"

"From the very second I laid eyes on you," he rumbles as his fingers tighten slightly around my neck. "I imagined what you would look like spread out for me, what you'd feel like, what you'd taste like."

"You kinda skipped the whole tasting step." I laugh as he fucks me harder.

His mouth twitches in what I think is the start of a smirk before he leans forward, grazing his teeth against my ear as he whispers, "Do you really think once would ever be enough for either of us? I'm just getting started, baby."

Dom begins rubbing my clit faster, his cock throbbing inside me like he's about to come at any minute when he takes me by surprise. His hand pulls back before slapping down against my clit, and I shout out in surprise before my orgasm rips me to shreds, starting at my pussy and sending an insurmountable wave of pleasure from my toes up to my head. I continue to moan and shout my orgasm, not a care in the world as to who is hearing us. Dom lets out a rough groan that more closely resembles a growl as his cock swells before jerking inside me.

We both wring every ounce of pleasure out of one another until our movements ease and all that's left is heavy breathing. We're silent for what feels like forever before Dom releases his hand from my throat, placing featherlight kisses against it before finding my lips again. His lips are soft and gentle, like he's trying to atone for his earlier aggression. It's a gesture that melts me in more ways than one as he slowly pulls out of me and walks over to the trash can, disposing of the condom before righting himself.

I go to stand, but Dom is there before I can, scooping me up once more and carrying me over to the small couch to the side of the room. He sits down first, with me straddling his lap. I pull my head back to look at him, but he just puts his hand on the back of my neck and forces me to lean into him. His arms are braced around me so tight that even if my life depended on it, there is no way I could ever get away. Not that I could even fathom a reason why I would do so.

Dom doesn't say anything. Instead, he just sits there quietly, holding me and playing with my hair the way that I'm coming to realize he loves, probably even more than I do. His phone eventually rings, and his grip on me tightens slightly before he releases one arm and answers his phone.

"Yeah?" he answers.

The person on the other end speaks briefly.

"Good," he says before hanging up and pocketing the phone.

I take the opportunity to lean back and look at him, a calmness across his face that I don't think I've ever seen before. His hand raises up to cup the side of my face, his thumb brushing against my cheek as he smiles almost sadly.

"Time to go, baby. Your car is fixed."

"Oh, that's good," I say, doing my best to mask my disappointment. I wouldn't have minded another round or two.

He doesn't say anything as he continues rubbing his thumb over my skin.

"So, is this the part where you ghost me again?" I ask with a laugh, only half teasing, really.

His eyebrows knit together at that as he shakes his head.

"It's fine, it's not like I was thinking about you every second of the day or anyth—"

"I was," he interrupts. "Thinking of you. Every second."

That catches me off guard, and I can't help but tilt my head in curiosity.

"Then why the vanishing act?"

"I had some things come up with work, and I knew if I saw you again, that would be the end of it."

"End of what?"

He shakes his head as he looks away for a moment, his eyes returning to me as he speaks. "Life as I knew it."

I try not to let myself get all swoony over his words but c'mon, would any woman stand a chance?

"So, what now?" I ask.

"Now," he starts, his hand on my thigh, squeezing tightly. "You're mine."

CHAPTER NINE

ZAYDEN

I barely feel the sting of the needle against my chest as my cellmate shadows in the angel wings. Since being transferred to State, I've been on my best behavior. It's taken an insane amount of control not to slit some of these pieces of shit from ear to ear, but I'm determined to get out as soon as possible.

I've tried to contact Dominic for almost eight days, and I've been met with radio silence. Something isn't right, I can feel it. I have my suspicions of what it is, but for my brother's sake, I hope it's not what I'm thinking. If he has so much as touched a single hair on my angel's head, I'll slice off each one of his fingers piece by piece.

The Polaroid of my angel is my only possession in this hellhole and my most precious at that. It's a picture of her walking from her house to the bar. She's about a block into her walk, and she's blissfully unaware of the cameraman's presence. She's gliding down the street, her blonde hair flowing in the wind around her as she wraps herself tight in that black jacket and dark blue jeans. Those headphones she loves so much are wrapped around her ears, and she's wearing her favorite pair of tennis shoes.

As soon as I get out of this place, I'm gonna take her away from that shitty city. Somewhere nice and secluded where it can just be us. I've already made some calls about purchasing a beautiful cabin on the Snoqualmie River, tucked away in the woods where we can be alone and she can be safe when I have a job. Or maybe I'll stop taking jobs altogether. The thought of leaving her even for a night sends a prickling feeling spreading across my skin and a shallowness in my breath.

It's been too long since I've seen her. Since I've held her. I have to get the fuck out of here, and I have a plan to do so if my fucking brother would bother to call me back.

"Alright, man. Done," the makeshift tattoo artist says as he begins packing up his prison-made tattoo gun.

I look down at his work and can't help but grin. Right across my chest is her name scrawled in a pretty font, and on either side is angel wings. It's not the best work I've ever had done, but it's better than nothing. I didn't have the opportunity to get a tattoo of her before I got arrested, and I couldn't go another night without her name inked into my skin.

Leaning back against my bed, I nod in response before closing my eyes, though my cellmate doesn't leave my side.

"What the fuck?" he says.

I peep an eye open as I raise a brow. "What?"

"You said you'd make it worth my while if I tatted you," he says as he grabs his pencil dick and shifts it in his pants.

I let out a laugh that sounds every bit as maniacal as I am before I sit up, standing to my full height and towering over the guy.

"You think I was gonna suck you off or something? Let you fuck me in the ass for some ink? When I said I'd make it worth your while, I meant that I wouldn't gut you like a pig and wrap your intestines around your neck while you sleep. Same can't be said anymore," I say with a tilt of my head and a smile that has his eyes rounding and his body shaking.

A pounding comes from our door before a guard's voice sounds through. "Lights out, inmates!"

I don't move an inch, forcing my cellmate to squeeze past me as he scurries off to the top bunk. I move back to my bed, laying on my back with my hands tucked behind my head and a smirk on my face.

"Sweet dreams."

CHAPTER TEN

BLAKE

After I get my car back home, I'm not even parked for ten seconds before a text message comes through, the contact's name reading Dominic. Did he add his number to my phone when I wasn't looking? Kinda creepy but kinda cute, I guess.

> Dominic: When can I see you again?

I smile to myself as I tap out my reply.

> Me: You literally just saw me.

> Dominic: Your point?

Practically giggling to myself like a schoolgirl, I text him back.

> Me: I work for the next four nights. Can you do early afternoon any of those days?

> Dominic: I'll see you tomorrow. Noon. I'll bring lunch.

> Me: Okay! See you then. Night.

I pocket my phone and grab my purse before locking my car and heading upstairs. It's not until I walk through my door and look up at my entryway mirror that I realize I'm grinning like an idiot. Fuck, I should not be getting this giddy over a guy I virtually just met. I mean, granted, I've known him for over a month, but almost all of that time he was MIA. I've only been around him less than a dozen times, and I can already feel myself falling down the slippery lust slope. I mean, god, how could I not? The man looks and fucks like a Greek god. He's fiercely protective and also surprisingly kind. Soak my panties and sign me the fuck up.

———————

MY ALARM GOES OFF EARLY THE NEXT MORNING. Normally, I sleep in, but Dominic is coming over, and to put it nicely, I'm a slob. It's not because I'm lazy, I really do try, but when one too many things need to be done, my anxiety gets the better of me. I get overstimulated, and I disassociate. But I don't want him to know that, so having a sex-on-a-stick man in my apartment is motivation enough to clean it up.

After I wash the dozenth dish and fold my second load of laundry, I'm just able to get a clean top and some jeans on when a heavy knock sounds from my apartment door. He texted me twenty minutes ago to let me know that he was on his way and to shoot over my apartment number, but I really thought I had more time. I glance at the random papers stacked on the kitchen island, shoving them into the first drawer I see before running my fingers through my hair and walking over to the door.

When I pull it open, Dominic is standing there in his typical black dress shirt and black pants. A bag of something amazing smelling is in his grasp as he lifts it up in offering.

"Hope you like Mexican."

"Love it." I smile as I awkwardly stand in the doorway before I step to the side. "Oh, sorry. Come in," I say and he nods his head with the start of a smile and steps inside.

His eyes scan the apartment, nodding to himself softly.

"What?" I ask.

His eyes come to me. "It's exactly what I expected."

"Is that a good thing or a bad thing?" I laugh.

"Good." He nods. "It's warm, lived in. Feels nice."

"Are you a vibes guy? Gonna lecture me about my chakras and all that?" I tease as I guide him over to the dining room table.

He lets out a short laugh as he shakes his head.

"More of a feeling guy. I think our gut is the most intelligent organ in our body."

I raise a doubtful eyebrow at him as he begins unpacking the food.

"Not the brain?"

Dom shakes his head. "Our brains are intelligent, of course, but when you're down to the wire and you need to make a split decision, more often than not, we rely on our gut when our brain can't handle that high-pressure situation."

I rest my elbow on top of the dining room table as I place my chin into my hand.

"What kind of high-pressure situations do you deal with, Mr. Graves?"

He raises an amused eyebrow as he looks me up and down.

"Plenty."

"Yeah? Like when customers don't pay for their flat tire or bunk engine?" I ask as I grab the container with what looks like beef fajitas.

Dominic watches me, nodding to himself, like he's noting which item I grabbed first before he grabs a container that has some kind of red burrito in it.

"The shop isn't my only venture."

"Oh?" I ask. "I was wondering about the nice outfits. Didn't seem fitting for an auto repair shop owner."

He nods as he takes a bite of his food, chewing fully before speaking.

"You're very right. I also own a security company."

"Like hired muscle men?" I ask.

"More like tech security. We mainly have contracts with the Department of Transportation and various high-profile companies that need to make sure their servers are protected. You wouldn't believe how many people a day try to hack into the street cameras or a financial institution's funds."

"So, you're basically a hero?" I tease with a wink.

A genuine laugh rips out of him, causing him to lean back in his seat as he shakes his head.

"I can honestly say I've never heard that one before."

"No? Did I never thank you for being my hero in the bar that night?"

A look of irritation flickers across his face at the reminder before it soon passes.

"Don't remind me about that guy. He got lucky."

"He almost got dead." I laugh. "Honestly, how have the cops not come knocking on your door?"

He shrugs. "Guess they have bigger things to focus their attention on."

"True. Well, I'm glad they haven't hauled you off in silver bracelets yet. I like having you around."

I cringe as soon as the words leave my mouth. Fucking hell,

Blake. Desperate much? Instead of looking spooked or turned off, though, he gives me a soft smile before he reaches his hand out across the table, lacing his fingers with mine.

"I'm not going anywhere."

I smile back at him, squeezing his hand but making no attempt to pull away as we begin eating our lunch one-handed.

"What about you?" he asks. "I'm assuming your passion in life isn't bartending?"

I snort at that. "Yeah, definitely not. But it pays the bills."

Dom nods at that. "What would you do? If you could do anything?"

I speak before I'm able to remind myself what a terrible idea it is.

"I want to be a social worker, one of the good ones. Place kids in good homes and make sure they're safe."

The air instantly thickens, and Dom's body stills as his eyes focus on me.

Fuck. This is why I try to avoid this topic, because when I do, the question that always follows is—

"So you were in foster care?" he asks.

Yup, that one.

I give him a short nod.

"Me too."

My eyes snap up to his. "Really?"

"It's an ugly story."

The shortness in his tone makes it clear that it's not up for discussion, and I can definitely respect that.

We eat the rest of our food in a comfortable silence. You'd

think that it would be awkward, eating quietly in your house with a guy you basically just met, but honestly, it isn't. There is something calming about Dominic, soothing almost. At first glance, I'm sure he would intimidate the shit out of you, but I see more to him, the softer side, the one he clearly tries to hide but for whatever reason, is allowing me to see.

Once we are finished, I clean up the containers before tossing them into the trash. Dominic stands, grabbing his phone and pocketing it. Disappointment fills me as I watch him.

"You leaving?"

He pauses, turning to face me fully. "I do need to get back to the office to look into some things."

"Oh, cool. Thanks for lunch," I say, doing my best to right my tone.

He's clearly not buying it. He slowly closes the distance between us, weaving his fingers through my hair on both sides of my head before forcing me to look up at him.

"You don't want me to leave?"

"Well, no. I mean, you have to get back to work. I just kinda thought you were coming over to...you know?"

He watches me for a moment before a sly smirk spreads across his face.

"You disappointed that I was gonna leave without making you come, baby? Need an orgasm or two before I head out?" he asks almost teasingly.

"I mean, I'd be stupid to turn down an offer like that," I huff on a laugh as I look away.

Dom's fingers curl into my hair, gripping it tighter before

forcing my head back, leaving me no choice but to make eye contact with him.

"I can't leave my woman wanting. I'll give you a ten second head start," he says as he pulls away his hands and begins rolling up the sleeves of his shirt to his elbows.

"Your woman?" I question dubiously, despite the hard thudding of my heart at his words.

"I told you that you're mine. I meant it."

"Does that mean that you're mine?" I say, biting back a smile as I do.

"Absolutely," he agrees seriously.

A giddiness fills me as I bite my lower lip and nod.

"Okay."

"Okay," he says. "Ten seconds."

"Ten seconds until what?"

"Until I catch you," he says as he finishes rolling up his sleeves.

I watch him with a small smirk as his eyes flick up to me.

"Seven, six, five."

I don't waste another second, adrenaline suddenly coursing through my veins as I take off running down the hall. There isn't really anywhere good to hide, so I figure just getting to my bedroom is the best chance I have.

I slip inside the room, slamming the door shut and plastering my back against it as my chest heaves. Excitement buzzes through me as I hear his heavy steps casually stroll through the house. He tries to push the door open, but I put everything into holding it back, an excited giggle slipping out of me as he almost gets it open before it's slammed shut again.

"Back away from the door, baby. I'm gonna break it down, and I don't want you hurt," he says through the thin wood.

"NO!" I shout as I throw the door open. There is no way in hell I can lose my security deposit on this place.

He's standing in the doorway with his hands braced on either side of the frame, a dark smile on his face as he speaks. "You need to work on your hiding skills."

In the next moment, I'm in the air, tossed over his shoulder as he crosses the room before dropping me onto the bed. I land with a bounce before his body covers mine. His hands are at the top of my jeans before he's undoing them, peeling the material down my legs. My panties go right along with them, and suddenly I'm completely bare in front of him.

"Christ, babygirl. Your pussy is so pretty."

"Thanks?" I laugh softly as he shoves his head between my thighs, flattening out his tongue as he runs it through my slit from top to bottom.

I let out a surprised gasp at the motion, quickly morphing into a moan as he does it again and again. My fingers tangle into the sheets as he devours me like a starved man. His tongue lashes against me, teeth nipping at my clit as my body begins to thrash. I don't know if I want more or if I'm trying to get away because it's too much. Either way, my efforts are futile. Dominic wraps an arm around my waist, pinning me to the bed as his attack only intensifies.

"Oh my god! Oh fuck!" I shout out as it all becomes too much, and I have no choice.

I dig my hand into his thick hair, curling it into my fist as I force his face to grind against me, giving me just the push I need to come.

I feel my pussy pulsate as a euphoric rush of pleasure envelops me. I hear Dom groan in between my thighs as he quickly licks me clean, only coming up for air when my orgasm has subsided. His mouth is glistening as he swipes his tongue across his lips, his eyes rolling into the back of his head before he smirks.

"You're fucking decadent. Better than I could have imagined."

"Help yourself anytime." I laugh on an exhale.

"Don't mind if I do," he says as he lies on the bed, lifting me up by my hips and lowering me right onto his face.

I squirm at the feeling, still extremely sensitive as he pushes on my lower back, forcing me down. I watch him undo his pants blindly, pulling his cock out before stroking it a few times.

"Open up your mouth and suck," he commands, his mouth rumbling against my inner thigh as he pulls me down to fully sit on his face.

I've only seen his cock once, and it wasn't for long before he was plunging it inside of me. But now, looking at it only inches away from my face, I can't help but swallow. I know women aren't supposed to complain about a cock being too big, but Jesus. I think he could have done with a few less inches for all of our sakes.

"Suck," he commands again before burying his face into my pussy.

Opening my mouth, I take his head first, allowing my tongue to run over the tip and causing him to let a low growl rumble through his chest. Slowly, I begin bobbing my head up and down, taking a little bit more of him each time. Apparently I'm too slow for Dom's liking, though, because in the next moment I feel his hand at the back of my neck, forcing me to take all of him.

I gag instantly, tears blurring my vision as he forces me down again and again. I feel his tongue increase speed against my clit as he slips a finger inside me, fucking me with it as he continues forcing my head down onto him. I do my best to swallow around him, but I can hardly fucking breathe the way he fills my mouth. Letting out another gag, I do my best to keep it together as I, quite literally, choke on this man's cock. Not that I'm complaining.

He pushes another finger inside me as he swirls his tongue around my clit, causing my body to shudder against him. I feel Dom's cock begin to swell as he pushes me down hard one more time before his warm cum hits the back of my throat, forcing me to swallow every drop as my own orgasm tears through me like a fucking hurricane.

I feel him lick and suck me practically dry until I collapse against him. We lay there breathing heavily for several seconds before he pulls me off him and tucks me under his arm. His hand cups my cheek as his thumb brushes away the streams of tears against my skin.

"Your tears are so beautiful, baby. So beautiful when they're just for me."

I do my best to smile as he continues tracing his fingers against my skin, almost like he can't stop himself, and like hell am I going to ask him to.

CHAPTER ELEVEN

BLAKE

The next week, I'm just finishing my closing tasks when a knock comes from the front window of the bar. I look up to see Dominic standing there with a patient half-smile. Unable to stop myself, I grin and walk over to the door, unlocking it as he steps inside.

"Didn't you have some meeting that would run long?" I ask as he locks the door behind him.

"I said long, not all night, babygirl. I can't let you go home alone, can I?"

I bite back my smile before turning to finish up my closing tasks, mainly because I don't want him to see the excitement on my face that he showed up tonight. Since we've been together, I haven't worked a shift that he hasn't been present for, apart from today. Obviously, he has a job, several actually, and he can't spend every waking minute with me, but I was unreasonably disappointed when he said he wouldn't be by tonight.

"How'd your meeting go?" I ask as I grab the mop bucket and begin mopping the front of the house.

Dominic holds a hand up, stopping my motion before he rolls up the sleeves of his no doubt ridiculously expensive dress shirt and takes the mop from me. I'm stunned for a moment as I watch this larger-than-life, powerful man doing something as mundane as mopping a dive bar floor. For me. He's gonna have to mop me up too, because the small action has turned me into a pile of goo.

"It went well."

He doesn't elaborate, and I don't pry, mainly because I know it's futile. We've seen each other nonstop for a week, and I hardly know a thing about him. Normally that wouldn't bother me. I like to stay as far away from the topic of pasts with others, but for some reason, I want more from him. I need it.

We close up the bar in comfortable silence, and I slide into his sleek black Audi before he drives us back to my place. Without a word, he parks in the visitor spot and gets my door for me, locking the car behind us as he ushers us up to my apartment.

"I'm gonna go change," I say.

He nods and moves to the kitchen, making himself at home as he scours through the cabinets. I watch as Dominic frowns when he noticeably comes up empty. Discomfort seeps in as I fidget under his stare.

"I haven't been to the grocery store in a while. I need to go soon."

"You went last week," he reminds me.

I flinch just slightly at the reminder. Shit, yeah, I guess I did.

Dominic stares at me for several more seconds before he nods, shutting the cabinet in front of him and pulling out his phone.

"Looks like a diner is the only thing that's available right now. That sound okay?"

"Sure."

"I'll go pick it up. Be back soon," he says, walking over to me and pressing a quick kiss to my lips.

Annnnnd there he goes. Running for the hills from the poor slummy girl. Okay, I don't think that's actually what he's doing, but I can't help but feel uncomfortable. Based on his obvious wealth, I'm sure he doesn't know what it's like to not have cabinets full. I'm sure he doesn't even go grocery shopping on his own, at least outside of here and there.

I ditch my clothes, slipping on a soft pair of cotton sleep shorts and a tank top. I skip the bra because those things are medieval torture devices, and I refuse to wear one for any longer than necessary.

I'm lying in bed, flipping through potential movies to watch, when I hear a knock come from my door. I frown, getting out of bed and opening the door, surprised to find Dominic waiting with a bag of what smells like takeout diner food.

"You look surprised," he says as his eyes flick across my face. "Did you think I wasn't coming back?"

"Oh, I don't know. Didn't think too much of it, I guess." I laugh lightly.

Liar.

Dominic doesn't seem to buy it, but he humors me by stepping inside and dropping the topic. He moves to the dining room table when I shake my head.

"Bring it to the bedroom. I do not have the energy to be anything other than horizontal right now."

An amused chuckle escapes him, but he nods and follows after me through my postage stamp-sized apartment. When we step inside my bedroom, I take the bag from him and begin unpacking the insane amount of contents inside. He always orders enough food to feed an army, I swear. I mean, I guess he is the size of a small army alone, but still.

Pancakes, french toast, eggs, hash browns, and even two club sandwiches litter my comforter. My stomach audibly groans in celebration, and I waste no time grabbing one of the orders of pancakes and the provided syrup. I dig into the stack, cutting through it with the plastic fork, before unceremoniously shoving it into my mouth. God, I'm so attractive when I'm hungry.

I look over to see Dominic watching me with a small smile before he shakes his head.

"What?" I ask over a mouthful of food.

GRAVES

"I love that you aren't afraid to eat in front of me."

My brows dip at that. "Why would I be afraid to eat in front of you in my own house?"

He nods and keeps his smile in place.

"Very good point."

I give him a wink and happily work through a solid quarter of the amount of food he brought, and the man, being a literal beast, eats the remainder. When we're all finished, he gathers up the containers before throwing them all away and coming back into the room.

He sits down on the bed, dragging my feet into his lap before he begins rubbing them. I practically scream out in pleasure as he digs his thumbs into the arches of my feet. It feels better than anything I've ever felt. Better than a hot shower on a cold day, better than sex. Okay, not that good, but god, it feels amazing, though.

"What did I do to deserve this?" I practically moan.

"You worked hard today, baby. Has no one ever rubbed your feet?"

"Never." I laugh immediately, causing him to apply more pressure to a spot that apparently is extremely sore. I moan and groan in pleasure as Dominic chuckles to himself but silently keeps working at me.

I'm practically a pliable mess in bed when I speak before thinking about it. "I don't know anything about you," I blurt.

His movements stall for a moment before he speaks. "What do you want to know?"

"Anything, everything," I say as my eyes collide with his.

They look so shielded, so guarded. I wonder if mine looks the same as his. I'm asking for him to let it all down for me, but I'm sitting here unwilling to do the same. So, I lean my head against the mattress, closing my eyes as I let out a slow breath.

"My parents died when I was six," I say.

Dominic is still for three more seconds before he begins massaging my feet once more, as if he were trying to coax the words out of me.

"My father got drunk one night, not out of the norm by any means, and confronted my mother. I guess she had been having an affair. I was upstairs while they were down in the kitchen. I didn't hear everything. All I heard was screaming, such loud screaming. I heard hitting like punches, and then I heard a gunshot."

I swallow as the pop from the gun, followed by the ringing, still plays in my head.

"I got up from my room and went downstairs to see what was happening when I heard a thunk. When I crested the corner downstairs, I heard another gunshot, followed by another thunk. This time I knew what it was. My father's body fell to the floor in front of me, his eyes wide and...blood. So much blood," I choke out, doing my best to remain composed.

I feel my throat tighten and tears beg to be let free, but I won't allow them. Instead, I breathe through it, risking a glance at Dominic. He's watching me with a steady gaze. It isn't necessarily pity in his expression, but it's definitely empathetic. It's a look that makes me feel seen, yet not victimized.

"I was young, you know. I didn't fully understand what had

happened, and there was just so much blood. I wanted to help, and so I tried scooping it up and pushing it back into their bodies. It didn't work, obviously, and when the police found me, I was sitting there just...soaked in their blood. Apparently I didn't talk for a few weeks after that. I don't really remember much after that night until I was adopted on my seventh birthday."

"Were they good to you? Your adoptive parents?" Dominic asks.

I smile sadly as I remember Mr. and Mrs. Harrison.

"They were until they passed away. Car accident."

Wow. Way to trauma dump, Blake. I would have been happy learning his favorite color or if he had any childhood animals. I didn't need to unload one of the darkest moments of my life like that. Oh well, at least I kept the darker memories to myself, the ones I never allow the light of day to see, the ones I never will.

We're silent for several moments before he speaks.

"My parents died when I was nine. Drug bust gone wrong. They were junkies, but they tried. My mom always sang to me before bed. Fleetwood Mac because it was the only songs her fried brain could remember," he says with a tone akin to fondness. "She swore she sounded just like Stevie Nicks, and I humored her because if she was singing to me, she wasn't fighting with my dad or doing worse in the living room."

I'm stunned into silence. I expected him to be sympathetic. Apologize because no one ever knows what to say in these situations and move on or get the hell out. I definitely didn't expect him to open up. I'm afraid to even breathe in risk of spooking him, so instead, I sit quietly and listen.

"Whenever they needed their fix, they would drop me off at the neighbor's apartment and head down the road. One night, they didn't come back to pick me up, and the cops knocked on the neighbor's door." He ends it with a casual shrug and an impassive face.

I frown at that. "You didn't have family? Anyone to take you in?"

"I had an uncle. He died," he says flatly.

"And then you went into the system," I guess.

He nods. "I was adopted shortly after their funeral and stayed at that house until I was eighteen."

"You were one of the lucky ones," I say wistfully, but my small smile dies when I see the look on his face. He doesn't agree or disagree, but something in me tells me there is way more to the story. But I've pushed him enough for one night, and I climb into his lap, wrapping my arms around him.

I feel him hesitate, as if he were still trapped in those memories, but reluctantly, he wraps his arms around me, squeezing me tight as if I could vanish out of thin air at any moment.

CHAPTER TWELVE

DOMINIC

I'm adjusting my watch as I step through the restaurant and make my way to the hostess.

"I'm meeting with Mr. Robinson."

She smiles a little too wide and sticks out her tits as she bends down to look at the seating chart. I can't hide my disgust at her desperation. If I wasn't completely infatuated with my woman, maybe I'd give her a second look. However I am, impossibly so, and she couldn't be more repulsive in this moment.

"Right this way." She winks.

I let her get several steps in front of me, putting as much distance between me and her overly poignant perfume before following her. We wind through the restaurant when a hand catches my arm.

I turn in a flash, surprised when I see my woman holding the cuff of my suit jacket as she smiles widely at me. I soften my posture and give her a small smile as she stands to hug me. Wrapping my arms around her, I hold her tight before cupping her jaw and pressing her lips to my own. It's just short enough to be appropriate but long enough to tell her how much I've missed her since last night.

"Sir," the annoying hostess says, clearing her throat. "Your meeting is this way."

She gives a nasty glare to Blake, and I feel her actually shrink slightly under the woman's gaze, which pisses me the fuck off. I stand a little straighter, slightly pushing Blake behind me so she doesn't have to witness the bitch a second longer.

"Please inform him I'll be a few moments. I'll find my way," I say before dismissing her with my back.

Blake flicks an uncomfortable look at her before I regain her attention, shaking my head, so I hope she knows she's worth a thousand of that woman. That the only reason she is trying to make Blake feel small is because she burns too bright.

She smiles warmly up at me before nodding.

"Dominic, these are my friends, Gabrielle and Christian."

Gabrielle extends her hand to me, a knowing smile on her face as she looks me up and down. It appears she has heard as much about me as I know about her. Like how she moved here from Chicago when she was ten. She grew up rather privileged and married Christian Aranda five years ago and gave birth to Alison Aranda on February eighteenth of this year. That's all the information I gained from her background check. Blake told me that they met in a foster home together.

I shake Gabrielle's hand as I nod.

"A pleasure to meet you, Gabrielle."

"Gabby, please." She smiles in a way that is just a touch condescending.

I turn to face her husband, who smiles at me genuinely. I ran a background check on him as well. He's in tech, a software engineer for one of the largest computer software companies in the country.

Shaking his hand, I nod and greet him. "Pleasure."

"Yeah, nice to meet you! We've been curious to meet the guy that's scooped up our Blake."

"Your Blake?" I ask with a dubious eyebrow raised.

The look Christian sends her when his wife isn't looking raises my hackles, and I take a seat beside Blake, wrapping my arm around her as I keep my eyes on him. He feels my gaze and quickly averts his eyes, pulling out his phone like he's answering an email, before I drag my attention back to my woman.

"What are you doing here?" she asks with a completely oblivious smile.

Her naivety is so refreshing in my life yet so frustrating because I can't be there to protect her from creeps every second of the day. Especially when she assumes they are friends. I'm going to have to work with her on that.

When her unique eyes practically twinkle from the daylight streaming in through the window, I can't help but soften a little. Fucking hell, she's stunning, and she's all mine.

My fingers rub across her arm, tracing over her tattooed sleeve as I look down at her.

"Business meeting. What about you?"

"We're just having lunch. They got a sitter—"

"And we are making the most of it!" Gabrielle smiles as she lifts her mimosa in the air.

Christian raises his as he laughs, and I eye them both carefully before looking at Blake.

"Do you need a ride?"

"No, I'm—"

"We're her ride," Gabrielle practically scoffs before she begins giggling.

I cut her a glance that has her giggles dying before turning back to face Blake.

"I don't want you getting in a car with someone that's been drinking. Wait for me? I'll make this quick."

Blake smiles and nods when her friend cuts in, again.

"Aww, that's so sweet! You're so sweet! Why aren't you that sweet to me anymore?" she complains, smacking her husband's arm.

He winces at the impact and rolls his eyes before sending a gooey look to Blake that has my fist clenching in my lap.

"Because you're not as breakable as Blake. She needs someone to dote on her."

"Fuck you," Blake scoffs with a chuckle, assumingly taking his words as teasing and not the hidden promise I plainly see them to be.

Yeah, the fuck she's going home with them. If Mr. Aranda has it his way, he will no doubt leave his wife passed out in the car while he tries to take advantage of Blake. Not gonna fucking happen.

I bend down, pressing my lips to hers once more in a kiss that is definitely not appropriate for the restaurant, but it is for marking my territory. When I pull away, I don't spare the two idiots across the table a glance as I look at my woman.

"Wait for me," I say softly, but in a tone that brooked no argument.

She smiles up at me shyly as she nods, and I give her a quick wink before standing.

"Nice to meet you, Gabrielle, Christian," I say, allowing my distaste for his name to linger on my tongue.

He frowns slightly at that, but his wife is oblivious as her hungry eyes rove over me, settling on my crotch. Okay, could this woman be any worse?

"Please, it's Gabby." She giggles before hiccupping.

I hum under my breath but don't give her anything else before turning to Blake.

"See you soon, babygirl."

———

I WRAP UP OUR QUARTERLY MEETING AS FAST AS POSSIBLE

and am out of my seat as soon as it's acceptable. With a quick shake of the hand, I'm on a mission to find Blake. Glancing down at my phone, I see several more missed phone calls from an unknown number. I know who is trying to get a hold of me, and I know it's gonna bite me in the ass if I don't get in contact soon. I'm not ready yet, though. I need more time. I need to get her out of here, somewhere safe.

She mentioned that she loved San Diego, and I immediately started sending her condo listings after that. She's laughed off each one, and I'm not sure if she doesn't take me seriously or if she's not willing to accept my offer. I'd whisk her away right this minute if she'd let me, but I just don't think she is there yet.

So, for now, I dismiss the notification and look up to find Blake waiting for me in the front waiting area, alone. I grit my jaw in irritation at that. If Gabrielle was a good friend, she would wait with Blake before abandoning her, and if Christian wasn't a piece of shit, he would wait to make sure the girl he's very clearly hooked on wasn't left alone for anyone to take advantage of. Whatever, I'm glad they're gone, and I'm glad she was a good girl and listened to me.

When she sees me, her smile is wide and makes my chest tighten at the sight alone. I can't fight a small smile of my own when she looks at me that way. Fucking hell, I don't think I've smiled as much in my entire life as I have over the last two months. She's changing me, I can feel it, but fuck if I want to fight it.

"How was your lunch?" I ask as I pull her into my arms, pressing a kiss to the top of her head before walking her out front. I hand the valet my ticket, and he jogs off to get my car.

"Good. Gabby got a little too drunk, so Christian took her home shortly after you left."

"That happen often?" I ask.

Blake lets out an airy laugh as she nods. "More than you know."

I want to ask her why she surrounds herself with people like them. She can clearly do better. She is totally oblivious to Christian's affections, so it can't be an attention thing. In fact, Gabrielle seems extremely threatened anytime the spotlight shines off her for even a moment. That makes for a terribly one-sided friendship, and my babygirl deserves a hell of a lot better. Something tells me that conversation won't go over well. So, for now, I'll stay silent, be there for her the way people in her life should, and I'll be keeping an extra-careful eye on Christian Aranda.

When my car pulls up, I grab the car door, opening it for her before moving to the driver's side. I tip the valet, and then we're off. I easily maneuver through the streets, pulling up to her apartment in no time.

"What are you doing tomorrow night?"

"It's my first night off in ten days. I'll probably lay in bed all day and relish every fucking bit." She smiles.

"Or you could let me take you out," I suggest.

"Out? Where?" she asks.

"Anywhere you want. We could do dinner or something else. I just want an excuse to show you off," I say with a small smirk.

"Well, as long as it's a ploy to boost your insufferable ego and nothing serious like enjoying my company," she teases.

I roll my eyes but chuckle, nonetheless.

"I'd love to. What time?" she asks.

"Seven?"

"It's a date."

"Fuck yes, it is," I say before grabbing the back of her neck and pulling her lips to mine.

She melts against me, her tongue darting out to stroke against my own. I grip her tightly, so tight I fear I might shatter her. My control shakes, and I do my best to breathe through it, reminding myself that I can't lose control with her, I'd never forgive myself.

I pull away quickly, resting my forehead against hers as I take deep, even breaths. When my pulse returns to a regular pace, I open my eyes to see her already watching me.

"I'll see you tomorrow."

"Definitely."

CHAPTER THIRTEEN

BLAKE

I'm going through my closet, pulling out my top two dress picks before I turn to face Gabby. As soon as I told her I was going on a date with Dom, she insisted on coming over, stating I couldn't pick a proper date outfit alone which was kind of insulting, but one hundred percent Gabby. I know she can be a lot sometimes, and she's definitely a friend you need in doses, but she's really all I have in this life, or at least all that's left.

"Okay, what do you like better?" I ask Gabby.

She glances up from her phone and smirks.

"They're both black, babe."

"Yeah, so?"

She shakes her head as she tosses her phone down.

"That one," she says, pointing to the off-the-shoulder black lace cocktail dress that hugs everything just right.

"Perfect." I smile as I slip it on, pairing it with a pair of black pumps.

My hair is already curled, but I run my fingers through it to give it a more relaxed look before I finish swiping on my red lipstick. Normally I don't care about makeup or dresses, honestly, but Dom is taking us to the nicest seafood restaurant in town. The waitlist is usually something crazy, like a year, no clue how he got reservations, but I'm not complaining!

My phone buzzes on the dresser, and I grab it quickly, disappointment fluttering in my chest when I see that it isn't Dom, it's just Christian.

Christian: Where are you guys going to dinner?

I scrunch my face at that. Why is he texting me, and why does he want to know about where we are going?

"Why is Christian texting me?" I ask.

Gabby looks up with an unimpressed eyebrow.

"How should I know?"

I shrug, leaving the message on read before Gabby speaks again.

"So, what's the reason Daddy Warbucks is taking you out

on the town?" she teases.

I roll my eyes as I call out to her.

"I swear to God, if you call him that to his face, our friendship is over."

She snickers as she comes and wraps her arms around my shoulders, kissing my cheek.

"You couldn't exist without me, and you know it."

"You confident in that?" I ask with a raise of my eyebrow.

She nods seriously. "Very."

We both chuckle as a knock comes from the door. I cap my lipstick and go to open it, smiling when I see Dom standing in the doorway with a bouquet of flowers in his hand and his body wrapped in a deliciously tailored suit.

I think it's his expression that is my favorite part of it all, though. His eyes are wide, mouth unhinged, as his gaze rakes over me, from top to bottom. I feel like a goddess in front of him, I always do.

"Baby, you are...exquisite," he says reverently before stepping inside.

He tosses the flowers onto the counter and wraps an arm around my lower back, hauling me into him as he leans down to kiss me. I put my hand against his chest to stop him.

"I don't want to get lipstick all over you."

"You think I give a shit?" he scoffs before crushing his lips to mine.

A flurry of butterflies rush through my chest as I wrap my arms around his neck. His tongue swipes out, tangling with mine when a very forced cough comes from behind us. We break apart, turning to face my grinning best friend.

"Hate to break it up, but you have to leave a little something for the honeymoon, kids," she teases.

I roll my eyes as Dom raises an eyebrow at her.

"How are you doing, Gabrielle?" he asks.

"Good, but I hate it when you use my full name, and you know that," she says with a smile that is just a little too flirty for my taste. I know it's just Gabby being Gabby, doesn't mean I like it.

He nods his head. "My apologies."

I take the flowers from his hand, lifting them to my nose before inhaling.

"They are beautiful. What are they?" I ask.

"Daffodils. They're associated with strength and resilience due to their ability to survive and withstand winter storms and come out the other side in the spring. They're beautiful and strong. Little fighters, just like you."

Hot tears prick at my eyes, and I do my best to blink them away before smiling.

"Thank you so much."

"Of course." He nods as I step into the kitchen, grabbing a vase from the top of the cabinet before filling it with water. I place the flowers inside and turn to find Dom patiently watching me.

"You ready?"

I nod with a smile before tossing a look at Gabby.

"Lock up when you leave, yeah?"

She winks at me as she nods. "Have fun you two!"

I wave goodbye as we step out into the hallway and make our way to the elevator. Dom's arm slides around my waist seamlessly as we ride down, before getting out and making our way to his car.

The drive to the restaurant goes by fast, and soon we are sitting at a fancy white-clothed table with soft music playing all around and the best view of Puget Sound in front of us. An entire bottle of white wine, two lobster tails, and one crème brulée later, I'm handing my plate to the waiter while Dom stares at me.

"What?" I say with a small smile.

"I just am...surprised," he says cryptically.

I lean toward him and rest my head in my hand.

"By?"

"You."

"In a good or bad way?" I tease.

"I haven't decided yet," he says seriously.

His words cause my smile to fall slightly. I lean back into my chair before sitting up a little straighter.

"Okay, what's going on? You're acting weird. If you're gonna break up with me, don't you know it's best to do it when you drop me off so there isn't the whole awkward ride home thing?" I laugh hollowly.

He lets out a short huff, like the very idea is ridiculous, as he shakes his head and stares off into the distance. It takes a moment for his eyes to come back to me, but when they do, they seem to be more clouded and confused than ever.

"I'd never. Blake, I didn't take you out tonight because I

wanted to end things. I wanted to take you on a date, a proper one. One that you deserved. You deserve far more than I could ever possibly give you, but I'm going to try to be worthy, always."

A small bit of relief passes through my chest as I relax.

"Okay, now you're sounding more like you're gonna propose to me, which would be insane."

"Would it?" he asks curiously.

"Uh, yeah?" I laugh. "We've known each other for like two months."

He nods like that makes sense before he knocks his knuckles against the table like he's made up his mind about something.

"Alright, I guess you'll just have to move in with me then."

"Excuse me?" I blink.

"Well, I respect the fact that you're not ready to get married, and despite my failed attempts, you don't seem to be ready to move to San Diego either. So I'll have to settle with you moving into my apartment."

I'm speechless at the matter-of-fact tone carrying his words. Does he expect me to just bow to his every command? Does he think that just because the time that we've spent together has been some of the happiest of my life that I'm just going to bend and twist to fit whatever desires he deems necessary?

"No," I say.

His head turns to the side slightly at that as he frowns.

"No?"

"Yeah, no," I huff, shaking my head at the beautiful yet stupid man in front of me.

"Why?" he counters.

"Why?" I scoff. "B-because we just met, we just started dating. Living together, that's such a...big step, and what if things don't work out? I'm on the street? Again? I can't do that. I won't do that. I like you, but I can't put myself at risk, and I—"

I don't even realize Dom is out of his chair until he's by my side, kneeling, his hands cupping my cheeks as his eyes search my face like he's looking for something.

"Baby, I would never let anything happen to you. If you didn't want to be with me anymore, we would figure it out together. You'll never be without a home again, I promise. Even more so, there is no possibility in this fathomable universe where you and I aren't together until the end of time. You're mine, Blake, and I'll never let you go."

The steadiness in his words and the certainty in his eyes cause my currently racing pulse to slow. My breathing evens as I nod carefully at him, a sense of ease washing over me that I didn't know I needed. I think it's safe to say that I have abandonment issues that are definitely unresolved. The idea of moving in with someone I'm crazy about shouldn't send me into a full-blown spiral like that, but on the same hand, the idea of losing the only sense of stability I've really had in my whole life is worthy of said spiral.

"And," Dom continues, "I'll keep your apartment. I'll cover this year's remaining payments, and this time next year we can talk about if you want to keep it or not. Whatever you want, baby."

"Next year?" I say. "You really think we're going to be together for that long? Already, at two months, you know that?"

"I do." He nods confidently.

All I can do is blink at him. What else am I expected to do or say in a situation like this? He's listening to what I'm saying, yes, but not accepting no. He has an answer for every potential question I have, a solution for every problem.

"Please?" he asks, softening his tone to the point where it's the lightest I've ever heard before.

Something in his tone, or maybe his eyes, has a strange feeling twisting inside of me. It's a feeling that is powerful enough to have the words spilling out of my mouth before I can even stop them.

"Okay."

"Okay?" he questions.

I nod with a small smile. "Okay."

CHAPTER FOURTEEN

BLAKE

The movers that Dom hired set down the last box in the living room before Dom signs their paperwork. They thank him and step out of his apartment, well, I guess, my apartment too. If you can even call it an apartment. It's more like a mansion in the sky.

I've been here a few times before, but we usually spend time at my place, so it all feels...different. Two strong arms slide around my waist, pinning me against his chest as his lips murmur against the sensitive curve of my neck.

"What are you thinking?"

"How crazy I am to let you move me into your place in less than twenty-four hours."

A low chuckle fills the room as he nuzzles deeper into my neck.

"It's your place now, Blake. Whatever you want to do, consider it done. I can give you my card, and you can buy all-new furniture. Or I can hire an interior decorator, and you can let them do all the work. I want you to be comfortable," he says as he turns me to face him.

I can't help but laugh and shake my head.

"I'm sorry. I know that you're well-off and everything, but this is like the shit billionaire men say in those romance novels. Your place is great, nicer than anywhere I've ever lived."

"You're not hearing me, baby. I don't want it to be my place, I want it to be *our* place."

I look up at his deep brown eyes, so intense, so focused. God, I feel way too much for this man, way too fast. I'm not being careful with my heart, and I know this slope is only about to get a whole lot slipperier now that we are living together.

Can't wait to explain this one to Gabby.

Leaning up onto my toes, I close the distance between us, pressing my lips against his as his hands travel down my body. They settle on my ass before he's lifting me into the air and pressing me against the wall. I swear, just a single touch is all it takes for us, and with the way his tongue is beginning to ravage my mouth, I wouldn't have it any other way.

His lips run up and down my neck, leaving small nipping

trails in his wake as I grind myself against his hard-on.

"Tell me what you want, baby. I want to hear you say it," he says against my skin.

"I want you to fuck me against this wall right here, right now."

His eyes flick up to mine as one of his hands releases me and goes to his pants.

"Done."

He crushes his lips against me once again while he pulls his cock out and rips yet another pair of yoga pants, making his access all the easier. The man is going to owe me an entire drawer full at this point.

I hear the shuffling of the condom wrapper before Dom pulls away from me, ripping it with his teeth and spitting the torn piece to the ground. My pussy pulses as I watch him roll the condom on before he pushes the head of his cock through my torn yoga pants and past my panties. It's tight at first, but Dom has never been one to take things slow, as he pushes all the way inside me until we're completely flush. He blows out a heavy breath as he presses his forehead against my own.

"You ready?"

I bite my lower lip and nod quickly. He smirks before his hips begin thrusting. From this position, I can't do much but be at his mercy, which, trust me, is not a bad thing. I still do what I can, bouncing on his cock and desperately trying to rub my clit against him before I say the hell with it. Reaching down beneath my pants, I rub my fingers against my clit, instantly forcing a moan to fall from my lips.

"Fuck, baby. You like playing with yourself while you ride my cock?"

"I'm not sure I'm riding it as much as I'm taking it." I laugh before he thrusts deep, practically all the way to my uterus, I swear.

"And you're taking it so. Fucking. Good," he says, punctuating each word with a thrust that has my eyes rolling into the back of my head.

"Dom," I moan.

"Yeah, baby. Say my name, I want to hear my name on your lips when you fall apart for me."

Dom's hands are gripping my ass tightly until one snakes up my torso, all the way up to my throat before his fingers wrap around it.

I should be terrified right now. In any other situation, I would be. I don't like tall men even standing over me, yet I'll let this one pin me by the throat against the wall and fuck my brains out. Dom isn't just some man, though. He's quickly becoming my favorite person. He knows me almost better than I know myself, and I think, in a way, I know him the same. It's crazy and fast and insane, but there is no one that I feel like I trust more, especially in this moment, than him.

I feel my pussy throb against his cock as he adjusts his angle, fucking me in a way that has his head rubbing against my G-spot over and over again. Before I can stop myself, my pussy clenches and my orgasm rips through my entire body. I scream out Dom's name at the top of my lungs as I rub my clit and use him to wring every ounce of pleasure out of this as I can.

"Fuck," he mutters before his cock throbs inside me. His grip on my throat and ass tighten as he rides out his own orgasm, letting out a ragged breath when it's passed.

Slowly, he lowers me to my feet before cupping my face gently. He lifts my chin up before brushing his lips against mine in probably one of the softest kisses we've ever shared. I find myself smiling when he pulls away before he whispers to me, "Welcome home, baby."

———

A WARM TONGUE RUNS THROUGH MY PUSSY LIPS. IT DOES it again and again, but it's not enough to fully wake me. I murmur for Dom to go to sleep, but I don't think I fully form words because after we fucked three more times before bed, I'm exhausted.

I'm almost fully back to sleep when I feel the pressure of something being pushed inside me. It's warm and hard, and I can't help but groan, half in pleasure and half in discomfort.

"Dom," I finally groan, turning my head to the side and reaching for his body to push him off.

"Shhh," he whispers into my ear before he begins thrusting softly and slowly.

I'm trapped in a sleepy daze, not really awake but not really asleep, only the feeling of being so full and small waves of pleasure running through me with each thrust. It feels different, though, and not just because I'm half dead to the world.

"Condom," I murmur as I blink hazily up at Dom's

shadowed form above me.

"We don't need one. I need to be close to you," he rumbles low.

"I'm not on birth control, dummy," I huff as I try to push him off me once more.

"It's okay," he says, his fingers dragging against my skin, drawing soothing circles that have me softly lulling back to sleep.

I think I hear him say something else, but I choose to lean into the sleep that is desperate to pull me under instead. I feel a warmth flood inside me and another wave of pleasure that I think is my own orgasm. Either way, in the next moment, it stops before Dom presses his lips to mine and whispers, "Sweet dreams, angel."

———

WHEN MY EYES BLINK OPEN, IT TAKES ME A MOMENT TO figure out where I am. Then I remember I'm at Dom's apartment, my apartment now. Rolling over onto my side, I see him asleep beside me, one of his hands tucked behind his head as he gently breathes in and out.

I go to stand up and use the bathroom but when I stand, something is wrong. I'm wet between my legs, really wet. There is no way I started my period since I just finished it last week.

As soon as I make my way into the bathroom, I'm able to confirm that I definitely didn't start my period. Then, the hazy memory of last night comes to me. Dom on top of me, him licking me and fucking me without a condom. What a fucking asshole! I can't believe he would do that. He knows I'm not on birth control, and he went and did it anyway.

Anger begins running through my veins as I do my best to control my temper. I need to help do inventory at the bar today, so I had to get up early anyway. I finish cleaning myself up in the bathroom and take a quick body shower before I wrap myself in a towel. I make fast work of grabbing clothes and am just getting my pants on when Dom stirs awake.

"Baby? Why are you awake?" he asks groggily.

"Gotta go," I say as I slip on my socks.

"To work? Want me to drive you?"

"I can drive myself," I snap before blowing out an irritated breath.

A look of alarm crosses his face before he slides out of bed and makes it over to me in three large steps. He rests his hands on my shoulders, to which I quickly shrug them off before he cocks his head to the side.

"What's wrong?"

I refuse to look at him, staring at the ugly abstract art painting in the corner instead. I feel his hand slip under my chin and force my gaze to his. I don't try to dim my irritation or disgust at his behavior as I look at him.

"You had no right."

"For?" he questions.

"Last night! I told you no, and you did it anyway. Now I have to go to the fucking pharmacy and spend sixty dollars that I shouldn't need to because you were too careless and too horny."

He blinks at me slowly like I've lost my mind before he reaches for me again.

"Baby, slow down. What are you talking about?"

I laugh hollowly and shake my head.

"Oh, that's cute. Is that how you get out of trouble? Play dumb? You fucked me last night, Dom. While I was sleeping. And you didn't use a condom. I slept with your cum inside me all night. Let's add a possible UTI to the equation. Thanks for that."

He shakes his head softly before his head stops moving, his body goes rigid, and his jaw clenches.

"You're sure?"

I roll my eyes. "Yeah, the wet panties gave it away this morning. Just get the fuck away from me right now."

I go to walk away, but he's too fast, wrapping an arm around me and spinning me around until I'm facing him again. I don't try to fight back, as it would be futile if I did. He holds me tight as he looks deep into my eyes.

"I'm so sorry, baby. I promise, it'll never happen again. I'll make sure of it."

"You do that. I gotta go."

"I'll get you the pill, just head to work. I'll drop it off with some lunch, okay?" he offers.

"Don't bother," I say with an irritated breath as I move out of the bedroom and to the kitchen. I grab my purse and slip on my shoes before heading out the door. Amazingly enough, Dom doesn't follow me. I don't know why I expected him to be the type to chase after me and not drop it until I forgave him. I'm relieved he isn't, though, because although a pill can solve it, it's the whole going rogue thing that has me more than a little pissed off.

CHAPTER FIFTEEN

DOMINIC

My knuckles turn white as I grip the steering wheel, turning left so hard that my rear end breaks loose around the corner.

Motherfucker. He wouldn't. He couldn't.

I got a message from him a couple weeks ago, along with all of the missed phone calls. It was short and unassuming, if you didn't know him.

Soon.

I, however, knew exactly what it meant, and though it meant that I'd get my brother back, I also knew that it would mean my woman would be in danger. Brother or not, I'm not foolish enough to know that once Zayden sinks his teeth into something, he won't stop until it's dead, and I've never seen him so infatuated with anyone or anything as he is with her. Ever.

I can't let him have her. He saw her first, but she was never his, she was always supposed to be mine.

Parking in my usual spot, I get out of the car in a flash, slamming the door shut behind me. Not like he doesn't already know I'm here. My feet pound against the pavement as I go around to the side entrance, entering the nine-digit code and using my thumb for the biometric scanner before the lock disengages.

I'm still frustrated Blake wouldn't just move with me. I had been subtly working on her ever since I got that message from Zayden. She said she loved San Diego, and though I was thinking more like Rio de Janeiro, it would have worked. I debated drugging her and moving her overnight for her safety, for our happiness. I knew she'd forgive me eventually.

I didn't want her to see that side of me yet, though. She has this image in her head of us, of me, and I like it. I want to preserve it for as long as possible. Besides, I'm certain there isn't a place I could take her on planet Earth where Zayden wouldn't track us down. It's what he does best.

As soon as I step inside Zayden's dungeon, because you can't really call this warehouse a home, a silver blade is flying through the air and sinking into my upper shoulder. Pain spears through me as I grip the knife, taking note that only half an inch is actually embedded in me, and decide to just pull it. I yank it out with a wince before looking out into the purposefully dark room. My back is against the door when another blade comes flying through the air. I miss it narrowly, ducking just in time before another and another come at me.

"Jesus Christ, stop!" I shout.

"Oh, now you want to talk?" Zayden's voice asks, an eerily calm lilt to it.

"Zayden," I sigh.

"Because I thought you were too busy for your own brother. Too busy fucking *my* angel to pick up the goddamn phone!" he roars before stepping out of the shadows and attempting to plunge a knife into my gut.

I grab his hand, twisting it away from me. His eyes are crazed, his pupils are blown, and his features are feral. My arm shakes as I hold him back. We've always been comparable in strength, but he has spent the last four months in prison and he's stronger, a lot fucking stronger.

Pinching a pressure point in his wrist, I force him to release the knife before I shove him away from me. My psycho brother I can deal with, my psycho brother with knives, not as easily.

While he's still on the ground, I hit him across the cheek, taking him by surprise and allowing me enough time to cover him. I pin him to the ground by his throat as I speak.

"You snuck into my apartment last night, didn't you? You *touched* her," I grit out, shame and disappointment washing over me. She was right beside me, two inches away, and she was violated by my own brother while I fucking slept. The level of failure I feel is insurmountable. Words don't cut it, so violence will have to do.

I deliver another hit on his other cheek, feeling a small sense of satisfaction when my knuckles burn from the impact.

Zayden's eyes come up to me, those piercing blue eyes turning to practical ice as his voice comes through, strained thanks to my hold on him.

"Of course I touched her, she's MINE!"

In a move faster than I can counter, he's bucking me off him and maneuvering us until he is the one pinning me to the ground. Instead of the usual unhinged smile he wears when we are fighting or he is killing, pure anger drenches his features as he looks down at me.

"She's mine and you stole her. I told you not to touch her, brother. You were supposed to protect her, nothing more," he says with a crack of his head against the bridge of my nose.

I feel blood pour from it instantly, but Zayden doesn't stop there.

"You fucked her!" he screams, hitting me so hard in the left kidney that I literally see white.

"You tainted her with your dirty fucking hands, and now I'm gonna cut them off," he says as he reaches for a knife in his back pocket.

Fucking hell. He doesn't make threats lightly. I know he has every intention of slitting my hands straight off my arms. Glancing to the side, I see a loose brick in the crumbling walls of this place. I yank it with all my might and smash it into the side of Zayden's head.

He falls over instantly, dropping the knife and cupping his profusely bleeding wound. A small part of me feels bad, but as I stand up and look down at him, brick still in hand, I remember what he did to Blake. To *my* woman. And all sympathies die in the stale air.

"She's mine," Zayden rasps, clearly not letting this go.

"She was never yours. You can't just claim people you've never even spoken to, Zayden. It doesn't work like that. Regardless, she's mine now, and you won't be taking her away from me."

"You sure about that, brother?" he says with a weak smirk.

"Positive, because if you step within a thousand feet of her again, I will shoot you on site."

He laughs, actually laughs, a delirious one that sends a chill down my spine. I do my best to ignore him as I continue.

"Now that this is out of the way, I need to go to the pharmacy and make sure that your wrongdoing from last night won't ruin her life."

Despite the amount of blood he's losing, a fire ignites in his eyes as he looks up at me.

"That is our baby in the making, you stay the hell away from both of them!" he snarls in outrage.

"No, it's the proof of your assault that will be gone by the end of the night. I mean it, Zayden, stay the fuck away from her, or I will kill you, brother or not. You will not take this from me."

Without another word, I turn on my heel and walk out of the room. When I get into the car, I text Doc to go to Zayden's and take care of his injury. He's the head of trauma at Seattle

Valley Hospital, who likes to do side work under the table for us since going to the hospital in our line of work is completely out of the question. We've used him for years, and he knows how to keep his mouth shut and fix us up, mainly Zayden.

I fire up the engine and make my way to the pharmacy. Zayden ruins everything he touches, like hell if I'll let him fuck this up for me as well. Yes, he saw her first, but he doesn't know her, and she doesn't know him. He doesn't have an unbreakable bond that sets his soul on fire with a single look from her. I do, me and her. She's mine, and I'll do whatever it takes to protect her from everything, most of all him. And if it comes down to it, I'll choose her every fucking time.

CHAPTER SIXTEEN

ZAYDEN

The cool blade slides between my fingers as I roll the knife over my knuckles. Doc watches me uneasily as he stitches up the parting wound Dominic left me with. Doc says I have a concussion, big surprise there. He says that I need to take it easy and have someone monitor me for the next twenty-four hours, but I have someplace to be, so as soon as he finishes the last stitch, I am on my feet and escorting him out of there.

I think his name is Henry, maybe Michael. I don't really care. All I do care about is that he takes cash, keeps his mouth shut, and always comes running when we call. He likes the under-the-table work. Or maybe he comes because, when he first started working for us, I rattled off his childrens' first names and schools.

Looking into the mirror on the wall, I notice the reddening on both my upper cheeks. No doubt it'll be bruised by morning. Dominic fucked up. If he wanted me to stay away from my angel, he should have just killed me, because that's what it would take to keep me from her. Then again, death might not be enough.

I'd had the idea of how to get out of prison for weeks, it was the orchestration that took a little time. I had exhausted my resources inside the walls, and since Dominic was unreachable, I contacted the only person I could. It's someone we cut ties with long ago, and I'm sure I'll regret taking his help, but it had been almost three months since I'd set eyes on her. I was about to suffocate. I had to get out of there. I had to see her.

Imagine my surprise when I showed up to her apartment to find it completely empty, not a scrap of her in sight. I began to spiral as vivid images of worst-case scenarios danced in my mind. I jumped on my bike and drove to Dominic's house, ready to tear him limb from limb for allowing something to happen to her.

When I opened his bedroom door and found another figure sleeping in his bed, it caught me off guard. Dominic doesn't allow people in his apartment, ever. But a single second more in that room, one smell of her scent and all the pieces clicked together.

My twin tried to steal my angel, and for that, he would

have to die, eventually.

I could have ended him right there, claimed her for myself, and we would live happily ever after. But I needed something more than revenge at that moment. I needed her. The way her pussy wrapped me up so tight, her buttery smooth skin, the sweet little moans that left her mouth with every thrust.

Christ.

I adjust my cock, trying to ease my growing hard-on at just the thought of her.

Before I realize it, I find myself outside the bar, watching her move from table to table in my usual spot. Goddamn, I missed her. I fucked my fist every day to the memory of her, but nothing compares to her.

A car turns around the corner, and I already know who it is. I take a sidestep down the alley, ducking into the abandoned Chinese restaurant. I'll let Dominic think that he has won, that he's somehow scared me into submission. And then when he's least expecting it, I'll take what's mine. For good.

THREE DAYS GO BY. SEVENTY-TWO HOURS WITHOUT MY angel, and I'm starting to lose it. My leg is bouncing, my skin is crawling, and I feel as though my lungs are about to eviscerate.

I can't. Fucking. Breathe.

I just got back into town from a job for my "bailor," a term of our new agreement. When he calls, I go. No questions asked. The fact that I just landed back in the States is the only reason I haven't dug out my own beating heart by now.

My bailor is satisfied for now, and Dominic is no doubt naïve enough to think I'm backing down, which gives me the perfect opening.

I debated packing our stuff and having it ready by the time my angel's shift was over, but then it occurred to me: why should I run? I have nothing to run from, certainly not a snakelike brother. This is my angel's home, and she wants to stay here, I know it. So, he can be the one to leave. In a body bag or a car, it makes no difference to me.

I know that my brother usually sits in the bar and watches her work, at least he's doing part of what he was told. But tonight, I staged a little distraction on the other side of town so I could have some alone time with her. He was called away for a security issue and had no choice but to leave her side.

There are only two customers in the bar, and the owner has left for the night, which means it's finally time.

I come through the back entrance, pausing in a shadowed corner until she comes into the back. She's oblivious to me at first, her eyes scanning the bottles of liquor in front of her before they settle on a red wax-dipped lid. Before she can reach it, I wrap my hand around her mouth and press my lips against her ear.

Her body locks up instantly before I begin to speak.

"Shhh. It's me. I missed you," I whisper lowly.

She relaxes instantly, pride waving through my chest that I bring her so much ease as I release her mouth.

"Dom." She smiles before attempting to turn around.

My hands go to her waist, forcing her forward as anger tears through me. *Dom?* How does she not know it's me? How can she not *feel* it's me?

The hot trails of fury run through my veins as my breathing becomes erratic.

"Dom?" she questions softly. "Are you okay?"

Looking to her left, I kick the supply closet door in before pushing her inside. She goes in with a stumble, and I follow after, slamming the door closed.

"What are you doing?" she whispers in the pitch black.

I don't need light to know every inch of her body, though.

Choosing not to respond, I undo the button of her jeans before peeling them and her panties down her legs. In the next moment, I bury my tongue inside her cunt, forcing her to let out a breathy pant as she digs her fingers into my hair.

"Fuck! What are you doing? I could get fired," she says in a needy moan.

I roll my tongue over her clit, groaning in delight when her flavor hits my tongue. So goddamn delicious. Her hand presses me into her more, a request I'm all too willing to fulfill. I slip a finger inside her and begin finger fucking her when her legs begin to tremble.

"Oh god, oh fuck. I'm gonna—" she whimpers.

When I feel her begin to tremble, I take away my tongue and bite down on her clit, forcing her to scream out in pain. That part only lasts for a moment, though, before pleasure wins her over and she coats my fingers with her cum. It's practically pouring down my hand, and I don't hesitate a second before I'm following the trail with my tongue, making sure not to waste a drop of my angel's delight.

"Wow, I...I don't know if I liked that or not. That hurt," she says as I slowly stand up.

"Pleasure and pain are a fine line, and if you do it right, they blend together beautifully."

Before she can retort or refuse, I'm spinning her around, bending her over, and shoving myself into her.

"Fuck. I'll never get used to you stretching me like this," she moans. "Are you wearing a condom?"

"Fuck no," I spit as I fuck her deeper.

Her back arches to accommodate me as she huffs. "We talked about this. The birth control won't be effective yet."

"Guess we're having a baby then," I say as my cock twitches at the thought.

My angel laughs, a beautiful melodic laugh that sends pleasure running through me.

"Definitely not. I'll just take another Plan B, I guess."

My hand slaps her bare skin as hard as I can, a painful scream escaping her that hurts part of me and fuels another.

"You. Will. Not!" I growl into her ear.

"I have to," she whimpers.

I slap her ass again and again, causing her pain-drenched screams to turn into outright crying. I can hear her practically sobbing as she begs me to stop. I can't, though. Anger has a chokehold on me at her words, and she has to be punished.

"P-please, you're hurting me."

"I'd never hurt you, angel. I love you too much," I say before

I slip my hand in front of her, rubbing quick circles over her no doubt sore clit before I come.

I can practically feel the confusion inside her, her battling emotions warring against one another, but pleasure rules all, and her pussy begins contracting against me. She whimpers and moans her release, though it sounds more painful than pleasurable. That's the consequence we must face sometimes.

When our bodies are drained, I lean forward, pressing a soft kiss just over her pulse point as I whisper.

"See you soon."

CHAPTER SEVENTEEN

BLAKE

I'm still having trouble catching my breath. The darkness of the supply closet is overwhelming, but I'm not ready to step into the light, mainly because I'm not sure what to make of what the fuck just happened.

Dominic is aggressive in the bedroom, no doubt about it, but this wasn't just aggression, this was pain. This was deliberate punishment. He got so mad so fast, and then he was back to being loving and sweet. I've never known him to have such extreme emotions, and he's never not stopped when I've asked.

Though all that is more than concerning, the bigger piece that has me feeling puzzled is how I was left feeling in it all. I should have been angry or scared or upset, and I was, until I wasn't. He hurt me until each sharp sting morphed into something different. Something strong and violent and... blissful. I've never known myself to be a masochist, but what else would you call it when my partner leaving me in pain gave me a rush of practical euphoria? Of excitement and adrenaline, and though it hurt in the moment, part of me wanted to ask for more, to push the boundaries, even if I was terrified of where they would take me.

When I finally get up the strength to leave the closet, I come out to find the bar empty and my two remaining customers' bills covered by the cash left on the bar. It made closing easy enough, and before I know it, I'm shooting Dominic a text saying that I will just meet him at home.

As soon as I step in the door, I see him at the stovetop, his back to me, as something aromatic and delicious fills the air. He looks over his shoulder and smiles at me, that smile that practically turns me gooey on the inside, like I'm sunlight, and he's lived in nothing but darkness his whole life.

"Hey, baby. How was your shift?"

"Good," I swallow, images of our little tryst in the back flashing to the forefront of my mind.

He smiles, but his brows furrow slightly as he watches me.

"You okay?"

I shake the images away, nodding and rising up onto my

toes before I place a kiss against his lips.

"Yeah, can I help?" I ask as I gesture toward what I now see as spaghetti and meatballs.

He shakes his head.

"I've got this. Go sit on the couch."

I smile and nod before making my way into the living room. I turn on the first thing that comes to life on the TV as he walks into the room, two plates in hand. We eat in relative silence, but that's definitely not unusual for us. However, I can't shake this nervous energy that I certainly know is coming from me. It's practically palpable, the endless questions rolling around in my head. I know I have to speak them, and have to get them off my tongue, but my nervousness wins each time.

Once we're finished, Dom takes my plate and sets it on the coffee table before taking my feet into his lap. He begins massaging the balls of my feet, causing my eyes to roll into the back of my head as I melt into the couch.

Dominic gives me a gratifying smile as he continues his godsent work. In my hazy, blissful state, the words I've been harboring since I got home finally spill out before I can overthink them for one more second.

"Tonight was different, not in a bad way either. I liked it, a lot. It was just...different."

He turns to face me with that same easy smile.

"What do you mean?"

I rest the side of my head against the couch cushion as I shrug, suddenly feeling slightly embarrassed.

"I didn't know I liked a little pain with it all. It was new, and I wasn't sure at first, but it was kinda...fun, I guess."

His smile slowly begins to fall as confusion clouds his face.

"Baby, what are you talking about? What pain? Did you get hurt at work?"

I let out half a laugh that comes out as more of a scoff than anything. Is he really gonna pretend that it never happened? Talk about whiplash.

"Uh, the closet in the back? Tonight? You practically shoved me in and fucked me until I saw stars," I hedge, staring at him as I wait for the pieces to come together.

Instead, he just continues to stare until a few seconds go by, and his body goes rigid.

"Excuse me?" he asks, his voice deathly low.

"Jesus Christ, Dom. You fucked me, and it was hot. I loved it, and I just wanted to talk about us trying more of that, but you're making it weird with this whole 'I don't know what you're talking about' thing. Fucking forget it," I say as I shove away his hands, standing to my feet and crossing the room. Embarrassment fills me from head to toe. He could have just told me it was never going to happen again, or he didn't mean to, or whatever his excuse is. He doesn't have to make me feel like I'm an idiot who hallucinated the whole thing.

His hand wraps around my arm, whipping me around to face him in a flash.

"No, don't go. I need you to tell me everything that happened tonight. Every. Detail."

"Have you lost your mind?" I ask with a shake of my head.

"We had sex?" he asks. "Tonight? At your work?"

"Yes, trust me, you were there!" I laugh hollowly.

His chest begins rising and falling quickly, sharp breaths escaping him as his grip on me tightens like iron.

"We shouldn't be having sex anymore. Not for a while. Not until I say, understand?" he says.

I scrunch up my face at that.

"Wh-wait. What? No. I don't understand. What the fuck is going on?"

"Maybe I can help clear this up," a voice says from the hallway.

Dominic and I turn to see a darkened figure step into the light of the kitchen. My eyes widen as my pulse slows. Carefully, my head turns back to Dominic before looking at the new stranger. The stranger with the face I know too well, with the voice I know too well. It's...Dom. Twice? Wait. Wait. It's—

"Zayden," Dominic practically growls.

Zayden? Who the fuck is Zayden? The man I'm looking at is an exact replica of my boyfriend. Or who I thought was my boyfriend. What the actual fuck?

He smiles slowly, a sinister look glinting in his piercing blue eyes as he focuses on Dominic.

"Good to see you, brother."

"Brother?" I echo as my eyes begin flicking back and forth between the look-alikes. Between the *twins*.

"Oh god. So, tonight. It wasn't you in the closet," I say to Dom. "It was—"

"Me, my angel," the guy in the hallway, Zayden, says with that same practically maniacal smile.

"I told you I'd kill you if you ever touched her again," Dominic says as he takes a step away from me and toward his brother.

"Wait, again? Are you saying he's switched places with you? With me?" I choke out.

My mind races as Zayden turns his attention on me.

"Think about it, angel. I know you can feel the difference between my inferior brother and myself. You said it just now. It's different with me, and you like it. You want more of it—"

"Shut the fuck up!" I shout as my breathing becomes erratic. "I d-don't even know you! You're a fucking rapist! A predator. It...it was you the other night. With no condom? Not Dom. That's why you were so—"

I turn to face Dom, a combination of sorrow and fury intertwined on his face.

"I'm so sorry, baby. I should have protected you better. I should have gotten you away from here before he could get to you."

"Now, we both know that would have been a very bad choice, Dominic," Zayden cuts in with a shake of his head. "All is well, I'm here now. She knows the truth, and we will be on our way," he continues before holding his hand out to me.

I stare at it like a serpent ready to bite. Does he think I'm going to take that thing? That I'm just going to walk out of here with the guy who literally took advantage of me twice? I think I'm gonna be sick.

"Angel," Zayden repeats as he takes another step closer.

Dominic puts his hand against Zayden's chest, stopping

him in his tracks as he practically snarls at him.

"Take one more step and lose that fucking hand."

"You're lucky I let you live last time. I should cut out your heart right here and now just for touching her, let alone thinking you could claim what has always been mine," Zayden scoffs.

"Are you fucking insane?!" I shout, causing both of their eyes to swing toward me. "I thought you were an only child? Huh?" I shout at Dominic.

He flattens his mouth and doesn't say a word as I continue.

"Was this a game? Some type of creepy parent trap twin bet? See who could sleep with me the most? How many times have I been on a date with Dominic when it really wasn't you? How many times did I pour my fucking heart out to one of you while the other sat back and laughed?"

"You have it so wrong, baby," Dominic says.

"No! No. You don't call me baby. You don't call me anything. I don't know what the fuck is going on here, but I want nothing to do with any of it."

I turn on my heel, reaching for my keys and phone on the kitchen island, before a hard body presses me against the wall. I push against it, but it's completely unyielding as he reaches down and pries the keys out of my hand, tossing them over his head and into the hallway before taking my phone and throwing it to the ground, grinding it under his heel as he speaks in my ear.

"You can't run from me, angel."

"Let me go!" I scream.

Zayden is ripped away from me in the next moment as

Dominic holds him back, delivering a punch to his brother before he's receiving a hit of his own. They are literally twins, same size, same build. Same everything. Though Zayden seems to be a bit more agile, he dodges more hits than Dominic and even manages to get him to the ground.

Dom's eyebrow is split open, blood pouring down his face as Zayden reigns down blow after blow. Slowly, Dominic stops fighting and instead just lays there. Something in me hurts at the sight, and I run toward him.

"Stop!" I scream, jumping in front of Zayden to block any more hits.

Unfortunately for me, either I'm too fast or he's too slow. Or for all I know, maybe it's on purpose. Zayden's meaty fist drives right into the side of my head, sending my vision flashing before I stumble.

"Goddammit!" he roars. "Angel?!"

I feel my feet slip before my body thunks hollowly against the hard floors, a second sharp pain ripping through my head. I can't open my eyes, can't even move. I just feel dizzy, light, and something warm begins spreading down my face and into my hair as I drift off into darkness.

CHAPTER EIGHTEEN

BLAKE

I try to blink my eyes open, but they won't budge. I move my head to the side, but an agonizing pain rips through me. Okay, don't move your head, Blake.

Taking several slow breaths, I lift my eyelids, thankful when light begins to pour in and I can see the world in front of me. I'm in one of the spare bedrooms, and it looks to be the afternoon based on how much sunlight is in the room. I try to slowly turn my head to assess the rest of the room when a voice calls out, "Angel?"

Dominic?

A man in a leather jacket rushes over to me, crouching down by the bed as he takes my hands in his. He looks like Dominic to a T, except for his eyes. Dominic's are a beautiful deep brown, but these...these are like two crystal-clear pools, so blue you could practically dive into them. They are a stark contrast against his jet-black hair that is currently wild and unruly like he's run his hands through it a thousand times. His knuckles are bloody and swollen, and the last moments I remember begin flickering to life before my eyes.

I rip my hands out of his as I attempt to scramble away from him before I let out a bloodcurdling scream from the pain.

"Shh, shh, shhh," he hushes. "Don't move, angel. You're hurt."

Pain is drenched in his eyes, like it hurts him that I'm injured more than the actual pain I feel.

"I'm so sorry. I didn't see you, and then you fell, and." He shakes his head before looking up at me with renewed fire in his eyes. "I'll never forgive myself."

In the next moment, the door is pushed open, and a swollen-eyed Dominic stumbles in as his eyes scan the room.

"You're awake. Are you okay? Did he touch you? I heard you scream."

"What's happening?" I ask as I flick my eyes back and forth between the two.

Dominic sits down on the opposite side of the bed, resting his hand on my thigh before I move it from his reach. Hurt flashes across his face before he nods.

"Last night, Zayden hit you, and then you hit your head on the floor. You lost a lot of blood."

"I was aiming for you!" he seethes.

"Well, you did a shit job!" Dominic snaps. "Look at her!"

Something akin to a flinch rips through Zayden's body before he stands up and storms out of the room, slamming the door so hard the wall shakes.

Once he's gone, the room is silent for several seconds before I finally speak.

"So, last night, all of that actually happened?"

He blows out a breath before nodding.

"So, you lied to me."

His eyes come to my own, so many unsaid things pass through them before he speaks.

"There is so much you don't know. So much I want to tell you."

"Then tell me," I say flatly.

He rolls his lips together and shakes his head.

"I can tell you, it's not what you think. We were not tricking you. We were not playing you. This was not a game. This is real, we are real," he says as he reaches for my hand.

I don't move it as I allow myself to absorb his words.

"So where does he come into all of this?" I ask.

Dominic clenches his jaw.

"He saw you first and became obsessed with you. Then he... had to go away for a while. He wanted me to look after you, and all it took was one look and I knew I couldn't let my brother have you. I knew I wasn't good enough to even set my eyes on you, but I wanted you anyway."

He saw me. So all those nightmares, the feeling of being watched. That wasn't my imagination, that was...him. Oh my god—

"He slept with me. Twice. More than twice?" I question.

Dominic shakes his head. "Not to my knowledge."

"How?" I whisper. "How did I not know it wasn't you? How did you not know?"

"We're identical twins, and he is incredibly...cunning."

"And sick!" I snap. "He tricked me, deceived me. Technically raped me!"

"I failed you," Dominic says in response. "Twice." He hangs his head low for several seconds before lifting it up until he meets my eyes.

"I don't fail, ever, and the most important thing that I've ever held, I failed. I won't ask for your forgiveness because I don't deserve it."

"Why is he still here?" I ask.

"What?"

"Zayden. He nearly beat you to death. He hit me. He took advantage of me. Why is he still in your apartment?"

"It's complicated," he says with a slight twinge on his face.

"Uncomplicate it."

He doesn't say anything for several seconds. Instead, he just stares at me, unmoving. I think he's never going to respond until he finally speaks.

"Zayden isn't good. There isn't a good bone in his entire body. But there are worse monsters out there."

GRAVES

Without another word, he stands, turns his back, and shuts the door. I hear the sound of a lock, which sends a chill running down my back. I'm locked in here and obviously injured. My phone is destroyed, and I'm trapped inside a house with my boyfriend, well, my obviously ex-boyfriend due to current circumstances and his crazy twin brother.

What the actual fuck?

CHAPTER NINETEEN

DOMINIC

I switch the lock into place, hating that I have to do it but knowing there isn't a better option at this moment. Things have changed so radically in the last twenty-four hours. Everything has gone to shit, and if I didn't need my fucking brother's help, he'd be half digested on a pig farm or quickly decomposing in a vat of acid by now.

He's leaned over the kitchen island, knuckles gripped against the marble edges, eyes locked on her locked door like he can burst it down with his gaze alone. Zayden has always been this way. He likes something, he fixates, and then that fixation turns into an obsession. First it was knives, then it was bloodshed, and now it's...her.

When I step into his line of vision, blocking his view of her, his eyes are the only thing to move, flicking up to me in an irritated scowl.

"Move," he grits out.

"Why? So you can stare at the door? No. We have work to do and plans to make to get us out of the shit situation you have now placed us in."

Zayden's knuckles tighten against the counter as he speaks.

"I've got it under control. I'll keep him happy, and you keep her safe when I can't be here."

I shake my head as I move into the living room, grabbing my laptop before I fire up my software.

"That isn't a life. What, should I just keep her locked in the bedroom until the end of time?"

"Yes."

"No," I scold. "She deserves more."

His eyes are on the door, confliction flickering past his face before he nods once in agreement.

"I still can't believe you called him," I mutter under my breath.

His eyes fly over to me as he moves across the room like lighting. My laptop snaps shut before he throws it against the wall, forcing it to shatter into pieces.

Fucking prick.

"I still can't believe my own brother, my fucking twin,

would leave me like that. You left me to rot in prison so you could steal my angel. So, yes, I did whatever I deemed necessary to get out, get her, and kill you."

I scoff and roll my eyes. The fact of the matter is that we both talk a big game. I think we would both do every single form of torture to one another gladly, but actually killing each other? Taking away the only other Graves this world has? We could never.

"You won't kill me, and you know it," I say with a shake of my head.

"For her, I would," he says, causing my head to tilt to the side. "If it was between you living or her, it would be her. Every. Time."

The seriousness in his tone and the manic look in his eye should irritate me, upset me at least. Instead, I feel a sort of peace with it as I nod.

"As you should."

Surprise flashes across his face before he nods once.

"So," I continue. "What's our next move?"

ZAYDEN

I'M SITTING IN THE CHAIR ON THE FAR-LEFT CORNER OF THE darkened room, the takeout bag firmly gripped in my hands. Her breathing is rhythmic, in, out, in, out. It's mesmerizing the way her soft exhale seems to fill up this room, her rosy cheeks and full lips laying perfectly still as if she were a porcelain doll. She's breathtaking like this. If I could keep her preserved like this forever, I would.

Maybe in death.

She must feel my presence because, in the next moment, she rouses awake, her eyes bouncing around the room before landing on me. Contempt fills her gaze instantly.

"What are you doing in here, Zayden?"

The sound of my name on her lips has me practically groaning. My cock stiffens to a steel fucking rod, and I do my best not to fall to my knees and eat her until she passes out right here and now.

"Dinner," I say simply. "How did you know it was me without seeing my eyes?"

"Because Dom isn't creepy enough to sit and watch me sleep," she snaps, her fire I love so much coming out in full flame.

I narrow my eyes at her though, as a piece of that sentence lingers that I don't like.

"You've called him Dom several times now."

"So?" she questions. "It's a nickname. Normal people use them from time to time."

"Normal?" I question, enjoying the irritation that passes over her face at my teasing.

"Yeah, I understand it's a foreign concept for a psycho stalker rapist like you."

I blink at her words but don't say anything more. The hate on her tongue is so strong, surprisingly strong. For some reason,

I thought she would understand why I did all that I did. Why I will continue to do all I do. It's all for her. For us.

"Eat," I say as I set the food onto the bed beside her.

"I'm not hungry," she mutters.

"I didn't ask if you were. Eat."

She looks like she is about to refuse when her stomach lets out a thunderous growl. Looking away quickly, she faces the wall but doesn't say anything. I let out a heavy sigh before coming to the side of her bed. I crouch down on my hands and knees, I know how much she hates being towered over, before I meet her eyes.

"Please."

My angel blinks hard once, shaking her head like she's confused by me, before she turns back over and opens the bag, grabbing the first fry she can and plopping it into her mouth. I stand up, walking back over to my chair where I left her milkshake on the floor. When I hand it to her, her eyes light up, just for a moment, because of me. It gives me a rush unlike any kill ever has.

She hesitates for a moment before I nod in encouragement. Taking the cup from me, she grabs another french fry and dips it into her shake. It's one of her favorite combinations. Sometimes she'd go to this little twenty-four-hour diner after work and order a side of french fries and a vanilla shake, never anything more or less. I started ordering the same thing too from the other side of the restaurant, and though I don't love it like her, it's not bad.

I watch as her chewing slows, and she looks up at me with

a frown.

"What's wrong, angel?"

"I feel like I should say thank you, but I hate you. You're a bad person. I don't think you deserve thanks."

I nod at that, confused as to her dilemma. Her eyes narrow at that.

"You're not even gonna try to refute it?"

"No. You're right, I'm a very bad man."

She swallows roughly for a moment but maintains her composure as she speaks.

"Are you going to kill me?"

I tilt my head to the side as I look at her.

"Why would you think that?"

"I don't know what to think. One moment, I was dating my boyfriend, moving in with him. The next I find out he's a liar with a secret twin brother who has been stalking me. Now I'm locked inside a bedroom with no way out."

"The door is right there." I gesture easily.

"So I'm free to go?" she asks.

"No."

An irritated huff leaves her as she tosses up her hands.

"See? I'm a fucking prisoner. So just do whatever you plan on doing and get it over with."

She grits her teeth and squeezes her eyes shut, bracing her body as if she's prepared for whatever comes next. I'm more intrigued as to why she feels the instinct to allow whatever is about to happen in order to escape. Most people would beg and plead. Try to run or fight. She's giving up, and that doesn't coincide with who I know she is.

Slowly, I reach a hand out, brushing my knuckles over her cheek as I speak.

"All I want to do is keep you safe, angel."

One eye slowly opens at that as she watches me for several seconds.

"Then let me go," she whispers.

I don't respond before leaning down to press a kiss to her forehead. She doesn't fight me off, which leads me to believe she's still doing whatever she thinks she needs to survive this, and I fucking hate that. I leave without another word, an idea sprouting in my mind. She has such intense survival skills. I'm beginning to see she's had to survive worse than me in her time, which is a chilling thought because I'm just about the worst there is.

CHAPTER TWENTY

BLAKE

The next morning, I wake up to yet another figure watching me from the corner. For some reason, though, I'm able to tell that it's not Zayden. I think it's in the way they carry themselves. Or maybe it's because for the better part of two months, I've practically eaten, slept, and breathed this man. Only now I'm looking back at that as the problem it is. I was blinded by lust, by infatuation. He was so quiet, so secretive, so dismissive. All the signs were there, every red flag. And I raced past them like it was all green from the start.

Stupid, stupid.

"You're awake," Dominic says softly.

"Yep."

We sit there in silence, knowing neither one of us is going to speak first, before he lets out a sigh and scrubs his hand through his hair.

"For what it's worth, I'm truly sorry. I didn't like lying to you."

"Then you shouldn't have," I snap.

"That's where we are gonna disagree, baby. I did what I thought was best to protect you, and I make no apologies for that."

"Protect me from what? Zayden?" I ask.

He stays silent as he watches me, seemingly choosing his words carefully before he shakes his head, dismissing whatever thought he has altogether.

"Whatever. We had a good run, but I want to leave. I want to go home, please let me go," I say, attempting to appeal to his softer side, at least the side I think is soft. I really don't know what to think of him anymore.

His brows furrow at that. "Baby, you are home."

"No, I mean my apartment. I haven't given up my lease yet, remember? I want to go back there and—"

"I gave up your lease," he interrupts.

I pause for a moment, not sure I'm hearing him properly.

"Excuse me?"

"I gave it up. Paid the remainder of your lease and told them you wouldn't be back."

"Wh-why?" I snap in outrage.

"It's not safe for you to be out on your own, not right now."

"You're fucking unbelievable! Let me guess, you told Mark I quit?" I snark with an eye roll.

But when he doesn't disagree, my eyes bulge out of my head.

"You're kidding me," I deadpan.

"You moved away, urgent family matters," he says without a hint of remorse.

I jump to my feet, closing the distance between us before I wind my hand back and slap him across the face. He rears back but doesn't do anything other than that.

"Fuck you!" I hiss. "What? You're just gonna keep me here? Forever?"

"Not forever," he says cryptically.

"This is kidnapping, you know that, right? You're gonna go to jail, you're gonna—"

"Christ," he mutters with a shake of his head. "Will you take a deep breath, please? You're gonna work yourself into a panic attack."

"A little hard not to panic when I'm being held against my will with no context!" I laugh hollowly.

He runs his thumb over his fingertips before he looks up at me, his cheek already reddening from my blow.

"If you take a deep breath and calm down, I will explain."

My breathing is still ragged, but I take several slow breaths before sitting down at the edge of the bed. Dom nods at me once before he speaks.

"There are some people that could be coming for Zayden."

I blink twice at that before I turn my head to the side.

"And that involves me...how?"

He rolls his lips together before he continues.

"Zayden's...affection for you won't go unnoticed by them. If they see him with you, or at least following you, they are going to take an interest in you, and believe me, you don't want that."

"I think I'll take anyone's interest in me over that psychopath," I scoff.

Dominic levels me with a serious look as he leans forward, resting his elbows on his knees.

"Remember how I said that Zayden was bad, but there was worse out there? Well, these men, they might as well be the devil incarnate. They will take you, they will hurt you, and they will kill you."

A pang of fear runs through me, no matter how hard I try to remain unaffected by his words.

"Why?"

"Because it will hurt Zayden and me." He grimaces before looking down at the ground.

"Well, what the fuck is wrong with you guys? How do you make enemies like this?"

Dominic shakes his head. "They aren't our enemies."

My eyes widen at that before I let out a sarcastic laugh.

"Well, I'd sure as shit hate to see how your enemies treat you."

He doesn't respond, clearly not having my dark sense of humor.

"Fine, whatever. How long do I have to stay here?"

"It's too soon to tell. I'm assessing the situation, and then if you still want to leave me—"

"I will," I agree quickly. "Maybe with the chaos of the last forty-eight hours, I wasn't clear. We aren't together anymore, Dominic. I don't like you, and I sure as hell don't love you. In fact, I fucking hate you."

I regret the words as soon as they spill from my lips, which is stupid because shouldn't I hate my lying ex-boyfriend? Shouldn't I hate the man who has deceived me, imploded my life, and is keeping me prisoner? None of my rationale seems to weigh out the regret I feel at the look on his face. He winces, just slightly, as if he's been dealt a blow and is trying his best to mask it.

He stares at the furthest wall for several seconds before turning to face me.

"I deserve that and more, but it doesn't make me love you less."

My mouth parts on instinct before I can help it, but I'm not even able to overanalyze his words before he continues.

"I came in to tell you that Zayden and I have decided you can't be stuck in this room. You're free to roam about the apartment and you'll be able to leave the apartment soon. Just not yet."

Well, that will make it a lot easier to break out of this place. If they're going to let me out of the room, I could just walk out the front doo—

"Don't think you'll be able to just escape out the front door, baby," Dominic says, literally reading my mind. "I have installed a biometric scanner on the inside of the door, only Zayden and I are able to leave the apartment as we've removed the fire escape exit."

My mouth hangs open at that.

"What if there is a fire?"

"Zayden or I will get you out. One of us will be around at all times for your safety."

With that, he turns to leave, gripping the doorknob before pausing. His back is still to me as he speaks.

"I'm sorry you got dragged into this. I'm sorry Zayden saw you and decided to latch onto you the way he did. I'm sorry I did the same. I really did try to fight it. I knew Zayden getting involved with you was going to ruin your life. I knew me getting involved would make it even worse. It couldn't stop me, but I am sorry."

Before I can respond, he slips out the door, leaving it open for the first time in days. I hear a door shut down the hall and assume he went to either his office or bedroom down there. I'm left sitting on the bed, more than a little confused at the warring feelings inside me. Really, Blake? It's been two days and already you're feeling sympathy for your captors?

Stockholm syndrome is setting in, apparently.

CHAPTER TWENTY-ONE

BLAKE

With my newfound freedom, I stay out of my room all night long. A form of protest, I guess. I made myself breakfast, lunch, and dinner. Well, I attempted to. I'm not a fantastic cook, but I can do the basics. I watched endless amounts of trash TV, listened to hours of music, and even cleaned just for the sake of boredom. Zayden tried to sit with me on the couch when he came back from wherever he was, but one death glare and he surprisingly got up and moved to a room down the hall. I'm assuming he has a room here, or maybe he too.

Dominic did say he was gone for a bit. I'm not sure where, though. For work? Does he even work? Vacation? Something tells me guys like Zayden don't go on vacation, though.

At some point around the fourth or fifth movie, I ended up falling asleep. I'm only awoken in the dead of night by a crash in the dining room. I bolt up from my position on the couch, tossing my blanket aside to see a man on top of Zayden with several dining room table chairs broken. One of the wooden legs is splintered into pieces as the attacker beats Zayden's face in.

Zayden just smiles through it, cackling at the man before grabbing one of the broken chair legs and plunging it into the man's stomach. My eyes widen in horror as blood begins to pour around the impaled leg. Oh my god.

The man screeches in pain before Zayden tosses him off, grabbing a knife out of the chop block in the kitchen and sinking it into his neck, sliding it across the skin, and practically severing his head right off. Bile begins to rise in my stomach as I stare at the gory scene before me.

Once finished, Zayden stands over the man, his own blood running down his face as his shirt and hands are bathed in the man's blood. He rubs his fingers together as if he were analyzing the blood before he smirks. He's not just a crazy stalker, this man is a straight up murderous psychopath.

In the wake of their grand entrance, the front door wasn't closed all the way, meaning I could have a way out. Zayden's back is to me, and I'm honestly amazed he hasn't noticed me yet. Then again, he was a little preoccupied.

As quietly as I can manage, I begin tiptoeing around him, only feet from the front door, when he speaks.

"Going somewhere, Angel?"

I freeze in place, my blood running cold, and my stomach bottoming out. My breathing begins to pick up as Zayden slowly turns to face me, looking like a blood-drenched grim reaper as he closes the distance between us. I do my best to walk backward, but he matches me step for step, slamming the door closed behind me, and officially sealing my fate.

"How much did you see?" he asks with a hint of a smile playing at his lips, his eyes crazed with what is seemingly bloodlust.

Shakily, I look up at him, meeting those crazed blue eyes as I speak.

"A-all of it."

He nods, lifting a red finger to me before gently tracing my cheek.

"Not some of my best work, but it was a matter of importance."

"Wo-ork?" I tremble as I look up at him.

He smiles down at me and shakes his head.

"Dominic doesn't tell you anything, does he?"

I don't even want to know what he means by that. I don't care. All I know is that if I want to make it out of here alive, I need to be compliant. Closing my eyes, I steady my voice as I speak.

"Are you going to kill me now?"

"Hmm," he hums. "Depends. Are you gonna tell on me,

angel?"

My eyes fly open at that, locking onto his.

"No."

I'm convincing even to my own ears, and for a moment, I have a small amount of hope of making it out of this. Until he gives me a wicked grin that sends a chill down my spine.

"Liar."

Fear trembles through my body as he lowers his head into the crook of my neck, inhaling deeply as he smells me before flicking out his tongue and running it over my pulse point. The exact place where he stabbed the man.

"Come with me," he rumbles into my ear before nipping at my earlobe.

I look up to see him pressing his finger against the biometric scanner, forcing the door to spring open. He pulls the door wider, gesturing for me to go first.

"B-but you're so bloody."

He looks down at himself, grinning, before lifting his shirt over his head and wiping his face and hands with it before tossing it to the ground near the growing puddle of blood on the floor. The first thing I notice is a smattering of tattoos across his chest. There are so many that it takes me too long to see them all before he's gaining my attention again.

I look up to see him holding out his red-stained hands for inspection as I stare blankly at him. He rolls his eyes, slamming the door shut once more as he saunters down the hallway.

"Be back in five."

Seconds later, I hear the sound of a shower fire up down

the hall. My gaze hasn't been able to leave the dead body on the floor, though. His eyes are still open, wide and terrified, with only tendons holding his head onto his body. The sight is enough to make my stomach roil, and yet, I can't look away. Like a car accident, my eyes are glued to the horror in front of me.

My first instinct is to call Dominic, ask him why the hell he would leave me alone with his serial killer brother. But then a thought hits me: what if Dominic is just like him? What if I'm not in danger at all, not outside these four walls at least? What if this is all an elaborate ploy? To gain my trust, let down my guard and gut me like the family pig.

Quickly, I look around the kitchen for something, anything. A landline, a cell phone, a fucking smoke signal. I need to get out of here. Get away from these psychopaths before I end up just like—

"Let's go," Zayden says with damp tousled hair, a new shirt, a leather jacket, and pants, along with a sparkling white smile.

The wolf really hides in sheep's clothing. Any woman would see either of them in the street and throw their wet panties directly at them just for a second of their attention. That's what makes them so fucking dangerous, though. Who even knows how many women they've killed, how many people they've killed, and how many more they plan to.

"D-dom said I wasn't allowed to leave the apartment," I stutter, despite my best effort. Every bone in my body is screaming at me, begging me not to leave with this man.

He grins at me, giving me a wink that sends my stomach roiling.

"Dom's not here right now."

He opens the door once again, forcing me out first before shutting it behind himself. We walk through the hall in silence before stepping into the elevator. The entire way down and all the way out to the parking garage, not a word is spoken.

Zayden stops short of a motorcycle before he tosses his leg over it.

"Get on."

I hesitate, looking the thing up and down, before he turns an almost irritated look at me. It's the first time I've seen him look at me with anything other than creepy obsession. And I have a feeling that is not a good thing, so I do as he says and climb on behind him.

He fires up the bike as I keep my hands tucked into my lap before he reaches back and yanks my arm out and around him, doing the same to the other side before he peels out of the garage in the next minute. We fly through the moonlit-drenched city streets, weaving in and out of cars and buses. It almost feels like we're flying.

The wind wraps around us, hugging us tight as we continue our drive. I've never ridden on a motorcycle before. Not for any particular reason, just never have. Now I kinda wish I would have before I was no doubt about to die. He turns to look over his shoulder, his eyes flickering over my face before he taps my hands. I'm assuming that means hold on.

I brace myself, and sure enough, he pops the bike into a wheelie. I let out a scream as fear rushes through me before the bike lands, and a giggle escapes me before I can stop it. Zayden does it again and again before he turns a hard left and we begin going down a heavily wooded road.

I'm not sure how long we've been driving for. Could be a few miles, or it could be fifty. Eventually, though, the trees become thicker until we come upon a graveyard. The temperature instantly drops by ten degrees, and an eerie feeling begins to sink low in my gut as he follows the dark, winding, uphill-paved path.

Out of nowhere, he slows down, pulling the bike off to the side before shutting it off. He pats my leg, and I am assuming that means to get off. I do as he says before he does the same, only he leans against the bike, sitting sideways on the seat as he pulls a cigarette out of his leather jacket and a lighter. He lights it as he pulls out a knife from his pocket and begins flicking it in his hands almost mindlessly.

"What did you see?" he asks, his eyes on me.

I glance around me, noticing no signs of life, literally, anywhere. Swallowing roughly, I decide to answer. "I saw you kill that man."

He nods. "Does that make you afraid of me?"

"Well, yeah. You didn't just kill him, you...you enjoyed it."

A spark lights up behind his eyes as he keeps his impassive face and nods.

"I did."

My eyes narrow at that.

"Why?"

A slow smile spreads across his face.

"It's human nature. Kill or be killed. Hunt or be hunted. We don't live in the Stone Age anymore, and things are a little more complicated, but the same remains. You're either a hunter or you're the prey."

"What does that make me?" I ask carefully.

A small smirk spreads across his face.

"That all depends on you, angel."

We don't say anything more. Instead, we both sit here and watch one another, neither making a move of any sort. After a minute or so of this, Zayden lets out a chuckle.

"Want to play a game?"

"No. But I don't think I have a choice, do I?" I ask.

"No." He smirks. "We're gonna play a little tag. If you win, you'll eventually run into someone, tell them the crimes you witnessed, and about the men who held you hostage."

"And if you win?" I ask with narrowed eyes.

His smirk transforms into a wicked grin as he watches me with an eager glint in his eyes.

"Then I get you."

A rush of fear hits me. I don't know if he means get as in *kill* or get as in *get*. Either way, I'm not too enthused. Then again, he's practically offering me my freedom on a silver platter. All I have to do is outrun him. Or his bike. Fuck.

"No bike," I barter.

He cocks his head to the side as I continue.

"On foot only, no cheating."

That smile returns as he nods once.

"Of course."

I blow out a shaky breath as I nod.

"I'll give you a ten second head start. Good luck, angel."

I take a small step back as he begins counting.

"One. Two."

I don't wait around for three or four. Like a lightning bolt, I'm gone in an instant, choosing to run downhill because of the slight advantage. I hear his voice continuing to count down in the distance, though his voice thankfully becomes quieter with each passing second.

I do my best to stay on my feet, but the broken headstones and protruding tree roots are tripping me up every other step I take. The crisp night air burns my lungs, and my limbs already feel like gelatin. I'm definitely not a runner, but hell, at this moment, I wish I was.

My breathing wheezes as I turn a corner, doing my best to follow the paved path, knowing that it'll take me to the main road. Unfortunately, I hear the pounding of footsteps behind me, and I risk a glance over my shoulder. Here comes Zayden, feet flying across the pavement toward me. Well, how fucking stupid am I for running through the graveyard and not on the fucking road?

I decide to cut to the right, pushing myself deeper into the cemetery in hopes he will get tripped up just like I did. I bob and weave around the smaller, more inset headstones, leaping over the occasional boulder or tree root. My heart is pounding to the point of pain, but I know I can't stop.

An eerie sound, a maniacal laugh, echoes through the graveyard, sending goose bumps up and down my spine as the thumping of his footsteps increases. A cold sweat has broken out across my entire body, and just as I try to dodge to the left, my foot gets caught and my shoe flies off before I even take my next step.

Stopping in my tracks, I turn around to grab it when I see Zayden is less than fifty feet from me. Adrenaline rips through my body, and shoe be damned, I'm gone again. Fuck, fuck, fuck. He's too fast. I'm too tired. I can't do this. I can't do this.

In the next moment, two strong arms wrap around my waist, hauling me off to the right before plowing me into the ground. My back takes the bulk of the impact, the wet midnight dew soaking through my shirt as a large body lands on top of me, pinning me to the cemetery floor.

"Gotcha," he rumbles into my ear.

CHAPTER TWENTY-TWO

BLAKE

We're both attempting to catch our breath, but I'm far less worried about catching my breath and more focused on the paralyzing fear that is gripping me. My body begins to shake, and the way he smiles at me chills me to the bone, the moonlight shadowing his features make him look like a demon of the night.

In the next moment, that knife from before is out, and it's slicing through my shirt like butter, forcing the fabric to fall to my side. He then hooks the blade under my bra, slicing through the middle like it's nothing, forcing my breasts to spill free. I try to cover myself, but he pins my arms to my side, bearing down all his weight onto me before he sucks my nipple into his mouth.

"Look at me, angel," he coaxes softly.

I grit my teeth and try to dissociate, but it's not as easy as it should be. Not when Zayden is forcing my eyes on him.

Slowly, I unpeel my eyes, allowing myself to look at him.

"Good girl. Now keep those perfect eyes on me until I'm finished."

He lifts up the knife once again, taking the back of the cool metal and dragging it down the middle of my chest, forcing a shiver to run through my body. Whether it's from the cool feel of the blade or the fear of what comes next, I'm not sure.

The knife makes its way down my stomach and to the hem of my leggings before cutting a line down those as well. Zayden's large hands wrap around the shredded fabric before yanking them down past my knees and off to the side, my panties going along with them. I'm suddenly lying in the damp grass, completely exposed and vulnerable. And though I feel a deep-seated fear inside me, I can't help but feel a lighter feeling begin spreading through me when I see the way he's looking at me.

His eyes greedily take in my naked flesh, looks of varying adoration and awe covering his face as he curses under his breath.

"You're perfection, angel. Absolute perfection."

"P-please," I stutter. "Don't h-hurt me. Don't—"

"Shhh," he whispers. "I'd never hurt you, only if you asked

for it."

My brows furrow at that. "So, you really won't kill me?"

He cocks his head to the side in confusion.

"Of course not. If you die, I die."

"Then you're gonna rape me again," I breathe out shakily, closing my eyes as I begin to accept my fate.

"I've never raped you, angel. You've never told me no, never pushed me away from you. You've always been willing and giving of your body, a gift I treasure."

"You made me think you were someone else, that's rape, Zayden!"

He lets out a groan as he drops his hips down against me, rubbing his hardening cock against me through his pants.

"I love it when you say my name, angel."

"Stop calling me that," I grit out, doing my best to keep my head through his fucked-up mind games.

"I can't. That's what you are. You're my angel, and I'll be your devil. Bound for all eternity. I'll do anything to protect you, always know that."

"From everyone but you, right?" I bite.

"Exactly," he says before cupping my pussy, grinding the heel of his hand against my clit. I try to repress a moan, but with a little more pressure, it escapes me before I can help it.

Zayden continues this move as he takes the knife in his other hand and begins dragging the blade against my skin again, this time on the sharp side. My pulse begins to thunder as fear grasps me in a chokehold when the silky tip of the blade pierces my skin just slightly, enough to allow a bead of blood to follow with it.

He makes two more cuts, each just below the other, on my inner thigh, the sharp pain morphing into something unnamed, something unknown, and a dark, recessed part of me enjoys it.

"Fuck, I knew you'd bleed so beautifully for me."

His eyes collide with my own, that same bloodlust-hazed look in his eyes like it was earlier tonight as he sets the blade aside and rubs his thumb over the cuts, smearing the blood across my thigh before lifting it to his mouth and rubbing it against his lips. His tongue flicks out, tracing over the crimson red before he groans and rolls his eyes into the back of his head. I feel his palm increase in speed against me, and when he plunges a finger inside me, I'm embarrassed to say that I'm absolutely soaked. He adds another finger before pulling out, rubbing those same fingers into my blood once more before sucking on them.

I should be repulsed. He's disgusting, sick, and demented, for sure. I should not feel my pussy pulsing, ready to fall apart at the sight of this psychotic man losing his fucking mind because of me, for me. Without another word, he pulls his cock out with one hand before he's shoving himself inside me.

A sharp scream tears through me at the aggressive thrust before it fades into an unwanted moan. I should be fighting harder, I shouldn't succumb. But when his hand digs into my hair, fisting it into his palm as he forces my eyes on his, I let go of everything, and I exist in this moment, no matter how wrong it is, it feels so fucking good.

"You're so perfect, angel. I need to have you forever," he

pants as he tightens his hold on me.

"Fuck," I moan as his pelvis grinds against my clit.

"Goddamn, your cunt grips me so good. Tell me how much you love my cock in you. Say my name," he groans.

I shouldn't be giving in to this at all, let alone obeying his commands, but his name slips past my lips like it was always meant to, and he rewards me with his fingertips now dancing against my clit.

"Zayden."

He doesn't last another second, shoving deep inside me, hitting my G-spot, and making me see stars as his warm cum fills me. Once his orgasm subsides, that doesn't stop him, as he continues fucking me for several more seconds, practically forcing the cum as deep as it can go before he finally slows, forcing my eyes to meet his.

"That was perfect."

Now that my own orgasm has subsided, I don't know how to feel or what to think. I'm disgusted with myself and confused and still kind of turned on. The sudden need to cover myself is strong as I try to cover my body with my hands. Zayden watches me carefully, and it's almost like he can see in my mind, like he's attempting to allow me inside his. I'm not sure I want to go to a place like that, though.

He shucks off his leather jacket before peeling up his shirt, revealing those insanely defined sets of muscles covered in the various shaded tattoos, before pulling the shirt over me. He continues to unravel it down my body until it hits my upper thigh, just barely covering the three cuts that are finally not bleeding.

I watch as his fingers dance around the puffy and swollen skin as if he were entranced by it.

"Will they scar?" I ask.

He shakes his head before looking up at me.

"When I mark you forever, it will only be when you beg me to."

I don't say anything to that, as we both just watch each other for several seconds. I feel his other hand come up to my lips, brushing against them reverently. Something is wrong with me. I can't describe it, I can barely comprehend it, but all I know is that right now, in this moment, I want him to kiss me more than I want my next breath.

Maybe I want it so I can confirm that I have nothing but disdain for him, that what just happened was nothing more than a lust-fueled haze. I was scared and running on an adrenaline high. That's all it was, and if his lips touching mine fills me with the revulsion it should, I'll know for sure that I'm not crazy. I haven't lost my mind. I was acting out of survival and a basic human reaction.

My mind made up, I lift a hand to the back of his neck, pressing forward slightly and making my intention clear. His eyes flash with surprise, and he doesn't hesitate, his lips are on mine in the next instant.

Butterflies tear through my body, soaring from my chest to my lower belly. My heart begins beating harder than it was when I was running for my life down this hill. A warm buzzing feeling begins from where our lips are joined all the way to my toes, and when his tongue peeks out to tangle with mine, it's officially confirmed. I've lost my goddamn mind.

Surprisingly, Zayden doesn't try to do anything more than kiss me. He is practically consuming me like I'm the meaning of life, his life at least. I need more, though. Pushing Zayden to the side, he rolls easily onto his back, and I climb on top of him, sinking down onto his already hard cock with only a little pain. I breathe through it before rising up and sinking down again.

"Fuck, angel. Ride my cock. Take what you want."

I continue my motions, chasing only my own pleasure as Zayden watches on in awe, digging his fingers into my ass cheeks as he guides my rhythm.

"Zayden!" I moan.

His cock hits each spot just right, forcing my body to shudder and shake as I do my best to keep myself upright.

"I've got you," Zayden says before he wraps his arms around me, holding me in place before lifting me up as he gets to his feet.

He carries us for several feet before pressing my back against a cool surface. Before I have a moment to look around us, Zayden's taking over, thrusting deeply inside me as his mouth is latched to my neck, sucking and licking me as he fucks me against this wall. The only thing I can do is toss my head back and enjoy the feel of him.

"Zayden! Fuck. I'm gonna—" I gasp as that familiar feeling is already setting in, causing my legs to quake as my breathing becomes choppy.

"Good. Come all over my cock, baby. I want to drown in

your cum."

I feel his teeth sink into the hollow point of my neck, and in the next minute, I cum. My vision spots, and my body practically locks up as I shout my release. I scream and squirm in his arms as he holds me up, fucking me until he's following right behind me, his cum filling me up for the second time. Thank fuck for birth control, though I'm still not one-hundred-percent confident that it's fully effective yet.

Letting out a ragged breath, I rest my head against the wall before looking up. I stare at the starry sky for several seconds before an archway catches my eye. I look up to see that we were fucking against a stone pillar on one side of an entrance to what looks like a private cemetery. My eyes squint as I try to make out the words better. It takes me a few moments in the dark before my eyes clearly read the word "Graves" scrawled across the top.

"Is this..."

"My family's plot?" Zayden fills in. "Yes. Say hi to my mom and dad." He laughs, forcing a demented laugh to escape me.

"Oh my god. No. This is disgusting. We fucked in a cemetery, in your cemetery," I say.

"Twice." He nods.

I cover my face with my hands as I shake my head. I feel Zayden slowly lower me until my feet are on the ground. A shiver runs through me as the crisp air wraps around us.

"Are you still going to tell on me, angel?" he asks, forcing my chin up with two fingers.

I squint my eyes as I look up at him.

"You're still gonna let me go?"

"Of course not," he scoffs as he runs his hand through my hair. "But I want to know if you still want to see me rotting in a jail cell or on the wrong side of this ground."

The way I can barely form a sentence proves I'm in no position to be making decisions or declarations, but for some idiotic reason, I no longer feel threatened by him. He's too obsessed with me, whether that's good or not. I truly don't think he'd ever hurt me or let anyone else hurt me. He's not a good man, he obviously feels no remorse for the man he killed today, and he's made it clear that wasn't his first kill, but a strange comfort settles with me that he's not gonna stake me with a chair leg at any given moment.

"Why did you kill him?" I ask. "The guy...in the dining room."

His fingers continue tangling through my hair, like he can't help but touch me as he speaks.

"He works for a man that wants information on me, on Dominic, on you. He knew you were in the apartment. He knew too much."

I'm quiet for a moment, secretly loving the feeling of my hair being played with as I speak again.

"So, this man, he's the one Dominic was talking about. The one who wants to hurt me?"

His eyes come to mine, a dangerous glint in them as he shakes his head.

"He doesn't want to hurt you, but he would never pass up an opportunity to control me. I'd burn heaven itself to the ground to keep you as mine. He'll know that and use it against me, against all of us.

"Why? What does he want with you? What—"

He presses his lips to mine, silencing me for a moment before resting his head into the crook of my neck.

"No more questions. Just listen to Dominic and me. Don't run. I need you safe."

I decide to stay quiet, and he seems happy with that as he wraps his arms around my shoulders and buries his nose into my neck, continuing to inhale my scent in a way that is still definitely creepy but not nearly as terrifying as it was just hours ago.

Silently, we walk back up to the bike, Zayden tucking me into his side so tight I can barely walk on my own. We find my shoe along the way, which is nice, and he slips his leather jacket on, which is honestly hot as shit since he's now bare-chested with only a leather jacket and his pants on.

One tattoo catches my attention more so than the others. It's a pair of angel wings with a scrawled name across them. It only takes me a second to recognize my own letters inked into his skin. My eyes come to his in surprise, but he only watches me impassively, seemingly waiting for me to speak. I choose not to, though, and he shrugs before leading us to the bike.

As I go to sit on the leather seat, I wince at the feeling of cum running down my legs. Zayden's eyes drop between my thighs, and he smirks before shoving some of the leaking cum back inside me. I inhale at the intrusion before he gives me a salacious wink and fires the bike back up, weaving his way through the cemetery and back to the main road.

GRAVES

What the fuck just happened?

CHAPTER TWENTY-THREE

DOMINIC

It took me nearly two hours to find Blake and Zayden. When I ran out of logical places they could be after finding a dead body in the middle of my dining room, I thought of illogical places, like our family grave site. I had been working late at the security office and hadn't thought much of leaving Zayden alone with Blake. She hated his guts, and he loved her with everything he was capable of. They were going to be fine for a few hours. Apparently, I was wrong.

As soon as my car crested around the corner of the paved

driveway and I spotted Zayden's bike, fear ran through me. I took off on foot since it was the fastest way to where they no doubt were. Zayden has been irrational since obsessing over Blake, more so than normal. I wasn't sure what he was capable of. Would he be crazy enough to pull off a murder-suicide, so they were together forever? No fucking question. If I found out that he had harmed a hair on her head, no amount of pain would be enough punishment. I wouldn't allow him to off himself. I'd torture him for the rest of his days if he took her from me.

When I finally came up to the Graves family cemetery, my feet slowed and my heart stopped beating for several seconds when I heard a moan, not a masculine one either. A feminine one. One that I had been well acquainted with. I heard the love of my life crying out in pleasure, "Zayden!"

He's taken advantage of her before, several times, and I wasn't there to protect her. This time would be different, though. When I stepped around the corner, there I saw them, her clothes cut up and strewn all around them. Only, instead of seeing her pinned to the ground, screaming for help, she was on top of him, his shirt drowning her frame as she rode him and shuddered in what looked like pleasure.

It was equally enraging and erotic. I was about to rip her off him for the sake of claiming what was mine when he lifted her up and started walking her toward me. For a moment, I almost allowed myself to be seen. To see what would happen from there, to see if Blake would be as happy for me to be here as I was to see her. For some reason, I didn't, though. I tucked myself behind the other side of the opposite pillar, and I watched them.

Blake's moans were loud and filled with ecstasy, while Zayden encouraged her with every thrust. My cock was painfully hard, and before I knew what I was doing, I was taking it out, running my hand over it once or twice just to take the edge off. It wasn't enough, though. I began working my cock faster and faster as I caught glimpses of Blake's beautiful ass and perfect pussy getting fucked raw. I imagined my hand was hers, that I was in place of Zayden right now, which wasn't all that hard since it's like looking in a mirror.

I was fucking my fist to the sound of my brother fucking my woman, and it only took one more pump before I was coming hard. My vision blurred, and I had to right myself against the pillar just as Blake screamed out her release, Zayden following right along.

I allowed myself one more minute for another breath before I tucked myself away and went back to my car. I drove out the back entrance before they could even see me and went straight home. I finished cleaning up the mess Zayden left behind, stashing the body into the deep freezer in the back room for now until we have better means to get rid of him.

When I finish throwing the last bloodied towel into the washing machine, I hear the snick of the door opening and watch as Zayden steps into the hallway, a sleeping Blake in his arms. He quietly carries her to her room, making eye contact with me and giving absolutely nothing away.

I follow after him as he lays her down on the bed, pressing a kiss to her lips that has my jaw tensing in irritation. Hasn't he had enough of her already? She broke up with me this morning, told me she hated me, but she's more than willing to fuck him? The anger and betrayal and hurt of it all are unfair and unjust, and I'm fucking pissed.

Zayden steps away from her, brushing past me as he makes his way down the hall and past both of our rooms. He comes up to the broom closet before pressing his finger down on the scanner, forcing the hidden door to swing open as I follow him inside the room.

He moves through the room casually, jumping up to sit on top of the deep freezer, where his latest kill currently rests. The wall of weapons on display is just across from me, and I seriously consider using some on my brother. Guaranteed, Blake will never fuck him again if he doesn't have a dick.

"What are you doing up late, brother?" Zayden asks as he swings his legs in a carefree way that very much does not represent my demented brother.

"Oh, you know, cleaning up your messes, driving through cemeteries," I deadpan.

A single eyebrow raises, but he doesn't react other than that.

"You been spying on me?"

"Kinda hard not to when you're fucking her in the middle of the goddamn cemetery!" I roar, not caring how loud I get since the room is soundproof.

"Jealousy is unbecoming on you," Zayden drawls lazily.

I close the distance between us, grabbing him by the throat and pushing him flat against the wall.

"Fuck. You. We had a deal. You agreed not to touch her. You

agreed not to—"

"Things change, brother. My angel and I made another deal, and it was far sweeter than the one you and I decided on."

"I don't want to hear this shit. I want you to back the fuck off. Her whole life is in ruins because of you!"

He scoffs. "Please, what life? To and from work? The occasional visit with her self-absorbed friend who has a whole-ass family and barely enough time for her? She wasn't being loved the way she deserves, now she can."

"At the risk of her life, Zayden! How do you not get that? If Maxim finds out about her, which he will, she's as good as fucking dead. Not today, maybe not tomorrow, but one day."

Zayden's eyes turn practically black as he easily shoves me away from him.

"Don't tell me what's at stake. You think I don't know this?" he snarls as he jumps to his feet and begins pacing. His hands are digging through his hair as he mutters to himself almost manically.

"I know! But I'll protect her. I'll keep her hidden from him for as long as possible, and when he finds out about her, I'll talk to him."

"Fat fucking lot that'll do. When he finds her, he will make you his bitch forever."

"So be it! It's better than living a life without her."

I shake my head. "You're so goddamn selfish. She can't live like this, Zayden. We need to set her up with a new identity, in a new country, and cut all contact. It's the only way," I say, the words tasting like acid on my tongue the instant they're out there.

His eyes go wild, and he leaps for the closest gun, cocking it and pressing it right to my temple.

"Suggest taking her away again, and I will blow your brains all over this room, brotherhood be damned!" he rages, his eyes panicked and wild.

He thinks I'm gonna take her in the middle of the night, not leaving a clue behind. He thinks he'll have to spend his entire life just trying to find her again, and he's not wrong. The thought has crossed my mind since the moment I learned about her. Sometimes I still think about it, but I'd like to exhaust every other possibility until then because, though I know Zayden would die without her, I'm not too sure I'd be much better.

"Just stay inside, under the radar. We need to dig some stuff up on Maxim, something that we can pin on him if he threatens her."

"You've been trying to do that for over a decade, and you've always come up short," Zayden throws out.

I nod. "I'll have to try harder."

He nods his agreement, and we both stay silent for several moments.

"She calls you Dom," he says, almost hollowly.

I tense at that, not knowing how to respond, so instead, I nod.

His head turns to the side, silently asking me if I've told her, which I haven't. Not really, at least. I shake my head, to which his shoulders seem to almost slump in relief. We're quiet for several more seconds before he speaks.

"I'm never going to let her go."

I look up at him, his stance evenly spaced and rigid. As if he is ready to fight me to the death should it come to that. From what she's said today and what I saw tonight, though, I'm not sure how much of a fight is really there. She doesn't want me, maybe she was just in the moment with him, or maybe she does want him. I don't care either way. At the end of the day, if she doesn't want me, what the fuck am I supposed to do? I'm not like Zayden. I won't force her to love me, even if I want to so fucking badly.

"If she wants me, I'll never let her go either," I say.

"May the best win, I suppose," Zayden muses.

"Suppose so."

CHAPTER TWENTY-FOUR

BLAKE

When I wake up the next morning, I'm in bed. Not my bed at my apartment. Not Dominic's bed, but the bed in the spare room. My prison bed, as I like to call it. Last night felt like a fever dream. It must have been, right? There is no way all of that happened. No way I willingly fucked Zayden twice. I look down at the dark gray shirt engulfing me before lifting it to see three lines that are already beginning to heal on my inner thigh.

Okay, definitely real. I don't suppose temporary insanity could explain away my lapse of judgment. I mean, maybe it could. That and the fight-or-flight mode that was activated with his little primal play chase game.

I force myself out of bed, noticing instantly how sore I feel between my thighs. God, he was not fucking around last night. I feel like I got fucked for hours.

While I basically hobble toward the bathroom like a newborn deer, I wince when I step inside the shower, allowing the warm water to hit my sensitive skin. I swear to God, I'm going to get a UTI if I sleep for one more fucking night full of cum.

Once I'm rinsed off, I grab the shirt I threw on the ground which, now that I look at it more closely, I recognize it as Zayden's, before I cautiously slip out of the bedroom.

When I step into the bright kitchen, a strong smell of bacon and something sweet fills my senses. There also seems to be a brand-new vase filled with daffodils on the island, and just the sight of the beautiful flower has my heart squeezing.

A muscular back is turned to me, and when those deep brown eyes land on my own, my stomach does a little flip. He gives me a soft yet hesitant smile that makes my heart hurt. In the wake of the insane night I had, I had almost forgotten about the other morning. What I said to Dominic and how I hated myself for saying it. Obviously, I should hate him, but if I can fuck Zayden, then what's stopping me from at least talking to Dominic, right?

"Hi," I say softly.

"Good morning." He nods.

I stand awkwardly in place as his eyes flick down to my

shirt, his jaw clenching in response, which makes me feel like shit. I've never been one for good timing, either, because I'm blurting out my words in the next moment. "I slept with Zayden."

Dominic just stares at me as I continue to speak.

"I mean, on purpose this time. Well, kind of not. The first time I was kind of against it but kinda not, and then the second time I initiated it. But I honestly think I need a lobotomy because who willingly sleeps with their stalker? Someone who wants to end up as a lampshade, that's who." I laugh hollowly to myself before shaking my head.

"Why are you telling me this?" Dominic asks impassively.

Something about his nonchalance bothers me, which is completely unfair and gross of me, but it does. I shrug in response, and he nods before turning around, focusing back on the food he's cooking.

"I know."

I frown at that. Zayden told him? What a fucking asshole. Did he come home and rub it in his brother's face?

"I'm sorry," I say softly.

He turns to look over his shoulder at me.

"Why are you apologizing?"

"Because shouldn't I be sorry? I mean, I slept with your brother and—"

"And you broke up with me. You're single and free to see whomever you deem worthy."

I look down at the floor, not sure what else to say, when suddenly Dominic is in front of me, his hand cupping my jaw and tilting my face up to his.

"Are we broken up, Blake?" he asks.

I open my mouth, not sure how to respond, as he continues.

"Because I would very much like us not to be. I would love to be able to say that you're still mine, but I also understand that I lost that privilege, and it's completely understandable if you choose not to see me anymore."

I frown at that, a sour feeling twisting my stomach.

"I don't want that."

I feel his thumb gently brushing against my cheek as he gives me a sad smile.

"Me neither. So? Are you mine? Can we start all of this over?"

"No more lies?" I ask.

He hesitates just for a moment before he nods.

"No more lies."

I let out a soft breath as I nod.

"I've missed you," I say as his lips crush against my own.

His hands go beneath my thighs, gripping them tightly, before he lifts me into the air. I wrap my legs around his waist as he moves us to the kitchen island, setting me on the edge before dropping to his knees. He pushes up the hem of Zayden's shirt on me until it's bunched above my thighs. Dom's movements falter for a moment as he stares at my inner thigh, his finger coming to the three little slits as a thunderous look crosses his face.

"He cut you?" he practically growls.

I look down at the cuts before I meet his eyes.

"Yeah."

His jaw turns to granite.

"Did you consent?"

Did I? I mean, no. He didn't say, "Hey, Blake. Mind if I slice and dice ya a bit?" But at the same time, I can't deny that a small part of me kind of liked it. It was kind of a rush. The sting of the pain and the needy pleasure on his face as he did it had warring feelings mixing inside of me. Couple that with the adrenaline of what came next and the potential danger I was in, and it was an erotic encounter like I had never experienced. I never thought I would be into the whole knife play thing, and maybe I only liked it in that one moment, but there is no doubt that I did like it. Too much, probably.

"Yeah," I answer softly, knowing that at the end of the day, he's really checking to see if Zayden cut me to hurt me or not.

That thunderous look doesn't leave his face, but he gives me a terse nod before he buries his face between my thighs. His tongue lashes against me in a violent way that I have never experienced before now. Without a second's notice, he spears two fingers inside me, finger fucking me as his mouth continues its assault against my clit.

I dig my hand into his hair, mainly because, fucking hell, I need something to grab onto as he basically attacks my cunt with no sign of stopping anytime soon.

The familiar feeling begins building in me with each swipe of his tongue and move of his finger. My legs begin to quake, and my breath becomes choppy and uneven as I try to hold off my orgasm, not wanting this to be over just yet. It's no use, though. My orgasm hits me hard. My back practically bows off the cool countertop, my screams echo through the house, and Dom doesn't stop until I'm a limp fucking mess.

When he pulls away, for a moment, I think that he's done. That is, until he pulls his cock out and slides into my still wet cunt, no condom in sight, as he lets out a groan of pleasure.

"What, are all the Graves brothers against condoms or something?" I rasp on a laugh.

His hand comes to the side of my ass cheek, slapping it so hard that a rip of pleasure and pain runs through me.

"He's not going to be the only one inside you with nothing between you two. You're mine, baby, and now I'm gonna fuck you like it."

I nod in agreement as he snaps his hips, causing me to let out a moan as he does it again and again, finding a fast-paced, practically savage rhythm. My hands grip the edge of the countertop, doing my best not to fall off as Dom literally fucks me straight into the island.

He lifts two of his fingers up, holding them in front of my mouth.

"Suck."

I part my lips, and he doesn't waste a second pushing his fingers into my mouth. The taste of me springs across my tongue instantly. I've never minded my own taste, in fact, I kinda like it. So I have no problem wrapping my tongue around his fingers, licking and sucking on the digits, and causing him to let out a panting breath as I do.

"Fuck, baby. You're so goddamn perfect. Come on my cock. Let me feel you fall apart while I fill your cunt up."

I moan around his fingers as I feel my pussy clench several times before I go off again. I feel myself pulse and clench around Dom as I moan. I feel Dom release inside of me, his cock swelling before warmth fills me. He fucks me through his own orgasm, collapsing on top of me with a shaky breath.

We stay like that for several minutes, Dominic still firmly buried inside of me with no sign of pulling out before he lifts his head to look at me.

"I love you, Blake. I love you, and I can't share you. I need you to be mine."

My heart thuds and seizes all at once. Not sharing me is the easy part to accept. I mean, it's not like I want to be shared. The thing with Zayden last night was obviously a mistake. It was a tension and adrenaline-fueled mistake. He's a psychotic stalking killer. The only reason I'm even alive, no doubt, is because he has it in his head that we are destined to be together or some crap. He's a lunatic. Dominic is the only man that I want, obviously. And he loves me?

"Really?" I ask stupidly.

He nods seriously, cupping my face the way he does.

"I love you too," I say, meaning it instantly and feeling a flurry of something unexplainable as he smiles a genuine, wide, blissful smile before pressing his lips against my own.

When he pulls away, I smile up at him as he pulls out and begins tucking himself away. My eyes catch a shadowed figure from the corner, two bright blue orbs piercing straight into me, and a look filled with so much anger, it chills me straight to the bone.

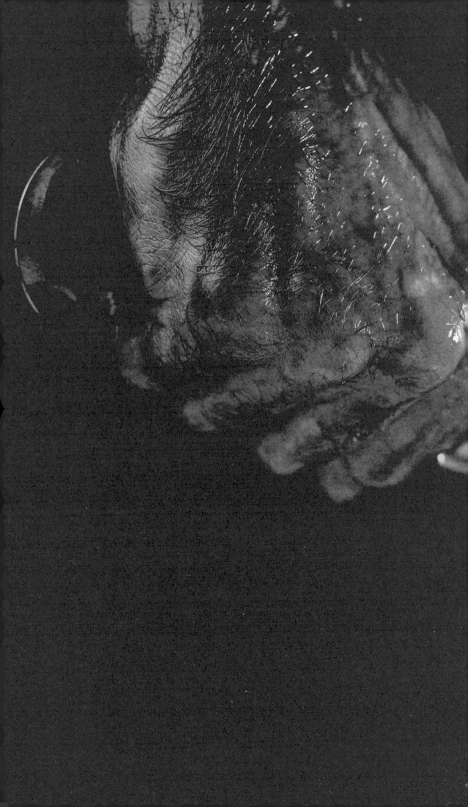

CHAPTER TWENTY-FIVE

ZAYDEN

I've been in my room all day. It's a better alternative than sitting out there watching my brother touch my angel. We agreed to let the better man win, but I only agreed because I know that I'm the better man for her. Clearly, she needs some convincing, though.

A heavy knock comes from my door, and I plunge my knife into the wall just beside it before Dominic pushes inside. He glances at the knife and at me before he rolls his eyes, almost like he's desensitized to me, before he speaks.

"I have to go. Jarod called. Someone tried to hack into the block's surveillance cameras."

I turn my head to the side at that.

"You think—"

"Yes," he finishes.

Shaking my head at that, I thumb the next knife beside me, running my fingers over the sharp edge of it, watching in fascination as that red line appears in its wake.

"We're going to have to jump in front of this problem before it gets worse," I mutter.

"No. Absolutely not. We are never going to let him anywhere near her, he's not allowed to know she even exists. Stick to the plan. Keep her inside, do not let her leave for anything. I'm still working on something. I dug up a job he did for the Mariano family over in New York. Looks like he didn't finish the job fully, and they're looking for him. Maybe that could work to our advantage?"

My head whips up at that.

"You think the way out of this mess, all of us alive, is to sic the mob on him? If he's evaded them for this long, what makes you think he can't continue to do so, this time killing everyone in this apartment in retribution?" I scoff.

Dominic clenches his jaw as he shakes his head and turns to leave.

"It's the best choice we have. We're sticking with the plan."

His back faces me, and he takes one step out the door as I call out to him.

"Feel good to be all patched up with her?"

He freezes mid-step as I go on.

"Nothing a good fuck on the kitchen island can't fix, am I right?"

"About the same as a fuck against our family grave gate."

His words make me smirk. I'm still shocked that I didn't know he was there that night. Then again, he learned from the best, just like I did. Also to his advantage, when I'm with my angel, my awareness dulls, my attention completely snapped up by her. She consumes every ounce of me just the way I like it, though I'll admit, if I'm going to keep her safe from Maxim, I need to be better. Allow my obsession to fill me within these four walls, as above all else, her safety is first priority.

Without another word, Dominic leaves, and a few minutes later, the front door opens and shuts. The blood on my hand has dried, and I move to the en suite bathroom in my room to clean it up before I make my way into the living room. When I do, I find my angel curled up in a ball on the couch, reading a book. I recognize the author's name. Must be a favorite of hers.

Her eyes leave the page for only a moment before she's fixating back on her story. I can't deny that irritation flits through me at her disinterest in me. Last night was too perfect for her to act like it never happened. That was supposed to be all it took to confirm for her that we were destined to be together. The way her body responded to me, even when I showed my proclivities. The way she wanted more. She's perfect, we're perfect. She'll see it soon enough.

I make quick work of a bacon and cheese omelet with some toast for her. It's about dinnertime, but she really likes having breakfast for dinner. Though she's pretty terrible at making omelets. I can't tell you how many times I've watched her attempt them, only to get frustrated and turn it into a scramble. So many times I wanted to come out of her closet to help her, and now I can.

When I'm finished, I plate it and carry it over to the coffee table along with one of those flavored sparkling waters that she loves. I set it down in front of her, causing her to lower her book and inspect it. She frowns before looking up at me.

"What's this for?"

"To eat," I say flatly.

Her eyes squint at that. "You made me food?"

I nod as I move to take the seat directly across from the couch, leaning back as I gesture toward her.

"Enjoy your book, eat. Pretend I'm not here," I say as my eyes greedily take in the sight of her beauty before me.

She scoffs at that as she sets her book down.

"Kinda hard to do when you're just staring at me."

"That never bothered you before," I counter.

Irritation passes across her face.

"That's because I didn't know you were there, creep."

A low chuckle escapes me as I lean forward, resting my elbows on my knees as I look at her.

"We both know that's not true. Sometimes I'd make a noise here and there just to make you aware. Your fight-or-flight instincts are terrible, by the way. Hiding under your blankets when you hear a thunk at night won't keep you alive, angel. Not by a long shot."

"Fuck you!" she spits out before taking the plate of food and throwing it at me. I dodge it easily as it shatters apart against the wall behind me, egg and crumbs half stuck to the wall with glass shards everywhere.

"You don't know me, Zayden. Just because you stalked me doesn't mean you know me. I don't really give a fuck what you think of my fight-or-flight skills. They've gotten me this far, right? I'm still breathing, I'm still fighting. So why don't you do me a favor and go fuck yourself?"

Her breathing is labored, eyes filled with a rage that surprisingly starts to dim. I just sit there in the chair, watching her patiently until she appears to be calm enough.

"Would you like me to remake you the omelet?" I ask.

She turns her head to the side as she looks at me.

"What the fuck? No. Fuck your food. I don't want anything you have to offer me."

I frown at that.

"You, me, and the cemetery know that's not true, angel."

She tosses her hands out by her sides and lets out a hollow laugh.

"The cemetery? Where I was literally running for my life? Where you tackled me to the ground, pulled my pants down, and cut my skin before you fucked me against my will?"

I'm across the room in a flash, my hand wrapped firmly around her throat as I pin her to the back of the couch. Her eyes are wide and afraid, but she makes no attempt to fight back.

C'mon, angel. Fight. Please.

"Don't delude yourself. You and I both know that from the

moment I took you to the ground, you wanted it. Your pussy was practically sopping when I got to you, and this," I say as I pull out my knife, conveniently the same one from last night. I slowly drag it against her skin, so featherlight it won't leave a mark, unfortunately.

Her pulse thunders to the point I can see it jumping out of her skin, goosebumps pricking against her skin as her pupils dilate. A look of something akin to want flashes in her eyes, lust even. *Exactly*.

"This," I continue. "I think you enjoyed more than you expected. The chill from the metal made your heart race and fear tighten its hold on you, and I think you liked the rush. The first slice is always the hardest. It's sharp and stings, but the sting blends with the fear, and soon, it's an addicting concoction you don't know if you should refrain from or overdose on."

That lust-drenched look has now taken up residence in her entrancing eyes. I'll never be able to decide which one I like more, it's impossible. I love the pair. Blue and brown together, two sides of the same coin, making up my beautiful woman.

"Do you want to feel alive, angel?" I whisper into her ear, allowing the blade to run along her collarbone and dipping beneath her T-shirt between her breasts. Her breath forces a soft gasp to escape her as she practically shudders in my arms.

The knife continues its descent, stopping on her bra. I don't plan on stopping there though, I need better visibility. I turn the knife in my palm, forcing the tip of the blade in my direction and cutting a line straight through her shirt. A few more inches, and the material practically falls to her sides. I slip the knife beneath the front clasp of her bra, ready to free her breasts when she breathes.

"Please don't cut another one."

I nod softly. "As you wish," I say against her ear, sending another round of goosebumps sparking against her skin before I lower my mouth between her breasts, freeing the clasp with my teeth and allowing her breasts to spill out completely for my eyes to see. The dusty pink of her nipples causes cum to leak from my tip.

The point of my blade turns back to her skin, tracing lazy lines down her torso before coming to her leggings. This time I don't wait for her to argue with me as I turn the blade once again and hook the fabric, tearing it and her panties easily in half until she's left completely bare for me. Fucking hell.

I drag the cool steel against her bald pussy, enjoying the quiver that comes from her legs when I pause just at her slit. Fear and adrenaline seem to course through her as I turn the knife in my hand and push the handle between her thighs. She doesn't fight me, but she doesn't open up for me either. It's no problem for me, though. I know she wants this, even if she can't admit it. I'll do it for both of us.

The handle of the knife slips inside her easily, almost too easily. Just as I knew she would be, her pussy is soaked, and she lets out a shuddering breath that slips into a moan before she can help it. I continue plunging it in and out of her, fucking her with one of my favorite knives as I speak.

"That feel good, angel?"

Her eyes are clenched tight, her hands gripping the couch

as she stays silent. She's fighting me so hard right now, it'll make her release all the sweeter.

"Eyes on me. Now," I say in a harsh voice that has her eyes flying open.

She looks conflicted and pleasure-drunk. Like she doesn't know which way is up or what to do next. I release my hold on her throat, shifting my stance and dropping to my knees in front of her. Her legs are still not spread, but they've parted slightly to make room for her new toy.

I pull it out of her, a thrill of pleasure running through me when she lets out a needy little whimper at the loss of it. Smirking to myself, I hold her eyes with mine as I raise it up to my mouth and suck on it, licking her juices clean off the handle. I can't help but groan as the taste, that is so undeniably hers, spreads across my tongue. I want nothing more than to bury my face in her cunt and eat her until the sun comes up, but she has to beg me. No claiming she didn't want it, that she didn't have a choice. She's going to beg for me to eat and fuck her pussy, and then I'll happily do so until the end of time.

"Do you want it? You want it back in you?" I ask, smirking when I look down and see that my hand is bleeding from where I was holding the blade.

"Look what you do to me," I say as I hold my hand up for her to see. "Look what your pleasure costs me, angel."

"I-I'm sorry," she says shakily.

"Shh, don't be," I say as I run my hand up and down her thigh soothingly, pride sparking inside my chest when I see my blood smeared across her perfect porcelain skin. "Give me your words, baby. Tell me you want me, that you're begging for me, and I'll give you that little push over the edge I know you're desperate for," I say as I take the blade in my hand once more, pushing the handle of the knife just to her opening, only a half-ounce of pressure more, and it would be inside her again. The way she's arching her back and wiggling her hips tells me she wants it too, badly.

To my irritation, though, she doesn't speak. I wiggle the blade side to side, teasing her more as her eyes roll into the back of her head and a small leak of wetness coats the handle. Her pussy is practically crying out in agony, desperate for any kind of attention.

"C'mon, angel. Let me hear your pretty little lips beg for me," I say again, hoping she'll finally comply.

Her eyes come to me, her hips still wiggling as they seek relief when she speaks.

"I'm with Dom. I only want Dom."

Fury blinds me as I rip the knife away and bury it in the couch beside her. I stand up without another word, grabbing my keys off the table and leaving the apartment. The door shuts with a bang so hard it shakes the entire wall. My feet move quickly from the elevator down to my bike. It's barely even started before I'm racing through the night as anger, bitterness, and a little bit of hurt all boil underneath my skin.

The buzzing of my phone vibrates in my pocket, but I ignore it because honestly, it's only going to be two people, Dominic or Maxim, and I don't want to speak to either of them. So instead, I focus on the road in front of me, driving as fast as I can in an attempt to outrun the overwhelming urge to kill my brother and my angel before taking my own life. I'm nothing without her, and if she won't have me, she won't have anyone.

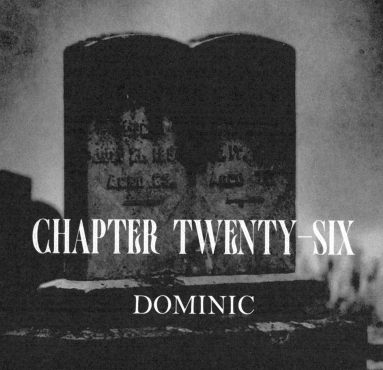

CHAPTER TWENTY-SIX

DOMINIC

"You're sure you've gone over everything?" I ask Jarod for the third time.

"Yes, triple sure. Whoever it was, they were definitely overseas, looks to be Russia."

My gut tightens at that. I know one person in Russia that I don't want watching the street cameras surrounding my apartment, and there isn't a doubt in my mind that out of over seven billion people in the world, it's him.

I nod at that. "Lock it down. I want to double the eyes on

these streets until you can figure out how to block them out completely. If the DOT finds out, our asses are on the chopping block."

Jarod, my operations manager and little prodigy, nods seriously as he begins typing away. I have a small team that runs the security company for me. Mainly because I don't trust easily. It would be one thing if we were actually doing what Jarod and our three other employees thought we were doing: providing cyber security for high-profile clients like the DOT, investment bankers, and such. It's even more important for covering up Zayden's reckless behavior, and now, keeping Blake safe.

I'm texting the other guys to apprise them of the situation when an unknown number begins calling me. Dread sinks into my stomach as I step out of the room to answer.

"Hello?"

"Finally, a Graves who knows how to answer the phone." Maxim's thick accent echoes through the phone.

"Maxim," I say curtly.

"Dominic. It's been quite some time. You don't stay in touch with friends?"

"Are we friends?" I ask dubiously as I move over to a free computer, logging into it before pulling up the phone tracking software.

"More so, we're family, *moy mal'chik.*"

I let out a short, dry chuckle at that as my fingers fly over the keyboard.

"No sense in tracing, why not just ask me where I am?" he

says.

My hands still as I stand up and look around the office.

"Where are you, Maxim?"

"I'm in Moscow still, though I hear Seattle is getting a much better summer than us. Maybe I should come pay a visit. See my boys."

The thinly veiled threat is hard to ignore. I glance over my shoulder before lowering my voice.

"What do you want?"

"Your brother to call me back. He's been ungrateful. I got him out of prison without so much as a thank you."

"He's been doing jobs for you," I point out.

"Yes, that's just business. I'd like a thank you as well. Tell him to call me. I have a new mark."

"When?"

"I want him in Miami no later than tomorrow."

I blow out a breath. Getting Zayden anywhere away from Blake will be fucking hard, but the further he is, the safer she will be.

"I'll try."

"You will do," he corrects before the phone goes dead.

Fuck.

Pocketing my phone, I grab my keys and head out the door without another word. Jarod will lock up behind me. He practically lives here, I'm honestly not even sure that he has a home. I've caught him sleeping in the break room more times than I can count. Whatever.

It only takes one ring of the phone as I turn out onto the

road when Zayden answers.

"What?"

"Maxim called," I say.

"Yeah, I know."

"You need to call him back or he's threatening to come to Seattle. Which may mean he already knows more than we'd like."

Zayden is quiet for too long before he finally curses under his breath.

"What does he want?"

"New mark. In Miami. He wants you there by tomorrow morning."

"I'll be home in five," he grumbles.

My brows furrow at that.

"You're not home? Who is with Blake?" I ask as I climb into my car, firing it up and backing out of the parking garage. A heavy feeling weighs on me that I can't quite explain as I wait for his words.

"She's fine. She's locked in the house, and I needed to cool down."

"Why?" I ask, to which I'm met with silence. "Why did you need to cool down, Zayden?" I ask again.

"She wants me, but she won't let herself have me because of *you*," he practically snarls through the phone.

I frown at that. "What do you mean?"

I'm met with silence again, and when I pull the phone from my face, I see that he has already hung up on me.

I can't deny that I'm more than curious to know exactly

what happened that made Zayden so upset, to push him to leave Blake's side willingly. Then again, maybe it would be best to live in the dark on this one for now.

When I get home, I'm just stepping in through the door when I see Zayden standing over Blake. She's asleep on the couch in a pair of sleep shorts and a tank top. He's just watching her silently, a small bag packed at his feet as he leans down to her, pressing a soft kiss against her forehead and whispering something that I don't quite catch before he grabs his bag.

He turns around to face me, giving me a stiff head nod.

"Get in, get out," I say as I clap his shoulder.

"In and out," he agrees before casting one more look at Blake over his shoulder as he sneaks past me and out the door.

I shut the door behind him and stay in place for several seconds before I cross the room to Blake, scooping her up into my arms and carrying her to my bed. I set her down on her side of the bed before stripping down to my boxers. Sliding in behind her, I wrap my arms around her waist, one of my hands resting on her chest. I rest my chin over the top of her head, falling asleep to the steady beat of her heart.

CHAPTER TWENTY-SEVEN

BLAKE

When I woke up the next morning, Dominic told me that Zayden had to leave for work. I didn't know how I felt about that news. Mainly because I had mixed feelings that hit me simultaneously. Relief because, after the whole thing on the couch, I wasn't sure how I was going to face him, happiness to have the psycho stalker far away from me for at least a little while, and then obviously the most confusing, disappointment.

I was disappointed the second the words left Dom's lips, and I can't tell you why. The relief and happiness hit a half of a second after like a chaser, but unfortunately, this chaser didn't remove the entire taste of that first shot.

I'm painting my nails because I've already watched everything worth watching on TV, did all the laundry, and cleaned the kitchen because there is nothing else to do trapped in this fucking apartment when a buzzing sounds from a side table in the living room. I frown at the noise before I follow after it, surprised to find a phone resting on the table with a sticky note on the front of it.

USE THIS WISELY, ANGEL.

I'M WATCHING YOU.

- ZAYDEN.

A rush of something flutters through me for a moment before I rightfully push it back where it belongs. I unlock the phone to find hundreds of unanswered phone calls and texts, ranging from my coworkers to my boss, ex-boss, I guess, to Gabby and Christian.

There is also one more text above the rest. It's a single letter, but obviously I know who it is.

> Z: I miss you, angel.

I debate whether or not to respond. I mean, I probably shouldn't. But he didn't have to give me a phone back, so I guess I should at least thank him, right?

> Me: What made you decide to give me a phone?

His response comes almost instantly, like he was waiting for me to respond.

> **Z: How else am I supposed to handle being away from you for so long?**

I smile, just barely, despite my better efforts as I respond.

> **Me: How long will you be gone for?**

> **Z: Three days at most.**

Again, warring feelings conflict me, but I don't have it in me to name them right now.

> **Me: Where are you again?**

> **Z: Working.**

I roll my eyes at him.

> **Me: What do you even do for work? Dom has the security company and the mechanic shop. What do you do?**

His response takes a few minutes to come before he responds.

> **Z: Text me before you go to bed, angel.**

I'm not surprised by his response, and I scroll over to the text thread from Gabby. Her messages started out friendly and normal but quickly turned panicked when days went by with no response. Christian's are very similar. They go from checking in on me to full-blown panic.

Deciding it's probably just best to call Gabby, I hit call and wait for her to answer. It doesn't ring for two seconds before her voice is rambling through the line.

"Thank God! I've been going crazy. What the fuck is going on? Your boss said you quit, and your landlord said you moved. What the hell, Blake?" she snaps.

I open my mouth, ready to respond, when Dom walks in from seemingly the shower after his workout in the makeshift gym next to his bedroom. A towel is wrapped around his waist, with a droplet of water falling from his jet-black hair before landing on his toned chest. He watches me with a self-satisfied smirk as I blink several times, shaking myself out of the self-imposed trance I suddenly found myself in.

"I'm sorry. It's been a crazy week."

"A crazy week? That's all you have to say? Where are you?"

"At Dominic's," I say, causing his eyebrow to lift in intrigue as he stalks his way over to me.

"Dominic's? So, what? You moved in with the guy you just started dating?" she scoffs in a tone that oozes judgment.

"It's not *just*. We have been together for—"

"Months, Blake," she fills in. "You barely know anything about this guy. And he made you quit your job and give up your apartment? That's toxic behavior, babe."

"He didn't make me do anything," I defend, though I don't know why I do. He technically did both of those things.

"Sure, he didn't. Look, I don't know what's going on with your head, but I'm not about to let some smooth-talking asshole grenade your life like this. You're gonna come stay with us until some sense is knocked into you. Do you think he will let you go willingly, or should we sneak you out tonight?"

I can't help but let a humorless laugh escape me.

"Whoa, what? No."

"No?" she questions.

"Yeah, no. I'm not sneaking out. This is my home, and if you don't like it, then I don't know what there is to say."

She's quiet for several moments before she finally speaks again.

"I'll call you later when you've calmed down. You're not thinking clearly. You need help."

I scoff and shake my head.

"I don't need you gaslighting me into thinking I'm in a toxic relationship, Gabs. I'm fine. You said you liked him, what's the issue all of the sudden?"

"I like him, sure, but there is something off about him. Something dark. He's fine as a casual getting out there kind of thing, but to up and change your whole life for? No, sweetie," she says in a patronizing tone that grates my nerves.

Looking up at the ceiling, I shake my head as I speak. "Whatever, Gabby."

Now it's her turn to scoff. "Whatever Gabby? That's really all I get? After everything me and my family have done for you? You're gonna throw years of friendship away because of some guy?"

"No, I'm throwing years of friendship away because you're a judgmental bitch."

"Fine. Don't come crying to me when you end up broken and battered, just like before. I won't be here. Good luck pulling yourself out of the gutter."

Without another word, the phone goes dead, and an unbelievable amount of sadness and anger rushes through me. I honestly can't believe that just happened. Gabby has always been my closest friend, my freaking person. When the world let me down, she didn't. I don't care if she had solid points, her attitude was way off. If this was the first time we've had a conversation like this over a choice I've wanted to make for myself, maybe I could look past it. But this isn't even close to the first time she's tried to manipulate me into doing what she thinks is best, what she wants. Even if she's trying to come from a place of love, she's out of line, and that last sentence did it for me.

Dominic is just standing there, staring at me as I clutch my phone in my hand and stare at the wall behind him. It takes me at least a minute before I even make eye contact with him.

"Are you okay?" he asks.

"It's fine," I bite out.

He takes a step closer to me, cupping my face in his hands as he looks down at me.

"I didn't ask if it was fine, I asked if you were okay."

I pause for a moment before I eventually nod.

"Good, she wasn't a good friend to you anyway," he says as he presses a kiss to my forehead. "But you probably shouldn't mention this to Zayden."

Frowning at that, I pull back to look at him.

"Why?"

He levels me with a "seriously" look that has me turn my head to the side.

"Because if he heard anyone tell you that staying here with me and him will leave you broken, battered, and in the gutter, he'd string them up by their toes and skin them alive."

I gulp at that, a small rush of fear tearing through me as I'm reminded yet again just how psychotic these men I've somehow found myself with are. I say men because, even though I haven't seen Dominic kill anyone, I don't doubt for a second that he's every bit as capable as Zayden. He just has more self-control, a bit of a moral compass steering him right from wrong. Zayden doesn't have such a device, and honestly, I think he enjoys it better that way.

"Hey," Dom says softly, shaking me out of my thoughts.

I look up at him, and he gives me a sympathetic look as his thumb brushes against my cheek.

"How about a movie night? We can order in, whatever you

want, watch comedy movies, and forget this day."

"It's not even night yet," I say, looking out to see the Seattle gray still intact, but it's not raining, so that's big for western Washington.

Dom shrugs. "It doesn't matter, we can't leave the apartment right now even if we wanted to, so we might as well do whatever the hell we want."

I open my mouth, ready to ask all of the questions that have been bouncing around in my brain for days, weeks now, but I know it's futile.

He seems to sense my resistance as he wraps me up in a hug, holding me tight, before whispering against my ear, "It's okay, baby. This is all temporary, I promise."

I can't help but smile, just a bit. All he's ever trying to do is take care of me, whether that is physical or mental. I swear I'm not sure the man knows there are much bigger things to life than constantly hovering over me. It's different from the way Zayden hovers.

Zayden watches me like I'm the most captivating thing in the world. Like he wants to dissect me piece by piece to understand the fascination of it all before hoarding those broken pieces to himself. Dominic is just always there, silent and stoic more often than not, but always unmoving. He cares deeply, so deeply, you might not even recognize it if you didn't know him. I do, though, and with him around, I've never felt so safe in my life.

Nodding to Dom, he gives me a quick wink before he's pulling out his phone and calling in an order to our favorite

Mexican restaurant. I cross the kitchen, heading for the upper cabinet, before grabbing the bottle I'm in search of. I cut a lime, grab the salt, and swipe two shot glasses to accompany the tequila before making my way back to the couch. Dom finishes our order a moment later and quirks an eyebrow at me.

"What are you doing?"

"Drinking. It's better than just staring at a box like a mindless zombie, and I've already done enough of that for today, so next best thing, yeah?"

Dominic chuckles as he comes to sit beside me, his towel loosening slightly as he does.

"Alright, what are we doing? Just shot for shot drunk? Drinking game?"

I think about that for a moment before I grin.

"Truth or shot," I say with a nod.

He seems to think it over for a moment or two before he slowly nods.

"Don't you think you're at a disadvantage? Seeing as I'll be able to drink five times as much as you."

"You're big talk, Graves. That means I go first."

He holds his hand out in an "after you" motion as he settles back against the couch, watching me with a hint of a smile.

"Alright. Truth or shot, did your parents actually die in a drug bust?"

His smile falls instantly, pain and anger passing over his face. For a moment, I think he's going to get up and storm away, but after a few seconds, he uncaps the tequila, pouring it into his glass before lifting the clear liquid to his lips. He tosses it back without a wince or a hint of a burn before he stares at me.

"Did your dad hurt you?" he asks.

A cold chill runs down my spine at the question. Fuck, I guess neither of us are pulling any punches here.

I debate on taking the shot, but if I do, we might both be drunk before we get anywhere tonight.

"No," I answer shortly.

His eyes squint at that, but he doesn't say anything, just nods.

"Do you think Zayden will ever kill me?" I ask.

He frowns at that, physically recoiling at the question as he opens his mouth to answer before he pauses.

"I hope not."

My eyes bug out at that, and Dom doesn't offer me any comforting words for several seconds before he speaks again.

"Zayden can't do anything halfway. He hates big, he fights big, he obsesses big. It's who he is. The only way I could see Zayden hurting you is the way a child hurts the new puppy they got for their birthday. He'll love you so big, want nothing more than to hold you tight. Only if he's not careful, it'll be too tight, and he'll snap your neck."

Confliction courses through me at his words. Mainly because I don't know what to do with them. Fear isn't an emotion that pops to the surface, and that's concerning for me. Disgust isn't up there either, again concerning. Instead, Dom's words just make sense. They confirmed everything that I suspected but didn't know how to verbalize. Zayden is clearly obsessed with me. He even thinks he loves me, and consciously,

I don't think he would ever hurt me, but with all that obsession and all that "love," there is a very real possibility that I won't make it out of this alive.

"I'm not gonna let that happen," Dominic continues, as if he can see my mind spiraling. "I'll die before harm comes to you."

My stomach flips at the ferocity in his words, the truth behind every syllable. He reaches out, cupping my hand in his and lifting it to his lips, pressing a quick kiss to it before squeezing.

We continue playing the game for what feels like hours. I start asking all the questions I know Dominic won't answer, like what Zayden actually does for work, what else he does for work that he doesn't tell me about, where Zayden went away to months ago, or where he is now. Each question was met with a shot that had the silent giant sinking deeper and deeper into the couch. Guess he can't hold his liquor as much as he thought.

Don't get me wrong, I'm three sheets to the wind myself. Dominic started getting really fine-tuned with his questions, asking if any boyfriends or kids in the foster homes ever hurt me. I chose not to answer instead of being honest because if I were honest, that would leave only a few more questions, and I don't want him even close to that trail.

"Okay, okay, I gots one," I slur with a giggle.

Dom chuckles and wipes his hand across his face like he can shake off the buzz he clearly has going on.

"Have you ever hads a th-hreesome," I say, the words struggling to roll off my tongue as I begin giggling once more.

I watch as Dom licks his lips, sinking his teeth into his lower one with a salacious smirk.

"Dominic Graves!" I gasp as my words evolve into a fit of laughter once more.

He shrugs his shoulders.

"My brother and I are a good team."

Heat rushes through me at his words.

"You had a threesome with Zayden and another woman?"

Dominic nods.

"Was it hot?" I ask, my pulse thundering and my panties soaking at the thought of it.

His eyes come to mine, heat flaring in the deep brown eyes.

"Very."

The next words that slip out of my mouth are unexpected and completely unauthorized.

"Zayden fucked me with his knife," I blurt. "Right here, where you're sitting, actually. He pushed the handle inside me and..."

My words die off as Dom grabs the tequila bottle, leaving behind the shot glass as he puts the bottle to his lips and takes three large gulps. When he pulls it away, he keeps it in his hand as he speaks.

"I know. I watched the security cameras last night."

I'm quiet for a moment as he stares at the nearly-empty bottle, tipping back the last remaining liquid as he leans his head against the back of the couch and closes his eyes.

"It's okay, baby. You like him, it's okay," he murmurs almost to himself before a soft snoring sound fills the room.

Holy shit. I outdrank Dominic. I mean, not really, since he had way more than me, but I put this practically godlike man on his ass, snoring away on his couch. His words echo in my head. Like him? Like Zayden? Yeah, there isn't a chance in hell of that. He's psychotic and demented, and Dominic is perfect. They are identical twins, one is good and one is bad. I'm already with the good twin. Why the fuck would I want the bad one?

Then, from no fault of my own, mental images of a twin sandwich pop into my head. God, that girl must have been in heaven. Jealousy spikes through me at the idea of someone else having them, of someone else knowing what it feels like to have their complete attention, four hands, two mouths, two tongues, and two huge cocks. My pussy throbs at the idea of it, and before I can stop myself, I'm grabbing my phone.

It rings for several seconds before that gravelly voice answers, sending a shiver down my spine and another pulse between my thighs.

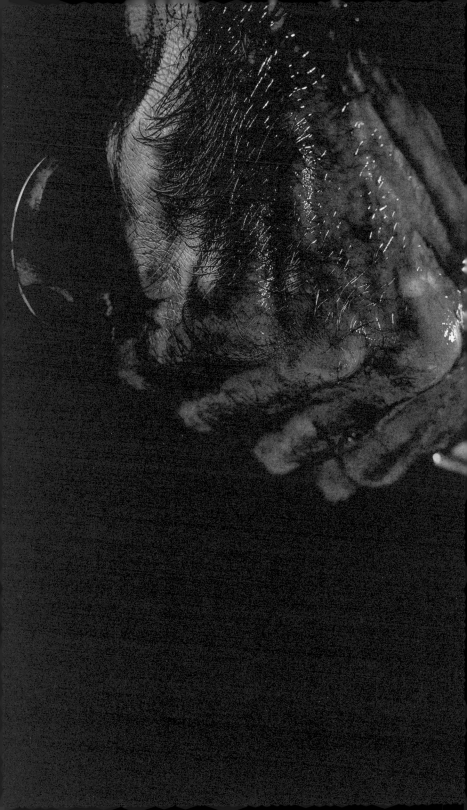

CHAPTER TWENTY-EIGHT

ZAYDEN

"Angel?" I answer.

She doesn't respond, setting me on edge instantly.

"Angel, what's wrong?"

Suddenly, a giggling sound comes through my earbud.

"Why do you call me angels?" she slurs lightly before giggling again.

I frown at that, looking around the empty rooftop I'm staked out on before speaking again.

"Are you drunk?" I ask.

"Nooooo," she says with a laugh. "But your brother is. We played a drinking game, and I won!" she cheers.

Anger pricks at my skin as I gnash my teeth together. Dominic is fucking drunk? When he should be watching and protecting her? When Maxim is out here watching us like a hawk, waiting for us to make a mistake, and he gets drunk and leaves her vulnerable?

The thought of packing up my shit right here and now and jumping on a plane back to her is tempting, but I know if I don't finish this job, there will be a lot worse things coming our way a lot sooner. It's best for everyone if I keep my head down and go to work.

"Are you safe?" I ask her.

"About as safe as I can get in this fucking fortress mansion in the sky thingy," she rambles.

A bit of amusement pulls my lips up into a barely there smile at her slurring. Of course she's goddamn precious when she's drunk. I'd expect nothing less from my angel.

"I want you to go take two acetaminophen and a big glass of water right now, okay?"

Instead of answering, she just giggles.

"You smell so good." Her voice practically moans through the phone. "You're such a bad man, how do you smell so goooood?"

I frown at that as she continues.

"I'm in your bed, Zayden." She snickers.

My eyebrows shoot up at that as I smirk.

"Oh yeah? And what are you doing there, angel?"

"Playing with my clit," she says, her nervous smile practically audible through the phone.

Fuck. My cock instantly hardens, which is not ideal seeing as I'm lying on my chest on a cold rooftop, looking down a sniper scope, and waiting for my target who should be coming up for his nightly cigar any minute.

"What are you doing playing with yourself in my bed, angel?"

"I think I miss you," she groans.

"You think?"

"Mhmm. I'm not sure because the idea sounds dumb, but I want to see you right now. I want you next to me in your bed."

"I want that too, sweetheart. Why don't you tell me what you're doing and what you're thinking about, and it'll be like I'm there?"

"Okay," she pants. "I'm rubbing my clit with my fingers, and it feels so fucking good."

I press my cock against the stone roof, seeking out any kind of possible relief as I speak.

"Yeah, angel? Why don't you go ahead and slip a finger inside for me."

"S-sure," she stutters as she inhales sharply.

"There you go, angel. Does it feel like I'm with you now?"

"N-no. T-too small. You're so big."

"Good point. Put three more fingers inside yourself."

"Three?" she balks.

"Three," I command.

A pause of silence comes before she's gasping into my ears.

"Fuck, Zayden. Yes."

"Good girl. Now I want you to fuck yourself with those fingers the way I would."

"Okay," she agrees all too easily before she begins moaning and whimpering through the phone.

Fuck this. I roll onto my back quickly, pulling my cock out and tossing my glove to the side before I begin stroking my cock. Her little noises already have my cock leaking with precum, and as soon as I get a tight grip on myself, I feel my balls begin to draw up.

"What are you thinking about, angel? Talk to me." I rasp.

"You and Dom," she gasps.

That has my movements pausing for a moment before she continues.

"He told me that you guys have had a threesome together. With some other girl. I'm—"

"Jealous?" I finish.

She whimpers in response.

"Aw, angel. No need to be jealous. I promise when I get back, my brother and I can make you feel so good. Don't even worry."

"He would never share me," she says, though it sounds more like a pout.

"Don't be so sure. There are things about Dominic you don't know. I think he might just love sharing you, it's me who won't share you, sweetheart."

"But please, Zayden. Please. I want you both. I want to feel both of your hands on me, your mouths, your—"

"Shhh, no need to beg. I'd do anything for you, including share you with my brother for a night."

"Just one night?" she asks, disappointment heavy in her breathy tone.

Sharing is definitely more up Dominic's preferences than mine, but how can I say no to anything my angel asks when she's begging so beautifully?

"Ask me nicely," I say as I begin beating my cock faster and faster. "Ask me if I'll let my woman have me and my brother together."

"Z-Zayden, can I please have you and your brother together?"

"Fuck! Such a good girl. Are you my woman, angel? All mine?"

She's silent for a moment, only her breathy pants coming in through the phone.

"I'm Dom's, Zayden."

Disappointment and anger bloom inside me, and I'm ready to fucking explode when her voice softens.

"But maybe I could be yours too."

It's not what I want to hear, but she's softening to me, opening up, and all I need is for her to open a little more so that I can break her open entirely.

"You're already mine, angel. Always have been. Now be a good girl and come. Come all over your fingers. If I don't find my sheets stained with your orgasm when I get home, I'm not gonna be happy."

"Zayden," she gasps. "Zayden, I—"

"Come," I command.

In the next moment, she emits a scream so loud it will no doubt be heard down the whole fucking block. A rush of pleasure blinds me temporarily as my balls tighten before releasing. I cup the head of my cock with my hand, making sure to catch every drop as my cock throbs with its release.

We're both silent for a moment as I grab a rag out of my duffel beside me and clean myself up.

"Zayden?" she asks softly, insecurity tinting her words as the sound of a door opening from across the way catches my attention.

I roll over onto my stomach, lining up the scope and emptying one into his frontal lobe before he can even light his cigar.

"I'm coming home, angel."

With that, I hang up the phone, pack up my gear, and run to my getaway driver. Technically, I don't need to run, I've got more than enough time before his security team will check on him, and since there are no cameras up here or in the alley where my car is waiting, I'm in the clear. I'm not running because of the job, though. I'm running because of her. To her. She better be ready when I get there.

CHAPTER TWENTY-NINE

BLAKE

I wake up with a drum inside my head. It feels that way, at least. It's the only explanation for the pounding in my skull. When I blink my eyes open, it takes me a moment to get my bearings. The feel of the black silk sheets beneath me already tells me where I am before my brain can catch up.

Zayden's room. I'm in Zayden's room? When did I come in here? I grab my phone beside me and open it to see several missed text messages from Gabby that I couldn't give a shit about and one text from Zayden.

Zayden: On my way, angel.

Like a flash, everything begins replaying in my mind from last night. Dom and my drinking game, confessions, my phone call with Zayden. Oh my god. My phone call with Zayden. Where I begged him to fuck me while his brother did the same, together. Oh my fucking god. Fuck you, tequila. I swear to God, I will never drink you again.

I push myself out of the sheets, forcing myself to stand on my feet and get the hell out of here. When I open the door, I see Dom sitting at the kitchen island, a cup of coffee in front of him as he holds his head into his hands.

Hesitantly, I tiptoe up to him, and when I'm only a few feet away he turns, giving me a soft smile before wincing.

"Hey, babygirl. How'd you sleep?"

"Good. You?"

"I was fucking out. I don't think I've ever been that drunk. What did you do to me?" He chuckles as he drags me into his lap, resting his head on the curve of my neck.

"You're the one that wouldn't give up the secrets," I tease.

He lets out a short chuckle as he nods, pressing a soft kiss to my skin.

"I may be regretting my choices now."

Yeah, same.

The front door opens in the next minute, and Zayden walks in, duffle bag tossed over his shoulder, arms bound in his form-fitting leather jacket. He doesn't even look at Dom, his eyes come straight to me, and fear mixed with anticipation whirls inside me as he drops the bag to the floor, crossing the room until he's inches from me.

"Hey, how did it go?" Dominic asks.

Zayden doesn't answer him, though, those blue eyes are practically electric as they bore into me. Whatever he's searching for in my face or in my eyes, he must have found it because, in the next minute, he's gripping my cheeks with both hands and crushing his lips to my own.

At first, I don't react. I'm in shock. I don't think it's possible to move. Then his tongue sweeps against my lips, practically forcing his way in before tangling with my own. From there, I lose what little bit of sense I had left.

I wind my arms around his neck, pulling him closer to me as he deepens the kiss. He holds onto me like I'll shatter if he lets go, like we will shatter. His lips move against my own hurriedly, like he's been thinking about this moment for too long. I'm so lost in this, in him, in us, that I almost forget where we are. That is, until Dominic's arms around my waist tighten, silently reminding me of his presence.

I pull away from Zayden quickly, shock and horror at what I have literally just done in Dom's lap, taking over me.

My eyes come to Dominic's, a million apologies on the tip of my tongue. I don't get to voice them, though, before Dom's mouth is on mine. It takes me by surprise, but I instantly sink into the comfort of his touch, of his kiss. This right here is the man that I love, and somehow he's still able to kiss me like I'm the woman he loves. Even if I just made out with his brother while sitting on his lap.

I feel another mouth on me, trailing up and down my neck before nipping at the sensitive part of my ear, forcing me to let out a moan into Dom's mouth. I feel Dom slip a hand between my thighs, rubbing against my leggings as Zayden's hands come to my breasts, slipping underneath my shirt before flicking his thumbs against my nipples.

All of it is too much and yet not enough. I can feel myself literally soaking straight through my panties, leggings, and probably onto Dom's pants. Excitement is overwhelming me for what comes next when someone's phone starts ringing. In true twin fashion, Dom and Zayden pause instantly before they both rip away from me at the same time. They share a heavy look before Dom looks at me.

"Go take a shower."

I frown at that.

"What? I—"

"Now," Zayden snaps, causing me to jolt at the heat in his tone before I move to stand. I look at them both with equal parts confusion and sexual frustration as I move down the hallway.

By the time I make it to the shower, I'm fucking pissed. It should be illegal to get a girl that worked up, to dangle a living, breathing wet dream like that only to shut it down in the next minute. So, as soon as I strip down naked, I grab the detachable shower head, knowing at least it won't let me down.

A KNOCK COMES FROM THE DOOR, AND I LOOK UP TO SEE who it is. I've been in the spare room for close to an hour, and I'm already satisfied and dressed from my shower when Dom pushes the door open.

"Hey, I have breakfast ready if you're hungry."

I wait for him to say more because food has absolutely been the last thing on my mind, but he just watches me for a few more moments before turning his back and striding away. Sooo, are we just supposed to pretend that whole thing never happened? I'm not sure I can do that. It was one of the hottest experiences of my life, and we barely got to a little bit of groping.

When I stand up and move to the kitchen, I notice that Zayden is clearly absent while Dom is plating some breakfast. He hands me five Belgian waffles, eggs, bacon, and a glass of orange juice. I look down at the massive plate before looking up at him.

"Sir, this is your plate, right? Because there is no way I can eat all of this."

He shrugs as he hands me a fork.

"Whatever you don't eat, I'm sure me and Zayden will have."

Something runs through me at just the reminder of the two brothers doing anything together, which apparently gets me excited. Jesus, I'm so fucked. Without meaning to, I turn my head over my shoulder, looking around the room but coming up empty.

"He's in his room," Dominic says.

I turn back around to look at him, my brows dipping in faux

confusion as he raises a "no bullshit" look to me.

"Zayden, you're looking for him. He's in the room."

"Oh cool. I wasn't looking for him. I was just—"

"It's fine, baby. You don't have to lie."

Suddenly, a notification comes from his phone, and he curses under his breath before grabbing his wallet and keys.

"I have to get to the office. I'll see you tonight," he says as he leans down, capturing my lips with his own before pulling away and heading out the door.

Looking down at the plate in front of me, I pick at it a bit before I decide to push it away. My disappointment from this morning aside, I'm getting really sick of being here. I know Zayden said there is a man out there that could hurt me if I'm seen out and about, but so what? He's either going to find out eventually and this will all have been for nothing, or I'm just going to stay locked up in this apartment for the rest of my days?

Absolutely the fuck not. I'll lose my mind before that happens. I can already feel myself dwindling. The only thing that seems to help the days go by these days is cleaning, something I used to fucking detest. Guess that shows you how a person can change if they're bored enough.

———

AFTER I SWEPT AND MOPPED THE FLOORS, DUSTED, AND folded the laundry with my music practically rattling the walls, of course, I ended up taking a long hot bath that resulted in an even longer nap. Have I mentioned that I'm sick of being on virtual house arrest by now? Because I am. So fucking sick. I want to work. I want to go to a coffee shop every morning. I want to have more purpose than just existing in a fucking bubble. Even if it is a really nice bubble.

I wake up blurry-eyed and check the time. It's already seven o'clock, so I've essentially fucked myself out of a good night's sleep tonight. Awesome.

When I make my way out into the living room, I see Zayden and Dominic sitting at the coffee table with a few takeout containers and a deck of cards. Zayden is puffing on a cigar, and the smell instantly turns my stomach.

They both turn to face me as Zayden smiles around the Cuban in his mouth.

"Hey, angel. Want to play some cards?"

"We're playing poker," Dominic supplements.

Those words instantly send my heart into palpitations. My pulse quickens, and any and all background noise fades away. All I hear is the thudding of my heartbeat and my quickened breathing. A cold sweat breaks out across my body from my head to my toes, and I do my best to swallow away the bowling ball that has formed in my throat.

I can practically feel the memories so feral coming to light they are eating me from the inside out. I can't, though. They belong buried, they need to stay that way. No, no, no. Quickly, I take a stumbled step backward, before another and another.

"No...thanks. I'm going to bed."

Dominic frowns at that, standing to come closer, but I hold up my hand to keep him back, not realizing how badly I'm shaking until I see my fingertips trembling. I tighten my hand into a fist, wincing at how incredibly weak I'm left from nothing more than a reminder of a memory.

Slowly, I take a deep measuring breath, opening my eyes to see identical looks of concern on their faces. I hear Dominic call out to me, or maybe it was Zayden. Either way, I ignore them and get back to my room, slamming the door behind me as I lean my back against the solid wood. I slide down to my ass, gripping my head on either side as I attempt to keep it together.

"It's okay, Blake. It's okay. You're okay," I wince as I squeeze my eyes shut, attempting to shut out the suffocating memories that seem determined on taking me down to the pits of hell tonight.

CHAPTER THIRTY

DOMINIC

Zayden is already to his feet, trying to follow after her when I catch his shoulder, squeezing tightly to gain his attention. His eyes snap to mine, a look of pure concern, purer than I thought he'd be able to conjure. I shake my head in silent explanation, and he takes the cigar out of his mouth, inspecting it curiously before his eyes come to the card game.

I give him another look, and to my surprise, he agrees with me and sits down, allowing Blake time to handle whatever she needs to.

"She'll be okay," I say more for my benefit than his.

"She needs to get out of this house, Dominic," Zayden says as I set up the cards for a new game.

"I know," I grit through clenched teeth. I don't want her trapped like a bird in a cage any more than he does. But it's not safe. Every step forward I take, we are met with a blow that takes us two steps back. We've been trying to figure out a way to get out from under Maxim's thumb for years. I thought that we had done that, until Zayden went and threw us right under there yet again.

"What do we do, huh?" Zayden snaps. "You're the idea man. You come up with the plans. Tell me a scenario where all three of us make it out alive. Where we all go along to be controllers of our own destiny."

I'm quiet for a moment before I speak.

"Kill Maxim."

Zayden scoffs at me, taking a large puff off his cigar before blowing it into my face.

"Genius plan. Bravo. Except for the fact that it's impossible. The man taught us everything we know, Dominic. You think he doesn't see every step we take ten steps ahead of us?"

"He does," I agree. "Which means we would have to hit him with something he doesn't see coming."

Zayden perks up at that, leaning forward in interest.

"Like?"

"Like...I don't know yet. I'm working on it."

He blows out an irritated breath and leans back into the couch.

"You're not working on shit."

I roll my eyes at his petulance as I grab my drink. We play the game in as much silence as virtually possible for the next hour or so before he speaks.

"So, you gonna bring up this morning?"

I flick my eyes up at him before going back to the cards.

"What's there to say?"

Zayden snorts a strangled laugh before he turns his head dubiously to me.

"I'll be honest, I was expecting a throat punch or something for kissing her like that. I didn't expect you to be into it. What happened to all the 'you touch her, I kill you' shit?" Zayden teases in a way that tells me he's looking for a fight. I won't give him the satisfaction, though.

"I abandoned it somewhere between you fucking her on top of our dead parents and fucking her with your knife where you're sitting," I say easily.

He grins wickedly as he pulls out the same knife from his pocket, lifting the handle to his nose and inhaling deeply.

"Still smells like my angel."

I roll my eyes at him, but don't respond.

"You know she called me," Zayden says.

"When?"

"Last night. You were passed out drunk, apparently, and she was horny in my bed," he says with the hint of a smirk that has me wanting to knock his two front teeth out.

I don't respond, and he doesn't expect me to as he continues.

"She said you told her about us having threesomes in the

past. That she was jealous."

"What did you say to her?" I ask.

He gives me a wicked smirk as he pulls the cigar out of his mouth and winks.

"I told her we'd take care of it for her."

I frown at that. "Why would you say that?"

"Because I meant it. What my angel wants, my angel gets. And if this morning is anything to go off, you're not as opposed to the idea as your pinched face looks right now."

"That was when we were young and dumb, Zayden. With women who meant absolutely nothing to us. This is Blake. She means—"

"Everything," he finishes.

I open my mouth to argue when a blood curdling scream erupts down the hall. Zayden and I are up and to our feet, running through the apartment in a flash. He's the first one to her door, literally kicking it down despite it not having a lock on it anymore. He has his knife drawn at the ready, and I pull my gun from the back of my pants, aimed and prepared as I scan the dark room.

It takes several seconds for us to realize there isn't a threat, though. None that we can see, at least. There is just Blake on the bed, thrashing and screaming.

"No! Please! Not again! Please!" she screeches, the very sound shattering a piece of me as the horrors of her past are brought to just a glimmer of light.

Zayden is on her left, slowly trying to wake her up as I tuck my gun back into my waistband and come onto her right.

"Shh, babygirl. It's okay. I'm right here. You're just dreaming. It's just a dream," I murmur into her ears, causing her eyes to fly open.

She fights back harder than before, kicking, hitting, and shoving us away. Zayden and I instantly step back on instinct, our hands raised as her eyes flit wildly around the room. It seems to take several seconds for her to place exactly where she is and for her to leave whatever fresh hell she was just in and breathe.

Blake blows out a choppy breath as she runs a hand through her sweat-soaked hair, dropping it to her side before she looks up at us. Her skin is as pale as a ghost, forehead dotted with beads of sweat, and fingers left with a tremble that looks like it may never fully disappear.

I've seen fear, I've seen torture. Though I never relished in it like Zayden, I've killed more people than I could ever count. I've seen hundreds of people an inch from death in my lifetime, but not a single one of them has ever looked so defeated, so lifeless, so broken as she does right now.

Zayden goes to speak when she holds her hand up to him.

"Out, please," she says, her voice breaking on that last word.

The sound alone is enough to send a painful pang through my chest, and we both nod as one before filing out of the room. I give her one more glance over my shoulder before stepping out of the room, but she isn't looking at me. She's turned away, hugging her knees to her chest and shaking like a leaf.

Once the door is shut, Zayden continues standing there,

fists balled at his sides and chest heaving. We have suspected she was hurt by someone in the past. The logical answer was her father, he was obviously an abusive piece of shit with anger issues, but she was so young when they passed that it doesn't seem like it could be that alone. No doubt her parent's death was an added trauma that she didn't need, and something tells me that's only the tip of the iceberg for our girl. I mean, my girl.

CHAPTER THIRTY-ONE

BLAKE

*T*he musty air is so thick I can hardly breathe, the damp concrete floor cold, so cold. My naked body shivers against it, but I can't move. I feel a wetness against my cheek, but I can't tell if it's from the floor, my tears, or my blood.

My skin crawls as the feeling from the last touch still remains, like an unremovable mark, no matter how hard I try to wash it off, it will never leave. Forever staining my skin, reminding me of what I have suffered and what I will continue to.

A pair of clammy hands grip my hips, lifting them into the air *as I begin to whimper. No. No. No. No. Not again. No more, no more. I try to muffle my cries as quietly as I can manage. They hit me extra hard when I make noise. When the impact comes, I'm not ready for it, though. The force of the thrust causes an audible tear, and I scream. I feel a glass bottle hit the back of my head before I can even breathe, and blood begins running down the back of my neck because of it.*

His jagged fingernails dig into the flesh of my ass as he pounds me into the floor, ripping me more and more with each thrust. My eyes meet him from across the room, a satisfied, lust-filled smile donning his face as he watches his friend destroy me. He already had his turn. He always goes first, and then the others follow. The other two that hurt me tonight are on either side of him, watching in a semblance of awe as their friend strips away what's left of me. At least for the night. They'll be back tomorrow night, they always are.

One minute I'll be sleeping, and the next I'll have hands on my body, carrying me down to the basement before pinning me to the floor like a pig for slaughter. He always starts by undressing me himself, whispering to me how I've been begging for it and tempting him all day while his wife sleeps soundly upstairs with her CPAP machine on, masking my torture and my screams.

He then runs his tongue up and down every inch of me, forcing the slimy feeling to linger with me longer than it should before he begins. Almost every single night this has happened for the last seven years. I'd fight to get away, fight to be free, if only I had anything left worth fighting for.

I wake up drenched in sweat, gasping for a breath I'm unable to catch when I look at my surroundings. Slowly registering where I am, that I'm safe, that I'm free. The sun streaming in from the window tells me that it's already morning and I could never be more thankful for that. I haven't had a dream like that in years. I've purposefully avoided any and all reminders possible, and it's a system that has seemed to work for me. Until last night.

The door is slightly open, and I remember them closing it behind them last night, so obviously they've been in here since then, and by they, I mean Zayden. I decide to take a shower before going out there, mainly because I'm uncomfortable but also because I'm embarrassed. I don't know what I was saying or how I was acting before they woke me up. I know the nightmares used to be really bad. All of my exes used to say so, at least.

I take my time lathering myself, shampooing and conditioning twice, as well as shaving myself from head to toe. None of it really matters, though, because once I'm dried and dressed, the knotted feeling in my stomach only amplifies with every step I take out of the bedroom.

They are both standing at the kitchen island, seemingly talking in hushed tones. It's almost like they feel me before they see me, because before I even say a word or make a noise, their heads look up at me in perfect unison.

"Do you guys ever sleep?" I joke, noticing how it falls flat.

"No," they respond together.

I give them a tight smile and nod before Dominic pushes away from the counter and comes to me. I flinch as he towers over me, something I thought I had gotten over, at least with him. Clearly, last night was a setback in many areas.

He frowns at that, smoothly dropping to his knees before me as he looks up at me.

"Are you okay?"

I nod. "I'm okay, you don't have to kneel," I say as I reach for him, attempting to pull him up.

"I want to," he insists steadily. The assurance in his words makes my heart skip a beat, and I think I fall in love with him a little more right then and there.

"What are you guys doing today?" I ask.

"Nothing. Was just planning to spend time with you," Dominic says as his phone begins to ring.

I raise an eyebrow at him, and he curses before grabbing his phone and silencing it. It starts ringing immediately, forcing him to silence it again. On the third ring, I catch his hand before he can cancel the call.

"Go to work. Do your thing. Protect the street cameras and all that stuff," I say on a small laugh.

He shakes his head when I soften my voice, my lower lip quivering as I do.

"Please?"

There is something about Dom. He makes me feel so seen, so weak. He makes me feel that way because I know I can be vulnerable and fall apart with him, and he will be there to pick up the pieces. Right now, though, that's the last thing I need. What I want is to feel in control and strong, and I can't do that with him staring at me like this.

"You're sure?" he asks.

I nod quickly, forcing him to blow out a breath before he

stands slowly, pulling me into a hug before he reaches his full height. I wrap my arms around him as he pulls back just enough to kiss me. His lips linger on mine, and it's enough of a contact to send butterflies racing through me before his thumb brushes against my cheek.

"I love you, babygirl."

"I love you too," I say with a soft smile.

My words cause him to grin before he gives me a sweet wink and turns to face Zayden.

"Take care of her."

"Always," Zayden responds quickly, his focused eyes on me the entire time his brother gathers up his things and heads out the door.

When the apartment is silent once more, I realize that Zayden and I are still staring at each other, unmoving, practically unblinking.

"You guys saying your I love you's," Zayden remarks.

It's not quite a question, but it doesn't seem phrased as a statement either. It feels like a test, and one I don't feel like participating in. I roll my eyes and turn around, intent on getting away from him, when he comes up from behind me, catching my elbow and turning me to face him.

"What?" I snap.

He forces me backward until my back is pressing against the wall. He cages his arms over me and just stares. Where Dom is worried about intimidating me, Zayden seems to relish in it. I try to act like it doesn't bother me, but with the menacing look in his eyes, the steel-cut edge to his jaw, and his face inches from mine, I'm doing all I can to keep it together.

"What do you need?"

I furrow my brows at that.

"What do you mean?"

"What do you need, angel? What can I do?"

I stare up at him for several seconds before I shake my head and look away.

"Nothing. I'm fine. Can you please just leave me alone and—"

"No. Now tell me how I can fix this."

"Fix what?" I ask.

"You."

I blink hard at that, my breath practically stolen from my lungs for several seconds before I speak softly with a shake of my head. "You can't."

"Then what can I do to make it all go away for a little?" he asks, softening to a tone I wasn't sure he was even capable of.

"I just want to be...in control. Free. Strong," I say more to myself than anything as I stare at the wall behind Zayden.

Slowly, my eyes come back to his when he doesn't respond, those blue eyes flaring to life before he nods his head once.

"Grab a jacket."

He heads for the door, and I don't hesitate. I'm in no position to be turning down a chance to get out of this apartment.

When we get downstairs and onto Zayden's bike, a thought occurs to me. The last time I ended up on an excursion on the back of his bike, I ended up getting fucked on top of his parent's grave. Maybe this was a very stupid idea. Clearly, I can't be trusted around him, or more accurately, he can't be trusted with me.

As soon as we hit that open road, though, with the wind whipping through my hair, all of my headache-inducing thoughts and worries fade, and I just...live. Zayden bobs and weaves through traffic so easily, it's as if he's more agile on a bike than his own two feet. He moves with each curve and bend of the road, and it feels closer to magic than just driving down the freeway.

It doesn't take long before we're exiting, and another mile or so down the road we're pulling off into the gravel parking lot of a building with the name Buckey's Shooting Range.

Zayden swings his leg off the bike, helping me with the helmet he slipped on me when we left before setting it on his handlebar. He offers me a hand, and I look at it hesitantly before I take it. His fingers intertwine with my own, and even when I'm off the bike, he refuses to let go, tightening his hold on me instead.

I shoot him an irritated look, but he just winks at me as he leads us toward the front door.

Within ten minutes, we are set up at a shooting lane on the very end with two guns and a box full of bullets. Zayden picked a human-silhouetted target to shoot at, and he loads one of the guns before gesturing for me to come to him.

"You ever shot a gun before?" he says, though I can barely hear him through the earmuffs they make us wear.

I shake my head and scoff. "When would I ever have shot a gun?"

He shrugs his shoulders as he pulls me to stand in front of him. Setting the gun in my hand, he straightens out my arms and has me hold it, pointing toward the target as he speaks.

"This is your safety, this is your clip, your rear and front sights," he says, pointing to various parts of the gun. "You want to line up your target in between your rear and front sight. It's okay to close one eye to practice, but I want you shooting with both eyes open."

"Why are we doing this?" I ask.

"Because someone hurt you badly and you weren't able to defend yourself."

My stomach drops to the floor as a rush of goosebumps cover my skin. I wonder if I look as pale as I suddenly feel, but I don't get a chance to speak before he continues.

"They took something from you, and you never got it back. This is how you get it back, one shot at a time."

I don't say anything as I look into his eyes. He waits for me to deny it or something, and maybe I should, but a smarter piece of me knows that would be futile. He's not guessing, he's not running with a hunch. It's obvious what happened to me, it's just that no one wants to form the ugly words into a single sentence.

Swallowing roughly, I nod, turning to face the target as I hold my arms out. Zayden's hands run over my form, making small adjustments to my hold and stance before he nods, resting his hands on my hips.

"Close your eyes for me, angel. Picture him. Picture the man who hurt you, who stole your voice, who stole everything.

I want you to picture him as vividly as you can."

My stomach revolts at the request, the very idea of reimagining his face voluntarily too repugnant. For some reason, though, I do as he says. I see everything, from his dirty blonde hair and scraggly beard to his beady green eyes and his overhanging beer belly. I can practically smell him, taste him. I'm ready to fucking lose it when Zayden speaks again.

"Open your eyes and shoot the son of a bitch."

My eyes fly open, and my finger on the trigger doesn't hesitate. I fire the gun as many times as it lets me until the clip is out of bullets. When it's done, my hands are shaking as I set the gun down onto the counter, blowing out a measured breath as Zayden hits the button that brings the target closer to us.

He pulls it down from the cable, grinning like a madman as he shows me. Four out of the six shots landed on the silhouetted body. Two to the head, one to the chest, and one to the stomach.

"Now that's one dead piece of shit," he cackles in a way that should sound completely unhinged but hits my ears, sounding of pure delight and pride.

"How do you feel?" he asks as he tucks a piece of hair behind my ear.

I nod. "Can we do that again?"

Zayden grins at me, nodding before hooking up a new target and sending it back down the lane.

"But first, I'm gonna show you how to take the gun out of someone's hands."

He takes out the clip, clearing the last bullet inside the chamber before testing it down the lane. Once he knows there are no bullets inside, he points it toward me.

"What do you do?" he asks.

"Beg for mercy?" I snark.

He rolls his eyes but smiles, handing the gun to me. His head nods, and I take it, pointing it at him like he did me.

"So, if they are holding it with one hand, you want to do this in one motion. If they are holding it in their right hand, you're going to grab the muzzle of the gun with your left and hit their arm with your right simultaneously."

After he explains it, he does it so fast it makes my head spin. Zayden's hand wraps around the muzzle, and he smacks my arm loose, forcing my grip to break as he holds the gun, spinning it into his hand and pointing it at me. I can't help but laugh at how utterly incompetent I just was as he nods encouragingly.

"Your turn."

CHAPTER THIRTY-TWO

ZAYDEN

My piece of shit brother has been lazy. He doesn't care about her, not even in the slightest. If he did, he would have found this guy by now. He's too worried about maintaining his legal businesses and keeping himself on the up and up to get his hands a little dirty. I have no such limitations.

It took me two hours to sift through Blake's background before I was able to pinpoint exactly where I could find him. She didn't give me anything to go on, of course, but she didn't deny that it was a him, and when she shot that fucking target up, I knew I was right on the money.

Dominic said it wasn't her parents, and though that would be a logical explanation, it didn't feel right. So, I started looking at her past relationships. Boyfriends, teachers, bosses. Anyone who could have been close enough to hurt her for an extended period of time. Then one name popped up, I took one look at his face and knew who it was.

So, that's what brings me to this shithole neighborhood in the slums of Chicago at two in the morning. Blake is tucked away in bed with Dominic, safe and sound, and I'm standing over a sleeping dead man. I had planned to do it quickly, make it discreet, something like natural causes, especially with his sleeping wife beside him. I have a better idea, though. One I think my angel is going to thoroughly love. After all, tomorrow is our seven-month anniversary.

CHAPTER THIRTY-THREE

BLAKE

The bed beside me sinks down for a moment before an arm wraps around my waist, pulling me away from Dom and into a warm body. I feel a gentle inhale against my head before a soft voice is whispered into my ear.

"Good morning, angel."

I can't help but smile.

"Good morning, Zayden," I murmur sleepily.

"I have a present for you," he says before pressing a kiss to my neck.

"We're sleeping," Dom rasps. "Get the fuck out of my room."

"Sorry, brother. My angel and I have a whole day planned. See you later," he says before slipping his arms underneath me, lifting me into the air and out of the room.

I cling to him quickly, giggling as Dom shouts at us.

"Where the fuck are you taking me?" I laugh as Zayden walks into the spare room, setting me on the bed before grabbing some of the clean clothes I've folded and put in the dresser in here.

Now that Dominic and I are better, I feel like I spend more nights than not in his room, but nights like the night before last, where I obviously needed my space, this room works. Is it bad how easily I'm adapting to this life of captivity? Probably.

Zayden sets out a black T-shirt, a pair of black leggings, and some black socks.

"Get dressed, angel!" he says almost giddily.

I raise an eyebrow. "All black? Are you trying to turn me into you or something?"

He looks down at his black shirt, black leather jacket, and black jeans before giving me a wicked smirk.

"It's a good look, yeah?"

I roll my lips together but choose not to respond. He definitely doesn't need an ego boost, and I'm sure as hell not gonna give him one.

Grabbing the clothes, I quickly move to the bathroom. Zayden takes a step to follow after me until I level him with a look that has him raising his hands in innocence and taking a step back. It doesn't take me long to brush my teeth, run a brush through my hair, and get dressed.

When I step out of the bathroom, Zayden is practically bouncing on his toes. He looks less like the thirty-two-year-old psycho stalker and more like a kid on Christmas morning.

"Ready?" he asks.

"Are you gonna tell me why the hell you woke me up at the crack of dawn?" I question with a yawn.

"I told you. I have a surprise for you."

With that, he strides out the door, and I follow after him. He hooks a left down the hallway and continues until he stops in front of the broom closet. Looking over his shoulder at me, he catches my furrowed brows before he winks and pops open a hidden compartment on the right side of the door. A biometric scanner whirs out, and Zayden presses his thumb against it before the wall of the closet clicks, swinging open to reveal a room.

What the fuck?

Zayden pushes it the rest of the way open, holding his hand out for me to take as he pulls me in. There are no lights in here, and I can't really see anything as Zayden shuts the door behind us, plunging us into total darkness.

"You ready for your surprise?" he asks.

"Okay, out with it, you're starting to creep me out." I laugh lightly, though the sensible side of me is slightly unnerved.

"Close your eyes," Zayden says.

I do as he says, and I can see the lights turn on from behind my eyelids. I smile in anticipation before he speaks.

"Alright, angel. Surprise!" he practically exclaims.

I open my eyes, my smile falling instantly as my eyes round in shock. There is a chair in the middle of the room and a large, tied-up man attached to it. His mouth is duct taped, his face bloody with a large red bow on top of his head, but I'd recognize those green eyes anywhere.

"What the fuck?" I whisper on a choppy breath.

"It's your present!" Zayden smiles, wrapping an arm around my shoulders as he does. "It's our seven-month anniversary, and I had no idea what to get you. It was kinda stressing me out, to be honest. But between the other night and yesterday, it just clicked for me."

My breathing is shallow, my body chilled straight to the bone as I'm locked in eye contact with my abuser. My tormentor. The devil himself. My foster dad.

"Why would you bring him here? Why would you do this to me?" I ask, my voice breaking as my eyes begin to fill with unshed tears.

Zayden's smile falls, and he cups my face, brushing away a stray tear.

"To kill him, angel. To take back everything he took from you. I thought after yesterday, you'd want that. Should I have just killed him in Chicago?" he asks softly, like he's asking if he bought the wrong ice cream.

"You went and got him in Chicago? Last night?" I ask.

He nods, his eyes flicking quickly over my face.

"I don't know what he did to you, and I don't need to know. What I do know is that he hurt you, and for that he deserves a painful death."

Jim whimpers behind the duct tape, stealing my attention from Zayden. At first, I felt this paralyzing fear, a fear I knew I'd feel if I ever saw him again. But the more I look at him, the more I see how truly vulnerable he is. His feet are tied together, his arms fastened behind his back, and his putrid mouth sealed shut. He's not in control, not even close, and that forces something to buzz inside me. Something strong and powerful. Something...different.

"What are you going to do to him?" I ask Zayden, keeping my eyes on Jim for several seconds before turning my focus back to the unhinged man in front of me.

"The question is, what are you going to do to him, angel? He's your present, to do with what you will. I hand-selected some of my favorite toys over here," he says, gesturing toward a small metal table filled with various weapons.

I take a few steps toward the table, running my fingers over them as I do. Needle-nose pliers, a meat tenderizer, a bone saw, a scalpel, some kind of metal hook, and more knives than you'd ever know what to do with.

"Of course, we have plenty of guns if you'd rather something less messy, or I can handle it all if you just want him gone. You say the word, and it's done."

I swallow before inhaling slowly. My morality should be at war right now, with my conscience telling me how horrific this is. I shouldn't even be tempted. The fact of the matter is I'm not just tempted, I'm exhilarated.

"What's the most painful one to use?" I ask.

Zayden cackles with glee before he rushes over to me.

"So if it were me," he says, pointing at himself, "I'd start by breaking every bone in his body before you even get to the cutting, but that could take a while, and I don't know how long you want to—"

"He abused me for seven years, I have as long as it takes," I say hollowly.

"Seven years?" Zayden asks stiffly.

I nod, not making eye contact with him. His hand grips the large meat tenderizer, gripping it in his palm before swinging around, connecting the metal tool against Jim's left cheekbone. He screams in pain as Zayden continues his assault, hitting his kneecaps with such ferocity that the crunch that sounds is downright sickening. The next move he makes is Jim's clavicle. His body bucks at that, forcing the chair to the ground.

Zayden turns to face me easily, tossing the tenderizer onto the table before he blows a piece of hair out of his face.

"Sorry, angel. I got him started."

A sick part of me forces a smile to spread across my face, an actual smile. Is it weird to swoon because a man kidnapped and beat your abuser? I don't think so.

"Zayden, do you have any more cigars?"

He nods, patting his chest before pulling one out and a lighter. He offers them to me, and I take them both, lighting the cigar.

"Please sit him up," I ask.

Zayden nods his head dutifully, lifting him and the chair up, all with ease. I continue lighting the cigar until the end is completely red hot.

"Do you need a cutter, angel?" Zayden offers, nodding to the cigar.

"Soon."

I don't intend on smoking this, though.

"Do you know why I only have tattoos on one arm, Zayden? Nowhere else on my whole body?"

He shakes his head, his eyes filled with fascination.

"To cover up these," I say before plunging the lit cigar into Jim's bare arm.

Since he's wearing nothing but a pair of boxers and a white wife beater, there is so much skin to choose from, and I plan on burning every inch possible.

His muffled screams are still extremely audible behind the tape, and a sick part of me enjoys the sound. I pull it away from his skin, re-lighting the end for the maximum amount of burn before I do it again and again. I litter his skin with so many burn holes that I practically black out, only the smell of burning flesh and tobacco mingling in the air.

Zayden, at some point, comes up to me, his fingers skimming over my tattooed arm as I continue my work. His fingertips delicately begin tracing over the slightly raised areas. They healed well since I was so young, but they're still there if you look hard enough, thanks to him.

I watch as Zayden's chest begins to heave and his eyes darken, anger seemingly having a vice grip on him as he looks up to me.

"I want you to have this, but I need to kill him. He hurt you, he needs to die."

I smile sadly, shaking my head at my deranged protector.

"I wish all he did was hurt me with a cigar."

Zayden's eyes narrow at that as I hold out my hand for him.

"Cigar cutter, please?" I ask.

He digs around in his pockets before producing one for me, his gaze heavily on me as I move to stand behind Jim, gripping his sausage fingers in my hand.

"These fingers." I laugh coldly. "They touched me and ripped me. Poked and prodded. They were the things that started it all."

The sticky blackness of my trauma begins seeping inside me, the safely guarded box it was trapped in has been busted open, and there is nowhere for it to go but everywhere. I've been trying to prevent this feeling for years, something I thought I had overcome once and for all. Oh, how wrong I was. Zayden's right, though. I need this to heal, to move on, and maybe to cause a little hurt in my wake.

I try to straighten out his fingers, but he curls them into a ball, squeezing and fighting against the restraints Zayden put in place. I try to peel them away from his fist, but he's too strong. I huff in frustration before I see Zayden raise his hand like an eager child in class.

I furrow my brows at him and nod.

"Can I help you, angel?"

"That would be great, why did you raise your hand, though?" I ask as he walks around Jim.

"I didn't want to interrupt your fun."

I can't help but laugh at that. God, he's fucked up, isn't he? Like really fucked up. Why am I liking him more and more by the minute, though?

Zayden grips Jim's left wrist tightly with one hand, forcing his fingers out with the other. I give him a grateful smile, and he winks at me. A wink that, for some fucked-up reason, sends my stomach flipping. This shouldn't be a cute moment. I shouldn't be getting all flirty and giddy as my stalker helps me torture my abuser. Apparently Zayden and I are just built differently, though, because it most certainly is.

I slide Jim's first finger through the cutter, wasting no time before I apply pressure and the digit slices clean off. He screams an agonizing sound of pain as I work one by one through each finger. The ring finger bled more than the others, which I thought was ironic seeing as his wedding band was still attached to it. His wife knew, she always knew, she just pretended not to, and so I don't feel an ounce of guilt for making her a widow by the end of the day.

Once we finish with the other hand, he's sobbing and moaning as blood is pouring out of his hands and creating two round puddles beneath them. The concrete floor has a type of epoxy coating that seems like it will be easy to clean up when we are done with him, so that's convenient.

"What next?" I ask Zayden.

He sweeps his hands out and smiles.

"This is your rodeo, sweetheart. I'm just enjoying the view."

I smirk at that, walking over to Zayden's tools of torture before grabbing one of the knives and bending down in front of

Jim once more.

"The Achilles hurts really bad, right?" I ask Zayden.

He makes a sour face and nods.

"Like nothing you've ever felt."

"Perfect," I say before taking the knife and slicing horizontally across both his Achilles tendons. Blood shoots out of the back of his ankles as he bucks and jerks against his bindings, forcing him to the floor once more.

Slit by slit, I tear him apart. Zayden even steps in for a bit and pulls out each of his teeth with the pliers. He says it makes disposal that much more seamless, and hey, he's the expert. We also figure why not cut off his toes, it's not like he'll need them where he's going.

Zayden grabbed some rusty barbed wire from a cabinet and coiled it around Jim's shoulders, pulling it tighter and tighter until he had no choice but to stay as still as possible or risk bleeding out faster.

Jim's eyes are surprisingly wide and panicked for the state he's in. I would have thought he'd pass out from blood loss by now, but I guess it pays to be a fat piece of shit. They're fixed on me currently and are practically begging me to let him go, to stop all of this. Zayden doesn't seem to like that much.

A low growl emanates from his chest as he grabs a knife and plunges it into his right eye without hesitation, twisting and pulling it clean out, still staked on the knife as he tosses it to the ground and grabs another.

"You will never set eyes on her again!" Zayden snarls before giving the other eye the same treatment.

Jim's screams are bloodcurdling as he struggles against the barbed wire, his once-white wife beater is now almost completely crimson. My hands are stained with his blood, as are Zayden's, with blood splattered across his chest from the eyes, but I've never been so completely unbothered in my life.

"Take the tape off," I tell Zayden, who does as I say without a second of hesitation.

Jim begins babbling profusely, his head whipping in either direction, as he tries to make sense of where we are due to his newly blinded state. Blood is still pouring from his empty eye sockets, and it's truly a grotesque sight as he begs, "Please! Please! Blake, don't kill me. Please. I loved you so much. I still do. I think about you all the time. I'm sorry. I love you!" he wails, his words coming out distorted due to the lack of teeth.

Zayden sends a punch to his gut that sends him wheezing as I grab the scalpel.

"Tongue," I command shortly.

Zayden delivers another punch to Jim's jaw, and with the sickening crunch that sounds next, I know for sure it's broken. I suppose that was the intent because, in the next moment, Zayden easily pushes the rest of his jaw open, allowing his hand inside his mouth before his fingers grip his blood-soaked tongue.

I don't waste any time slicing through the thick muscle as I speak.

"You stole my voice before I even knew what it meant to have one, so why should you deserve to speak?"

The cut is clean and quick, which surprises me. I thought

it would be harder than that. He moans and groans in pain as his mouth makes a gargled sound. He's losing too much blood, and I know it won't be long now. Zayden gives me a nod like he agrees that these are his last few moments, so I decide to make the best of them.

I nod down at Jim's underwear, refusing to touch him anymore in my life, and though Zayden looks inconvenienced by this, he does it happily for me. Zayden's large hand grips Jim's limp cock, holding it out at the perfect angle for me.

The scalpel slices through even easier than the tongue. Blood sprays against both of our faces, and though I cringe at the initial impact, I'm not all that bothered when I see that it's done. Zayden is now holding the severed remnants of Jim's worthless dick when I nod toward Jim's mouth, my intent clear.

Zayden seems to nod in approval before he shoves it into his mouth, pushing it so far back that it blocks his airway. Jim fights against it, though his movements are weak and his effort futile. Slowly, his muffled screams stop, his muscles cease their straining, and Zayden shoves the chair to the floor, echoing in the room with a solid thunk.

For a moment, the only sound in the room is our breathing and the faint sound of Jim's blood dripping on the floor. The puddle is enormous, taking up a third of the room as it continues to spread.

My eyes are still on Jim, unable to look away, unable to erase what I have just done. I did it. He's gone. Forever. And he went in one of the worst, more excruciating ways I could imagine. He can't hurt me anymore, not even in my dreams, not after today.

I'm free. I'm free.

Zayden is watching me carefully, like he thinks I'm about to break at any moment. I don't feel like breaking, though. What happened here wasn't tragic, it was joyous and celebratory and I've never been on a high quite like this in my life.

I close the distance between Zayden and me, our bodies clashing together instantly. My mouth is on his as his hands are on my lower back, hauling me into him until every inch of each other is touching.

His hands peel my leggings and panties down my legs while I'm grabbing the hem of his shirt, pulling it over his head before tossing it to the side. He does the same to me, unclasping my bra with one hand before throwing it to the floor. I practically tear off his jeans in the next moment, dropping to my knees and taking his cock into my mouth.

Zayden lets out a throaty groan as I suck him deep down my throat, his blood-soaked hand brushing across my face and into my hair. I look up at him, hoping I'm conveying everything I'm feeling, everything I don't even understand myself.

How grateful I am that he gave me this, that he freed me. That he sat by silently and allowed the ugliest parts of me out, and he welcomed it with open arms. There is so much wrong about Zayden, but there is a lot that's right about him, right for me.

He pulls away from me, practically tackling me to the ground as he begins eating my pussy. I let out a scream as his tongue viciously attacks my clit, flicking, sucking, and nipping at it with his teeth. He devours me like he's never tasted anything better in his life, and the way he grinds his cock against the floor as he does tells me he's just as ready to lose it as I am.

"Fuck me," I pant. "Please, Zayden. Fuck me."

His arms snake underneath my back, palms supporting me as he makes a quick move, flipping onto his back and taking me with him until I'm sitting on his face. His eyes roll into the back of his head as he continues feasting on me before he murmurs against my thighs.

"Ride me, angel. Take what you want. I'm all yours to do with as you please."

I don't hesitate, raising my hips off his face as I wiggle down his body. I slide onto his cock easily and let out a pleasured moan once I'm fully seated on him. As I rise up and sink down on him, I feel a wetness coating my legs.

When I glance down, I see the puddle of Jim's blood slowly beginning to surround us. For a moment, I'm disgusted. That is, until Zayden glances over, a dark lust-filled look consuming his eyes before he looks back at me.

"Look at that. Look what you did, angel. You're so perfect, so incredible."

His praise feels strange, and yet, it's like a rush of dopamine to my brain. I continue thrusting, grinding my clit against Zayden's pelvis as more and more blood begins to surround us. I won't lie, there is something erotic about it. In a super-damaged, PTSD way, but I'm turned on all the same.

I feel Zayden's cock begin to pulse, and he groans as he smacks the back of my ass so hard I yelp in reaction.

"I'm gonna come, angel. I can't help myself when you're

riding my cock like a blood-soaked goddess. You're every dream I've ever had wrapped in one," he moans.

"You're sick, you know that?" I pant, grinning as I fuck him faster, my own orgasm just out of reach.

His piercing eyes come up to mine, his grip tightening on my hips as he speaks.

"So are you."

That hard truth mixed with the quick, deep thrust against my G-spot is my undoing. White light blinds me as my mouth drops open and a scream erupts from me. My body shakes as my pussy pulsates. I feel Zayden's cum fill me up as I practically clamp down on him, pure euphoria tearing through my body, leaving nothing to hold me up.

I collapse on top of Zayden, my breathing heavy, as my eyes begin to flutter closed.

I did it. I did it. I'm free. I'm free.

CHAPTER THIRTY-FOUR

DOMINIC

When I got out of bed, I couldn't find Blake or Zayden anywhere. I wasn't sure where they could have gone since Zayden's keys were still on the kitchen island. At least he didn't leave the house with her again. As I walked down the hallway, I noticed the closet door was open, and I instantly knew something was up.

I peeked inside, not sure I was truly seeing what I was seeing. A man was tied to a chair, bloodied, beaten, and currently having his tongue cut out by Blake. I was about to barge in there and ask Zayden why the fuck he would involve her in our business, but I looked for a second longer and I saw it. This wasn't a job he wrangled her into, this wasn't Zayden pushing her past her limits for his own sick satisfaction. This was for *her*.

The look on her face said it all, whatever this was, it was personal, and I knew I couldn't ruin it for her.

Zayden watched her with such awe and such adoration as she butchered a man, practically drenched in his blood as she did so. If I didn't know my deranged brother was in love with her before, this would have confirmed it. And the way she looked at him once she had finished, that shit hurt.

I've been sitting at the island ever since, drinking, pretending that I didn't see what I thought I saw. That there was something real between them. It wasn't just fear and adrenaline to get out of a graveyard with a madman. It wasn't the forbidden temptation and built-up lust on a couch. This was real, their connection raw, messy, and true.

I sat with it for a while, doing my best to convince myself that, in the end, she'd still choose me. That I was better for her, but when I heard her moans, that's when I poured my first glass. They left the room twenty minutes ago, Zayden carrying her in his arms as they made their way to his room. I heard the shower start up shortly after, and it only turned off a minute ago.

The right thing to do would probably be to accept defeat. Accept the fact that while she cares for me and no doubt loves me, something about Zayden understands her on a level I never can. Something about his twisted, fucked-up soul heals a broken part of her own. He has more to offer her than I do, in ways I never could.

So, yeah, the right thing to do would be to walk away. That's the thing about the Graves brothers, though. We aren't known for doing the right thing.

My feet are light as I make my way down the hallway, my pulse pounding with each step I take. I can sneak into a government building and download encryption codes without a bead of sweat. I can slip into somebody's house in the middle of the night, execute them while they're fast asleep beside their spouse, and not have my heart rate elevate even a single beat. But right now, I feel like I'm going to be sick, because if she looks at me and turns me away...if she tells me it's him...

I shake my head at the thought. I'd rather fucking die than lose her.

When I step into the room, Zayden and Blake are curled up in bed. The lights are off, the blinds are drawn, and she's lying in the middle of the bed, her head on his chest with his arm wrapped around her. My heart squeezes at the sight before Zayden makes eye contact with me.

His eyes aren't apologetic or sympathetic, not in the slightest, and why should they be? Roles reversed, I wouldn't be feeling bad for my brother. I'd be basking in the high of having her, in fact, that's exactly what I did.

In the next moment, her eyes flit open, landing on me. Goddammit. Those eyes. Like nothing I've ever seen before. The dark brown one has always been my favorite, but maybe because the blue always reminded me too much of Zayden's.

"Please?" she asks softly, forcing my eyebrows to dip.

Please what? I'll do anything she wants, even if it means tearing my own heart out. Even if it means walking away and letting them ride off into the sunset while I sit on the sidelines, silently loving her. But I have to hear her say it. She has to tell me she doesn't love me, that she doesn't want me. It's the only way.

Zayden rolls his eyes before reaching over her, flicking the blankets back on her other side, and giving me a pointed look. I'm surprised for a moment, but I don't fight it. I kick off my shoes and pull my shirt over my head, leaving my sweats on as I slide into bed behind Blake.

Her back is bare, and it isn't until I'm completely pressed against her that I realize she's completely naked. I can't help but grow hard at the feeling of her silky skin pressed against me. She must feel me because her ass presses against my hard-on as she turns her head over to smile at me. Her wet hair is fanned out against the pillow behind her as she nuzzles closer to me.

I take full advantage of her move, wrapping my arms tightly around her waist before my hand brushes against Zayden. Blake smiles happily as Zayden takes up the space she created, plastering her between us before she closes her eyes. Zayden and I share a heavy look, a million things being spoken silently between us.

She's not choosing him. She's not choosing me. She's choosing us. We could both fight it, tear each other apart in the process, but in the end, it will only hurt her. She wants us, and whatever she wants, she gets.

GRAVES

I'M WOKEN UP BY THE SOFT SOUND OF RUSTLING. MY EYES blink open to find Blake now facing me, her eyes staring up at me softly.

"Hi," she whispers softly as the sound of my brother snoring echoes in the background.

"Hi," I say, pulling her just a little closer to me.

Zayden is lying on his back, arms above his head, while Blake scoots closer to me, smiling as she cuddles in closer. I press a kiss to the top of her head as she nuzzles her head against my chest. We're silent for several seconds before she speaks.

"I'm sorry."

I frown at that, pulling back slightly to look at her. A tear escapes her eye, sliding down her cheek as she looks up at me.

"Baby, why are you sorry?"

"I cheated on you," she says with a wince, curling her lip up and shaking her head. "With your brother," she chokes out, shaking her head in disappointment.

"Hey," I say gently, trying to soothe her as I grip the back of her neck with my hand. "It's okay."

"It's not. I thought you were gonna kill him when you came in last night, or me, or both of us. You didn't, though, you just looked...sad. And I'm terrified that I've ruined everything with us. That I blew it, that you don't love me anymore," she cries softly, her voice shaking as her face pinches and tears stream down her face.

"Shh, shhh," I hush her as I cradle her close to me.

"Please don't cry, baby. It's okay. I love you so much, nothing could change that."

"Don't tell me that just because you think it's what I want to hear, please. You should be pissed at me. I'm a fucking whore."

My grip on her tightens as my tone becomes stern.

"That's enough. I will never tolerate anyone speaking about you that way, yourself included. It's okay, Blake."

Her eyes come to my own, flitting back and forth between them as she shakes her head.

"How are you okay with this?"

I stare at her for a moment, using my thumb to brush away her tears as it grazes her cheek.

"Because I'd rather share you with Zayden forever than risk losing you. Let's be honest, if I forced you to choose, I'd lose you."

She shakes her head quickly, and I think she even believes herself, but I don't.

"No, I would," I insist. "The fact is, there isn't just room for me in your heart. You love him too, or at least you're getting there. Even having half of your heart is the greatest gift I've ever been blessed with, and I'm not letting that go for anything."

I press a kiss against her knuckles, her fingers intertwining with my own as she shakes her head softly again.

"I don't know what I feel. I don't love him. He's creepy and controlling and psychotic, obviously, but he also...gets me. Better than I get myself, it seems. Or at least a piece of me. He makes the darkness inside me feel...okay."

"Yeah," I sigh as I squeeze her hand. "He has a way of doing that. Of making bad things seem okay, allowing you to embrace yourself to the fullest."

She nods in agreement.

"So, you're okay with this? With me being with...both of you?" she hedges carefully.

"If it makes you happy. That work for you, brother?" I ask Zayden, who woke up at least a minute ago.

Blake startles in my arms, turning her head to see Zayden watching her carefully. His hand reaches out, tangling in her hair several times, like it soothes him, before he responds.

"You know, if it was anyone else, I'd kill them?" he asks Blake, obviously referring to me.

Surprisingly, she laughs at that, nodding her head softly.

"Good, but you better figure out what you feel for me soon, angel, because I'm so fucking in love with you that I'm ready to carve your name into my heart."

She cocks her head to the side and smiles.

"That's oddly sweet of you, Zay."

The nickname seems to roll off her tongue, and my eyes shoot to his instantly. His body tightens in response, though, so he answers my unasked question.

"Zay?" he questions, the word seemingly having a sour effect on his tongue.

"Short for Zayden," she draws out sarcastically. "You know, a nickname. We've talked about this with Dom, remember?"

Zayden stays quiet for several seconds.

"That's my nickname? I get one?"

She shrugs as a wide smile breaks out across his face, one

brighter and wider than I've seen him wear in years. There isn't a hint of wickedness or deranged anger hidden in the corners, just joy and bliss. It's a good look for my brother.

"You love me," he grins.

She scoffs and shoves him away. "I gave you a nickname, Zayden. We aren't picking out wedding rings."

"We should soon. Your fingers are too slim. I'm going to have to have something custom-made. Size four," he says, directing that last part to me like it's crucial knowledge for me to have as well.

Instead of being creeped out by the obvious fact that he's already measured her finger for a wedding ring, she sighs dryly.

"This right here is why I still refer to you as a psycho stalker in my head."

"Yeah? And what about when we're in bed?" he asks as his hand moves from her hair and disappears under the blankets.

Her breath shutters in the next moment before her eyes flutter. It doesn't take a genius to figure out what my brother is doing, and when he gives me a challenging look, fuck if I'm gonna back down.

"I seem to remember a certain phone call was made in this bed. Do you remember that, angel?" Zayden asks casually.

Blake's jaw tenses as she stares up at the ceiling, shaking her head to the side.

"Can't say I do."

Zayden gives her a crooked smile before Blake inhales sharply yet again.

"No?" he hums as I slide my own hand out of her grip and

skim my fingertips against her bare thigh.

Her head turns to me, a questioning look in her eyes as I find her bare cunt. I rub my fingers against her clit, forcing her to let out a choppy breath as I continue. My wrist brushes against Zayden's as he continues finger fucking her.

"You don't remember asking for a threesome with my brother? How you wanted four hands on you, two mouths, two cocks?" Zayden asks.

Blake's eyes roll into the back of her head as Zayden peels down the blankets, exposing her beautifully naked body to the both of us. I move my fingers further down, and when Zayden pulls his back, I slip two fingers inside her, forcing her to take both of us at the same time.

She lets out a pant that turns into a scream as we do it again and again. Zayden and I smirk at each other as she begins quivering and shaking.

"F-fuck. Oh my god. Please don't stop. Please, please, please," she begs.

I'm prepared to continue teasing her, but with one more thrust of our fingers, I feel her cunt wrap tightly around us, squeezing until I hardly have a pulse in my fingers before her cum hits us.

I gather as much of her cum on my fingers as I can before bringing them up to her mouth. She opens instantly, not even hesitating as she begins to suck. Her tongue swirls around my fingers as she lets out a throaty moan. I look down to see Zayden has his mouth latched onto her, and he's eating her like he's trying to tongue-fuck her. Actually scratch that, I know that's exactly what he's trying to do.

As she continues to suck on my fingers, I reach my other hand down to my sweats, pushing them down to my ankles before gripping the back of Blake's neck and pulling her toward me.

"Come suck my cock, baby."

She practically scrambles over to me excitedly, taking my cock to the back of her throat eagerly. I bury my fingers into her hair and clench my fists, using it as a way to guide her motions. Not like she needs any help, goddamn, my woman can suck dick.

I look up to see Zayden pull away from her now-bent-over pussy with a popping sound before he lines himself up to her. He gives me a mischievous wink before he thrusts inside her. Her back arches, no doubt giving Zayden a gorgeous view as he begins fucking her.

Matching his rhythm, I use her mouth, fucking her throat as deep as she lets me go. She begins to gag, and I back off for a second, but she doesn't let me. She forces herself to take more of me, her throat constricting around my cock as she gags again and again.

Fucking hell.

I feel my balls begin to draw up, and I hear Zayden's breathing become choppier. His hand sneaks around the front of her, rubbing her clit as his other hand begins massaging her ass.

"Shit, angel. Look how good you're taking us. Such a good fucking girl. I can't wait for us to fill you up. I'm gonna fuck your pussy, and Dominic is gonna take you right here," he says as he pushes against her asshole.

Her back arches, and she moans around my cock, causing my cock to twitch in response.

"Oh, does my angel like ass play?" Zayden smirks as he puts more pressure on her, forcing her body to buck in response.

Her head nods quickly, which I'm only benefiting from.

"She says yes," I say through clenched teeth. "She's gonna be so perfect."

"I can't wait," Zayden smiles. "Now come for us," he says, thrusting against her hard at the same time as I push myself down her throat.

Her body shakes in response as I come, my vision blurring and my body shaking as my orgasm tears through me. I hear Zayden and Blake both moan and move as they follow their own orgasms.

Blake collapses on top of me, and Zayden falls onto his back, heavy breathing is all that can be heard in the room. After a few minutes, I press a kiss against her head and move to get up. Zayden stops me, though, shaking his head as he points to her. She's fast asleep against my chest, and I lay back down, keeping her on top of me as he grabs his phone.

"Food?" he mouths.

I nod, looking down at her before looking back at him.

"I don't know what she wants, just get everything," I whisper softly.

He gives me a thumbs-up before stepping out of the room.

You'd think Zayden and I would need to talk about this,

hash things out, draw some ground rules, or something. I don't feel the need, though. He would rather die than ever hurt her, and I feel the same. He loves her more than he loves his next breath, and honestly, if it means keeping her happy forever, I don't give a shit. He's my brother. I love him almost as much as I love her, and I want him to be happy too. He deserves it. This thing might be as temporary as today or as permanent as forever. It's all in Blake's hands, she's the driver, and Zayden and I are just the happily-accompanying passengers.

CHAPTER THIRTY-FIVE

BLAKE

The smell of food rouses me from my sleep. I feel groggy and sore, so sore. My eyes blink open to find Dom looking down at me with a barely there smile.

"Did you sleep well?" he asks.

"Yeah, how long was I out for?" I ask.

"Just another hour. Zayden got food. Are you hungry?"

My belly roars in celebration that there is sustenance nearby, and we both chuckle at that before he nods. I stand up first, feeling a rushing of wetness between my thighs.

Fucking Zayden.

I awkwardly penguin-wobble my way to the bathroom and clean myself up quickly before coming back out. Dom has his sweats back on but his shirt is off. His skin is free of tattoos, unlike Zayden. That's an easy way to tell them apart. About the only way to tell them apart besides the eyes.

He walks toward me, holding a shirt up for me. I lift up my arms with a giggle, and he rolls his eyes at me before dressing me. The shirt falls down to my mid-thigh and smells just like him. I lift it to my nose, inhaling the clean masculine scent before he gives me a wink and intertwines my fingers with his.

I smile at him, walking out into the dining room, where there are seven different takeout foods sprawled across the table. Chinese, Mexican, Italian, Brazilian, sushi, and two types of American food are all opened and waiting for us. Zayden practically lights up when he sees me, making his way toward us. For some reason, I drop Dominic's hand when he does, feeling guilty.

There is no way I can smile at one brother while holding the other's hand, right? Zayden looks down at my hand before shaking his head.

"Don't stop holding hands on my account, angel. You'll hurt my brother's feelings, and then he gets all moody and punches holes in walls."

Dominic rolls his eyes at Zayden, and I look between the two of them quickly.

"I-I just want to be respectful. I've never done this before, and I don't want to hurt anyone's feelings."

"You won't," Zayden assures me, taking a step toward me and forcing me to move backward.

I bump into Dom's chest, and his hands catch my hips easily. Zayden plasters himself against my front, and I look between the two, silently asking what I'm expected to do.

"Stop looking for direction, babygirl. What Zayden is aggressively trying to show you is that we don't care. We want you to be happy. Do whatever makes you happy, and we'll be happy. Just make sure you spend time with both of us, and everyone will be good," Dom says with an encouraging nod.

My eyes come to Zayden, who is nodding with a smile before pressing his lips to mine. It's a slow kiss at first, our lips moving against one another in perfect synchronization. Then a pair of warm lips touch my neck, moving up to the sensitive part of my ear all the way down to my collarbone.

We just had a threesome, and though that was hotter than I could have imagined, I've never felt so worshiped, so cherished, as I do in this moment.

I expect one of them to progress things, but they don't, both just enjoying my skin against their own before they pull away at the same time, smiling down at me and leading me over to the table. Zayden pulls me down to sit on his lap, and when I try to get up, he only pulls me down again. I glance at him, and he just winks at me before wrapping an arm around my waist. Meanwhile, Dominic grabs two plates, putting a little bit of everything on both before he sets them in front of Zayden and me.

"Thank you," I smile shyly, not sure how to act or react

right now.

He gives me a tender smile before bending down and pressing a kiss to my cheek.

"Of course, babygirl."

Dom makes a plate for himself and takes the seat beside me, holding my hand in his as we eat in comfortable silence. Unfortunately, all good things always come to an end.

"I need to make a drive to the farm tonight," Zayden says.

Dom nods. "Need some help?"

Zayden shakes his head.

"What farm?" I ask.

They both pause, sharing one of those twin looks before glancing at me.

"It's a friend's farm," Dom says cryptically.

I raise an unimpressed eyebrow before turning to face Zayden, who doesn't hesitate.

"It's where we take bodies to disappear from time to time, a pig farm."

"A pig farm?" I ask slowly, his words running in my head for several seconds. "Jim is going to be eaten by a pig?"

The laugh that escapes me can't be contained. I giggle and cackle and even start to cry a little bit. That is honestly the cherry on top.

"Yeah. We have other ways we could do it, but the fucker is so fat, I think it's the easiest. I don't want to spend all night hacking him up piece by piece," Zayden agrees, laughing along with me.

Dom is the only one not laughing as he looks between the

two of us.

"Who was he?"

My laughter dies instantly, my appetite instantly souring. I expect him to apologize and drop it, but he only stares at me patiently. I look to Zayden for assistance, but he doesn't seem to be willing to offer any. Dom's eyes are begging me to open up fully and with Jim dead, I guess I don't feel the fear to do so that I once did.

"He is...was my foster dad."

Understanding clicks behind Dominic's eyes as his jaw hardens to granite.

"He hurt you," he states.

"Yes," I agree.

I feel Zayden's thighs tense beneath me, and I place a hand on one of them, causing him to relax instantly.

"He used to have his friends come over. 'Poker night,'" I say, using air quotes as I continue. "They'd play, smoke cigars, and then they'd get bored and wake me..." My voice trails off as I turn away from their prying eyes, swallowing through the next part.

"The first time I was nine, the last time I was sixteen, when I ran away."

The air is filled with dangerous tension, so thick you could practically choke on it.

"Names," Dominic grits out.

"What?" I ask, turning to face him.

"Do you remember their names? The friends?"

I shrug. "Yeah."

"Give them to me, babygirl. Right now."

"Why?"

He gives me a flat look and understanding dawns on me.

"Gerald, Bernie, and Slinky. I never learned last names or Slinky's real name. He was...one of the worst, though," I say as a shiver runs up my back.

Dominic seems to take mental note of the names, nodding as he cups the back of my head and presses his forehead to mine.

"I'll take care of them. You'll never have to think about them again."

"Unless you want the honors, angel," Zayden chimes in.

I turn to look at him, pausing only for a moment before I shake my head.

"Tonight was...enough."

Though I have absolutely no regrets and can't deny the rush and high I got from killing Jim, I don't want it to be a regular thing. I've slept more than I've been awake today, and I know it's my body's way of protecting me. I'm going to crash soon. I don't need to put more bloodlust on my agenda for the next day, week, or even year.

"So, what? You guys kill a lot of people? Like hitmen or something?" I chuckle, my laugh dying when they don't correct me.

"Hitman seems too basic, I prefer mercenary," Zayden says.

"And he does the killing, I do the planning," Dominic continues.

"Now," Zayden adds.

Dominic hesitates before nodding his agreement.

"Why? Why do you do it? Because they did something to you or—"

"Money, angel. It's how we make our livelihood."

"But you have your security business and the mechanic shop," I say to Dom.

"You mean the business to ensure Dom has access to wipe our jobs from evidence, and the shop where we launder our large sums of money?" Zayden asks on snicker.

My mouth drops open as I turn an accusing look to Dom, who has the decency to look a little sheepish, at least.

"Are you kidding me?" I ask. "Why didn't you tell me?"

"Babygirl, I love you, but you didn't need to know. Honestly, the less you know, the better. You shouldn't even be hearing half of this stuff," he says with a pointed look at Zayden, who shrugs.

"Why not?"

"Because if you ever get taken in by the police or an enemy and you have knowledge, they could hurt you," Zayden says over a mouthful of food.

"You don't seem too concerned about that." I point out.

"I'm not," he says with a shake of his head.

"Then why can't I leave this apartment?"

The guys share a look for several seconds before Dom speaks.

"We've been discussing it. I think things are...contained well enough. I still want at least one of us with you at all times, but I don't see why you can't get out more."

"Really?" I ask, my eagerness slipping through into my

words.

Dom smiles softly and nods.

"Tomorrow, angel," Zayden pipes in. "I'm taking you on a date, wear something warm."

He stands in the next moment, setting me to my feet before kissing the top of my head.

"If you'll excuse me, I'm gonna go take care of that little mess my woman made so beautifully," he says with a wink before sauntering down the hallway.

I shake my head, smiling softly, before facing Dom.

"Shouldn't we help him?"

"Nah, he'll be fine. He likes it."

"Why?" I ask with furrowed brows.

"Because he's fucked up, baby." He laughs, forcing me to laugh too.

Is it actually funny, or are we just disassociating? Probably both.

CHAPTER THIRTY-SIX

BLAKE

I'm wearing a pair of jeans, a long-sleeved shirt, and a leather jacket despite it being nearly eighty degrees out today. The sun is setting, though, and if Zayden and I are going out, it's going to be on his bike, and that shit gets cold even on the warmest of days.

He was gone for most of the night, taking care of what remained of Jim. Dominic cleaned the floors while Zayden went to the farm, and then Dominic and I fell asleep on the couch together. It was a perfect way to end an emotionally taxing day.

Tell me the last time you woke up in bed with one brother, went and slaughtered your childhood abuser with the other, fucked said brother in the man's blood, only to have a threesome with both brothers? Yeah, it was a first for me too.

Dom has been gone all day today, though. He's been at the office looking up all of Jim's friends, and according to Zayden, Dom is so good he will have names and addresses for them within the night. The only thing they will have to be careful about is when they take them out, seeing as Jim's disappearance has been blasted all over Chicago news outlets. They don't want to let the police make any connections when all of the men go missing too, which seems smart. It's not like they haven't done this a hundred times before, literally.

Why was it almost comforting to know that Zayden isn't just a lunatic with a short temper? To know that he kills people for money, that Dominic does too in a way. I assume he doesn't actually get his hands dirty, at least anymore, if Zayden's comment was anything to go off of. Knowing that they have an order to their chaos makes it somehow justifiable in my mind, which sounds crazy, I know.

I asked Dominic last night if they ever took jobs on women and children, and he said only women who truly deserve it and never children. So, that's something, I guess? At least they aren't out here slaughtering innocent families. More than likely if someone's name ended up on one of these lists, it's for a good reason.

Zayden is waiting for me in the kitchen, his fingers flying across the screen of his phone before his eyes come up to mine.

They rake me over from head to toe, and he smirks before pocketing his phone and closing the distance between us.

"You look way too beautiful to be leaving this house, someone is gonna end up dead, angel."

"Here's hoping it's not you. You're my ride."

Zayden barks out a laugh before pressing his lips to mine, pulling away with a shake of his head as he wraps an arm around my shoulders.

When we get on Zayden's bike and leave the parking garage, we don't get on the freeway like I expect, but instead, we head toward the industrial district of the city. He looks back at me and grins, though he can't see me smiling through my helmet.

A few turns and another mile later, and we are in what can only be described nicely as a sketchy part of town. Motorcycles are lined up for nearly an entire block on either side of the road. There is a car blocking the roadway that we pull up to. A guy is sitting in the driver's seat, and his eyes light up when he sees Zayden's bike.

"What's up, Ryan?" the guy shouts out to Zayden.

Zayden nods at him easily as he pulls a wad of money out of his pocket. He tosses it to him, and the guy catches it, inspecting the cash before nodding.

"Race starts in two minutes."

Zayden nods once more, and we swerve around the car. Someone is bumping music so loudly that it's filling the music all the way down the street. There has to be at least one hundred people out here, whether they are spectators or racers. It's like those racing movies but with motorcycles.

We don't park to the side like a lot of the other bikes do. Instead, we pull up to a start line of sorts before Zayden puts the bike into neutral and turns to face me.

"Surprise." He smirks.

I flip the visor up on my helmet and shake my head with a smile.

"This is your idea of a first date? Street racing?"

"You'll love it. I always hear you giggling on the back when I get into it."

I roll my eyes but don't lose my smile.

"What's up with him calling you Ryan?"

"Everyone does. No one uses real names around here. It's an unnecessary risk."

"In case the cops come?" I ask.

He nods.

"Are the cops going to come?"

"Maybe, but they won't catch us."

"A little cocky, don't you think?" I laugh.

"Yes." He winks before pushing my visor back down and kicking the bike into gear.

A girl comes to the start line in booty shorts and a bra before she holds up what looks to be a pair of panties. She smiles at the lineup of bikes on either side of us before blowing a kiss to Zayden. Irrational jealousy rises inside me, but I don't have any time to do anything before she drops the panties, and we peel out.

A few of the bikes shoot in front while we remain in the

middle of the pack. I wiggle in the seat, hoping somehow it'll make us go faster. Zayden reaches back and squeezes my thigh. It's as if he's telling me to calm down before we come up on a corner, leaning into it easily while one of the guys in the front wipes out, taking out a guy behind him as he does.

I cringe at the sight. Those are going to be some nasty injuries.

Zayden keeps it very casual as he bobs and weaves through the streets and other racers. I'm not sure how long we have, but when we come around one more corner, I see the finish line.

The bike kicks into another gear, and Zayden increases our speed. My adrenaline begins to spike as we get closer and closer, my blood practically buzzing in my veins.

The wind is biting straight through my leather jacket and sending my hair whipping from side to side. Zayden's hand is still on my thigh, and he taps it once more, signaling for me to hold on before he pops into a wheelie just as we cross over the finish line and edge out the guy beside us.

We drop back down smoothly, and a flurry of people rush over to us, cheering and celebrating Zayden's win as the guy from the car earlier runs up to us. He hands Zayden a small brown paper bag before clapping his back in celebration.

The girl that started the race comes up to us, batting her eyelashes at Zayden as she does.

"Congratulations, Ryan. I knew you'd win. Want to come back to my place and celebrate?"

He sneers at her like he couldn't think of anything more repulsive before he turns around, taking off my helmet and crushing his lips to mine. I slip my arms around his shoulders, smiling into the kiss as he very publicly claims me. I love every fucking second of it, especially when I hear the bitch huff and stomp off like a toddler.

Zayden pulls away, looking at me like I didn't just hang the moon, but I am the moon, before he places my helmet back on, turns around, and drives back down the road. We come closer to downtown before Zayden pulls up to a taco truck. He orders more tacos than we could possibly eat before we sit down at the picnic table to the side.

"That was something else." I smile before I take my first bite.

"I told ya you'd like it," he says as he picks up his taco.

I nod. "Do you go often?"

He shakes his head. "Haven't been in a while."

"How come?"

"Been busy. I was gone for a bit."

"That's what Dom said. That you saw me first, claimed me in your creepy stalker way, and then, what? You left? For a job?" I ask.

"I was in prison," he states casually before taking another bite.

My eyes widen.

"Prison? For what? For...one of your jobs?" I ask, lowering my voice.

"Fuck no," he scoffs. "I never leave a job messy, and I never get caught."

I furrow my brows at that.

"Then what got you locked up?"

He pauses for a minute, mulling over his words before he speaks.

"You."

"Me?" I ask, pointing to my chest. "What the hell did I do?"

He shakes his head and leans across the table as he speaks quietly.

"I was making sure you got home safe one night after work—"

"Stalking me," I correct.

Zayden smirks and nods. "And I noticed a man following you. He was close to you, too close. I knew he was going to rob you, hurt you, or worse. You always listened to your damn headphones too loud, so you didn't know he was coming up on you. It helped, though, because you didn't know when I took him down behind you. Before I could finish him off, some cops rolled up. I tried to give them this bullshit self-defense charge, but unfortunately, they didn't buy it." He laughs lightly like he's telling the world's funniest joke.

"Anyway, I ended up getting sentenced to prison for five years. I didn't take that well. I couldn't waste five years in that hellhole rotting away when you were out here, alone, unprotected, and not in my arms," he says, forcing my heart to skip a beat.

God. He's not joking when he says that he's loved me from the moment he saw me.

"Well, I thought you were alone and unprotected, apparently Dominic had that part covered," Zayden scoffs, a hint of irritation still in his tone.

"So, how'd you get out? Good behavior?" I tease with a small smirk.

He doesn't say anything before eating another taco. After a minute or so, he finally speaks.

"Called in a favor with a friend."

My eyebrows raise. "That's some good friend."

He doesn't agree or disagree, just stares at me before he goes back to his food. I want to pry more because Dominic never opens up like this, but it feels like the topic is very firmly closed. So I'll drop it...for now.

CHAPTER THIRTY-SEVEN

ZAYDEN

After the taco truck, I drive us home. Fuck, what I wouldn't give to just keep her wrapped around me forever. We would drive and drive until we ran out of road. Though I think my brother would take some issue with it, he could always track us down and meet up later.

See, look at me. I'm sharing.

I open the front door to Dominic's apartment, my arm wrapped tightly around my angel as we step inside. She turns to face me as soon as the door shuts, a wide smile on her face that makes my chest tight.

"Thank you for tonight. I had a lot of fun on our date."

"You think it's over, sweetheart?" I smile, tracing my fingers across her silky skin before I bring her mouth to me.

Her velvety plump lips practically melt against me as my tongue licks at the seam. I will never have enough of her, it's impossible.

I feel another presence in the room, and my eyes fly open, locking onto Dominic, who is leaned against the wall, his arms folded over his chest as he watches us with a pissed-off expression. Though based on the hard-on in his pants, I don't think he's actually that mad.

Pulling away from my angel, I lean down into her ear and whisper, "I think we have a voyeur."

She turns her head, smiling beautifully at him in a way that spikes jealousy inside me. I watch as she takes a step in his direction, but I wrap my arms around her waist, stopping her in place. This is still our date, and my brother isn't taking her before I'm ready.

I slip one of my arms around her shoulders, leading her down the hallway. We pass by Dominic, and I level him with a look he seems to read easily. I guide us into my bedroom, leaving the door open as my brother follows close behind. He shuts the door behind him, and my angel turns to face us, her eyes flitting back and forth between us.

"It's just you and me tonight, angel. Dominic is just going to watch."

She frowns at that. "I don't want him to feel left out."

A deep chuckle comes from Dominic, who is taking a seat in the chair in the corner of the room.

"Trust me, babygirl. I won't," he says as he starts stroking his dick through his slacks.

Confusion still tints her face as I press my lips to hers once more, stroking her tongue with my own as I walk her backward until she's falling onto the bed. We land with a bounce, and I quickly cover her body with my own, kissing across her cheek and down her neck. I rest my nose against her skin, inhaling deeply before letting out a rough groan.

Goddammit, she smells so fucking good. Like heaven on earth.

I trace a line with my tongue, starting from her pulse point all the way to where the neckline of her shirt starts. This isn't gonna work for me. I roll off her, kicking my boots to the side and shucking off my leather jacket before I speak.

"Strip for us, angel. Show us what's ours."

She glances between the two of us before she nods softly, shrugging off her jacket and gripping the hemline of her shirt, pulling it up and over her head. She's facing Dominic right now, and though I still feel the white-hot burn of jealousy, I know I'll have her all to myself soon.

I watch with rapt attention as she slides her pants down her legs, leaving her panties on before reaching up for her bra. When she undoes the clasp, her breasts spill free, and Dominic groans at the sight. His hand slips inside his pants as he watches her, and his arm begins moving faster when she lifts her hands to her breasts and begins playing with her nipples. Fuck, I'm ready to start beating my own dick if she doesn't get over here.

Peeling off my pants as fast as I can, I pull my cock out and sit on the edge of the bed, pulling my angel over to me. She falls into my lap, which gives me the perfect angle to bury myself inside her as soon as I get rid of these fucking panties. I reach for one of the knives out of my jacket on the bed and flick it open, slipping the blade between her hip and the thin cotton of her panties. I slice through the material easily, causing her to shudder in my arms as I wad up the wet material in my hands.

Lifting them to my face, I take a deep breath before groaning, lining myself up to her soaked pussy, and sinking inside. She gasps at the intrusion before it quickly morphs into a groan as she raises up, only to sink down on me again. Dominic has a perfect view of her as she bounces on my cock while facing him, and I grab his attention when I toss her panties to him.

He catches them easily, lifting them up to his nose. His eyes roll into the back of his head as he pulls his cock out and wraps her panties around it. My angel's breath hitches sharply as she watches him fuck her panties, and I make sure to reach around and pinch her clit so she doesn't forget which brother is doing the real fucking right now.

Her head tips back, making eye contact with me as she moans my name.

"Fuck, Zayden."

"Good girl. Say my name again."

"Zayden," she groans as her movements become uneven and jerky.

I continue rubbing her clit as she lifts a hand to her breast, rubbing her thumb against her nipple as she rests her head against my shoulder.

"That's a good girl. Play with yourself, angel."

Her pussy squeezes at my words. She's such a little slut for some praise, and I'm more than happy to shower her with all the words of appreciation she needs to soak my cock.

I grip her jaw, forcing her head back further until I'm able to reach it. My tongue tangles with hers again, savoring the feel of her mouth on mine while I'm buried in her. When we pull apart, she's a panting, needy mess, and based on the low groans coming from the corner, my brother doesn't have long.

Slipping my knees between her legs, I force them apart, exposing her even more for him.

"Go ahead, angel. Spread your legs for him. Let him see that pretty pussy while I fuck it."

"Oh my god," she gasps at the same time Dominic curses violently.

His fist is practically punishing his cock, and with one more pinch to her clit, she's coming. She practically flies off my lap, and I have to wrap an arm around her just to keep her seated as I empty myself inside her. I curse out my release, and Dominic seems to do the same until the room is silent and everyone is still.

"Wow," she sighs before looking between the two of us.

"Feel good, babygirl?" Dominic asks as he stands up.

"Would have been better if you were touching me too," she says breathlessly.

He humphs at that with a smirk on his face.

"Next time."

Dominic offers a hand to her, and she takes it, pulling off of me and forcing me to groan at the loss of her. I could stay buried in her tight cunt all damn day. He walks with her into the bathroom, and I hear the shower start up. I debate going in there to rinse off as well, mainly because I just want to touch my angel. My eyes start to flutter, though, and I decide my brother can have her for a few minutes, I guess.

―――――

THE NEXT MORNING, I WAKE UP WITH MY ANGEL'S HEAD resting against my chest and my brother holding her on the other side. If this is going to become a regular thing, we are definitely going to need a bigger bed. She doesn't take up much room at all, but Dominic and I are both six foot five and well over two hundred and thirty pounds. We need space.

My phone buzzes to life on the table beside me. I reach around for it, checking the caller ID before groaning. I ignored three of his calls last night, which was probably three too many. He has a short temper, and right now, my and Dominic's plan is to keep him happy for as long as possible. At least until we can figure out how to get out from under his thumb. Keeping him happy keeps him off US soil.

I slide out of bed quickly, careful of my angel's head, before I slip out of the room, phone in hand. As I answer, I go to the closet, opening the door to Dominic's torture room before shutting it behind me.

"Yeah?" I answer.

"You need to work on your people skills, *moy mal'chik*. That is no way to answer a phone call, especially when you have missed so many."

"Apologies. I was busy last night."

"Yes, I know," he draws out, his thick accent practically masking his words. "Street racing seems beneath you. Did you enjoy the prize you took home?"

The hairs on the back of my neck stand up at his words. Dominic and I obviously knew he was keeping an eye on us, how close of an eye, we couldn't be sure. Apparently, we have our answer.

I do my best to keep my tone uninterested as I shrug my shoulders.

"She was subpar at best. Kicked her out before she could even get her panties on." I fake a snicker.

Maxim bursts out in laughter at that.

"*Moy mal'chik*, you're despicable. Whores are tolerable for an hour or two, no more. Remember this."

My teeth crack at his words, even if he doesn't know he's insulting my reason for existence I still have the irrational need to gut him like a pig.

"How could I forget?" I scoff, causing Maxim to laugh one more time.

"I need you in New York, today."

Internally, I curse. Dominic better sort his shit out and quick. Not only am I sick of being Maxim's bitch boy, I'm sick of doing all these jobs for free.

"What's the mark?"

"Deveny Delecourse."

I furrow my brows at that. "The diamond company heiress?"

"One and the same."

"What did she do? You know how I feel about killing women."

The line is silent for several seconds, and with his first word spoken, I know I've fucked up.

"How dare you question me? You are a spoiled child, acting like you have a say. You are my puppet, and you will do as I say without a word. If I tell you to gut a pregnant woman in the street, you do so without a hint of remorse. I raised you better than this, you are better than this! Take orders, ask no questions, or I will be on the first flight to Seattle and behead you myself!" he snarls before the phone goes dead.

My breathing becomes ragged as I clench my phone so tightly the screen cracks. The door behind me opens, and I whirl around to face Dominic. His eyes scan over me once before he speaks.

"What's wrong?"

"Maxim called. I'm going to New York right now. Have you even been trying, or are you more than fine with my life being in the hands of that prick, forced to bend and break under his every whim?" I bark.

Dominic raises an unimpressed eyebrow at me as he folds his arms over his chest.

"I'm not the one who contacted him. We were fine, we were

square. He didn't have a thing over us. Then you blew that all to shit—"

"Because you wouldn't answer my calls! You were too busy fucking my girl that you left me to rot in prison!" I shout.

"Because you are the dumbass that landed yourself in there in the first place," Dominic scoffs.

"I was protecting her! She could have died. She could have been raped! Worse! I protected her, and I would do so again in a heartbeat. You're the disappointment, you're the letdown. So fix this, get him off our back once and for all, or I'm running. I won't do this much longer. If you don't fix this, I'm going off the grid, and I'm taking her with me," I say as I shoulder-check him, walking toward the door to grab my things.

Dominic catches my arm, whirling me around to face him before shoving me against the wall. He holds his forearm against my throat as he lowers his face to mine.

"If you so much as leave the county with her and don't notify me, you will regret it, I promise."

"Fix. This. Now," I snarl, not at all bothered by my brother's empty threats. He doesn't scare me. The moment he stopped completing jobs was the day we stopped being equals. He knows it, and so do I.

Without another word, I shove him away from me and head out the door. I storm into my bedroom, shoving some clothes inside a suitcase, before grabbing my keys and wallet. I need to head back to the warehouse to grab my equipment and call in a flight.

I have such a one-track mind, I almost miss her. Looking

to my left, I pause in the kitchen when I see my angel staring at me with a small, hopeful face. She's holding a plate out to me with some eggs and a burned-looking thing that appears to have been a pancake in another life.

"I, uh, I'm not a very good cook, but you guys always make me food, and I just thought I could make it for you this time," she says, her weight shifting from foot to foot like she's nervous.

I've never found anything more adorable in my whole goddamn life. I drop my bag to the floor and cross the distance between us, taking the plate from her, setting it on the island, and cupping her face as I press my lips to hers. She leans into my touch, her tongue darting out first. She tastes like fresh mint, and I chase the flavor as my grip on her tightens.

It's not enough that I'm doing jobs for free, especially ones I don't agree with. The fact that I'm constantly being taken away from her is too much. I can't think without her, can hardly fucking breathe. I need her by me at all times, and Maxim is ruining everything. I can't do this much longer. I can't be without her.

Pulling away, I bury my face in her neck, inhaling her sweet scent as I murmur against her skin, "I have to go."

"Oh, where are you going?" she asks.

"Away, for a job."

"Oh," she says, a twinge of sadness in her words that pangs my heart.

"I'll be back as soon as I can, okay?"

She nods softly, and I press a kiss to her neck before pulling back to look at her. Her eyes are sad, and it fucking guts me.

I watch as she pulls away, taking the plate of questionable-looking food as she heads toward the trash.

"Hey," I say as I catch her elbow before she can dump the contents. "I have time for breakfast before I leave."

"Really?" she asks, her face brightening a bit.

I smile at that, nodding as I take the plate from her and pull her with me to the table. I set her on my lap, wrapping my arms around her as I eat the barely digestible food. I grin through the whole damn thing like it's a five-star meal, though, because the smile it puts on her face is worth everything.

CHAPTER THIRTY-EIGHT

DOMINIC

With Zayden gone and Maxim satisfied, I decide to take Blake to work with me. She needs to get out of the apartment more, and I need to be spending more time at work. For several reasons. I've almost dug up all the men she listed, everyone except Slinky. Once I have their habits and routines finalized, I'll send it all to Zayden, and he will take care of the rest. Then again, a larger part of me wants to participate for the first time in a long time. This isn't a job. These aren't meaningless kills. These are necessary and essential, and they fucking burn.

Blake is helping Jarod sift through some data reports. I told her she didn't need to help, but she insisted she wanted to. Jarod's ears instantly turned pink when she smiled at him and took up the desk beside his. His eyes were practically glued to her while my own narrowed on him, and when he noticed, he quickly dropped his gaze and focused on his work. I'm not threatened by him in the least. Doesn't mean I appreciate him staring at my woman.

My eyes come to her, and I feel my body soften. God, I never thought I'd fall in love, ever. Look at Zayden and my childhood, we didn't necessarily have great examples or a solid start, but here I am, so fucking gone for the woman in front of me. The way I worry about her constantly is maddening. I'm not sure if this is how love always is, or if we just have a unique situation that forces me to feel this way. It goes past her safety, though. I worry that she's happy, I worry if she doesn't laugh enough. With one look into her eyes, my entire world flipped on its lid, and suddenly all I could eat, sleep, or breathe was her.

She looks up at me, obviously feeling my eyes on her, and I give her a quick wink that sends heat rushing to her cheeks before she winks back at me. I chuckle in my seat before focusing back on the screen, determined to track down Slinky and exhaust all avenues possible to get Maxim out of our lives. Killing him may be what it comes down to, but if we were even going to attempt that, we would need to buy off the handful of personal guards he never goes anywhere without, at the minimum.

I've already reached out to a contact that is in touch with

the Mariano Family. It would make things easy to just have the mob take him out for us, no guilt or blood on our hands to be found, but my contact said not to hold my breath. So, I'm working on alternative plans.

"Babygirl, can you come here?" I call out through the open door.

Blake smiles and nods before getting up. I watch Jarrod carefully as she does, checking to see if he will sneak a peek at her ass. Lucky for him, he doesn't. Good, I wouldn't want to have to kill my protégé.

"Close the door," I say as she steps through the doorway.

She raises a mischievous eyebrow before sauntering toward me. Her long legs eat up the distance between us before she perches herself on top of my desk in front of me. I lean back in my chair to allow her room before scooting closer to her.

"I got you something," I say as I reach into my desk drawer and pull out the black leather box.

Her eyebrows knit as a confused smile touches her lips.

"What for?"

"Well, Zayden got you an anniversary present. Seems only fitting I give you one as well."

A choked laugh escapes her as she hesitates to open the small black jewelry box.

"It's not someone's finger or something, is it?" she teases.

"Afraid not," I say as my mouth stretches into a smile. "Though if you need some fingers chopped off, you direct me to them, and I'll take care of it."

She squints her eyes at me before wearing a dubious smirk.

"I thought you didn't kill people anymore."

"I don't, doesn't mean I can't."

Something sparks in her eyes at that. It's not fear, it's not disgust, it almost looks like excitement. My babygirl is a lot more twisted than I ever would have imagined, maybe that's how she's able to love two broken men like us so well, even if she denies loving Zayden just yet.

When she flips open the lid, her breath catches, and her eyes come to mine. I rest my palm on her thigh, squeezing it softly as she looks back down at the necklace.

"It's beautiful," she whispers.

"May I?" I ask as I gesture toward the box.

She nods with a smile, and I pull it out as she lifts up her hair. My hands wind around her neck as I clasp it together before pulling back to admire it. It's nothing too extravagant, not even close. It's a white gold pendant custom-shaped into a daffodil. It was too unique of an item to simply purchase in-store, and I enjoyed having it custom-made, it made it more unique, more special.

"I love it, thank you." She smiles, a tear dropping down her cheek as she smiles.

I frown at that, catching the tear with my thumb.

"Why are you crying, baby?"

"No one has ever given me anything like this before. This is—"

"Just a necklace. You deserve far more, and I intend to give you the world."

She leans down, wrapping her arms around my neck and

pulling me into her. Her soft lips move against mine easily, like they were always meant to, and I just begin weaving my fingers through her hair when my phone rings. I debate on ignoring it, but Blake is the one to break the kiss, pulling away and glancing at the screen on my desk.

Without hesitating, she picks it up and answers it.

"Hello?"

I know it can only be one person that she'd be bold enough to answer on my phone, so I ease back into my chair and overhear Zayden's rough chuckle.

"Hello, angel. You're not my brother."

"Nope. How is your...trip?" she says with an exaggerated pause.

"Finished early and am in need of a mood lifter. Got any ideas?" he asks her.

I'll bet. Though Zayden might not have the same conflictions as I do, and despite him seeming like a cold sociopath, he does have a heart and a conscience, and he had to go against both today in order to protect the beautiful woman in front of me. A price he's happy to pay but taxing all the same.

"Hmm, we could go dancing!" she suggests, a spark lighting behind her eyes as she speaks.

"Angel, do my brother or I seem like the type to go dancing?" he asks, voicing my own thoughts perfectly.

I watch as her smile dims slightly at his words, and I narrow my eyes in response.

"We're going dancing, Zayden!" I shout so he can hear me.

Blake looks to me in surprise before I give her a reassuring nod and smile. Her light is back instantly as she does a little happy dance on the desk.

"Alright. Whatever you want, sweetheart. I'll be home in five hours, and the first thing I want is a kiss, and then your lips around my cock."

Blake giggles like a schoolgirl before she smirks.

"We could probably arrange something like that," she says as she gives me a sly wink that has my cock stiffening in my pants.

BLAKE IS FINISHING GETTING READY, AND ZAYDEN IS TAKING a shower when my phone buzzes in my pocket, alerting me that there is someone trying to access the fire escape. I frown at that, pulling up the camera to see a familiar face. Christian Aranda.

Quietly, I slip out of the living room and onto the balcony, glancing down to see the walking dead man horribly attempting to shimmy up the broken fire ladder. Broken for a reason, we don't need easy access for anyone to get to this place. It's honestly impressive he's more than halfway up.

I glance at the lock bracing the ladder to the side of the building before looking down at the patio below. I flick the lock, forcing the ladder to free fall. His screams rip through the night sky, but lucky for him, he lands with a rough thud onto the patio beneath him. Stepping on the outside of my balcony, I drop down to where I'm holding onto the edge before dropping beside him. I land easily despite the close to ten-foot drop before

I stand to my full height.

Christian is still on the ground, but when he sees me towering above him, his face pales by three colors. I don't waste any time, fisting his shirt in my hand before dragging his face to mine.

"Tell me, Mr. Aranda, because I may be mistaken. Are you attempting to break into my home?"

"N-no, he stutters. Of course not. I just...I wanted to check on Blake. She and Gabby had a fight, we haven't heard from her in so long. I'm worried."

"You're such a good friend to care so much," I say calmly.

He stares at me hesitantly like I'm trying to trick him before he nods slowly.

"Of course, she's practically family. I'd do anything for her."

"I'm sure you would. Most men will do anything for the woman they love."

He scoffs, attempting to throw me off, but he's a really fucking terrible liar.

"Yeah right." He laughs. "She-s...I'm married. To her best friend! We're all friends, just friends."

"Really? Because she admitted to me the other night that she's had feelings for you for a while, but she wasn't sure if you reciprocated them."

"Really?" he practically gasps, light and hope shimmering in his eyes.

I can't help but let out a curt laugh as I shake my head.

"Fuck no. You're a fucking idiot. She hasn't spoken about you once. To her, you're her controlling bitch of an ex-best friend's husband. That's it."

Disappointment shadows his features, and if I was a nicer guy, maybe I'd give a shit. He should be happy I'm the one who found him snooping. Had it been Zayden, he'd be sent home in pieces.

Lowering my voice to a deadly tone, I look down at him, commanding all of his attention as I speak.

"Listen very carefully, Christian. You will never come here again. If you try to contact Blake, I will break your hands, if you chance a glance at her, I'll pluck your eyes out, and if you so much as breathe a word in her direction, I will slit you from ear to ear."

His body is shaking in my grasp, but he doesn't respond. I shake him once, and he whimpers in response.

"O-okay. Okay," he sobs, tears pouring down his face. Pathetic.

I scoff, throwing him to the ground before moving to the slider door of the apartment, pressing my thumb against the scanner, and forcing the door to whir open. It's not like I'm going to buy a penthouse apartment and not buy out the surrounding units for added security.

Grabbing Christian by the scruff of his neck, I drag his sniveling ass through the empty living room, opening the front door, and jamming my finger against the elevator button. When the elevator doors open, I toss him inside, rolling my eyes as I smash the bottom floor button and close the doors.

God, he really is a worthless man. He and his wife deserve each other, and as long as they both stay away from my girl, they can have each other. If not, well, let's hope they're smart enough to stay away.

CHAPTER THIRTY-NINE

BLAKE

We're walking down the busy streets of Seattle, the city lit up by the night lights. I'm wearing a black bodycon dress that has a scoop neck but is completely backless. It's my favorite for two reasons. One, it shows off everything in just the right places, and two, no bra is required. Win-win.

Zay and Dom are both wearing black dress shirts. While Zay wears black jeans because I don't think he owns anything else, Dom is wearing black slacks because, again, I don't think he owns anything else. There isn't a pop of color on any of us apart from my red lip stain, and honestly, if that doesn't sum up our personalities, I don't know what does.

We come up to a club, and Dominic and Zayden both skip the line, both on either side of me, arms wrapped around me as we walk straight up to the bouncer. One look at the guys and he's opening the rope and letting us through. I glance at both of them suspiciously, but Dominic's face is impassive, and Zayden gives me a smirk and a wink as we move through the long hallway.

Dominic tosses out cash for our covers to one of the employees before we step into what is practically another world. The music is thumping so hard the walls are shaking, and the dance floor is absolutely packed. We don't make it five steps through the door before a man in a nice three-piece suit is rushing up to us.

"Mr. Graves." He addresses Dom before doing the same to Zay. "It's a pleasure to have you join us tonight. We have a VIP section reserved for you if you'll follow me."

"Thank you, Sean," Dom says easily as we follow after who I'm assuming is the manager up the stairs.

"How does he know you guys?" I ask in Zayden's ear.

"You know Dominic. Always an entrepreneur," he teases.

I frown at that before turning to Dom.

"You own this place?"

He looks down at me and nods, pressing a kiss to my head before we crest the corner to a lavishly decorated area. The black leather booth and jet-black table top oozing simple elegance as a waitress in lingerie comes up to us, smiling widely.

"What can I get you all?"

"Tequila?" Zayden suggests.

"No!" Dom and I shout at the same time, turning to each other and chuckling before I look at her.

"Can I do a vodka tonic?"

"Same," Dominic and Zayden say simultaneously.

The girl nods and rushes off to the VIP bar as my eyes roam over the area. There are four other booths up here, two of them taken up by a group of well-dressed guys. My eyes linger on one in particular. He looks familiar. His arm is wrapped around a gorgeous woman with jet-black hair as she tells him something that makes his blonde head throw back with a laugh.

I feel a sharp pinch come from my side, and I look to see Zayden glaring at me. I roll my eyes at his insecurity before I speak.

"I feel like I know him. Who is that?"

Dominic and Zayden both look at the guy before Dominic speaks.

"Trevor Michaels, quarterback for the Crusaders."

Ah, that makes sense. I don't watch football personally but the guys at the bar usually have me put it on every Sunday during the season.

"Two boyfriends is plenty, angel," Zayden scolds with a tight jaw.

I scoff at him before pressing a kiss to his lips. His bunched-up shoulders relax immediately as his hands begin running up and down my body. I pull away from him, though, and reach a hand behind Dom's neck. He comes to me easily, bending down to deepen the kiss, while Zayden seems to refuse to let go of me.

Feeling a presence beside me, I see the waitress set down our drinks on the table, giving me a subtle wink of encouragement as she does. So she's obviously a girl's girl, and I instantly love that.

I pick up one of the drinks, tossing it back in one go before I hand it to her. She laughs lightly.

"Another?"

I nod eagerly. "Keep them coming, please."

Zayden chuckles. "Better take it easy, angel, or we're gonna be carrying you out of here."

"That's the plan." I wink.

Three more vodka tonics later, I'm bordering the line between super buzzed and drunk when I grab the guys' hands and drag them to the dance floor. They dance with me for a song or two, but both end up pulling away and watching me with appreciative smirks. I watch as Dom and Zay both take turns sending murderous glares to all the men around me. Slowly, the packed dance floor begins to part around me, and it actually makes me a little sad. I want to dance and have fun, but they aren't dancing with me and forcing everyone to back away from me like I have the plague.

When I turn my head, I lock eyes with a gorgeous brunette. Her hair is in large barrel curls, touching her low back as she dances. The red dress she's wearing fits her like a glove and makes her tits look like they defy gravity. My eyes rake over her from head to toe. God, she's literally perfect. What I wouldn't do to have toned legs like that or practically glowing, creamy skin like hers.

She gives me a slow smile before curling her finger toward me. I don't hesitate, slowly making my way deeper into the thick of the crowd, as I come to stand a bit in front of her before I continue dancing. Now that I'm closer, I can tell that her eyes are emerald green, so bright they practically shine despite the near pitch-black club around us.

Her eyes seem to look me up from head to toe, assessing me the way I just did her. When her eyes come back up to mine, she gives me a smile that has heat flushing through me.

"Your eyes are incredible," she practically shouts to be heard over the music.

"So are yours!" I say.

She smiles at me before wrapping her arms around my waist, dragging me into her until I'm straddling her leg. I take up the same stance as we start dancing together, using each other to grind and move our hips. Her hands don't stay on my back for long before they're wandering lower, cupping my ass and pulling me against her harder. I feel my dress rise at the move, but I don't bother to pull it down, enjoying the friction her thigh is providing me as I continue grinding against her.

We dance like that for a minute or so before she releases my ass, riffling through her purse and coming out with two white tablets. She puts one on her tongue before offering me one. I frown at her.

"What is it?"

"E, baby." She smiles, pushing some of my hair away from my neck as she leans in to talk in my ear.

"I've never done it before," I admit.

"I'll help you," she says, her lips accidentally brushing my earlobe as she speaks.

Before I have a chance to speak, an arm is wrapping around my stomach and yanking me backward, a deep voice in my ear.

"What the fuck are you thinking, baby?" Dom's voice practically growls as he begins dragging me through the club.

I look to see Zayden practically screaming at the girl, his hands twitching at his sides like he's having a hard time controlling them. They fall out of view, though, when Dom begins practically carrying me down a hallway. We aren't near the VIP section, this looks more like an employee's only area before he pushes a door to our left open and drags me inside.

There is a couch and a couple of chairs, almost like it's a private little hangout area. The club music is still thumping in the room, and I can't help but move to the beat. Dominic is staring at me with an unimpressed look when Zayden slips into the room, an equally grumpy look on his face. God, it's almost hard to tell them apart when they are both sulking like this.

"Whatttt?" I draw out with a soft giggle, the buzz from all the drinks hitting me at full force.

"That was reckless," Dominic says.

"And stupid," Zayden finishes.

I roll my eyes as I continue dancing.

"I didn't do anything."

"You were about to take drugs," Dominic says.

"From a fucking stranger!" Zayden fumes.

Do they always finish each other's sentences, and I'm just

now realizing it?

"But I didn't," I point out unhelpfully before I break off on a laugh.

Zayden closes the distance between us, coming up from behind me and whispering against my neck as he speaks.

"You wanted to, though. You were letting her run her hands all over your body. What else were you going to let her do to you, angel?" he asks, his hand running down my body before coming to the hem of my dress, slipping underneath as he pushes a finger past my panties and inside me.

I inhale at the intrusion before a breathy moan falls from my lips.

"She's fucking soaked, brother. I think grinding with that little club rat got our girl all hot and bothered."

"Oh really?" Dominic says, moving toward me and caging me in from the front.

I feel his hand slip beneath my dress as well before he also forces a finger inside me. My head rolls back, resting against Zayden's chest, as Dom practically purrs, "Fuck, baby. Did you like her smooth body against yours? Were you wondering what it would be like to feel her lips on yours, her tongue on you?"

My pussy pulses at his words, and I nod my head. She was beautiful, no doubt about it, and in that moment, I probably would have done more than kiss her. I've never been with a woman, and never really thought I was attracted to women, but I may be retracting that prior way of thinking because the idea of hooking up with her has my pussy practically drenched.

The guys, my guys, continue finger fucking me together,

forcing my pussy to spasm and clench with each thrust.

"I know she'd love it," Zayden says. "I don't know how I'd like that, though," he says with almost a pout.

"Aw, come on. Every man loves a little girl on girl." I smile lazily as I look up at him.

"Fuck yes, but I can't be certain I wouldn't snap her neck the instant you were done with her just for touching you."

"Zayden!" I laugh in both shock and horror.

"What?" He shrugs innocently, like there is nothing wrong with using a human for pleasure before killing them.

I shake my head as Dom's thumb drops to my clit, rubbing quick circles against me that have my hands bracing against his shoulders.

"Let go for us, baby. Let us see you soak our fingers with your sweet cum."

One of them pushes deeper inside of me, pressing against my G-spot and sending a white light sparking behind my eyes. I practically scream my release as I begin thrusting against their hands, desperate for every bit of pleasure possible. Once my orgasm subsides, I let out a choppy breath before giving them a sloppy smile.

I open my eyes, looking to see Dom first. I loop my hand behind his neck, forcing his mouth against my own as our tongues tangle together. We're roughly broken apart when Zayden yanks me away, claiming my mouth for his own. Again, we're only together for seconds before Dom rips me away from him, picking up where we left off. I'm in the middle of a metaphorical, or not so metaphorical, I suppose, game of tug of war. Honestly, between these two godlike men, I'm not mad about it.

CHAPTER FORTY

DOMINIC

Thankfully, that night at the club turned out to be nothing more than an hour or so of police questioning and closing the club early for the night. I expressed my deep sorrow for the loss of one of my customers in my club and was overly eager to provide as much assistance as I could.

Because of this, the detective at the scene deemed it to be a suicide attempt. Apparently the girl had a history of depression and drug abuse, kind of sad, actually. Fortunately, that was the end of that, and no strings were left untied.

Over the last week, one by one, Zayden has been plucking off Blake's abusers. One shot himself in his apartment and left a suicide note. Another emailed his wife that he was leaving her, providing a confession about how he has been having an affair. He even attached a video of him committing said affair. I can't believe the idiot had the video saved on his desktop of all places.

That just leaves one left. Slinky. It took me until literally this very second, but I've done it. Ivan Samson, a.k.a. "Slinky." He was born in Rochester, New York, before moving to Chicago when he was twenty-two. He lived there until three years ago, when he very conveniently moved to Portland, Oregon. That's a quick drive. Few hours there, a few hours back. We'll be home in time for dinner with Blake.

I didn't go with Zayden to take care of the other two, but according to him, their deaths were absolutely horrific, and I hoped my brother did his very best work on them. They deserve it and then some. This one is different, the way Blake talks about him. The way she flinches just slightly when he is mentioned. He was bad, maybe even worse than her foster dad was, and something about it has old habits and old instincts rising to the surface inside me.

A knock comes from my office door at the apartment before Blake peeks her head in. I shut my laptop, sitting back in my chair, before gesturing for her to come in. She quickly does, perching herself in my lap before looking down at me.

"You've been in here all day. What are you doing?"

"Working."

"On?" she asks.

I run my hand up and down her back before slowly kneading at the back of her neck. She sinks into my touch and hums out a little pleasure-filled moan as I speak.

"I found Slinky."

She tenses instantly, but I don't stop massaging her, hoping my actions and words can ease that tension.

"I know where he is, and Zayden and I are going after him."

"Tonight?" Zayden asks, popping his head through the doorway.

I look at him before looking into Blake's eyes, a promise potent on my tongue.

"Tonight," I say.

A look of something dark passes behind Blake's eyes, she almost begins zoning out as my pressure on her neck increases enough for her to face me. When she does, she looks hollow and broken, and her words come out so empty.

"He was the worst. Jim was bad, bad in so many ways and the orchestrator of it all, but when I was there, in the moment, he was the worst. He hurt me for the fun of it, he took the most amount of time. They all made me feel less than trash, but him..." She trails off, a slight chill running up her spine. "His touch was vile."

If I was on the fence about going, her words have confirmed it. I'm going and I'm killing the son of a bitch with my bare fucking hands. He lives alone, no wife, no girlfriend. The motherfucker is so ugly, I don't think he could get hookers to pay him any mind. It's the perfect opportunity to spend as little or as much time as I want with him.

I DON'T LIKE THAT WE LEFT BLAKE ALONE AT THE apartment. We sure as hell weren't going to bring her here with us, though, and my security system is practically impenetrable. I know she will be okay logically, but I'll never not worry about her.

"You ready?" Zayden asks.

I turn to look at him, nodding my head.

Zayden grins widely as he opens the passenger door.

"Just like old times."

Yeah, old times.

I wouldn't go so far as to say I regret or that I am ashamed of my past. Neither are true. Over time, the more kills added to my belt and the more time I spent submerged in the thick, murky waters of this lifestyle, the more I knew it wasn't for me. Not the work on the ground, at least. I prefer being the eye in the sky, the reason behind Zayden's madness.

All that being said, I still get a high from it all. The anticipation, the thrill of the hunt, the capture. The euphoric wave of victory overwhelms you. There is never a more powerful moment you will ever experience than when you take another life. It's after that things become complicated. The guilt, the crash, the nightmares. Zayden is lucky enough not to experience those aftereffects, but I do, and it's why I leave it to him, typically. I can confidently say, though, that I know I'll sleep like a motherfucking baby tonight.

I pop the trunk, and Zayden lifts it fully, grabbing the two five-gallon gas cans before I grab Zayden's special bag of toys before shutting and locking the car. We casually stroll through the upper-class neighborhood, skull masks securely in place like we don't have a care in the world. I've already disabled the street cameras and every home's security cameras on the block. We're completely under the radar, so there is no need to sneak.

Bending down, I pick up the fake rock that he purchased online six months ago before grabbing the spare key. Zayden snickers and rolls his eyes as I put the key into the lock, turning it easily before pushing the door open. I allow Zayden to step in first before I follow, closing the door quietly behind me. We wouldn't want to wake the sleeping prince just yet.

I head upstairs while Zayden takes one of the gas cans, emptying the contents all throughout the bottom floor. The house is lavish for someone who comes from a shitty background like him. He lives off a trust fund and gambles away more than he can afford. He currently owes an obscene amount of money to several gangs, including the Italian Mafia and the Chinese Triad. One of whom will be pinned for what happens here tonight, and all of whom will get off scot-free because no one will miss this piece of shit.

Navigating through the home is easy since I memorized the layout. The architecture is quite beautiful, it's a shame it will be burned to a crisp by the end of the night.

Pushing open his bedroom door, I find him face down on his bed, snoring his life away with a tray full of coke and a meth pipe beside it. Lovely.

I slowly begin setting up, pulling out each tool and placing it on his side table so that Zayden and I can have our pick.

Zayden steps into the room the next minute, shaking more gasoline on the ground as he does.

"Did you start the gas stovetop?" I ask.

"All five burners," he says happily.

"How do you want to do this?" I ask.

"I'll let you take the lead, brother. In honor of your comeback." He snickers.

I roll my eyes, but I take him up on his offer, walking up to Ivan before rolling him onto his back. The fucker is so out of it he doesn't even wake up. I scoff before turning to Zayden.

"Rope."

He makes quick work of handing me the rope, slicing through half of it as he begins tying up the legs while I take the wrists. To make things even easier, Ivan has a four-poster king-size bed, and each pole makes tying him up that much easier.

Eventually he rouses, and I'm honestly tired of waiting for this asshole, so I give him a nice little wake up call. My fist drives into his cheek, shattering the bone instantly as he screeches awake.

"AH! What the fuck! Who are—"

His words die on his tongue when he looks between Zayden and me. His strung-out eyes then look at his tied-up legs and hands. He strains against the rope, which only forces it deeper into his skin.

Fear instantly fills his beady black eyes before he looks back at me, or at least my mask.

"W-who are you? What do you want?" He quivers.

"We're friends," Zayden says, his smile audible through the mask.

"Friends? I don't know you guys," Ivan says.

"Friends of Blake," I supply.

He looks confused as he shakes his head.

"I don't know any Blake. You got the wrong guy. I swear!"

"She was nine when you first met her, she used to scream and cry 'no' as you raped her. Ring a bell yet?" I grit through clenched teeth.

Understanding dawns across his face as he begins bucking against his restraints and screaming, "FUCK! I'm sorry! That was a lifetime ago. I'm a good guy now!"

Zayden lets out a chuckle, and I deliver another hit, this time to his mouth. His lip busts apart, instantly seeping blood as Zayden comes on the other side with his knife, sinking the blade through his palm and effectively pinning his hand to the headboard. He lets out an animalistic squeal that has me actually smiling. Oh yeah, I'm gonna enjoy this.

———

ZAYDEN AND I DESTROY HIM, PIECE BY PIECE. THERE ISN'T an inch of him left that hasn't been stabbed, smashed, removed, or severely broken. He pissed himself when Zayden took out his eyes, and he passed out after I took a dildo wrapped in barbed wire, Zayden's idea, and shoved it into his ass. I was pissed off that he passed out because I really wanted him to experience every rip, tear, and ounce of pain, just like Blake had to.

He's finally coming to, and there isn't much left to do to the piece of shit except to finish this. Zayden takes the remainder of the gasoline, dumping it onto Ivan and forcing him to cough and spurt. He shouts and screams, but since we took out his tongue as well, he can't speak.

I turn to pack away all of our tools, leaving the dildo inside of him as a parting gift of sorts, before Zayden leans down into his face, speaking loud enough for his blood-filled ears to hear him.

"See you in hell, fucker."

With that, we turn and walk out of the room, making our way down the stairs and out the front door. I turn around, lighting up the cheap Zippo I bought at the gas station before tossing it inside the hallway. The fire catches quickly, and I watch as the trail of flames races up the stairs, all the way to Ivan's bedroom.

We move so that we are at a safe distance from the fire as we begin to hear Ivan's screams. They're fucking music to my ears, and I wish I could stay and listen to his dying breath, but a neighbor will surely see the fire soon, and I want to get home to Blake. So, we get in the car, reeking of gasoline and covered in blood, before I start the car and drive off.

CHAPTER FORTY-ONE

BLAKE

I frown when I open the bathroom cabinet drawer and come up empty. Where the fuck did my birth control go? Leaving the spare room, I slip into Dom's bedroom, moving into his bathroom. We all slept in there last night, so there is a chance that I brought it in yesterday.

Nope. Shit.

The last place I can think of is Zayden's room, though we haven't stayed in there in several nights. I walk into his bathroom and begin rifling through his drawers when Zay appears out of the corner of my eye, freshly showered, as he leans against the doorway and cocks his head to the side.

"What are you looking for, angel?"

"My birth control. Have you seen it?" I ask as I meet his eyes in the mirror.

His brows furrow as he takes a few steps forward, gripping my hips as his mouth meets the back of my neck.

"You know what, I have," he says as if the location just came to mind.

"Really? Where?"

I feel him grip my leggings, slowly peeling them down my legs before he lines his cock up to me. Slowly, he pushes inside of me, bending me over the bathroom counter to grant him easier access as he smirks.

"I think I saw them when I put them down the garbage disposal."

"What the fuck!?" I shout, whipping my head around to meet his eyes.

He begins thrusting inside of me, completely unbothered by my anger toward him as he groans.

"Zay, you can't fuck me raw. We need a condom because you're a psycho, apparently."

"Shh, it's okay," he says as his grip on me continues.

"It's not!" I say as I push away from him.

"What the hell is going on in here?" Dom asks as he steps into the room, harsh judgmental eyes coming straight to his twin.

I turn my head so I can face him. Thank God the reasonable

twin is here.

"Zayden dumped my birth control pills down the sink! And he's fucking me without a condom. He's gonna knock me up, Dom!"

Dom's eyebrows knit together as he takes several steps forward, his hand reaching out to cup my face in a soothing way as he speaks.

"Why did you tell her?" he asks.

I balk at that.

"You knew?!"

Zay cackles. "Of course he did, I was just going to throw them away. He gave me the idea to put them in the garbage disposal. Said you might look through the trash for them."

"Why do you want me pregnant *so* bad?" I ask with a scoff as I look up at Zay, who is still happily fucking me against the counter.

I'd like to say it doesn't feel good or that I'm not absolutely soaked, especially since Dom walked in. Both would be lies, though.

"Why don't you want to be? Why don't you want my baby? Our baby?" he asks as he looks to Dom for support.

I glance over to see Dominic tilting his head thoughtfully as he nods, like he actually fucking agrees with him! Unbelievable.

"I...I don't know. I've never really thought about having kids."

"Well, think about it, baby. We would have the most perfect babies together, all of us." He nods.

"You both want to get me pregnant? Like several times?"

"Like as many times as possible," Zayden groans as he pushes deeper inside me, his cock twitching at his words.

I whimper at the move, my toes curling as I try to stay focused. Dom and Zay share one of those silent conversations they're always having before Zay pulls out of me. I feel uncomfortably empty and more than a little disappointed when he scoops me up into his arms and carries me into the bedroom, laying me down on the bed as he begins fully stripping me down.

Lifting my hips, I help him as I watch Dom strip, Zay following quickly behind once I'm completely naked. Both of them stand over me, stroking their cocks slowly as they look at me, raw hunger in their eyes as their gazes devour me like starved men.

Wordlessly, they both start moving toward me, Zay on my left and Dom on my right.

"Relax, angel. Let us relax you," he murmurs before pressing his lips to mine.

Who could refute a request like that?

I settle back against the bed, enjoying the feel of Zay's mouth on my own, when I feel another mouth touch me. Dom's lips are brushing against my hip, making their way down to my inner thigh before landing on my pussy. The first swipe his tongue has me groaning, and when he does it again, I reach my hand down and fist his hair, forcing him to not stop.

Zay pulls away from our kiss, trailing his lips down my neck before settling on my breasts. He gives them both equal attention before closing his mouth around my nipple while rubbing the other between his two fingers. I've always been a slut for nipple stimulation. I swear I could come from it alone. The combination of one man eating my pussy while the other sucks and plays with my breasts is overwhelming, and I feel my core begin to clench.

"Fuck, guys. That feels too good," I groan.

I feel Zay's hand disappear from my breast, trailing over my stomach and down to my pussy. He slips past Dom's mouth, which is currently latched onto my clit, before pushing a finger inside me. Oh my god. Fuck, fuck, fuck.

A heavy pressure settles inside of me, and I can't even attempt to fight it before I'm coming. It feels different, though. There is so much cum, like I can physically feel the difference. Dom's tongue moves away from my pussy as he begins eating me like he's seen food for the first time. That only lasts several seconds before Zay practically rips him away, taking his place between my thighs.

When he comes up for air, I look to see both men have glistening lips and matching crooked smiles that take my breath away.

"Wh-what was that?" I breathe heavily.

"That was you squirting all over us, baby," Zay says.

Embarrassment takes over me before Dom's hand cups my face, forcing me to look at him. He shakes his head reverently as he speaks.

"That was the hottest fucking thing I've ever seen in my life."

I smile tentatively up at them before Zay moves up next

to me, lifting me up and flipping me until I'm straddling him. His cock slides into me effortlessly, thanks to me squirting apparently before he slowly starts thrusting into me. I try to push myself up so that I can ride him properly, but he just holds me to his chest. I frown at that until I feel Dom's body come up behind me.

"Got the lube?" Zay asks over my shoulder.

Dom grunts as he grips my hips tightly.

"Not sure I need it, she soaked herself all the way to her ass."

I turn my head to see Dom, applying a bottle of lube to his fingers regardless, before he rubs it against my asshole.

"Wait, while he is still inside me?" I ask Dom as I turn to Zay. "Together?"

"Together," they agree in unison.

A thrill runs through me at that. We have yet to do this. More often than not, we have one-on-one time, or someone fucks my pussy and the other my mouth. We haven't played with double penetration yet, and as excited as I am, I'm nervous.

"Don't be nervous, babygirl," Dom hushes, like he can read my mind before he slips a finger inside of me.

With the way Zay is slowly working me over, it doesn't feel too bad. Not until he slips a second finger inside.

I wince for a moment, slightly uncomfortable, before I allow myself to relax.

"Good girl. You're taking me so well. I'm so proud of you," Dom says, forcing a moan to rip through me as my pussy pulsates.

"Fuck!" Zay yelps. "Our woman loves being praised, Dominic. Keep talking to her, she's squeezing the life out of my cock."

"You love it, baby?" Dom asks as he leans over me, continuing to fuck me with his fingers as he presses his lips to my spine, working his way down languidly.

"Mhmm," I whimper with a nod.

"Perfect," he rumbles softly before pulling his fingers out.

The feeling of only having Zayden in me feels weird now, and I'm not sure what to think when I feel the head of Dominic's cock pressed against me. I tighten instinctually, and Dominic tuts at that.

"None of that, babygirl. Relax. Let me in. Let me and my brother fill you up completely. I promise it'll be worth it."

Another throb tears through my pussy from his words, and I do my best to breathe as I nod my head in agreement.

After a moment, a burning pain radiates through me as Dom begins pushing inside of me. I want to make him stop, but I know it'll get better soon. I'm just too full as it is. There isn't enough room for him. Somehow he seems to make room, though.

My fists are clenched in the sheets, my mind solely focused on the way Zay is making me feel right now until Dom is fully seated inside of me. I feel his cock twitch in my ass, and I let out a shaky breath.

"You okay, babygirl?" he asks.

"Yeah, I'm okay. Just go slow, please."

"Anything for you," Dom vows reverently as his grip on my

hips tighten, and he begins slowly matching Zayden's rhythm.

I gasp at the feelings. Oh my god. Having their cocks in perfect unison, pulling out and pushing in. It's so overstimulating, so overwhelming, and I've never felt anything better in my whole fucking life.

"You love this, don't you?" Zay grits through clenched teeth. "You're practically leaking all over my lap, angel."

"I'm sorry," I pant as I stay plastered to Zay's chest, allowing Dom to happily fuck me into submission.

Zay barks out a laugh as his pace increases.

"Never apologize. Your cunt is fucking heaven, the closest I'll ever get to it, that's for sure."

"Zay," I breathe out. "I don't know how long I can last. I want to come again," I whimper.

"That's okay, angel. Go ahead and come for us. I'm gonna stuff your cunt so full of my cum, and then my brother is going to finish inside you."

"But no birth control," I remind choppily.

"That's why we're doing it, angel. We want you pregnant with our baby." Zay smiles.

"I'm already yours, I'll always be yours."

"So will the baby. We will give you two the world," Dom promises, pressing his lips against my neck as he continues fucking my ass.

My pussy throbs at that, and suddenly this whole breeding kink is actually turning me the fuck on. Or maybe it's the double penetration. Either way, I'm coming hard. Zayden moans, his cum shooting inside of me almost instantly as Dominic stills, letting out a muffled groan before he quickly pulls out. I hear the snap of a condom and look to see Dominic discard an empty condom. Shit, I couldn't even feel that on him.

I feel Zayden coat the inside of me, filling me to the brim, before his movements stop. The instant they do, I'm lifted off of him. Zayden easily rolls out from under me before I'm placed back on the mattress, chest down, while Dominic pushes his bare cock inside of me.

Gasping at the feeling, he begins fucking me with long, deep thrusts. I feel Zayden's cum leaking out of me, but with the way Dominic is fucking me, it's like he's trying to fuck it deeper.

"Fuck yes," Zayden groans. "Thank you, brother. Push my cum back into my angel. Fuck her nice and pregnant for me, will you?"

"Get fucked," Dominic gnashes, his movements and voice practically animalistic. "If my babygirl is getting pregnant by anyone's cum, it's mine."

"You guys are twins. Does it really matter?" I ask.

"Yes," they both answer.

I don't bother arguing as Dominic slides a hand around the front of me, rubbing his thumb against my clit as he does. Pleasure sparks through me at his touch, and I arch my back to allow him easier access to continue. When I glance to the side, I see Zayden lying on his back, arm tucked behind his head, as he watches us with a smile.

"C'mon, Dominic. Fuck our woman right. I know you can let loose more than that."

I frown at that. Not sure what Zayden is talking about.

Dominic is practically destroying me with his powerful thrusts and aggressive touch.

"Can't," he grits through his teeth. "Too precious."

Turning my head to the side so I can see him, I look up to see so much confliction on Dom's face, so much tension. Glancing over to Zayden, he gives me an encouraging nod accompanied with a mischievous smirk.

"I can take it," I say as I face Dominic again. His practically crazed brown eyes come to me as he continues playing with my clit and fucking me from behind. "Use me, Dom."

Something seems to snap in him. His hand abandons my pussy, going straight for my throat as he squeezes tight, so tight my breathing constricts for a moment before he adjusts his hold, applying pressure to the sides of my neck instead.

His thrusts become punishing, slamming into me so hard it's shaking the bed against the wall. I always thought Dom was an aggressive lover, but I didn't know aggression until this very moment. He smacks my ass hard before doing it again, still holding my throat tight as he fucks me straight into the mattress.

"Think you can take it? Think you can handle me when I'm like this?" he practically seethes at me.

"More," I beg, though I regret it as soon as his hand smacks my ass so hard I see stars.

My entire body tenses under each blow, and apparently that includes my pussy.

"Goddammit. You've never squeezed me so tight, babygirl," he grits out.

"You've never spanked me like this." I gasp as he does it again and again, switching sides each time.

"I will now. Now that I know how good you are, how perfect you are for me. For us. I'll spank this ass bloody and fuck this cunt raw every day for the rest of my life," he grunts before his cock swells and he explodes.

I didn't realize I was getting turned on through all the pain, but one more sharp slap to my ass sends me spiraling into an orgasm I didn't know I was capable of having. Dominic's grip releases from my throat, allowing a full amount of oxygen to hit me and effectively making me dizzy. My orgasm is amplified as I breathe and pant through the pain and pleasure mixing inside of my body. My brain is literally fried, unsure what to do with these conflicting signals. So instead of trying to figure them out, I just collapse on the bed, moaning and groaning through them both.

Several seconds go by, or maybe minutes, before Dom finally pulls out of me, rolling out of the bed and opening Zayden's bedroom door. I go to call out for him, but I don't have it in me. Zayden's hand tangles through my hair, pushing it to the side and revealing my face as he smiles down at me.

"You did so good. I'm so proud of you."

I smile hazily at him as Dominic comes back into the room. I feel his thighs come on either side of me, my ass still in the air as a cooling feeling touches my skin. I wince at the feeling, pain still very present as he slowly begins massaging me.

"Shhh, deep breaths, baby," he says as the cooling spreads to the other side.

"What is that?" I ask.

"Arnica cream. It helps."

He's quiet for a moment as he continues rubbing the cream all over me before he speaks.

"I'm so sorry. I lost control. I swore I never would with you. I—"

"Hey," I say as I turn my head to face him. "It's okay. I enjoyed it a lot. Apparently, I like a little or a lot of pain during. It's the after part that sucks."

Dominic nods. "That's why aftercare is so important."

I turn an accusing stare at Zayden.

"Why have you never done aftercare for me, after we've played with your knife?"

He rolls his eyes. "Because every time the knife came out, you ran away right after acting like you didn't love or want me."

There is a bitterness behind his words that stings something inside me. I reach my hand out for his, and he intertwines our fingers immediately before I speak.

"I do. Want you and me." I pause for a moment, swallowing lightly as butterflies begin fluttering through my stomach. "I do love you, Zayden."

Joy like I've never seen on his face before spreads, enveloping all of his features and leaving nothing untouched by it. He crushes his lips to mine, holding my face in his hands as he gives me a smile that takes my breath away.

"I'll love you until the end of time, angel. In this life, the next and every single one to come. It will always be you."

My heart skips a beat at that as I turn to see Dominic

watching us with a pleased smile. Like seeing his brother so happy brings him joy as well.

"I love you, Dominic, so much."

He smiles at me, another smile I don't see very often as his hand rubs soothing circles on my back.

"I love you so much more, babygirl. Forever. It's always going to be us. All of us," he says, sharing a look with Zayden before resting his hand underneath me, cupping my belly.

Something shifts inside me at that. I turn on my side to see his hand on me, and Zayden's hand comes right beside his, both of them wistfully staring like they are imagining me six months from now pregnant with their baby. The idea doesn't fill me with the fear it should. Though I'm not ready to start cranking out a bunch of Graves babies left and right, if it happens, I guess it wouldn't be the worst thing in the world.

CHAPTER FORTY-TWO

BLAKE

Despite Dominic and Zayden's best efforts, I am not pregnant. My period came two days after the guys literally shoved all of their cum inside me, and to say they were both disappointed would be an understatement. Dominic frowned but tried to hide it while Zayden threw an outright tantrum, shouting at Dominic for not pushing it deep enough. I honestly couldn't help but laugh at the ridiculousness of his irritation, which he did not appreciate.

I'm currently curled up on the couch with Dom tucked

around me. The cramps didn't really hit until this morning, and I'm currently in six levels of fresh hell. Of course, Dom noticed immediately and grabbed my heating pad before he began massaging my stomach. He's since moved to my back, and we are on our third season of some trash reality TV show when his phone rings.

He curses as he answers it, talking to someone about some financials that are skewed at the club.

"I'm not a finance guy. Have someone else handle it," he scoffs before his body tenses and irritation fills him.

"Oh really? On tape? I'll be right there, don't let him leave."

Hanging up the phone, he presses a kiss to my cheek before going to stand.

"I'm so sorry, baby. I need to go take care of some business at the club. I'll be back shortly."

"Is everything okay?" I frown at his tense demeanor.

His jaw clenches before he nods.

"Do you remember the manager?"

I nod.

"Apparently, there is a video of him stealing money out of the safe. Fifty grand."

My eyebrows shoot up at that.

"What are you going to do?"

He levels me with a look that has me smirking.

"Are you going to go beat him up like some Vegas pit boss?"

Dom scoffs but doesn't deny it, which makes me grin.

"I like seeing this side of you."

"What side?" he asks.

"The dangerous side. The rough and tough badass. It's hot."

He gives me a dubious look then crouches down over me, pressing his lips against mine before pulling away.

"You're a little fucked up. You know that, right, baby?"

I nod. "I'm coming to terms with it. How could I not be when I have two sexy as sin mercenary boyfriends?"

Dominic scoffs but gives me a small smile before heading out the door. I smile at him before focusing back on the TV, a new wave of cramps taking over that has me curling into myself.

"Angel? Are you okay?" Zayden says as he comes into the living room, a fluffy towel wrapped around his waist, his inked skin dotted with several beads of water, and that jet-black hair wet.

I look up at him and give him a weak smile.

"I'm fine. I just fucking hate periods."

"No shit. You should be pregnant with my baby right now. Not in pain." He frowns before coming down to kneel in front of me.

"What can I do?" he asks, running his fingers through my hair.

"Nothing. The heating pad isn't doing much right now, and I just want a little relief," I groan.

"Relief?" he questions. "I can do that."

I frown at him before he tosses the heating pad across the room, turning my legs so they hang off the couch as he begins peeling down my sleep shorts.

"Zay, what are you doing?" I ask as he bunches up my

shorts and panties in his hand, throwing them to the ground.

"Giving you relief."

"I'm on my period, though. I don't have cute little light periods. I'm bleeding a lot," I argue.

He raises an unimpressed eyebrow at me as he speaks.

"Angel, what would ever make you think that would be anything other than a turn-on? I love your blood, and for me to have it without even having to hurt you? Fucking priceless," he says before pushing my legs apart.

I go to argue when I feel him pull my tampon out. My mouth practically falls open when he tosses it to the side of the room like it was an inconvenience in his way, before he latches his mouth to my pussy. A rush of pleasure immediately courses through me from the first swipe of his tongue. I've never had anyone even try to touch me on my period, let alone go down on me. I always thought it was cruel that I somehow always felt hornier on my period with no way to handle it. Apparently all I needed in my life was an unhinged Graves brother.

Zayden moans and groans like he's having the time of his life, while I just try to stay upright as my fingers curl into the couch, arching my back and forcing my pussy into his face even more so. If he's going to offer, I'll give him whatever he wants, I guess.

When his tongue flicks against my clit before sucking it into his mouth, I physically shake as he slips two fingers inside me, slowly fucking me with them before his speed increases.

"Oh my god! Zay! That feels so fucking good," I moan.

I feel him chuckle against me, vibrating my clit in the

process.

"Good, angel. Now hold on to something."

"Hold on to—"

Before I can finish, Zayden is motorboating my thighs, I shit you not. At least that's what it feels like. His head is moving from side to side, vibrating my clit in the process, as his tongue is out, licking me from side to side. Fucking hell.

I dig both of my hands into his hair, using his face to dry hump against it, and it's just what I need to find my release. My orgasm hits me like a freight train in the best fucking way possible. I come for so long I'm almost positive it's two orgasms that have joined together back-to-back.

Zay continues licking my pussy for several seconds after I've finished before he sits back on his heels. I'm horrified at first, his nose down is literally covered in smeared blood, along with his two fingers. I swear to God, he looks more blood-soaked than when we killed Jim. I look around for something he can wipe his fingers off with when he lifts them to his mouth, keeping his eyes on me as he begins sucking on them. My pussy clenches at the way his eyes roll into the back of his head. This is so gross, so fucked up. Right? Definitely. Right?

Before I can say anything, he stands up, lifting me into the air and tossing me over his shoulder as he takes off running to his room. I can't help but giggle the entire way. Okay, maybe periods aren't the worst thing anymore.

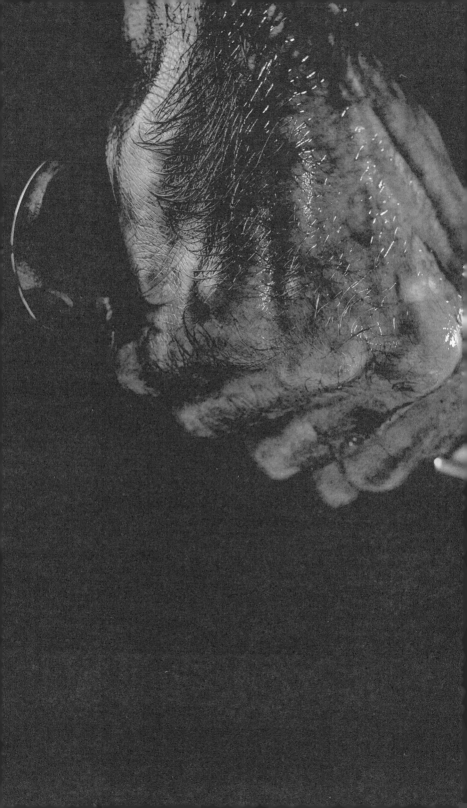

CHAPTER FORTY-THREE

ZAYDEN

My angel is sleeping soundly in my bed, tucked beneath my arm. Part of me wants to let her keep sleeping, while the other wants to wake her up with my face between her thighs. Decisions, decisions.

My phone lights up beside me, and I frown when I see who it is. Why the fuck is he calling me now? I've kept him on fucking cloud nine these last few weeks. I took care of the diamond heiress seamlessly, an overdose with her meds, and I've done two more jobs since then. The last I knew, he was happy as a clam and said that I had earned back my debt enough to start getting paid.

Of course, he didn't mention when I would be allowed to stop altogether. We both know why. I won't ever be able to stop working for him, not as long as he's breathing. The only reason we were able to escape last time was because we disappeared from the grid for long enough that he gave up on us and settled his sights on new little bitches at least.

I know I fucked up for calling him, I do. I was desperate, I was thinking short-term. All I was thinking about was getting to her, seeing her, touching her. Making her love me as much as I loved her. Now that I have that and more, I'm desperate to get away from Maxim permanently so his ugliness never even touches my angel.

Grabbing the phone, I slip out from underneath my sleeping love, heading out into the living room where I won't disturb her as I answer.

"Hello?"

"*Moy mal'chik*. How are you doing?"

"Well, what can I do for you?"

He laughs a throaty chuckle.

"That's my boy, straight to business. I have a little local job for you and your brother."

I frown at that.

"Dominic isn't involved, you know that."

"Ah, that's not what I heard. Little bird says he's taken up the old ways with a certain house fire in Portland."

"How did you know he was involved?"

"Zayden, do you honestly think there is anything I don't know?" His intent is heavy, hiding in his thick accent, but I don't acknowledge it. Acknowledging it would be like pulling the pin on a grenade.

He knows about her, undoubtedly, and as long as we do what he says, the peace will be kept. If not...

"What's the mark?"

I can practically hear his slimy smirk from the other side of the phone.

"There is a warehouse on the East Coast of some enemies. I want it gone."

"We don't really do destruction of buildings. It's a lot messier than a murder."

"That house in Portland went up real nice, I'm sure my boys can get creative. Besides, you're officially out of my debt. The job pays one hundred thousand, per Graves brother."

If he thinks I give a shit or need his money, he's deluded. Though I think he's smart to know that's not the case. Regardless, I don't have a choice, so I simply nod my head despite him not being able to see me as I speak.

"We'll get it done. Send over the details, and Dominic will begin planning."

"Glad to hear it. Chat soon."

Yeah, I fucking hoping not.

CHAPTER FORTY-FOUR

BLAKE

Dom came home later in the evening, knuckles split and swollen, with blood splattered across his dark gray shirt. I threw it in the wash for him and cleaned up his hands. He insisted he was fine, but he's always the aftercare guy in the house. I figured having someone take care of him for once was the least I could do.

The next day, Zayden and I are having lunch on the couch while Dominic is at a quarterly meeting with one of his customers. Zayden made us bacon grilled cheese sandwiches, and I happily munch away at it when an advertisement for a restaurant comes to life on the TV. A decadent slice of cheesecake is shown in slow motion, forcing my mouth to water in anticipation.

"Fuck, angel. Don't make me jealous of a piece of cheesecake. You're only supposed to look at my cock like that," Zayden says, though I'm not sure how much he's teasing.

"You know that diner by my old apartment?" I ask.

He nods as he leans back into the couch.

"They have the world's best cheesecake, I swear. They do a little chocolate swirl in it, and...ugh, it's so good," I groan in want.

"If you want me to go get cheesecake, just say that, angel." He smiles lovingly, playing with my hair before resting his head into my neck, inhaling slowly.

I've come to find that it relaxes him to smell me. It sounds strange, but the peaceful look that takes over his usually troubled eyes when he does it makes me sink into his touch, allowing him to hold me a little tighter.

"No, you don't have to. It just sounds good." I laugh lightly.

"What my angel wants, my angel gets," he says, pressing a kiss to my neck before he stands up, grabbing his wallet and phone before slipping on his leather jacket.

"You really don't have to," I say as I sit up, pulling my knees to my chest as I tuck the soft blanket Dom bought for me around myself.

He gives me a quick wink as he puts his thumb to the front door scanner.

"You can make it up to me later," he says with a salacious smirk before he strides out the door.

I smile after him, falling a little more in love with my beautifully broken, unhinged man. My love for Zayden hit me hard and fast. It happened before I even realized it, and once I did, I knew there was no going back, ever.

Grabbing our plates from lunch, I carry them to the kitchen and begin washing the dishes when I feel a presence behind me. My mouth pulls up into a smirk. Zayden and Dominic are both so light on their feet, so stealthy. They love sneaking up on me, but they won't get the upper hand this time.

I turn on my heel quickly, smiling in triumph. That smile dies instantly as a lead ball sinks into my stomach.

"Who are you?"

A large man stands on the other side of the island, dressed in a black sweater and peacoat. He has blond hair that has turned more silver than anything and a matching beard that is perfectly trimmed and neat. His cold gray eyes drill into me, an amused smile pulling at the corner of his mouth.

"Maxim. I'm sure the boys have told you all about me," he says, a thick accent coating his words.

I shake my head slowly, doing my best to hold my composure. My eyes dart around the room, landing on my phone that is sitting on the couch across the apartment. Fuck.

Turning my eyes back to Maxim, I do my best to give him a nonchalant shrug.

"Sorry, they haven't. I'm assuming you are a colleague?"

He chuckles lightly as he lifts a hand donned with faded

ink, scratching his beard as he nods.

"Something like that, I suppose. And you are?"

"I have a feeling you already know the answer to that question," I say cautiously, keeping my eyes narrowed and my expression bored.

His light smirk transforms into a sinister smile that sends goose bumps scattering across my arms as he tips his head back and lets out a deep, raspy laugh.

"I see what has my boys all twisted up now. You have fire, *kratsoka*."

"What are you doing here?" I ask, the unsettling feeling in my stomach growing with each second he's here.

"I came for a visit. It's been too long, and I wanted to see what all the fuss was about," he says as he takes several calculated steps around the island and toward me.

The closer he gets, the more I want to shrink in on myself, my past insecurities and instincts coming to the forefront of my mind. I do my best to stand tall, not moving a muscle. Men like this thrive on weakness, they want you scared and running.

"They aren't here. I'll tell them you stopped by," I say tersely as he closes the distance between us, backing me up against the kitchen counter.

His chest presses against my own, his head looking down to keep his eyes on me.

"So perfect. Your eyes, they are something special, *kratsoka*."

I try not to breathe through my nose as his breath fans across my face, the smell of vodka and mint intermingling and turning my stomach inside out.

"And your skin," he continues, as if he isn't even speaking to me but instead just talking out loud.

He reaches a tattooed hand out, brushing against my cheek when I quickly whip my head away, gnashing my teeth in reaction. In a flash, he has a gun to my head, pressing the cold steel right between my eyes.

"Careful, *kratsotka*. I don't tolerate disrespect."

My heart is hammering, my chest heaving as I keep my eyes on his, not moving a single muscle as I wait for his next move. I've never felt so close to death than at this moment. Not with Zayden in the cemetery, not even from all those nights at Jim's. This is different, the air is thick with danger and tension, and I can hardly fucking breathe.

Slowly, he drags the gun down my face, not removing it from my skin as he begins tracing a line down my cheek to my neck, settling over my breasts for several seconds before coming back up to my mouth.

"Open."

My jaw quivers, but slowly, I do as he says, parting my trembling lips as he pushes the barrel inside. He slowly begins pushing in and out of my mouth, forcing it so deep that I gag around the metal before he pulls back and does it again and again.

"You do so well, *malishka*. My boys are lucky indeed," he says as he forces it deeper than before.

I try to breathe around it, but it's practically blocking my airway. I feel a tear hit my cheek, slowly sliding down, but I don't react other than that. His eyes drop to it, tracking the path slowly before he leans forward, sticking his tongue out and catching it on the tip, drawing a long, slow line up my cheek all the way to my ear.

"Tell my boys to call me. We have business to discuss," he whispers roughly into my ear, his accent sending my stomach roiling as he lets his mouth linger on my skin for another moment before he pulls away, taking the gun with him.

I take a greedy breath now that my airway has been restored, and I watch as Maxim doesn't spare me another glance, easily opening the front door without even needing to use the scanner as he slips out of it.

My body stays frozen in place for several seconds, unable to move, to think, to process what the fuck just happened. I look down to see my hands are trembling, no, my whole body is. Before I know it, the floor is slipping out from under me, and I'm falling. I land on the floor with a rough bang, but I don't feel it.

I lay there trembling and shaking, curled up into the tightest ball possible as I focus on the bottom of the kitchen cabinets. I can't hear anything. I can't feel anything. All I can do is shake and stare.

CHAPTER FORTY-FIVE

ZAYDEN

I unlock the front door easily, pushing it open with a smile.

"Alright, angel. I got the whole damn cake, so you should be set for a—"

My words die on my tongue as I look to see the living room empty, TV still on. I frown at that, heading for the bedrooms. I check each one, all coming up empty.

"Angel? Angel! Where are you?" I begin to shout as I start running through the apartment.

My heart is racing but instantly settles when I find her in

the kitchen. Though it starts right back up again when I fully take her in. Dropping the bag in my hand to the floor, I fall to my knees as I crawl to her.

"Angel, what happened? What's wrong? Are you hurt?" I ask as I begin patting her down for injuries.

She's curled up in a ball, shaking like a leaf, not speaking, not even blinking. I push some hair out of her face and look to see her face is soaked with silent tears streaming down her face.

I lay flat on the floor, forcing her eyes to come into contact with me. I'm sure my own look terrified, I feel terrified.

"Sweetheart, talk to me. What's going on? What can I do?"

Her eyes finally come to mine, pain and fear mixing together in a heartbreaking combination. She lets out a gut-wrenching sob that stabs my heart. Her silence is gone, replaced by the horrific sounds of her painful cries. I scoop her into my arms, forcing her to straddle me as I lean my back against the oven. She buries her face in my neck as her arms wrap around me, holding on so tight it's almost painful. I want the pain, though. I'll take whatever pain she wants to throw at me with a fucking smile on my face.

I wrap my arms around her tightly, hoping the compression will help calm her down, but they only set her off more. Feeling panicked, I pat my pocket for my phone, pulling it out quickly, and call Dominic.

"I'm busy," Dominic answers in a hushed tone, no doubt in the middle of his meeting.

"She won't stop crying!" I shout hysterically. "I don't know what happened. I don't know what to do!"

I hear something crash and labored breathing as Dominic responds.

"I'm coming. Where are you? Is she hurt?"

"Home. I don't think so. I left to get her some cheesecake, and when I got back, she was like this."

The sound of Dominic's car firing up sounds in the background before the squealing of tires.

"I'm two minutes out," he grits out.

My angel lets out another soul-crushing cry, my grip on her tightening as if I could stop it from continuing if I just hold on tight enough.

"Put the phone up to her ear," he says.

I hold the phone beside her head as my brother talks in the softest tone I've ever heard come from him.

"Hey, babygirl. I'm on my way home. Okay? Just hold tight. I'll be there in less than a minute. I promise."

She lets out a cry that almost sounds like she says okay, but I can't be too sure. I lift the phone back up to my ear as I talk to him again.

"Have you checked her out for injuries?"

"Yes, of course. Externally, she's fine. Should we call Doc?" I ask before hearing the slam of a car door and Dominic's jostled breathing.

"I'm here. Coming up the stairs now!"

Ten seconds later, my brother blows in through the door, chest heaving as his head whips around, landing on us in an instant. He drops to the floor, crawling over to us as he wraps his arms around her.

"Baby, baby, baby," he coos softly. "What's wrong? What happened?"

She's hyperventilating, but she turns her head to face Dominic, sinking deeper into my chest than before as she stutters, "M-maa-xim."

My gut clenches as I look at my brother, whose eyes are still on my angel.

"Say that again?" he asks softly, though a steeliness has passed behind his eyes.

"Max-im. H-he w-was here. He-he—" She breaks off into another round of sobs, worst-case scenarios flashing before my eyes.

Dominic is pulling out his phone, his fingers flying over the screen as he no doubt pulls up the apartment's security cameras. I reach out for his phone, forcing him to turn it, so I can watch as well. Fury passes across Dominic's face when Maxim enters the room seconds after I leave. We watch the entire thing, my muscles tightening with each second.

My stomach turns when I watch him shove his loaded gun into her mouth, forcing tears to fall down her face before he licks them off her. As much as I want to look away, I don't allow myself, letting the anger I feel inside of me fuel me for what's next.

"Take her," I say stiffly.

Dominic looks at me with pure rage on his face as he stares on.

"TAKE HER!" I snarl before he does as I say, scooping her out of my arms as I leap to my feet.

GRAVES

I reach for the glass bowl on the counter, smashing it against the wall as I begin to spiral. I destroy anything and everything in sight, letting out an animalistic roar as I do. He knows about her, he's seen her, touched her. There is no more time for waiting, no more plans. He has to die. Right now.

Running down the hallway, I hear Dominic call out to me, but I don't waste my energy entertaining him. I enter the war room easily, loading a bag up with any and every weapon I can get my hands on before I'm tearing out of there.

My feet carry me to the front door quickly, and I have my hand on the knob when I hear a soft, broken voice call out to me.

"Don't go, p-please, Zay."

The sound shatters my barely beating heart, and I turn to see my angel's tear-filled eyes begging me. Doesn't she see I don't have a choice? That I have to go? I have to protect her, I'll die a hundred deaths before I let anything like this happen to her again. Still, I'm no match for those watery eyes and crestfallen face. I drop my bag to the ground, covering her back with my body as Dominic and I hold her between us.

"We've got you, angel. We'll take care of this. You're safe. You're always safe with us."

Dominic and I share a murderous look, our minds firmly made up. Prison or someone else taking him out won't do, not even close. He crossed a line, and now he will die a bloody death at our hands once and for all.

CHAPTER FORTY-SIX

DOMINIC

It took a while for Blake to calm down, and I understand why. Maxim can make the strongest men break with just a look. He pulled nearly every intimidation trick he could have with Blake, and she didn't waver. She was composed and calm until he left, then the dam burst, and rightfully so. She's so fucking strong, I don't even think she sees it. Zayden and I do, though.

Zayden ended up scooping her from my arms and carrying her into the bath. They just sat there silently as I massaged Blake's head, slowly lathering her hair until the water ran cold.

Afterwards, we got her dressed in comfortable clothes and tucked her into my new bed. I've been tired of staying in the spare bedroom or Zayden's room since mine is the largest in the house, and since there is no way Zayden would sleep without Blake for even a single night, I purchased an Alaskan King, the biggest and best on the market.

Blake is lying in between us, her head resting on my chest and her legs intertwined with Zayden's, before she breaks the silence.

"Is he the man? The one you've been worried about from the start?"

I share a look with my brother before turning to look at her beautifully mismatched eyes, giving her a tight nod. She lets out a disappointed sigh as her head nods.

"Makes sense. I get it now."

The room is quiet again for several more minutes before she swallows roughly.

"How do you guys know him? He's not from here, right? His accent..." She trails off, goosebumps smattering her skin as she does.

Zayden reaches over, rubbing his hand up and down her arms like he's trying to soothe them away. I know he won't talk about it. He never does, and part of me doesn't want to go there either, but a larger part of me knows it's important.

"The night our parents died. I didn't lie when I said I was the only one at the neighbors. I was. Zayden snuck out to follow them. We were nine, and he was too curious for his own good."

I pause, looking over to see Zayden spacing out, a tortured

look on his face as he stares blankly at the back of Blake's head.

"He followed them out of the apartment complex and one block over to their dealer's house. He hid in the bushes and peeked in through the side window. Zayden watched as our dad was getting high, his brother, our uncle, was trying to force himself on our mother." I grit my jaw, remembering the way Zayden recounted what he saw, what he felt, and how he wanted to help her but didn't know how. Peeking over at my hollow brother, I mourn who he used to be, who he was before that night.

"She fought with him, and then when the police barged in and guns started blazing, our uncle was too pissed Mom wouldn't give in, and he slit her throat, right then and there. Somehow he was able to sneak out the back before the cops could find him, and everyone else in the house died, so no one was sure who was in that house. Except for Zayden."

I pause for a moment, smiling sadly.

"You know she used to call us Dom and Zay? Never our full names. That's why it threw us so much when you started to. It felt...serendipitous."

Blake looks at me, her eyes practically drowning in empathy before she turns to face Zayden. He won't meet her eyes, though, so instead, she grabs his hands, wraps them around her waist and forces his head into her neck. I watch as he goes easily, doing whatever she asks of him, and I even notice his muscles relax the smallest amount when he smells her scent. It's something comforting, a basic human comfort, and the fact that she gets that about Zayden, especially, just proves how perfect she is for us.

"He was our only living relative, and since no one tied him to being there that night, he was given emergency custody of us. Knowing what we knew, though? What Zayden saw?" I shake my head as that day comes back to me, more vivid than I'd prefer.

The weeping friends, coworkers, and neighbors of our parents slowly start to leave once the caskets are lowered. The sun is setting fast, and the priest walks away with a sad shake of his head toward Zayden and me. I know that my cheeks are wet, but I don't want to wipe them away. That's my mama's job, but she can't do that anymore, and if she can't, no one will.

Zayden hasn't cried since the night they died, the night he ran home, bursting into the neighbor's apartment and found me. I've never seen anyone cry so hard.

Since then, though, not a drop has been found. He's angry instead and quiet.

We were moved into our uncle's house the next day, and we hate it. We can't stand being in the same home as our mother's killer. I tried to get Zayden to go to the police, tell them what he saw, but he said there was no point. That cops wouldn't believe a junkie's kid. Maybe he's right, but maybe they would believe him, and he can rot in prison. That seems too easy for him, though.

Slimy hands land on Zayden and my shoulders, a convincing sorrowful sound to his voice as he speaks to us.

"It's time to go home, boys. Say your goodbyes."

Anger fuels me as I stare at the holes in the ground where our parents now lie. The cops showing up may not have been his fault, but something tells me based on the way Zayden described things, our mother would have ended up here regardless. Probably our father too once he witnessed his own brother killing his wife.

Zayden and I share angry looks, and I notice that Zayden has something silver in his right hand. His knuckles are clenched around it, half of the knife hidden up the sleeve of his long shirt. His eyes are begging me to help him, and without hesitation, I do just that.

We move as one, and I spin around, stomping on his foot. It takes him by surprise before I punch my fist into his face as hard as I'm able. While he's disoriented, Zayden swings around, sinking the knife into his side. His mouth opens in shock, and he leaps for Zayden before I kick him in the balls. Dad always told me only cowards kick other men in the balls, it's not fair in a fight. There isn't anything fair about cutting open our mother's neck, though, so fuck fair.

He groans and cups himself, falling to the ground as Zayden stabs him in the back. Somehow, he's able to reach his hand around, gripping the handle of the knife and pulling it out. He swings it around, aiming for Zayden, when I leap on top of him. We wrestle with the knife, and I'm able to bend his wrist enough to force the blade toward him.

I put all of my muscle into pushing it into him, but I'm not strong enough. That is, until Zayden practically climbs onto my back, increasing my efforts as his hands come over mine. Together, we sink the blade into his chest, his mouth opening and making a croaking like noise for several seconds before he stops breathing.

Breathing heavily, I move to stand, and so does Zayden. We stare at our dead uncle's body for several seconds before Zayden leans forward, grabbing the knife out of his chest and putting it to his neck. His hand moves last, slicing a line straight across our uncle's neck. Blood squirts out from the move, soaking Zayden and my shirt, neither of us seem to mind, though.

Suddenly, a slow clapping sound comes from behind us, and fear grips me. Oh god. We're gonna go to jail. We just killed our uncle, and we've been caught. I look to Zayden, silently questioning if we should run. He doesn't give me anything, though. He just stares at me blankly as if he wasn't there anymore before we both turn to face our witness.

A tall man, wide as a building, with blond hair and silver eyes smiles down at us with a grin that turns my stomach. His hands are still clapping as his eyes look over Zayden and me from head to toe before looking at our uncle.

"Moi malchiki, that was impressive," he says, his thick accent making it hard to understand his words at first.

"Who are you?" I ask.

His eyes swing to me as he smirks.

"You can call me Maxim."

I sneer as I continue recounting the story, Blake's eyes unblinking as she stares at me, begging me to continue.

"He helped us move the body, took it to a local pig farm, and we watched as he was eaten completely within a matter of hours. Then he gave us a proposition. Go into foster care and more than likely be separated or come live with him. Train under him. Work for him."

Blake frowns. "You guys were only nine, though."

I nod. "The perfect grooming age, according to Maxim. Obviously, we chose to stay together, and Maxim legally adopted us. We were moving out of the US and into Russia practically overnight. For four years, we trained seven days a week, fourteen hours a day, and on our thirteenth birthday, we were sent on our first job."

Her beautifully full lips part in disbelief as she looks back to Zayden, who is seemingly coming out of his haze.

"How long did you guys work for him?" she asks him, no doubt testing to see if she can get him to talk about this.

He doesn't say anything for a while before he begins running his fingers through her hair.

"Until we were eighteen. Dominic had been planning our escape for years, and he was able to arrange fake deaths for us. We were careful for years, never using our real names until recently, when we knew he had no doubt forgotten about us."

"Why use your names at all? Why not ensure he never finds you by changing altogether?" Blake asks.

Zayden doesn't respond for a moment or two before he shrugs.

"They were just strung-out junkies, but they loved us with everything they were capable of. To let the name die felt like a—"

"Dishonor," I finish for him.

He nods his agreement as Blake smiles sadly.

"And he's the friend you called from prison?" she asks Zayden before he nods. "And what, now he's showing up at your house, asking you guys to call him?"

I frown at that. "That's what he said? That he wants us to call him?"

She nods. "Why? Is that weird?"

"Yeah," Zayden says. "I talk to him often. He even calls Dominic once in a while."

"So, he just said that as an excuse for why he was here?"

"Definitely," Zayden and I say.

"Well, then what does he want? Why did he come?"

"Oh, I'm sure he does want us to call him. I think he also wanted to get a look at you in person, assess you. He doesn't view you as a person, he views you as a bargaining chip, property, something to be lorded over our heads."

She cringes at that, staying quiet for several seconds.

"So, what do we do?"

"We do nothing," I say. "You are on total lockdown until we can kill him."

"You guys are going to kill him?"

"Of course," Zayden scoffs as I continue. "It's the only way for all of us to stay safe forever, baby."

I cup the side of her face, and she blinks up at me.

"I'm so sorry for the pain you've suffered."

Turning on her side, she faces Zayden as she speaks to him as well.

"I'm so sorry you saw what you did. That you lived through literal hell with no one to be there and hold you through it."

His arms tighten around her, to the point I'm concerned he will hurt her before he nods tersely.

"I have you now, angel. Everything happened so that I could hold you in my arms. I don't regret a thing."

She smiles sadly, knowing that isn't the truth. I think it's

Zayden's truth, but in the grand scheme of things, she doesn't believe him, and that's okay. Her lips come to Zayden's, their kiss slow and passionate at first, as if she was trying to heal all of his pain with this kiss.

I curl my body around her, hugging her as close to me as I can when she breaks the kiss with Zayden, pressing her lips to my mouth as he transitions to her neck. We sandwich her between us, and she groans in pleasure as she rests one hand on each of us.

"Use me," she murmurs against my lips. "Both of you. Let me take the pain away, at least for a little while."

I smile sadly at my sweet girl. Her heart is so big, so big for us, and as she brushes her ass against my cock, it's rock solid and ready for that tight little ass. I love being in her warm cunt too, but there is something about being buried in her ass that does something to me. My tip leaks a bead of precum just at the thought of it.

Pressing one more kiss to her, I push her toward Zayden, allowing him to entertain her while I make quick work of my clothes. They begin devouring each other. Blake is in her sleep shorts and tank top while Zayden, ever the confident man that he is, is laying there naked from the bath. I watch as Blake grinds herself against Zayden, whimpering as his cock rubs over her clit even through her clothes.

Once my clothes are on the floor, I slip behind her once more, hooking my fingers into her waistband and peeling the shorts down her legs until I'm greeted with her perfect bare skin. She's still dry-humping Zayden, which is fine by me because I want to get her prepped for me anyway.

Cupping the bottom of her full ass in either hand, I spread her apart for me before lowering my face, resting my tongue against her pussy before dragging my tongue all the way through her until I land on her asshole. She shudders against me as she arches her lower back, encouraging me to do it again. I oblige, licking her from cunt to ass over and over again until I just start eating her ass.

Slipping a finger inside her pussy, I lick and suck on her while Zayden grinds against her clit. It's enough to have her moaning and panting with every touch until I take my finger that is now soaked from her pussy and push it into her ass. There is a little resistance without the lube, but something about her taking me with only her own arousal easing the way is so goddamn hot.

Her body tenses at the intrusion, and she lets out a strangled breath.

"Zayden, play with her pussy," I say, and he happily complies, pushing two fingers inside of her as I slowly get her to relax around my finger.

Eventually, she begins moaning again and even starts moving against my hand. I gather enough saliva in my mouth, spitting directly onto her beautiful ass before pushing another finger inside her. She's panting heavily, and I know she's about to come, so I stop my movements and Zayden does the same.

"Wh-what's going on?" she whines. "Make me come!"

"We will, angel, but we want to play some more first."

"But you always give me several orgasms," she pouts,

causing me to let out a chuckle as I press a kiss to her back.

"Patience, babygirl. A little edging never hurt anyone."

"I'm pretty sure it has. They don't call it blue balls and blue ovaries for nothing."

I roll my eyes at her but can't contain my smirk. I look over her shoulder at Zayden, gesturing for us to roll, and he nods in agreement. I slowly ease my fingers out of her, moving to lay propped up against the headboard on my back. I wait as Zayden rolls them, plastering Blake to my chest as he covers her.

My hands go to Blake's hips, and I lift them up until I get the right angle before I grab the lube from my bedside table. As much as I'd love to see how wet I can get her, how much I can use to fuck her ass, I want this to be pleasurable for her. So, I gather a good amount onto my fingers, circling her asshole a few times before I push two fingers back inside of her.

"Fuck," she groans.

I only push in and out of her a few times. Her muscles relaxed and more than ready for me as I pull out once more, and line her up. She begins to whimper, I'm assuming in protest, until she feels the head of my cock on her. When I push her down, it takes a moment for her muscles to relax enough to let me in.

Letting her set the pace, I allow her to slowly sink down onto me, inch by inch, until my base is nestled in between her ass cheeks. I groan at the feeling, my fingers digging into the front of her hips as she half sits, half lies on me.

"My turn." Zayden smirks before lining his cock up to her pussy and pushing inside.

She gasps at that, her back trying to lift off of me in an attempt to flee from the pressure. I don't allow her to though, pinning her against me as Zayden slowly works himself inside of her.

When she's completely stuck between us, I begin pressing light kisses to her neck as Zayden leans forward and begins sucking on her nipples.

"Oh god, yes," she groans as we slowly begin fucking her.

Our pace is languid and gentle when her lust-drunk eyes come to me.

"I told you I wanted you to use me, this feels like you two are worshiping me."

"We do, baby," I say as I cup her face gently.

She shakes her head at that.

"Worship me another day. Use me today."

My cock throbs at her words, the temptation to fuck her until her asshole is raw is strong, so strong. She seems to decide she's going to take matters into her own hands, though, because she grabs my hand on her face, lowering it to her throat and forcing me to squeeze. Fuck. I love the feeling of her slim throat in my palm. It's so fragile, so breakable, and it makes me feel like a god that I have the power to decide whether she breathes or not, lives or not.

Without meaning to, my thrusts become deeper, more frantic, and the beast inside of me beats its chest at the pleasure it gives me.

CHAPTER FORTY-SEVEN

BLAKE

I do my best to swallow back the painful cry I want to release as Dom begins fucking my ass so hard I see stars. He needs this, I need this. We all do. My eyes come to Zayden, who is still fucking me gently.

"Where is your knife, Zay?"

He frowns at that. "Nightstand. Why?"

"Get it," I say.

He pauses for a moment, slowly pulling out of me before he grabs it. It's the same knife he's used on me before, obviously his favorite, and when he flicks the blade out, fear clenches inside of me. I push it away, though, as I speak.

"Use me."

For some reason, he hesitates, shaking his head as he sinks his cock back inside me.

"Not today, angel. You don't need it today."

"You do, though. All that anger is still inside of you, Zay. From your parents, your childhood, from today. You need this, and I need you to have it. Let it out, make me bleed."

He closes his eyes tightly, a hazy look taking over when he opens the knife again. Zayden begins tracing my skin with it like he always does, the sharpness of the blade a mere tease for what's to come. Goosebumps erupt across my skin regardless, as he drags it over my nipples and between my breasts.

Dom's grip on my throat tightens as he grunts and groans through his own trauma and horrors. They are everything for me, everything to me, and I want to be everything to them, even in the darkest of times.

Without warning, Zayden slices my stomach just to the side of my belly button. I wince as I look down at the four-inch cut. Fuck, I think that's the biggest he's ever done before. Blood immediately comes to the surface, and he leans down, his tongue licking at the seam. It stings at first, but the pleasured groans that come from him make it worth it.

He lifts his face up, his lips tinged red before he greedily licks at them, his thumb coming to the cut, massaging over it lightly like it's my clit. Maybe it is because, for some fucked-up reason, it makes my pussy pulse, that pain and pleasure overwhelming me as Dom continues fucking me like he's trying to ruin me.

"Do you like being cut up, baby? Does it feel good?" Dom asks in my ear.

"Yes," I moan. "I like what it does to Zay. He goes feral for me, and it fucking soaks me," I moan as Zayden makes another cut beneath it, smaller this time, but it bleeds quite a bit all the same.

Zay stares at the blood, completely entranced, as he fucks me deeper than before.

"So perfect, angel. So goddamn perfect," he grits through clenched teeth lifting the knife to his mouth, running his tongue along the bloodied blade as he does.

Something about this moment shakes a memory loose from the first time I experienced this, something he said. The words spill from my mouth as I moan, "Mark me, Zay."

His thrusts skip a beat as he looks down at me, his clear, crystal blue eyes practically a dark indigo right now.

"What do you mean, angel?"

"Make me yours. Mark me forever, please," I beg.

His eyes practically roll into the back of his head like that is the most erotic thing he's ever heard before he lowers the knife.

"Right here," I say over my heart. "Just like your tattoo. I want to match you."

He hesitates for a moment before he cups my left breast, lifting it up and pushing the tip of the blade against the skin, just a hair beneath it. It's lower than his, and I want to say that when he speaks.

"I don't want anyone to see it but us, it's only us, angel."

In the next moment, the knife bites into my skin, causing my body to clench and both of the men to groan as I do. Fuck, fuck, fuck. It hurts way more than the other little cuts, but I don't think Zayden would stop even if I asked him to right now, he's power- and blood-drunk as I look down and watch him carve a perfect Z into my skin.

"And a D," I grit through clenched teeth.

Dom's thrusts falter as I turn to look at him.

"Mark me for Dom too, please."

Zay watches me for a moment before nodding, cutting a D right beside it. Once he's done, Zayden presses his hand over the Z, and I feel Dom's hand come around me to cover the D.

"Even in death, forever mine," Zayden says.

"Forever ours," Dominic agrees.

I nod my head as my orgasm begins to creep up on me. Zayden's other hand reaches down and begins rubbing my clit, causing me to pant out my words.

"Forever."

His hand slaps down across my clit in the next second, forcing a scream out of me as my entire body tenses and both Dom and Zay to release.

We all still as one, heavy breathing and sweaty skin, Zayden presses his lips to mine before forcing me to turn my head to Dominic, kissing him right after. I can't think of an easier promise I've ever made in my life. There isn't anywhere or anyone I'd rather be with, ever. No matter what happens, I know that will never change. I'm forever theirs, I always have been.

CHAPTER FORTY-EIGHT

BLAKE

It's been two days since Maxim came to the house. After we all got cleaned up, Dom headed for the office. He said he needed to pick some things up before he came back to the house. Once he was back, he locked himself inside his office at the apartment and refused to come out.

I ordered lunch, because it's not a secret that I'm a shit cook, before I knock on the door. He doesn't answer, and the door is locked. I frown at that when Zayden walks by, raising a curious eyebrow.

"Is my angel in need of some lockpicking lessons?"

I laugh at that. "Of course you know how to pick a lock."

He nods like that is obvious before he runs into his bedroom, coming out with a small plastic case with several metal pins of varying-lengths. Zay explains how each lock is different and needs different tools and angles, but with practice, it will become second nature. He shows me how to feel around for the locking mechanism and how to push it back, accidentally unlocking the door himself.

Quickly, he pokes his head inside, grabbing the handle.

"Zayden, get the fuck out," Dom growls.

"We weren't ready! It's my angel's turn. One second," he says as he locks the door from the inside and shuts it once more.

"Your turn," he says as he hands me the pins.

I attempt to mimic his moves, but it takes me at least four times longer, and it's not done as well by any means. When I hear that satisfying click, though, pride swells inside of me as I push the door open, grinning like a maniac as Dom stares at me with an exhausted yet small smirk.

Bending down, I grab the food I ordered for him as I walk into the room.

"Pick your first lock?" Dom asks.

I jump up onto his desk, handing him his burger and fries as I nod.

"Yep."

He gives me a quick wink as he cups my thigh and opens his food with his other hand.

"I'm proud of you, and thank you, baby," he says as he picks up the burger, brushing his thumb against my leg as he eats.

When he leans forward, his shirt shifts, a small amount of what looks like plastic peeking through. I frown at that, unbuttoning his top two buttons.

"What—"

There is a fresh tattoo right over Dominic's heart, right where Zayden's is. It's a black-and-white daffodil with my name twisted around the stem. My eyes begin to water as I look up to him.

"Is this your first tattoo?"

He nods quietly. "Do you like it?"

I scoff at that, a laugh falling from my lips.

"Like it? I love it. You didn't have to do that, though."

"I wanted to. I couldn't think of a better first tattoo."

Leaning down, I press a kiss to his lips, sighing against him as he drags me into his lap. I wrap my arms around his neck while I straddle him before pulling away and resting my head against his shoulder.

"Why haven't you taken a break? You've been in here for days," I murmur.

His hand runs up and down my back as he speaks.

"It's important work."

"Are you almost done? Do you have a plan?" I ask.

He nods as I pull back to look at him.

"I do."

I wait for him to elaborate, but he doesn't, at least not for a solid minute before he blows out a breath and shouts.

"Zayden, get in here."

Zay comes strolling in, leaning against the wall as he groans.

"Bout fucking time. What do you got?"

"I found an itinerary change in Maxim's private plane schedule. He's got a flight to LA in four days. I cross matched the dates with his email and found a hotel reservation."

I expect him to say more, but he doesn't. Apparently he doesn't need to, because Zayden nods at that and claps his hands together.

"Alright, four days."

"Four days," Dom agrees. "I've contacted Precision Security. They are going to send a guy over to watch the place while we are gone."

"We?" I ask. "As in both of you?"

The brothers share a look between each other before both looking at me.

"It has to be this way. We both started with him," Dom says.

"And we are both going to end him," Zay finishes.

Something about this twists my stomach. I don't like knowing they will both be gone. Both be in danger. What if they need help? They don't have backup, the eye in the sky. Nothing. They could walk in on an ambush with no reinforcements.

"Hey," Dom says, pulling my eyes to his as he cups my cheeks. "We are going to make it through this together. I promise."

I swallow roughly and give him my most convincing smile. It still doesn't sit well with me, though.

CHAPTER FORTY-NINE

ZAYDEN

"I miss you." Her soft words are like the sweetest melody to my ears.

"I miss you too, angel. I can't wait to hold you when all of this is over," I say as Dominic and I are standing on the second story of Maxim's hotel, overlooking the reception area.

"I can't wait for that too. Will you tell Dom that I love him?"

I roll my eyes at her, not able to fight the flicker of irritation that she didn't deem it necessary to tell me that she loves me first.

"What about me?" I scoff, making no apologies for sounding like a pouty child.

Her smile is practically audible through the phone as she speaks.

"Aw, Zay. Are you feeling left out?"

"Yes," I state simply.

She laughs at that before sighing.

"I love you, Zayden. More than I should, more than I knew I'd ever be capable of. I love you so much it physically hurts to be away from you."

The normally limp beating of my heart goes into overtime at her words, an overwhelming sense of satisfaction filling me as I grin.

"That's better. I love you, angel. More than my next breath, more than this entire planet. I'd happily sacrifice every man, woman, and child if it meant protecting you, keeping you."

"Okay, that's a bit much. That's over seven billion murders, Zay." She laughs.

"All of them, gone," I state seriously.

Dominic shakes his head, and I send him a warning glare but don't engage when he bumps my arm. I look down to see Maxim and two men walking up to the concierge desk. Perfect.

"Got to go, baby. Stay inside. Keep your security outside."

With that, I end the call, and Dom and I head for the room. We already swiped a maid's key card, and as soon as we step out of our hidden alcove away from cameras, we slip on our masks, leaving nothing to chance despite Dom already playing a loop over the footage.

Moving into the elevator, we hit the penthouse button, easily being taken up to the top floor before we slip inside. We've already studied the suite extensively and decided the longer we wait to do this, the higher the risk for things to go wrong.

Dominic moves to the bathroom just inside of the front entrance while I take up residence behind the back-facing couch. I'll take out at least the first security guard that will undoubtedly step out first, Dom will grab up the second, and the rest we are planning on the fly since we know better than to expect anything from Maxim. He's one of the most unpredictable humans that has ever lived, hence why he's still alive.

I watch as Dominic peeks out around the corner, sharing a nod with me as he cocks his gun. Usually I prefer knives, and though I have plenty on me, a gun is more sensible in this instant. Dominic tucks himself away just before the elevator doors whir open. I don't hesitate, shooting a bullet straight into the head of the first security guard. He drops to the floor as Dominic darts out, snapping the other's neck before he can even reach for his gun.

Leaping over the couch, I run toward Dominic, where he now has Maxim pinned on his stomach to the floor. I push the gun to the back of his head as I chuckle.

"I've been waiting a long fucking time for this. I'd say it's been a pleasure, but I know how much you hate liars."

"P-please don't hurt me," the man whimpers.

Dominic and I share panicked looks. Maxim would never beg, ever. The other problem is that it's not Maxim's voice, it's not even Russian. My brother flips him to his back, our eyes rounding as we see a stranger before us. From behind, he looks identical to Maxim, literally. Same height, build, and hairstyle. What the fuck!

"Where is he!" I snarl as I press the gun to his throat.

"I-I don't know. These thugs picked me up when I was running in the park. They told me they'd kill my kids if they didn't cooperate. They just said I had to check into this room for a few days. I'm sorry! I'm sorry!" he weeps.

Fuck. Fuck. Fuck. Fuck.

I look up to see Dominic already on the phone, no doubt calling my angel. I stare at him anxiously, waiting for him to sigh in relief, for him to start talking to her, but he doesn't. The phone rings and rings before he hangs up.

His fingers fly across the phone, pulling up the live stream of our security cameras. Each room is empty, and he pulls up a different screen, watching the events play out. Sped up, I watch as two thugs kill the security guard outside the door, busting down the door and chasing after my girl.

She runs as fast as she can, grabbing a steak knife on the counter as she does.

Good girl. Get a weapon.

They are too fast, though. They tackle her to the ground, and when she stabs one of them in the leg, the other smashes her face into the floor. I let out a roar at the sight as they lift her like a rag doll, forcing a cloth to her face before she quickly goes limp and they carry her out the door.

In the next instant, Dominic's phone is shattering apart

on the wall. He lets out a feral shout that I thought only I was capable of before turning to the decoy man, wrapping his gloved hands around his neck, and snapping roughly.

His chest is heaving and his hands are shaking as he faces me.

"Where would he have taken her?"

I have an idea. I just hope I'm wrong.

CHAPTER FIFTY

BLAKE

The smell of something like acetone is the last thing I remember. It was slightly sweeter, almost like a cleaner of sorts. I remember smelling it, and then...nothing. I feel myself slowly trying to pull out of whatever haze I've been put under, but it's hard, so fucking hard.

My head lulls limply in front of me, forcing a tired groan out of me. I try to push my hair out of my face, but my arms are stuck, trapped. Slowly, understanding begins to hit me, and I muster up the strength to open my eyes. I find a ceiling, not just any ceiling, a crown-molded extravagant ceiling with a crystal chandelier.

I slowly allow my gaze to travel down the cream walls, coming to the large bed I'm lying on. No, tied to. Each of my hands is tied to the headboard. My legs aren't tied, and I should be grateful for that, but the fact that I'm completely naked gives me no such comfort.

"Good morning, *kratsoka*." A chilling voice smiles from a lavish chair in the corner.

"Maxim," I whisper on a choked breath, yanking at my restraints, only to find them tightening with each movement I make.

My eyes whip around wildly, landing on a tall man in a black suit. He's standing in the doorway, his hands folded and his eyes forward. I beg him with my own to save me, spare me, anything. However, he won't even look in my direction.

Maxim chuckles a filthy sound filling up the room as he does.

"Good try. My men are quite faithful to me. They wouldn't dare sign their death certificates for a pretty pussy."

He stands up to his full height, striding toward me as he smirks in a way that flips my stomach and chills my bones.

"Though I have to say, it is a very, very pretty pussy," he says, his hand reaching out to touch me.

I snap my legs closed, forcing them to the other side of the bed as fast as I can. He doesn't look irritated by my move, more amused than anything. Like he expected it, like he was testing me. I'm not sure if I passed or failed. I'm not sure if I wanted to pass or fail.

"Where am I?" I ask.

His eyes come to me, raising an unimpressed eyebrow.

"Did your mother not teach you manners, *kratsoka*?"

I clench my teeth in irritation.

"Please," I grit out. "Where am I?"

A satisfied smile curls across his face as he spreads out his arms.

"My home. How do you like it so far?"

"It's a little cold," I snark, goose bumps covering my body, though I'm not sure it's just from the temperature in the room.

He barks out a laugh as he scratches his beard.

"Yes, that is Russia for you."

Panic rushes through me. Russia? I'm in fucking Russia?! Oh my fucking god.

Taking another step closer to me, he shakes his head reverently.

"You really are a spitting image of your mother."

My brows furrow at that as I look at him.

"You knew my mother?"

"Very well." He smirks. "You have her nipples, the perfect rosy shade," he says, leaning over the bed and tweaking my left nipple between his thumb and forefinger painfully.

I do my best not to react, not to give him the satisfaction, but that only seems to egg him on. He palms my breast, squeezing until I whimper in pain. As soon as I cry out, he smiles but it falls almost immediately. His other hand comes to the skin under my breast, brushing against the healing skin, and a thunderous look crosses his face.

"You let them mark you?"

"Of course I—"

My words can't be finished, a sharp slap snapping my head to the side as he fumes above me.

"I'm very disappointed in you, *kratsoka*. I'm going to have to punish you for this."

I don't respond, which seems to be the right move at the moment because his anger seems to dissipate as he grips my cheeks, forcing me to face him.

"It's amazing you have her eyes, such a rare beauty."

"How exactly did you know my—"

I stop midsentence, worst-case scenarios fluttering through my mind. No. There is no way.

"Yes, *kratsoka*." He smiles, that sinister way he seems to have perfected over his lifetime. "It's been far too long since I've seen her. Having you here is like a serendipitous reunion."

My stomach rolls and saliva pools in my mouth, my body feeling the need to retch instantly. I do my best to swallow it back before I look away from him, squeezing my eyes shut.

"You're the man she had an affair with. The reason my father killed her and himself."

A darkness passes across his face as he practically snarls at me.

"That worthless pig was a coward! Your mother was getting ready to move here when he took her from me."

I shake my head. He's lying. There is no way. I was only six when my mother died, but I remember enough about her. She was warm and kind. There is absolutely no way she would have fallen in love with this monster of a man, no way she would have left me behind. I don't believe him.

"How did you even meet her? She was a secretary."

"For one of my business partners, yes. I'd worked with Harold for years. He handled all of my...assets in Chicago. One day I came in for an annual meeting and saw her." He pauses for a moment, an almost wistful look on his face as he stares at the wall to his left.

"I pursued her for months and she denied me at every turn. She was certainly a force," he smirks almost to himself before his smile drops, that stone cold killer mask back in place.

"I'm sure you wouldn't believe it, but your mother was the only woman I ever loved. Her death hurt me deeply, and even at that age, you were an exact replica of her. I always kept eyes on you, though. Even sent my brother Ivan to the States to look after you."

I stare at him before laughing in his face.

"Ivan?! You mean, Slinky? Oh yeah, he took great care of me. Especially when he'd rape me into the concrete floor, tearing and beating me until I was bloody!" I shout, waiting for his anger or shock.

Surprisingly, he remains completely impassive as he speaks.

"Was he not a man? There is only so much time you can spend around someone of your beauty and not do something about it."

My mind reels at his words. What the actual fuck? Disgust,

pain, and so much confusion rip through me as I let out a pain-filled scream, breaking into a rough sob as I do. Maxim stands there, watching me stoically until my sobs have quieted. I sniff as I look up at him through watery eyes before he begins speaking again.

"When the Graves brothers took an interest in you, I thought it would be the perfect opportunity to get them back in my reach. I had only learned of their supposed survival after Zayden began following you. Imagine my surprise when I find out my two most promising proteges had become infatuated with my ex-lover's daughter. The coincidence is fantastic." He smiles with a gnash of his teeth.

"Then Zayden made it all too easy, getting himself thrown in prison for you and coming crawling to me for a way out while Dominic fucked you instead of answering his calls." Maxim laughs.

"So, what happened? Why am I here? I'm not much leverage when you've taken me from them."

He nods his agreement.

"I quickly realized how deep their infatuation for you truly ran. They wouldn't allow me to use you as leverage, they would kill me before they did. Look what they did to my brother just for retribution in your name," he says with a pained glare, looking away as if he were trying to hide the fact that he's upset his brother is dead.

When he turns back to me, all of his emotion is wiped clean again as he levels his eyes on mine.

"They have become liabilities, and now they will come to

me, on my own property for you, and I will behead them before they can even set eyes on you."

His words scare the living shit out of me, mainly because I know he isn't bluffing. The guys will absolutely stop at nothing to find me, to try to get me back. When they do, they will be walking into their own death trap. I wish I could tell them, beg them not to come for me, to forget me. My fate is already sealed, it sounds like it has been from conception, but theirs doesn't have to be.

Maxim's hand begins drifting across my skin, skating down my stomach before slipping beneath my ass, kneading it in his hands.

"Wh-at are you doing? Don't touch me!"

"*Krasotka*, I told you. What is a man expected to do when such beauty is laid out before him like a feast?"

"You're disgusting! What the fuck do you think you're doing?"

"Reminisce about the past in your body until you're no longer of any use to me."

Tears spring to my eyes as his hand skates around to cup my pussy, forcing my thighs apart no matter how hard I try to keep them together.

"P-please. Don't do this. I'm her daughter. Y-you loved her, right? She wouldn't want you to do this."

"Mmm, you are. Let's hope you have your mother's cunt," he says before peeling my thighs open more, preparing to shove a finger inside me.

Before he can, the guard from the door comes up behind

him, hitting him in the back of the head with the butt of his gun. He hits him again and again until Maxim falls to the ground. My eyes look up to the intimidating man, my body shaking as he stands over me.

I try to choke out words, to ask him what's going on when he pulls out a knife, slicing me free from my restraints, before offering me a pair of sweatpants that are four sizes too big and a T-shirt that drowns me.

Silently, I get dressed quickly before he takes my elbow, guiding me to the door.

"What are you doing? Where are you taking me?" I finally ask.

He opens the door, sticking his head out and looking both ways before pulling me with him.

"Away." His thick Russian accent rolls.

"Why?" I whisper, unsure if there are others around.

"Dominic has secured my loyalties."

Dom. My sweet, brilliant man. Relief begins to slowly consume the gut-wrenching fear inside of me when the man escorts me to a running car in the front driveway. He opens the back door, holding it for me before looking from side to side.

"Thank y—"

Pop. Pop. Pop.

Suddenly, the man's body is riddled with bullet holes. His body jerks in response before collapsing to the ground. Three guards similarly dressed close in on us, or, I guess, me, before shooting the awaiting driver in the front. They begin yelling at me in Russian, and I don't speak a lick of it, but I have enough common sense to show them my hands and get on my knees.

My arms shake as I sink to the floor, knowing that the best chance I had at escape has now slipped through my fingers. Not only will I not make it out of this, if Dom and Zay come for me, I don't think they will either.

CHAPTER FIFTY-ONE

BLAKE

My legs and arms are tied now. I'm strapped to a chair, much like how Zayden tied Jim up. I'm not in the bedroom anymore, but instead in some kind of musty basement. The room around me is a literal jail cell with bars and everything, and I even spot a puddle of fresh blood on the ground.

I sit down here, for I don't know how long until the opening of the cell has my head whipping up, only to have me sinking back into the chair as far as I can, desperate to put as much room between us as possible.

When Maxim moves through the room, I don't see the extent of his injuries until the moonlight catches on his face, revealing a rapidly swelling and bleeding face. His jaw is granite, eyes manic as he winds back his fist and punches me across the face. He hits me again and again until I'm spitting out blood before gripping a handful of the sweatshirt. He yanks me toward him as close as I can go while still being strapped to the chair.

"You stupid fucking bitch! I don't know how you got him to turn on me, but make no mistake, I'm going to enjoy destroying you more than my fucking brother ever did."

He pulls out a knife, cutting a line in the crotch of my sweatpants before pulling out his alarmingly small cock. He lowers himself to line up with me when a knife sinks into his shoulder, pausing his movements as he stumbles. Another knife sinks into his shoulder, a few inches shy of his throat, before Zayden runs into the room, like the devil himself, nothing but wrath and murder covering his features.

Dominic is right on his heels, his eyes coming to me first. I must look pretty bad because the look he gives me is one of absolute horror and devastation before it quickly turns to rage. Zayden closes the distance between him and Maxim just as Maxim yanks one of the knives out of his shoulder and swings at Zayden. He dodges Maxim's swing easily, but the evil monster doesn't stop, backing Zayden against the wall as he continues to land hit after hit.

I feel hands come to my own, a knife freeing me for the second time today.

"Babygirl. Are you hurt? Fuck, of course you are. Can you walk?" he asks as he slices the bindings holding my feet together.

"Yes. I just—"

Dominic lifts me into his arms, throwing me over his shoulder regardless as he turns to leave.

"Wait! Zayden!" I shout.

Dominic shakes his head. "This is the plan. Hold on tight, babygirl. I'm gonna get us out of here."

I begin thrashing against him, screaming and shouting for him to put me down. Just as we are about to crest out of view, I watch as Maxim sinks a knife into Zayden's leg, forcing him to let out a rough growl. I scream in response, forcing Dominic to stop.

"Zayden! Help him! We have to help him!" I shout.

He hesitates for a moment before setting me down.

"Stay here," he says before he runs back into the cell, tackling Maxim to the ground before he can hurt Zayden again.

Zayden's eyes frantically go from his brother, landing on me instantly. Those bright blue eyes widen as he screams at me.

"RUN! Get out of here!"

But like hell am I leaving them to die. If they die, I die. I run back toward them as Zayden tries to stand before he collapses. He must be hurt really badly.

Looking at Dominic, I see him and Maxim wrestling with a gun before a shot rings out. My heart stops when I see blood beginning to pour from Dom's shoulder. He presses his hand to it tightly, but the blood is pouring through his fingers. Maxim kicks him for good measure before standing, looking down at

Zayden and Dom, gun in hand, before he swings his wild eyes to me.

"Perfect, come here."

I know better than to defy him at this moment. Slowly, I make my way to him as he speaks.

"You seemed to have trouble choosing, so here is your chance. Who should I kill first? Dominic? Or Zayden?" he asks, pointing the gun at both of the guys.

I shake my head, tears pouring down my face.

"Please, please don't do this. Don't hurt them. Please," I beg.

He snarls at me, shaking his head. "You're so weak. Are you sure you were her daughter?"

Maxim levels the gun toward them, and I just react. I jump in front of him, gripping the gun in an attempt to change its direction. Unfortunately, I'm not fast enough, and the bang that sounds is deafening. Everything quiets, though I hear two screams that tear my soul in two. I feel as if life is moving in slow motion as I look up to see Maxim's surprised expression.

Gripping the muzzle like Zayden taught me, I take advantage of Maxim's surprise, hitting his hand as hard as I can and forcing his hold on the gun to break. I twist the gun in my hand, firing blindly until the gun runs out of bullets before I fall to the ground.

My eyes land on a body in front of me, and something fulfilling replaces the pain for a moment as I see Maxim's dead eyes. Two holes in his head and one in his chest. That's one dead piece of shit.

Zayden and Dominic both drag themselves to me, pinning me between them as Zayden rips his shirt off, pressing it against my sternum. I inhale a pained breath as he does, and I look to see Dominic shaking his head, his mouth moving quickly. A few seconds go by before the ringing in my ears subsides, and I'm able to focus on the words.

"Baby, baby, baby! NO! No," he sobs as one of his bloodied hands begins pushing my hair away from my face.

"FUCK! She's bleeding too much!" Zayden shouts. "I-I don't know what to do! What do I do?!" he screams in panic to Dominic, who continues sobbing over me.

I want to tell them how much I love them. How I don't want them to worry about me. How they made my shit life worth living, no matter how short our time was together. I want to tell them how I'm so thankful that they tried, how lucky I feel to have their love, but I don't think I could physically say any of that, so instead, I settle for what I can.

"Even i-in deat-th. Foreve-r y-yours," I rasp before I begin coughing, blood filling my mouth as Zayden and Dominic begin screaming.

"No, baby. No! Keep your eyes open! Keep your goddamn eyes open!"

"Angel, please! Please don't leave me!" Zayden cries, tears hitting my arm as he does.

I want to tell them I don't want to leave, but I don't have a choice. I'm out of time, though. Everything turns dark and my eyelids flicker before the breath in me is stolen and I fade away, loving them with my absolute dying breath.

EPILOGUE

DOMINIC

It's the six-month anniversary of that night, and I don't think it will ever not be painful. I still wake up in a cold sweat, the look on her pale face permanently ingrained in my brain. The guilt will never not be there. If I would have been smarter, faster. If we would have been there ten minutes sooner, would it have made a difference? The what-if game is a mentally disparaging one, but it's one I'll never not play. Not when it was her.

Finding out that Maxim was the reason for Blake's parents' deaths was something that shook us both. The way he sanctioned his brother to rape her for years and no doubt had plans to do the same to her given the chance. The only peace I hold from that day is that he is rotting in hell, at the hands of my babygirl, no less.

Zayden was never the same from that day, rightfully so. He told her from the beginning, if she ever died, he would die. I think we all died that day.

A pair of lips presses against my neck, and I look away from the ocean in front of me to the beauty above. Her perfect smile spreads as she drops herself into my lap, her blue eye practically sparkling in the San Diego sunlight.

"You're looking entirely too serious over here," she teases, pressing another kiss to my jaw line.

I wrap my arms around her, one of my hands palming her stomach, brushing my thumb against the long scar separating either side of her sternum to her chest. We almost lost her that day, honestly, I'm pretty sure we did for a while.

Zayden gave her CPR while I held pressure to try to keep as much blood in her as possible. We had already called in some contacts for backup when we arrived, and to our luck, they arrived within a minute of Blake taking what I thought would be her last breath. Would have been nice if they would have shown up before we had to take out all of Maxim's men before we could even get down there, but it all worked out, I guess.

A doctor came with the reinforcements, and we were able to bandage Blake up enough and keep her heart pumping long enough for us to get her to a hospital. Zayden did compressions for over forty-five minutes, and he had to be physically pried off her by five hospital security officers.

We ended up being forced to be seen for our injuries, which seemed so small in comparison. I had a through-and-through shot to the shoulder, and Zayden happened to get hit in the same leg he was shot in last time. When the cops came around, one of our contacts was able to all but waive them off, and I'm grateful for that. In the moment, I wouldn't have doubted Zayden would shoot them dead in the middle of the hospital. Hell, maybe I would have been the one to pull the trigger.

Blake ended up being in surgery for over six hours, and they said she coded twice on the table. Thankfully, they were able to bring her back after having to repair a punctured lung, two fractured ribs, and a cardiac tamponade. The doctors were not overly confident she would wake up, which destroyed a piece inside Zayden and me both.

When she did open her eyes, we wept, literally. It was as if we had been given a second chance, the most precious gift in the world, and neither of us planned to ever forget how miraculous that gift is, how miraculous she is.

As soon as we were all healed enough to travel, we came home for all of two weeks before deciding to move. Seattle held too much pain, too much burden. Zayden and Blake laid in bed together for those two weeks, scrolling through beach house listings while I began offloading all of my businesses around here to newly assigned managers since I would no longer be able to operate in person. We've all agreed to take time for just us, maybe one day we will get back to business, I don't think Zayden could survive without it, if I'm honest. Then again, I think he could if Blake really wanted him to.

They ended up settling on a beautiful house that has its own private beach. We have three chairs on the back porch, all facing the ocean, in the most picturesque view imaginable. Blake comes out here every morning for the sunrise, but today I've beaten her by a few.

"You gonna go for a swim, baby?" I ask with a soft smile.

"I was thinking about it."

"Or you could let us make love to you," Zayden says, coming up from behind us before placing a kiss to her shoulder.

She smirks at him as she shrugs her shoulders.

"Well, gosh, when you give a girl options like that, how can I refuse?"

I chuckle at that, palming her bare thigh before my fingers slip beneath her bikini bottoms, sinking into her already wet cunt. Babygirl already knew what she was in for when she came out here looking like this.

Zayden leans down and kisses her, a hand on her throat as his hand traces over her breasts, settling on his mark. Blake has thought about getting the Z and D tattooed so they would never fade, but I personally like the natural look of it. Like our initials aren't just inked into her, but a part of her, the same way she is a part of us.

I watch as Zayden wraps his fist around her long blonde hair, yanking her head back as he pulls out his cock, forcing her to take him into her mouth. She looks so beautiful when she's full, and I can't help but increase my speed, wanting to see her fall apart on my fingers with his cock in her mouth.

As usual, it doesn't take much. Babygirl always gets too excited too fast. She's clamping around my fingers and screaming around Zayden's cock before I can even properly work her over. It's a good thing this is just our warm-up.

She continues sucking Zayden's cock while I remove my fingers, sucking them into my mouth as I groan at the taste of her on my tongue. Goddamn delectable.

Pulling my cock out, I stroke myself a few times before pushing her bathing suit to the side, forcing her to sit on me until I'm wrapped tightly inside her cunt.

"Fuck, baby," I groan as she moans.

Zayden snaps his hips as his grip on her hair seems to tighten. I feel my balls begin to tighten as she circles her hips, practically pulling the cum right out of me as she murmurs something around Zayden's dick.

"What's that, angel?" he asks as he pulls out of her for a moment.

"I said I'm ovulating, and I got my IUD taken out, so who's going to knock me up?" She grins.

"Goddammit! Dominic, get the fuck out of my fiancée before I gut you," he snarls.

"Fuck you, brother. I'm gonna take my time filling up my fiancée with as much cum as her sweet cunt can handle."

He glares at me, and Blake chuckles, gripping Zayden's cock with her left hand, two sparkling diamond rings shimmering on her left finger.

As soon as we were back in the States, we proposed, each of us presenting her with our own choice of rings. Mine was bigger. It wasn't fancy or over-the-top, we could have done that and would have. We had all talked about it, though, and Blake said she didn't enjoy all of the fuss. She wanted something intimate and simple, and that's exactly what we did.

Zayden and I wanted to get married immediately, but she insisted on waiting. She won't tell us why, just that she wants to have a long engagement. I think she's still waiting for the other shoe to drop. She's worried about being with both of us forever, that something will happen, and that we will make her choose. Zayden and I both know that will never happen. If we want her, the other comes too. Like a package deal, and if I really have to spend my life with the only two people in this world that I care about, then my life isn't all that bad.

Blake takes Zayden into her mouth, pushing him down until she gags. He mutters out a curse as he curls his fingers in her hair, beginning to fuck her mouth while I sink into her, lifting her up and slamming her down on me. I feel my grip tighten, and I glance down to see her hips are nearly white from the hold. She'll have bruises no doubt, but she bruises so beautifully for me.

I feel the tingling begin at the base of my spine, and before I know it, I'm coming. My cum shoots inside of her, her pussy contracting around it as she comes with me, moaning and groaning around Zayden's cock. I haven't even fully finished coming before she is out of my arms and face down, ass up on the ground. Zayden is already sunk inside of her, snapping his hips before finding his own release. He fucks her so violently, and I know part of it is because she feels that fucking good, but the other more dominant reason is because he wants our cum as deep inside her as possible.

When he's finished, Blake collapses to the floor, lying on her back as she gives us a lust-drunk smile. She's glowing, happy, and looks perfectly fucked.

Just the way I love her.

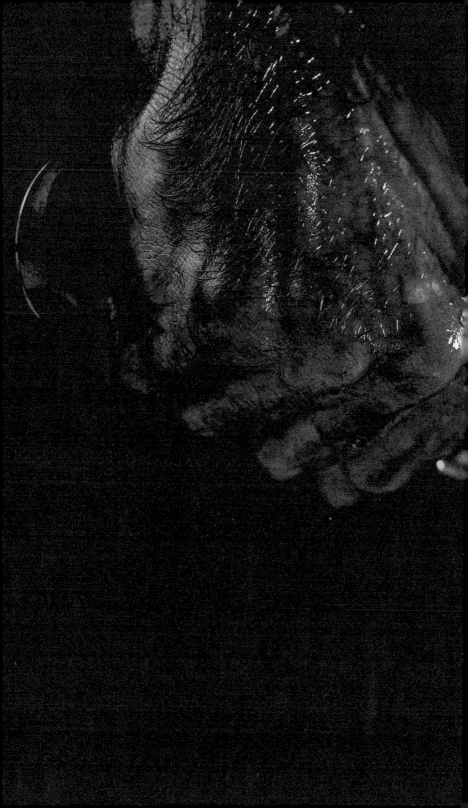

EXTENDED EPILOGUE

ZAYDEN

My beautiful new bride is currently breaking my hand, and I wouldn't have it any other way. Not that I would ever say it to her, but she had this coming. If she had just married us over a year ago when we proposed, she wouldn't have her feet in stirrups, her flowy white wedding dress discarded on the other side of the delivery room.

We had an intimate wedding, just us three and an officiant. Since our government is a bunch of prudish, close-minded bitches, my angel was only allowed to legally marry one of us.

Obviously, my brother and I handled it in the only way we knew how to. We bare knuckle boxed each other until there was only one winner, and I am proud to say that I am that winner.

Dominic said it didn't really matter since we have the same last name and she loves us equally, but he said that to make himself feel better because it sure as fuck does matter.

Our ceremony itself was a commitment ceremony, though, where my angel promised and vowed to love both of us even in death. It was just our names that were on the actual legal paperwork. Paperwork that wasn't in our officiant's hands for longer than ten seconds before her water broke.

We're having a little boy, and I couldn't be more thrilled. Though Dominic and I are nervous about what kind of fathers we will be, we know that my angel will be the most incredible mother so we will follow her lead.

After every test imaginable, it was proven that pinning down exactly whose baby is inside my angel is undeterminable. Because we are identical twins, our DNA is virtually identical, so all tests came back inconclusive. She was actually happy about it, she was worried if we found out one of us wouldn't love the baby enough, which is the stupidest thing to come out of her beautiful mouth. I would have loved the baby with all I am because, at the end of the day, he is half her, so he's already half perfection. I like to think it was my sperm that eventually won, though. I mean, the last time we tried, Dominic was the one to finish and she wasn't pregnant. We switched, and she is pregnant. Can't tell me that's a coincidence.

Dominic and I take jobs from time to time, not as many as

we used to and only local. I refuse to spend nights away from my angel, and now that we are having a baby, it's a hell fucking no. I don't crave the bloodshed like I did, but I can't deny it still fills me with an amount of thrill, a release, and I'm thankful my angel gets it. She's even come on a job or two with me when we get a mark on a rapist or abusive piece of shit, much to Dominic's chagrin. For the right reasons, she loves the kill, relishes in it almost as much as me, and it gets me hard every fucking time.

"Okay, okay. One more big push," the doctor says between her legs.

Dominic is on her left and I'm on her right, we both hold her hands as we support her the best way we can as husbands. By shutting the fuck up and letting her do and say whatever she wants.

"I fucking hate you both. Vividly. This is the worst way to spend a wedding day everrrr," she groans as she pushes until her face goes beet red.

She collapses against the bed at the same time a soft cry sounds out. It's a sound that immediately has my heart melting, and when I set my eyes on that little guy, I know that I'm a goner.

"Oop," the doctor says.

"Oop?" Dominic questions. "What the fuck does that mean?"

"Sorry, I'm just the on-call midwife, and your chart said you were only having one baby."

"We are!" my angel practically snaps at her.

She shakes her head as a nurse takes our son, clipping his cord quickly before taking him to the side of the room to weigh and measure him.

"I see the baby's head. Okay, here comes another contraction. You ready, Blake?" she asks.

"What? No!" she shouts before sharing panicked looks between Dominic and me.

"It's okay, babygirl. You've got this. Let's meet our other baby."

Her eyes clench tight as she nods, pushing again. This baby seems to somehow be able to come out in one push, and a louder, raspier cry comes from them.

"Another baby boy." The doctor smiles before quickly clamping the cord and bringing both babies to my angel.

Tears begin pouring down her face as she looks at them, and I'm in awe. They're so tiny. So perfect. I press a kiss to the side of her head as I whisper, "Thank you. Thank you for making them. They're just like you."

She cries harder as Dominic whispers something to her that I can't quite hear, but I don't mind. My eyes can't stop going back to my kids. My sons. My whole family.

THANK YOU

First off...are you okay? How you doing? That was a ride, a blood soaked, pleasure filled ride. I hope you enjoyed it and maybe even learned a thing or two about yourself along the way, whether you're proud of said information is irrelevant.

Not ready to be done with Blake, Dom and Zay? Click here to read an alternate chapter from the club where the girl and Blake don't just dance...

Thank you so much for reading Graves! I adore this throuple in all of their dysfunctional, beautifully imperfect glory. Though their story is over I have a few more smutty delights to keep you satiated in case you're not ready to say goodbye just yet. If I had it my way I'd keep you forever!

ACKNOWLEDGMENTS

To my Alpha, Sara, I'm so thankful for you! This book was months in the making, countless voice messages, incessant questions and the entire time you were my biggest cheerleader. Your work on this book was completely invaluable and I'm so blessed to have you as my alpha and one of my best friends.

To my Beta's, Elena, Thalia, Rachel, Lynds and Brittany, I adore you all! Each of you brought something unique and incredibly valuable to this book. From absolutely unhinged voice messages and stories, to hilarious reactions and life saving edits. You all are truly the difference from me putting out a book I love to a book I'm truly proud of! Thank you all for your hard work, patience and just being flat out amazing.

To my street team and ARC readers, thank you all for your support! Every page read, every review left, and every post made truly means the world. I'm not even a little shy to admit that I have hands down the best people behind me.

To my readers, whether this is your first book by me, or you've been by my side since day one, thank you. There are millions of authors out there, billions of books and you chose mine. Each one of you pushes me to write when my fingers ache, plot when my brain is mush and keep moving forward when I'm ready to give up. You all are the best readers anyone

ALSO BY

Gallows Hill Series –
A dark academia reverse harem
Deceit
Descent
Demise

The Alphaletes Series –
Interconnected football romance stories
The Loyalties We Break
The Walls We Break
The Hearts We Break
The Rules We Break

Stand Alones –
Gratify – A forbidden age gap
Jagged Harts – An MMA enemies to lovers